A HOLE IN THE WORLD

WESTON OCHSE

First published 2021 by Solaris
an imprint of Rebellion Publishing Ltd,
Riverside House, Osney Mead,
Oxford, OX2 0ES, UK

www.solarisbooks.com

ISBN: 978-1-78108-914-9

A CIP catalogue record for this book is available
from the British Library.

10 9 8 7 6 5 4 3 2 1

Designed & typeset by Rebellion Publishing

Printed in the UK

A HOLE IN THE WORLD

WESTON OCHSE

SOLARIS

For my daughter, Alexandra

Author Note

On the use of the word *Indian*. I chose a location on the Pine Ridge Indian Reservation in South Dakota, United States of America as a prime place for the plot of this novel to begin. The inhabitants are largely Ogallala Lakota Sioux Indian. While many countries use the term *First Nations Peoples*, the usage of this term was developed as part of a non-binding United Nations Declaration that the United States did not sign. Other terms, such as *Native Americans*, have been rejected by tribes because they don't see themselves as natives and largely find the term derogatory. It has also been argued that anyone born in the Western Continent is Native American. I have read that supporters of the term *Indian* argue that it has been used for so long that it has become the norm and are no longer considered as exonyms. It is not the intent of this author to insult in any way. I am merely striving to refer to a people by the most socially accepted means. This novel is meant for pleasure and not for political or social critique.

Born dead this spring,
an ancient & skeletal elm
in our backyard scratches
the face of the sullen sun.
Sliced ribbons of sunlight
wrap the fact that nothing
can save you this dry July,
not even bleeding dancers
tethered by medicine prayers
to a freshly cut cottonwood
tree twenty miles from here.

from SUN/DANCE/SONG
by Adrian C. Louis, member of
Lovelock Paiute Indian Tribe,
Pine Ridge Indian Reservation

PROLOGUE

FRANCIS SCOTT KEY Catches the Enemy woke up in a ditch, which wasn't all that uncommon. People had their own ideas as to why he chose such places to sleep, but the truth was that he had narcolepsy and would often wake up in the most curious places. What was uncommon was that he was in the middle of nowhere. He checked his pockets. He still had a few dollars and his wallet with his Tribal ID card and food stamps. So, what was he doing there? He scratched an itch only to see it was an ant. He pinched it between two fingers and flicked it onto the empty roadway. He still had his work boots and jeans. He still wore his favorite T-shirt he got from a Minneapolis Starbucks. He still had on his Cleveland Indians baseball cap that he wore as a joke that no one seemed to get. If he had everything, then why was he here?

The landscape was as flat and dry as the rest of the Res. West he could just see the smudge of the Black Hills, their sacred place turned into tourist place by the white man eager to make more money than they could spend in two lifetimes. Prairie grass grew in clumps along the road and metal fences separating the properties. Quail led their families from clump to clump, mastering the fast waddle. The cloudless blue sky already promised to be another scorcher and without a piece of shade in sight, he was going to get one hell of a burn. He could thank that to some-as-heretofore-unknown white man in the woodpile.

Nearby on a cutoff stood five white FEMA trailers that had been repurposed for permanent use. Each of them looked as if they'd gone through a hurricane or two. It was too early for anyone to be out except a few goats and a mangy cur. A free-standing basketball hoop lay on its side as if it had been shot. Three of the five trailers had blue tubs for rain catchment. Each one had a satellite dish on the power pole at the end of the house. An industrial-sized garbage can rested at the juncture of the cutoff and the main road, already half full with trash and, by the swirling black mass of flies, fresh mule deer carcass.

He pulled himself to his feet through sheer willpower and staggered to his left before he was able to get his balance.

Other than the trailers, an odd street sign was the only thing that rose any higher than he did. Anyone from the Res didn't need any signs to know where they were. The signs were for the government men when they came so they could get around. He knew this one especially because he was on the work detail that put it in. It said No Flesh Road, named after a famous Sioux Chief who went to Washington with Chief Red Cloud. A semi-dry creek of the same name paralleled the road. Those in the FEMA trailers were No Flesh ancestors, the last of an important line.

Francis Scott Key Catches decided to sit and wait for a ride back into Iron Hat. He pulled himself up an old tire and sat on it, wishing for something to quiet the murmuring in his empty stomach. He'd been expecting cars and trucks for some time. Little Wound School in Kyle would be opening and it served not only Kyle, but Iron Hat, and other places nearby. With no cars on the road, Francis Scott began to wonder if he hadn't missed a Tribal Emergency Warning.

He was just considering getting up and going to one of the No Flesh trailers to see if they knew what was going on when a car appeared coming from the direction of Kyle. It skidded to a stop even with him. The driver looked around in confusion, then used the cut-off to pull in, back up, and turn around.

Francis Scott watched it go back the way it came. They must have forgotten something, he figured. Had to get back home. He craned his neck towards Iron Hat to the south and didn't see a thing.

Soon cars and trucks began to come with more frequency, in ones and twos and threes. But the odd thing was, they all stopped in the same place, turned around, and went back. It was as if on reaching the spot in the road they received a warning on the radio to turn around.

Once again, he looked towards Iron Hat.

Nothing at all from that direction.

Was there a chemical spill?

He saw nothing on the horizon to prove the notion.

He spoke for a few moments with the people in the nearest trailer. They hadn't heard of any warnings. There were no alerts. The only thing that confused them was that they claimed to have never heard of Iron Hat.

Five hours later a feeling began to dawn on him. One he'd learned to listen to—one that had kept him alive on many occasions. It was strange being on the right side of things. Francis Scott—never Francis—had been largely misunderstood since Desert Storm. But that never stopped him from trying to be understood. His problem was he had too much time on his hands. He noticed things. And when he took the time out of his busy day noticing things to point things out to people who didn't notice things, they tended to dismiss him or not believe in him.

Like the time he saw giant butterflies coming off the surface of Devil's Tower in Wyoming when he was out delivering a load of lumber as part of a tribal interchange. No one had even taken a second to think what he said was true. But he'd proved it. Sure, they had been sky divers free basing off the top of the monument with butterfly-pattern-shaped parachutes, but that didn't mean he'd been wrong.

It meant he'd been paying attention.

Or like the time he saw the herd of Ghost Buffalo stampeding from Custer along Highway 16, their rumbles like thunder in the middle of winter, Hell's own sulfur pouring from their noses as they puffed their way down the iced roadway. Sure, it turned out to be actual buffalo who had run through twelve-foot-high snow drifts and been covered from horn to hoof by iced snow, but anyone seeing what he'd seen would have believed they were Ghost Buffalo as well.

Or even like the time when he'd been in North Dakota on a sixty-day work team at the oil fields and had seen several UFOs come, land, and remove cattle for some sketchy experimentation. He'd reported the information and had worked with a sketch artist to create a proper rendering. As it turned out, he'd been watching the events unfold over several nights on a drive-in movie screen erected in the middle of nowhere by a Silicon Valley billionaire who'd created a reproduction of the drive in from his youth for his own personal enjoyment and just loved cheesy cheap sci fi movies from the fifties and sixties.

Who knew there was a giant movie screen in the middle of nowhere? Was it his fault a billionaire wanted to recreate his youth?

Still, Francis Scott Key Chases had been paying attention.

He refused to believe that he was a poor witness with bad eyes and a loner's sense of the universe. He'd just been put in situations where his ability to witness was at odds with the curious folks and conditions that were presented before him. But now he had witnesses. And now it seemed as if an entire town had gone missing and it was only him who seemed to know about it.

An entire town.

Since when had that happened before?

And he, Francis Scott Key Catches, son of the Homecoming Queen of Kyle, South Dakota, Class of 1966 and Francisco Morales, itinerant worker and traveling magician, was the first one to see it happen when a car bound for the booming metropolis of Iron Hat, South Dakota, skidding to as stop in the middle of the road, the driver glancing both ways, then pulled a U-turn and went back the way they came from.

In fact, traffic had been like that for hours, cars and trucks and semis rumbling down the road, only to stop dead in the middle of it, then turn around as if they'd never intended on coming that way in the first place. At first it was just him watching the gigantic clusterfuck, but then came Freddie Makes Room who pulled up on a Razor ATV and asked what was going on.

The conversation had gone:

"No one's going to the town anymore," Francis Scott said.

"There's a town there?" Freddie Makes Room asked—something he shouldn't have to ask. Iron Hat was famous on the Res because of the Department of the Interior's intrusion after a well-digger found a Rare Earth metal deposit large enough to make a boardroom of billionaires.

"Of course, there is, Freddie. We've been there. Don't

you remember Big Sal?" he asked referring to the triple-sized gal who slung beer from the back of her trailer, party lights, and everything.

"Never heard of her."

"You and her made out last Thanksgiving."

"Don't remember and we don't celebrate Thanksgiving."

Then Little Frank Wounded showed up—all five feet of him, dressed in jeans and workshirt and boots.

"Whatcha doing, Francis Scott?" he'd asked as he hopped out of his pickup.

Francis Scott grinned. Little Frank was perfect and would be his ride. He angled his head towards the empty road before them. "Let's go into town and get some lunch," he said. "I'm buying."

Little Frank shook his head. "I just came from there. Traffic is a lot more than usual. People are driving in circles. Don't want to mess with that again."

"No, I mean Iron Hat. The town down that way."

Little Frank pushed back the rim of his cowboy hat and squinted at Francis Scott much like Clint Eastwood would have done minus the cheroot. "What the hell is an Iron Hat? I thought you gave up the hard liquor and were sticking to beer?"

There was a time after Desert Storm where no bottle would have been safe from Francis Scott. But that was an age ago. Still, he licked his lips at the memory of the taste of rye. Memories are rough things to ignore, but he was having too much fun living life to succumb to one with memories of mortars and blown out Iraqi tanks.

"Where do you think you bought your truck? And your clothes? You live in Iron Hat for god's sakes."

"Nothing of the sort." Little Frank looked up at Makes Room. "How long has he been like this?"

"A couple hours at least. Think he sprung a sprocket?"

"I think it's worth checking into." Little Frank strode over to Francis Scott. "Maybe we should check you into the clinic. See if there's a fever or something."

"Saw on Nat Geo about this brain worm from Africa that can make people see things that aren't there," Freddie Makes Room said.

They watched another car come up, stop, the look on the driver's face pure confusion, then turn the car around and head back into Kyle.

"See that?" Francis Scott said, thumping Little Frank in the shoulder.

"What I saw was a driver realize they'd taken a wrong turn then go back the way they came. Happens every day."

"But why here?" Francis asked, gesturing to the road. "Why this exact spot?"

Little Frank shrugged. "Good as place as any. Really, Francis Scott. Aren't you taking this a little too far?"

What had been fun was becoming anything but. What's the good of having a good time if you're the only one having it? Then he had an idea. He strode over to the pickup, climbed in, grabbed the leather book where Little Frank kept all of his meticulous maintenance records. Sure enough, he got his oil changed in the same location every 5,000 miles and the address was in Iron Hat.

He brought it down and showed it to Little Frank.

The diminutive man removed his cowboy hat, flattened his hair, then put the hat back on.

"I see what it says, but it makes no sense."

Francis Scott thumped the paper. "What you see are receipts from a place that existed right up until this morning. The questions are, why doesn't anyone except me seem to remember that it existed and what's going on in there? I mean, the residents can't just be gone. They have to either be trapped and can't get out or they don't think anything else exists outside of their town."

"What you're talking about is Twilight Zone," Freddie Makes Room said.

Francis Scott shrugged.

They all watched another car come, make a five-point turn, and go back the way it came.

"I don't care what it sounds like. I'm tired of being called crazy. I'm going to report it."

"How do you report a missing town?" Little Frank asked. "You and I both know the tribal police will lock you up in a second."

"He's right," Makes Room said. "That just means we need to think outside the box."

"Does that mean you believe me?" Francis Scott asked.

"Oh, hell no. But you're my friend. If you believe, I'd be a dick to think you're crazy." Little Frank nodded to the truck. "Follow me back to my place. We're going to blast this thing all over the internet."

CHAPTER 1

LAURIE MAY—AKA Preacher's Daughter—annotated the results of the experiment, darkened the screens on her computers, and sat back in her chair. She detested office work. She especially hated science. She had a Master of Arts in Religious Studies with an emphasis on monotheistic religions. Although there were some who tried to apply science to explain religions, most frequently the suspect science of psychology, she knew better. After all, who else had she known who'd been captured by Sufi mystics and held hostage in order to power the mind of a dying demi-god? She'd been up to her eyeballs in real life games between gods and men and didn't need any PhD trying to placate her beliefs with their scientific theories.

"Ms. May, can you run through the results one more time," came a voice over her desk speaker. "I want to verify before I input them into the master database. Remember what they say. Measure twice, cut once."

She imagined emptying a thirty-round clip from an HK416 into the speaker.

"Ms. May, do you copy? I need to know if you hear me."

His name was Dr. Norris Fields. He was a thirty-year-old wunderkind who held a PhD in Cognitive Neuroscience with an emphasis in extrospection from the Berlin School of Mind and Brain. Fields had done his thesis regarding Non-Linear Memory Retention. He eschewed the Ebbinghaus Forgetful Curve and had created his own topological model that they were trying to prove through experimentation.

Which was not the sort of thing she'd imagined herself doing when she'd joined Special Unit 77. She was a gun jockey and not a research monkey. Not that research wasn't important, it was just that she felt her talents were best used elsewhere. She was a five-foot-ten-inch thirty-two-year-old combat veteran of two wars with multiple tours, capable of equally identifying supernatural entities in the wild without resorting to theism and breaking down any man-held or crew-served weapon currently or historically in use. Truth be told, when she'd been informed of the opportunity to be assigned to an excitable freshly-minted scientist who wanted to change the world, she naïvely thought that it was a grand idea and a great way to break her teeth on the ins and outs of her new unit. But now after three months, six days, and seventeen hours of not being in the field she was afraid she might pop off like a fifty-year old Soviet-made land mine.

"Ms. May, are you there?"

"I'm here, Norris. I will recheck the data and send it to you."

He hesitated to respond. She knew why. He hated being called by his first name and much preferred Doctor, but he was young and full of himself and she felt it her duty to disabuse him of his notion that he was anything more than a newly-minted excitable scientist fresh from the educational womb.

She did as promised, and spent another forty-five minutes ensuring that the computational data was correct, then fired it off to him. She didn't give him a chance to react, instead, grabbed her pack, turned off her workstations, and headed to the indoor firing range. She was into her three hundredth round when Lieutenant Poe arrived wearing his 1950s standard issue OD green Army uniform complete with tie and belt. The uniform was as much an anachronism as he was. He was too old to be a lieutenant and the military hadn't authorized that particular uniform in over sixty years. Still, he was one of the only members of Special Unit 77 who wore a uniform of any sort, probably as a reminder to everyone that it was a military organization and not some pseudo mercenary outfit operating outside the jurisdiction of any actual government. Otherwise, no one would ever know that the complex of abandoned warehouses which were once part of a Chevrolet assembly plant on the edge of Muncie, Indiana, was now a secret government enclave with an even more secret mission. Every week the guards reported locals coming to see if there were any jobs at the plants, hoping beyond hope that they could go back to what their families had done before it had all been taken away.

"You come to watch me fire, or to dress me down?" she asked when she was finally through and cleaning her weapon.

In truth, she was still a reserve lieutenant in the military intelligence corps of the United States Army. So, on the surface of it, she and Poe were equals. But he wore lieutenant's bars to throw people off. No one put a lieutenant in charge of an entire organization like Special Unit 77. Her former mentor and friend, Boy Scout, figured that Poe had to be at least a lieutenant colonel if not a full bird.

"A little of both," he said. He was the Midwest all-American—fit, six feet tall, crew cut blonde hair, square-jawed—everything American wanted in its fighting man, but he seemed more at ease with himself than most people were with themselves. "Doctor Fields is doing important work, PD."

She so loved that he still referred to her by her call sign. She still felt awkward using her real name. "Norris is a good kid."

He sighed. "That's what I mean. Why do you have to call him Norris? Why don't you call him Dr. Fields?"

"It's his name."

"He's only a year younger than you."

She gave him her best smile. "He's just such a cute little scientist, isn't he?"

Poe sighed. "I'm sending you on a mission."

She stopped cold.

"A mission?"

"I'm putting you in charge."

She smacked her pistol back together. "About damn time. When do we leave?"

"A little under three hours. You have a mission brief and need to be at the special weapons armory."

"Special weapons?" She felt her heart skip a beat. "Can you tell me what we're after?"

"That's all going to be in the brief." He turned to leave. "Oh, and Preacher's Daughter?"

"Yes?"

"You're taking Professor Fields with you as an observer. Don't get him killed."

Her jaw dropped as she struggled to say something, but her body knew better. If she complained, she might lose her chance to get out of this place. She had to play nice. And that included her treatment of Norris.

Three hours and forty minutes later she was already regretting Poe's order to bring him along.

He had his own personalized gear, which was the first thing that should have been a concern. He wore gray and blue urban cammies with matching body armor and ballistic helmet. He wore yellow shooting goggles and had his own personalized set of 9mm pistols in matching shoulder holsters. A knife the size of a baby's arm was strapped to his right thigh. Combat knee pads and elbow pads were in place. He looked like he'd just modeled for

Soldier of Fortune magazine or a video game while the rest of them looked like practical urban terrorists.

She and the other four men on her team wore 5.11 tactical pants in black, not because of the popularity, but because of the stretch, give, and durability. The T-shirt of their choice—hers was an Iron Maiden concert T-shirt. Black combat boots, ballistic helmets, and body armor rounded out their non-traditional uniform. The idea was that they should go in with as little as needed and with absolutely no attribution. So, no flags, no patriotic patches, no well-known sayings. Just what they needed.

As it turned out, their special equipment was actually special ammunition and it wasn't as special as one might think. There were no silver bullets. There was no holy water in hand grenades. All they had were 410 gauge pistols made by Taurus called the Judge which used shotgun shells filled with Himalayan Rock Salt and lead balls. They each carried two and had several bandoliers of 410 shells. Which according to the mission brief was just what they required if they were going to take down a monster's nest of homunculi.

She'd let Norris keep his pistols but had taken all of his ammo.

He was furious at first, but when reminded that she was mission commander, he resorted to fuming, resembling a teenager who'd just been told he couldn't play any more video games. She knew he'd make her pay, but for now, it was best for him and the mission if he stayed in the rear with the gear and didn't have anything he could accidentally shoot them with.

The other four men on her team had no trouble with her being in charge. During the relatively short time she'd been in Special Unit 77 she'd interacted with all of them either on the combatives mat or on the range and they knew her to be as much a professional as they were. Plus, they'd been allowed to read the file about her last mission, where she had survived interaction with Zoroastrian demons. That alone gave her enough street cred for a thousand miles of bad decisions.

The mission was to travel to a Western Pennsylvania farmhouse that had been taken over by an infestation of homunculi. Special Unit 77 would normally allow another of the country's special units, like SEAL Team 666 or the Pathfinders, to take them out, but 77's proximity to the supernatural outbreak made them a prime candidate. Their mission was normally to protect the continental United States and her technology from supernatural exploitation from other countries. 77 had been around since the Cold War and was the tip of the spear in protecting the West Coast of America for decades. Since the advent of global media and travel, the mission was expanded. Their traditional headquarters of San Francisco was moved to Indiana where they could better respond to threats to the homeland on and in between all coasts and borders.

The other four shooters on the team were all ex Special Forces or Rangers. Their names weren't necessary and neither were complicated call signs representing any past deeds. Instead, for this mission, they were Alpha, Bravo, Charlie, and Delta and she would be Zulu. Norris would be November but he should never be in the position to ever touch a radio or likewise be mentioned on one.

The infestation had been discovered by a 77 tech specialist monitoring Instagram accounts. Detected initially by an algorithm, the short 46-second video dubbed over with Nikki Minaj's 'Superbass' showed the tiny figures swinging from the rafters of an unknown barn. It was later during video forensics that it was discovered that they were using the entrails of a large unknown animal for their ropes. Although there were no humans in the video, it was a presumptive fact that the person holding and recording the video was human and it was within the metadata that they discovered the location. That was thirteen hours ago. Not only did they need to ensure that they kept the infestation local, but also that other entities did not get their hands on the homunculi.

They rode in the back of a UH-53J PaveLow Helicopter flying at 120 mph towards the microscopic Amish community of Mascot in Lancaster County, Pennsylvania. The county itself was the largest grouping of Amish in the United States with upwards of 35,000 residents. She'd laughed when she'd seen the map. Thinking how conservative the Amish must be, having towns with peculiar names like Intercourse, Blue Ball, and Bird in the Hand was something out of a fiction novel instead of real life. They were headed towards a chicken farm. They planned on hitting the buildings at 2AM and ensuring that the infiltration was eradicated. Once mission accomplished, another crew would go in to investigate who it was and why they'd decided to create the artificial creations—basically trying to determine whether it was an accident of curiosity or a full-scale intentional engagement of the mysterious and forbidden.

Lights went out when they descended beneath the clouds.

Everyone checked their coms which ran through a basic special operations multi-interband team radio or MBITR. She lowered her NODS—night vision devices—over her eyes and adjusted them to her vision. She watched the red glow form the bulb over the rear door and listened to the flight crew as they flared in for a combat landing.

Preacher's Daughter had a sense of déjà vu. She'd been on so many combat missions in the last few years but only with a select group led by Boy Scout. She hadn't heard from him since she'd last seen him near Fort Irwin and Death Valley. And then of course there was McQueen and Narco and Criminal and Bully, all now deceased. They'd been the best brothers and sisters in arms she'd ever worked with. Was it true that she was the last one alive? She could hardly believe it. Part of her wanted to be with her lost brethren but then she knew that's not what they would have wanted. Boy Scout and McQueen especially—oh, McQueen—would have wanted her to live life to the fullest, grab it by the throat and throttle it until it gave her more.

If this wasn't doing that then she didn't know what that meant.

She thumped against the inside of the helicopter as it slammed to the ground.

The red light switched to green.

The ramp lowered and before it even hit the ground they were down and past it, single file, Alpha, Bravo, November, Charlie, and Delta behind her. The air was crisp but the sky was clear. The ground had been mown within the last few days and still had clumps of dead grass along the rows. They moved as a team for twenty meters, then stopped, got down, and made an arrow formation.

To the right sat a two-story farm house, a light on in the kitchen above the stove but otherwise nothing else. To the left stood an immense three-floor red barn with Pennsylvania Dutch Hex signs on all sides. The Daddy Hex tulip star was high up on the front of the barn which generally meant goodwill and was present to avert famine. But intermixed with traditional Dutch hexes on the sides were wiccan witch hexes that she absolutely didn't expect to see.

She relayed the information into her microphone, not for common knowledge, just so it would be recorded for post mission briefings and posterity. They also had video cams affixed to the sides of their helmets.

"Traditional Pennsylvanian Dutch hex symbols. Father Hex. Single Distlefink. Double Distlefink. Maple. Colonial Eagle. All common Teutonic symbols brought from Europe as pagan vestiges. Intermixed, however, with Seax Wiccan symbols. SW is a syncretic wiccan religion of Saxon origin codified in 1974 by Raymond Buckland. It's not considered real wicca, but something for housewives to mess around with and not burn their homes to the ground or invite a wandering soul to inhabit their babies. More new age than real magic."

"Then why is it on the side of a building with homunculi?" Norris asked, out of breath.

"Radio silence, November," she snapped. She didn't need his margin notes on her verbal report.

But it was a good question. It begged the idea that whoever was inside had been messing around and things had gotten out of hand. She much preferred that than the alternate which mean there was a dedicated sorcerer determined to create aberrations to do his or her own will.

One was plain evil.

The other was plain stupid.

She signaled them to move out.

Their order of march was the same.

They moved to the front door of the barn. She'd considered splitting the group, but they were such a small force as it was, she didn't want to put them in a position where they had to be on the defense. Also, with November along, it took one of her men out of the formation to take care of him so she really had herself and three pax to conduct the assault.

Given all of that information it might as well be frontal.

"Alpha. Prepare to breach."

Alpha moved next to her and tested the door. It was locked. He placed a small wad of plastic explosive on it along with a wired device. He spun around to the side of the wall as did she. The others moved to the side.

"Breach."

He depressed a button on his remote and the sound of a gun going off along with a puff of smoke came from the shattered locking mechanism. He shoved the remote into a bail out pouch on the side of his gear, grabbed the door and gave her a look.

"Enter."

He jerked the door open and slid inside, tactical crouch, a Judge in both hands held low at a forty-five-degree angle.

Bravo went next.

Then Charlie.

She followed with November behind her and Delta bringing up the rear.

The inside of the barn was wide open, reaching three full stories. Far in the back were double-stacked haylofts, but they only took up a fifth of the internal volume of the structure. The floor looked like it could hold hundreds of Amish and was probably used as a meeting place. No horse stalls or closets. Just space. In the Starlight created by the night-vision devices everything was cast in a green glow whether it be dark or bright. The only light inside the barn came from ambience outside the line of windows which were high on the walls near the ceiling. Everything else was variegated shadows of multifloras green.

Movement out of the corner of her eye made her head twist, but she couldn't see what it was. She dialed up Alpha's view and watched as a roughly human-shaped figure two feet tall with extra-long arms slid along a cable, then swung into the shadows at the back of the barn.

"Zulu, are you seeing what I'm seeing?" Alpha asked.

"Roger. I'm tied into your feed."

"Looks like they might be gathering at the other end."

She switched to Delta's feed who was watching this end of the barn. He was staring at things high up in the rafters. It looked as if children had been hung there or perhaps babies.

"Delta, what am I seeing?"

"Your answer is as good as mine. I don't know. No heat signatures on the bodies so if those are what I think they are they've been dead for a while."

She cursed internally. The thing about homunculi was that they were more than pests, they were collectors. If left to their own accord, they would latch onto one of the first things they saw and then search those things out to collect. They couldn't help themselves. It was the way their tiny fabricated brains were wired. And if the first thing they came across had been a human child in the home, then there was a tremendous chance that children from all over the county were missing as well, now hung from the rafters, thirty feet above them.

"Charlie, Delta. Other side."

Now that she'd seen the internal layout, she felt

comfortable deploying her men on the other side of the structure. More importantly, she needed to see what was above them.

"Anyone see the junction box?"

"I got it over here," Charlie replied.

"Check it. I want these lights on. Want to see the cockroaches swarm."

Sounds began to creep into her consciousness.

Titterings.

Slidings.

An occasional thump from above.

"Got it. Want me to light 'em up?"

She grinned, holding a single Judge in her right hand. "Sure."

She dialed back her night vision in time not to go blind as lights from six different hanging lamps came to life.

Her gaze went directly to the figures hanging above them.

"Dear god!" November exclaimed. "Are those children?"

"Incoming," Alpha called.

She crouched and swung her pistol around with two hands counting dozens of creatures running across the floor towards them, while others descended from the rafters on cords. Half of the children she'd seen hanging from the ceiling dropped as well—not children, but the little creatures, previously misidentified and hidden in shadow.

"Take them out," she cried.

She fired at the nearest target, its legs moving impossibly fast as it ran across the floor towards her, arms out, fingers eager to grab. While she'd never felt their strength, she'd read how improbable it was. The weapon kicked in her hands unexpectedly. She'd forgotten she was essentially firing a shotgun shell from a pistol.

The creature's chest evaporated as the lead eviscerated the skin, followed by the salt which on contact immediately began to melt the nasty little thing wherever it struck. It cried piteously as it rolled on the ground, its arms hugging its chest. A smushed face held thin lips with sharp baby teeth, a little pug nose, and extra-wide marsupial eyes that were not only capable of seeing more color but were as accurate in the dark as their own technology.

Other members of the team fired around her.

She fired four more times, then reloaded, each round catching one of the tiny thugs center mass. She'd just begun to reload, when she heard a scream from behind her. She turned and saw that November was firing one of his pistols at a homunculus which had latched onto his leg. The first question was why did he even have any ammunition and her second was why had he left her side.

After a quick check she saw that the rest of the team was positively engaged.

She finished loading, flipped the revolver closed and took seven tactical steps towards him.

She put the pistol to the back of the homunculus's head and fired.

Green and gray matter sprayed all over November's leg and gear.

She grabbed him and pulled him back to the side of the barn.

"Holster that weapon, November. I don't want you firing anymore."

He stared at her through wide eyes but made no move to comply.

"I said holster the weapon."

He complied, his hand shaking so much it took him three times to get the pistol secure.

She cursed and turned back to the ruckus.

At first glance it looked as if the floor had been littered with dead babies. But a closer examination revealed that they all had the face of Batboy from the *Weekly World News*, a picture that most people believed to have been a fake but was really that of a homunculus. Because they were arcanely made, they'd start to decompose soon and when they did, she wanted to be nowhere near the scene.

"Zulu, this is Alpha. We have a situation."

With all of the creatures down and out, she left Delta to babysit November and she, Bravo, and Charlie rushed to Alpha's side. What she saw made her heart sink. What had been nothing more than shooting apples in a barrel had just become serial murder. Two adults were nailed to the wall under the lower hayloft. She recognized the hex symbol they'd been nailed to—two doves above two hearts above the trinity tulips—which was ironically the marriage hex.

Fucking homunculi and their sense of humor. The hands of the man and woman had been sewn together, as had their faces. Their eyes were missing as was their hair, which had probably been braided and used as thread by the homunculi. Their chests had been cracked wide open and their entrails were missing. She didn't have to look up to know what they'd been used for. She was close enough to touch the pair but would let the next team remove them along with all the other evidence. The woman's nipples had been cut off as well as the man's genitals. Then she noticed the teeth marks. No, not cut off.

"Bravo and Charlie. How are we doing?"

"This is Charlie. Not sure. Feels anticlimactic. I can't help but feel we're missing something."

"This is Bravo. What he said. Something feels off."

"Delta. Status."

Silence.

She turned to look at her team but Delta wasn't where he should have been. Neither was November. She spun them up in her optics, but those were dark where Delta and November were concerned. A yawning pit opened in her stomach. Fate chose this moment to remind her that this was the first time she'd led operators into combat. She'd taken it for granted how easy it would—should—be, but then she remembered back in ROTC when eight of her former classmates had gotten lost supporting a ROBIN SAGE Exercise at Fort Bragg—the final two week test for US Army Special Forces. She'd had to go in and rescue them, showing them that it should have been impossible to get lost at Fort Bragg, especially with all of the roads bisecting the fort like incisions in a great military Frankenstein.

And now this.

Her own team.

She was as out of her element now as the other eight had been then. She knew this because her first inclination was to doubt herself, something she was sure Boy Scout never did and she hated herself for it. She'd been involved with such a great team she'd forgotten that all teams weren't made—they were forged. And she'd never had the opportunity to forge her own. She'd taken for granted that they would all follow her lead, even if it was unspoken.

"Everyone on me," she commanded. She turned and surveyed the space. There had to be three dozen dead homunculi scattered on the floor and another ten dangling from the ceiling. "Shoot anything that moves under thirty-two inches."

She moved with purpose, slowly, examining the walls, ceiling and floor as she did. When she came to where Delta and November had been, she couldn't help but note that there was a trap door in the floor. The reason they hadn't noted it in the beginning was they'd been so focused on what they'd thought were dangling children on the ceiling and the onslaught on the ground, that she'd failed to note that they'd been standing on the door the entire time.

She tried to call Delta and November again but received no response.

She ordered the door opened.

While Alpha and Brave did as told, she and Charlie covered the opening as it gaped, then yawned, revealing a set of wooden stairs slanting into the darkness.

"Charlie, stay in position and watch our six. The rest of you with me."

She led the way down the stairs and into the darkness, flipping to IR. She immediately saw movement, but couldn't make out what she was seeing. It was as if there were hundreds of undulating bodies surrounding a lone figure. The IR wasn't helping. They needed light. She dialed up the flashlight on the right side of her head.

Alpha and Bravo followed suit.

Three bisecting beams of light revealed that the undulations were actually homunculi being formed— gestating from the corpses of the chickens that had once been used to lay eggs—and standing in the middle of it all was a teenage girl who couldn't be more than sixteen, Middle English spells dripping from her lips as she urged the bitty creatures to birth forth.

She didn't want to kill a kid if she didn't have to, but that didn't mean that she couldn't wound one. She pulled a 9mm from a thigh holster and fired three times, catching the girl in both of her legs. She screamed as she fell, but the undulations continued.

The basement seemed to take up the same space as the meeting room above. She finally spied lights, but Charlie got to them first and lit up the scene.

She had her men begin killing the creatures before they were fully formed, most of them still in various stages of transformation.

In a far corner she spied several figures on the ground.

She ran for them and noted that there were six in all.

They were three dead teenage boys, their overalls draped around their ankles, their hands cupping their privates. She'd suspected something of the sort. Besides a body to grow from, homunculi also needed sperm for their creation. Another was a middle-aged man, perhaps a farm hand or the brother to the father. He was also stripped, but his hands were at his sides. What was left of his genitals had been chewed away.

But her eyes were for the last two.

Delta was dead, his eyes gone, stolen by god knew what.

November whimpered and screamed into the crook of his right arm as a new born homunculi suckled at the fingers of his left hand. No, not suckled—it was eating the fingers of his left hand.

She ran over and shot the fucking arcane abortion in the back of the head, then knelt, jerked out her first aid kit, and began to wrap the man's mauled hand.

She looked into Field's crazed eyes and knew he'd never be the same again.

She wouldn't be either.

She'd underestimated the threat and gone into the situation without knowing the layout of the area of operations. And because of her lack of planning, she'd gotten one person killed and the other permanently crippled.

Yeah.

She was one hell of a leader.

Get the statue ready.

CHAPTER 2

She stormed out of the out brief the minute it was over. She didn't need anyone else to tell her what she'd done was wrong. She didn't need Poe to reiterate again and again that she should have done X instead of Y and she should have thought of A, B, C and fucking D. She knew all that. She'd been led by real leaders before and remembered after the fact everything she should have done to begin with. What bothered her the most was that she couldn't write a letter to Delta's family laying out how awful she felt and how great an operator he was. Instead, they'd be informed that he'd died in a training accident and be provided with five million dollars paid over a twenty-year span as part of his special life insurance. They'd mourn, but they wouldn't investigate. They had five million reasons not to.

Then there was Dr. Fields—aka November. All that remained of his left hand was his pinky. The rest had to be removed. He was just beginning to speak, but there was a strain behind everything he said and a twitch to his head, as if he was concerned that a threat might pop out at any moment. She'd never wanted him to come along, but that didn't matter. He had and she was responsible for his safety and his life and she'd failed miserably.

Now all she wanted to do was forget.

Forget Delta and the twin black holes where his eyes had been.

Forget November and the baby homunculi chewing off his hand.

Forget Boy Scout wherever he was if he was even still alive.

Forget McQueen—damn McQueen—the heart and soul of her old team.

And all the rest.

So may friends lost.

She was in the elevator about to head down when Poe shoved his arm out, stopped the doors from closing, and got on.

"Where you going?" he asked. His voice was even, but his eyes were curious.

"I have a date with a bottle of scotch. I know he's only twelve years old, but it's legal in some places."

"That's some pretty raw humor, Preacher's Daughter."

"I feel pretty raw right now."

"You know, we've all—"

"I don't care fuck all," she said. "I don't want to hear that everyone has had a bad leadership experience and that everyone makes mistakes. In fact, I don't even know the fucking word for a mistake that costs a human life. There should be a special word for it. Accident. Mistake.

Mishap." She laughed. "Fucking mishap. I drop an egg it's a mishap."

"What about tragedy or catastrophe or calamity?" he asked.

"Those are better." She hung her head and bit back a sob. She tightened her jaw. "Fuck, Poe. I just feel so helpless."

"I know. There's no 'save game' in real life. There are no redoes. We get one chance to fuck things up and we normally do it."

The door opened to the lower level where they had their quarters. They also had a gym, a TV room, a bar, and a cafeteria that was open twenty-four hours a day.

She headed for her room.

"The bar is that way," he said.

"I'm going to get a work out in. Then I'll hit the bar."

He nodded and continued in the other direction.

Ninety minutes later, after remembering sadly that it was leg day, she strode into the bar, freshly showered wearing shorts and a T-shirt she'd picked up in Bagram on one of her deployments. Her legs were still shaky and she knew the backs of her quads would be screaming in a few hours, but the adrenaline and serotonin that poured into her system while she'd been mauling her muscles with weights was exactly what she'd needed. As would be a couple of glasses of Macallan.

She found that Poe was still there, sitting with a gin and tonic, reading from a tablet.

"I didn't take you for a reader. Let me guess. Cozy

murder mystery? Something with cats and old women?"

He grinned. "You got me. Guilty as charged."

"Really?

He laughed. "This is a proposed mission brief, but it reads like a sci-fi book."

"Tell me about it," she said, glancing at the ice in her drink. She liked the scotch only after a certain amount of melting took place. Without the ice it was too strong. With too much it was too watery. There was a moment in time, however, when the scotch was near perfect.

"Not now. Let's talk about you."

She pointed above the bar and the sign that said 'Welcome to the DMZ.' "This is a demilitarized zone. Nothing military. Right?"

"I wasn't going to talk about anything military. I thought we might talk about relationships."

She leaned back and appraised him. "If this is an opening line—"

"It isn't."

"Oh. Then what about them? Relationships can be sticky. They can suck or be great or even both at the same time." It was time for her to take a sip. Perfection. "What exactly are we talking about?"

"Your last team."

"My last team."

"I knew when I first met you guys that you were closer knit than a family. That's both good and bad. The bad is that you might never find that again. How many people do you know that continue to be operators and deploy to warzones because they had that one perfect tour and they were looking to relive it just one more time."

"Too many."

"Good. Because I want to make sure that you understand that what you had you will probably never have again. I don't want you to be constantly on the lookout for something perfect only to be disappointed."

She paused, then said, "All that is great psychology, but why are you telling me this?"

"Because I've been where you are. I've felt what you are feeling. Now that Boy Scout is out of the picture, you're like the lone survivor. It's not a good feeling."

She hung her head. "No. It's not." Then she raised her head. "Have you checked on him? Do you know if he's still alive?"

Poe gave her a stern look, then softened. He took a sip of his G&T. "I have something more important for you."

She sighed and took another sip. Poe was always changing the subject when it came to figuring out whether her old boss and friend was still breathing on planet Earth. "What is it? Am I going to walk an old woman across the street? Pet some dogs? What menial skill will you trust me with after I FUBARed the last mission?"

"I was thinking about the conversation we had about walking through doors."

"You mean the doorway theory?" she asked. She and her team had applied it on their last mission and it had helped them conquer millennia-old Zoroastrian demons.

It was more than just a theory. The doorway effect was absolutely true.

She remembered the conversation she'd had when she'd introduced the concept to McQueen and Boy Scout. She'd been ribbing McQueen, who was in perfect physical shape, about being fat when she'd brought up the idea that had ultimately saved them.

"There's this thing that scientists call the doorway effect. They based the title on research done at the University of Notre Dame. The idea was to try and explain why the brain partitions information a certain way. For instance, when you carry something from one room to the other, once you leave the room you came from, there's a better than average chance you'll forget why you were going to the other room or what you were supposed to do with the object in your hands. Because the subjects were tested in the room and then after they left the room, scientists were able to determine that moving through the doorway had an effect.

"Distance didn't have the same effect as the doorway," she continued. *"Subjects were tested after walking the same distance with the only differing operand being a doorway and, in every case, going through the doorway affected the ability of the subject to remember. What is it about a doorway that causes the mind to partition or replace a human's random-access memory? This suggests that there's more to the remembering than just what you paid attention to, when it happened, and how hard you tried. Instead, some forms of memory seem to be*

optimized to keep information ready-to-access until its shelf life expires, and then purge that information in favor of new stuff, like a computer would have RAM."

"Aren't you talking about ROM?" McQueen asked.

She shook her head. "That's Read Only Memory. Think breathing, the heart beating, etcetera. The body's ROM is what it needs to merely survive. By being read only it can't be overwritten. Imagine if it was and suddenly you stopped breathing because the code would no longer be there."

"Deleterious," McQueen said, nodding sagely.

"Deli—" She laughed. "Deleterious indeed? Were you just playing Scrabble or something? More like devastating. If that happened you might not have enough time to even say deleterious." She sighed. "Where was I before Mr. Scrabble joined in?" She snapped a finger. "Right. So, ROM covers everyday functions. RAM is short term memory that gets you through the day, and the hard disk is where memories are stored. So again, what is it about a doorway that makes the brain decide to overwrite the mind's RAM?"

"The mind is a strange machine. My PTSD proves it," Boy Scout said. "There are those who have done far less than I have whose minds can't deal with what they've seen and done. Do you think that the more doors you've gone through—metaphorically—the easier it is to deal with everything you've seen?"

"Certainly, the more experiences one has, the better their mind should become in organizing the information," she said. "For instance, a person who has never traveled might find themselves completely lost in a large airport because they have no frame of reference—no information on the hard drive. But me, or you, or even our fat gay hipster over there—"

"I'm not fat," McQueen said.

"Wouldn't have a problem, even in an airport in a foreign country without any signs in English. Know why?"

"Because we can bring our experiences to bear and use them to figure out the current configuration," Boy Scout said.

"And this is all done by the mind accessing the hard drive and placing the needed information in the RAM."

"I am not fat." McQueen repeated. "This is muscle." He flexed his arms and sucked in his stomach. He seemed disappointed that it wouldn't suck in more.

"Sure, it is, dear," Preacher's Daughter said.

"How does this apply to the doorway effect?" Boy Scout asked.

"I was thinking about the entities inside of you. They knew who they were and what they were back before they passed into The White. Then they passed into you. That's two completely different doorways. The White was a universe that could be molded by those within. The reason we called it The White was because it was featureless until we did something to it. I bet that's the same thing with your mind and I don't think they know where they are."

McQueen nodded. *"Like the airports. These entities had never been in an airport or the mind of a middle-aged semi-broken former Army Ranger, so their minds don't know how to explain it to them. And I'm not fat."*

"As they go from one door to the other, they forget what they were going there for," Preacher's Daughter said.

She smiled wistfully as she returned to the here and now. "You are too fat, my big dead gay hipster," she said to the universe. Then she took a drink and wiped the corner of her eyes.

"What about the doorway effect?" she asked Poe. "You missing a set of keys?"

"More like an entire town."

She grinned at the joke, then realized it wasn't a joke. "A town? How can we have an entire town missing?"

"We think a town is missing, but can't be sure."

"Wait a minute? Either it's missing or it isn't missing. What are you talking about?"

"Our computers say it's missing. There are references to it everywhere. We even have satellite imagery. But no one believes it. Everyone thinks the information is fake, including me."

She pursed her lips, then took a drink. "If no one believes it, then maybe it never existed."

"That's what makes the most sense, right? But if that's the case, why does all the information on the computers, including an algorithm that we have to track such things, say that it does exist." He raised a hand. "And oh yes.

One more thing. We also have an eye witness who claims that one day people just decided to not go there anymore because no one believed in its existence."

"That doesn't make sense at all. What is this place?"

"Iron Hat, South Dakota. It's on the Pine Ridge Indian Reservation."

"Never heard of it," she said.

"I knew you were going to say that," he said.

"How did you know?"

"I've been reading your resume and it states that before you joined the army, you were a missionary for your father."

"That's why they call me Preacher's Daughter. My father was a Baptist Minister."

"And according to your resume, you spent half a summer in Iron Hat performing missionary duties for your father when you were twelve."

"It didn't happen."

"Maybe," he said, "Just maybe, you've walked through so many doors you've forgotten about it."

"Seriously? It actually says that? I was a missionary in Iron Hat? Then why don't I remember?"

He raised a finger. "That's the million-dollar question."

CHAPTER 3

DR. FIELDS INSISTED on returning to work. He looked like a shrunken version of himself. He no longer held his head high, nor did he cock his chin like he owned the world. He looked more like a scared little man in a lab coat and Preacher's Daughter hated herself for it. As much as a pain in the ass Norris had been, he didn't deserve to spend the rest of his life this way. They'd fitted him with a prosthetic for his hand, with the promise of something more permanent later.

She and Poe sat midway in a small classroom for the best view of the screen. Fields stood near a table with a projector. He dimmed the lights and then began his presentation.

"Let me introduce to you the town of Urkhammer, Iowa," he began. His voice was far from normal and just on the edge of a shriek. He had developed a nervous tic that made his head twitch. He held his left hand protectively against his chest when he spoke. He stopped speaking, seemingly lost in a vision.

"What's so special about Urkhammer?" she asked,

throwing him a safety line to bring him back to the present.

He blinked and returned to them. "It doesn't exist." Fields showed a series of pictures of an old town taken from an airplane. Streets. Houses. Cars. But no people could be seen on the streets. "This is Urkhammer taken in 1929. Note that we have tangible evidence of its existence."

"How do we know that the pictures are of Urkhammer?" Poe asked.

"Annotations on the flight log and on the backs of the original pictures. Could they have been faked from the beginning? Sure, but let's posit a hypothesis that it existed as we see it in 1928. Fast forward to 1934 and there are reports that a caravan of families from Illinois heading West during the Great Depression sent men into town for supplies. The men were unable to enter any of the stores."

She asked, "When you say unable to enter, you mean—"

"Their feet would pass through the entrance steps and they couldn't walk into any of the stores."

She grinned. "Impossible."

"Later, when it was reported, police went into town to talk to the local sheriff. They couldn't knock on the door because their hands passed through the wood."

"This sounds like an episode of *The Twilight Zone*," she said.

"Indeed," he said, followed by a giggle. "A year later the town was reported as completely missing. All of the buildings were gone. What was left were the fields and the fences and the sidewalks." She was about to say something, but he held up his hand. "Then, in the late 90s, it was reported on the then nascent internet and became a product of an urban legends website. Or rather, it was claimed to have been completely made up. Invented. As in it never happened."

She frowned. "Then why tell us all of this if it was just a story to keep grown children living in a basement happy?"

"What if it was true? What if it did exist? What if everyone forgot about it? The natural assumption would be to say then that all evidence leading to it was made up. Then there's Doveland, Wisconsin."

He went through a sequence of pictures showing signs that said 'Welcome to Doveland.' T-shirts that advertised various Doveland businesses. Even a postcard that had been dated in 1956 from Doveland, Wisconsin.

He turned to them and nodded sagely. "Doveland does not exist either. It's not on any map. Reddit lists it as an urban legend. It's not real, yet we have this evidence.

"Then finally, there is Langville, Montana. It appeared on Google Maps but not in person. No one ever heard of it or has seen it, but there has been over seven million searches for Langville, Montana in the history of the internet. Why would people search for something that doesn't exist? And why does Google Maps have saved images of Langville from street view, but no actual map of the town?"

She turned to Poe. "This can't be all about doorways. It sounds more like Hyperstition."

"Tell me," he said.

"Hyperstition. Some gave a UK philosopher and eugenicist credit for the term, but the idea goes back to Plato's *Republic* where Socrates, Glaucon, and Adeimantus decide to create Plato's City in Speech to see how justice can be formed. In doing so, they have to populate the city and create all the relevant infrastructure and constructs."

Seeing the strained look on Poe's face, she tried again. "Hyperstition is a portmanteau of 'hyper' and 'superstition.' The term posits that hyper, the state of being abnormally or unusually active, and superstition, which is a widely held but unjustified belief, can come together and become an entity unto itself. Nick Land says that hyperstitions by their very existence as ideas function causally to bring about their own reality. In modern times that would be the idea of Atlantis, which is widely believed but lacking in fact. Or the Bermuda Triangle or the Illuminati. Or in political terms, the idea that America is run by a coven of pedophiles who traffic in children, which is what QAnon is trying to show for their own purposes. Once the ideas are posited, society creates facts around them that justifies the belief. These facts aren't necessarily facts, though. They were merely data points that can be applied to best give weight to either side of an argument.

"Take QAnon for instance. They insist that everyone do

their own research rather than provide proof themselves. This is genius really, because the average person doesn't know that original sourcing is the only way to prove things reasonably. Instead, they will search for any data point that adds proof to their argument, rather than searching for substantiating fact. It's a problem of the internet. It has provided a democratization of data points with an entire section of society unable to viably provide proper weight to the points."

"Aren't you being a little harsh?" Poe asked.

"Not at all. I'm not being academically prejudiced, either. Hyperstition is everywhere. Borges wrote about it in 1941 in his story 'Tlön, Uqbar, Orbis Tertius'. The story is about a city that is discovered because of a missing entry in a fictional encyclopedia that takes on a life of its own. The idea of hyperstition has been around for a long time."

"You're saying that the belief in Urkhammer, Loveland, and Langville is hyperstition," Poe said.

"I'm positing that it could be." She smiled. "I don't have enough datapoints to prove or disprove, but the idea of towns suddenly going missing is mysterious unto itself."

"Let's look at datapoints, then," Dr. Fields said. "Let's look at them with regards to Iron Hat. An internet search shows no record of Iron Hat ever. There are no data points."

"But I thought you said I went there," she said to Poe.

"Your resume was kept on a closed system. It lists Iron Hat."

Fields flipped another picture. This one showed her resume. For the most part she recognized it but the inclusion of missionary work in Iron Hat was as unfamiliar to her as if she suddenly had an afro.

She snapped her fingers. "Wait a moment. I thought Poe said that we had satellite imagery and websites that detailed the location."

"We did," Fields said. "Those data points no longer exist."

She sat back in her chair and oofed. "Could you have been wrong?"

Fields shrugged. "I suppose I could have been."

She decried his lack of confidence. She used to hate it and now she missed it. "But you doubt it?"

"I doubt it."

"Is this the only data point we have?"

"We also have the eye witness reports of a Sioux Indian called Francis Scott Key Catches the Enemy." He dialed up a video which showed a fifty-something Indian with deep creases in his face, long black hair tied into a braid beneath a baseball cap, speaking to the camera.

"Then they'd pull up, stop, look around like they didn't know where they were going, then turn around. Know why the jobless rate went up by thirty percent overnight in Kyle? Because those people used to work in Iron Hat and now they have no place to go and nothing to do because they all think the place doesn't exist."

"And you do, Mr. Catches. How does that make you feel? Lucky?" asked the blonde reporter with Rapid City call letters on her microphone.

"Lucky, hell. Makes me feel cursed. Why is it I know all this and no one else does?"

"Why indeed, Mr. Catches? Why indeed?"

Then the young reporter did her sign off and she and the handsome reporter in the studio joked about how crazy the man might be.

Preacher's Daughter pointed at the screen where it froze on Francis Scott Key Catches the Enemy. "We need to talk to that man."

"We sure do. A team is going out tonight to pick him up and bring him in to find out why he might be right when everyone else is wrong."

"Measuring him as a data point," Fields added.

"Makes sense. I'll get ready," she said, preparing to stand. Already, she was going over everything she would need to get ready. She wasn't going to be caught flat-footed again.

"Hold on," Poe told her. "You're not going."

"What do you mean?" She glanced at Fields who was staring at his left hand. She sagged back into her seat. "Is it because of the last mission?"

"Nothing of the sort," Poe said.

"Then why did you go to all the effort to brief me on a mission that I am not going to be a part of?"

"Who said you weren't going to be a part of this?"

"Wait. I don't get it."

"You do need to pack up and be ready. You are leaving tomorrow."

She realized he was parceling out information like a stingy neighbor parcels out candy to kids during Halloween. One. Bit. At. A. Fucking. Time. "Okay, Poe, enough of your games. What's the scoop?"

"You're leaving for Heathrow in the morning. Turns out this is not an isolated incident. A town went missing in England three days ago and the only one who seems to remember it is the member of parliament who represents it."

"Data point," said Fields.

"What about the Black Dragoons? Aren't they on it?"

Poe grinned. "Oh, they are. But because this happened in both places, this is now a joint venture. They're sending someone over as well."

She crossed her arms and stared at him for a long moment. "How come this feels like a hostage exchange?"

"It's not as bad as that," Poe said, standing and exiting the row. "You're being overly dramatic."

"Am I? Ever heard of mushy peas?" She made a look of disgust on her face. "And their chips are limp. Who wants a limp chip?"

Poe paused at the door. "I'm counting on you not to make this an international incident, Preacher's Daughter. America's various organizations have been friends with England and partners with the Black Dragoons for hundreds of years. Please don't ruin that in an afternoon."

Her frown deepened. "I got your international incident," she muttered.

CHAPTER 4

SHE'D MANAGED TO sleep for exactly two hours between the mission brief and landing at Heathrow. She'd been too excited and had spent the trip doing all the research she could do regarding hyperstition and Great Britain. The theory was interesting in that it could explain the way a lot of impractical things came into being. How someone could create a third point of a triangle which created the first two points after the fact. She'd plugged in and listened to a podcast called *Weird Studies* that had an episode about hyperstition. She'd made notes on the subject because they were getting into areas that interested her.

All great fiction is a refrain. All refrains are aesthetic constructs. A great work of fiction is an instrument for gathering specific forces within a milieu or territory and connecting them to the Cosmos that undergirds all things. Every fiction, in other words, is magical. In its cosmic function, every fiction brings forth a world. That's why you can use David Lynch's *Twin Peaks* to talk about the atom bomb and it works.

A concrete example how refrains work. *The first punk song was 'Blank Generation' by the band Television. The chorus "I belong to the blank generation" set to that particular melody and that particular rhythm— this is a refrain. What the song establishes is a territory, whereas the older proto-punk songs ('Helter Skelter,' 'My Generation,' 'Louie' covered by Kingsmen, etc.) are still at the milieu level—they exist within the territory of pop music. With Blank Generation, punk is born as a territory with its various intrinsic milieus. It's more than music: it's a setting (garbage- and graffiti-strewn alleyways), it's a way to dress, it's a set of beliefs, and it's a vision of life—a whole world of punk. Think of the poster for the film* Sid & Nancy. *You see the eponymous lovers embracing in a garbage-strewn alleyway. Would the image have communicated the essence of the film if the two punks were in a strawberry field or in front of an altar? Of course not, because the garbage-strewn alleyway is part of what these characters signify, a punk world. That entire world was called forth cosmically in that first song. Everything that happened afterwards was a kind of deployment or unfurling.*

Therefore, the punk scene created itself before there was even a scene based on an aesthetic concept. She couldn't help but laugh. The very idea that if a punk knew he or she had been envisioned before they were ever made would make them not want to be a punk.

They provided other examples in the podcast like fiction writer H.P. Lovecraft's Cthulhu mythos and the notion that there were elder gods, which he created out of whole cloth but which are conceptually worshipped by believers around the globe as real entities. Entire cults have been created surrounding these elder gods and if questioned, they treat Lovecraft as if he were Jesus or a prophet who received the information from the gods themselves and decided, instead of creating a bible, to popularize them in fiction.

She'd believed that she'd understood hyperstition, but the more she read, the more it delved into the increased speed of capitalism, the devaluation of social contracts, and the pragmatism of conceiving of and inventing a future. She couldn't help but feel some of the authors had absconded with the word and were using it for their own use, where she merely needed to understand the intersection between truth and the creation of something to become truth.

She was contemplating this and more when she was met in the greeting area by a tall man wearing a shirt and tie with a Tweed sports jacket. He wore jeans beneath this with turn-ups, and expensive-looking brown brogues with commando rubber soles hugged his feet. She felt completely out of her element. She'd dressed for travel and had sweat pants and a sweat shirt from Monterey, California, and a baseball cap that said 'Don't Feed the SEALS' with a circle and a slash drawn through a SEAL operator. She definitely gave off the soccer mom vibe or possible even a military spouse. She subtly raised her left arm to determine if she smelled. She knew how disheveled her hair was beneath the cap. *Oh Dear God.*

"Ms. May, I presume?" came the lilted British voice.

He seemed a bit standoffish as if he wasn't sure if a woman dressed like that could be an elite operator.

Damn it, but why was it that whenever a Brit spoke, she felt as uneducated as a heel of day old bread.

"That's me. You are—you're Colonel McDonnell?"

"Call me Mal."

"Then call me Preacher's Daughter."

He raised his eyes but made no other move. "Do you always go by your call sign?"

She thought for a moment, then nodded. "Pretty much always." She glanced at him as they started walking. She only had her carry-ons, so she was following him to a security door. He badged a camera and a moment later the door buzzed and let them through.

"Good thing I was wearing a disguise," she said.

She caught him raising another eyebrow. It seemed to be his only facial muscle. "Is that why you are dressed like an out of work housewife on a holiday."

She closed her eyes and felt her face redden. She considered returning to America and maybe starting over, but knew it was too late. So instead, she shuffled along behind the regal man like the combat soccer mom that he thought she was.

They took an otherwise empty bus across the tarmac until they came to an unmarked but distinctly military helicopter. She wracked her brain for the model. She knew the British military used the Apache and the old Vietnam warhorse the Bell 212. But they also had their own aircraft. With some air frames they partnered with France to develop a joint helicopter. But she believed this was the MK1 Wildcat, named after the airplane that fought in World War II. This one didn't have any armament, but it did have the nose mounted MX-15 Wescam Electro Optical Device (EOD) enabling it to detect targets by day and night at significant range.

Waiting in the door was another man in civilian clothes. He wore a thin-looking roll-neck beneath a navy blue Harrington jacket and sunglasses, looking a little like Steve McQueen. He had a ready smile, a mop of blonde hair and a deep tan. He reached down to help her on board. "Ma'am."

She accepted the hand and felt his firm strength as he pulled her into the craft.

"This is one of my sergeants. Andy MacKenzie. Call sign Munro."

She saw the questioning look that MacKenzie gave to his superior.

"Apparently call signs are all the rage in America," Mal said.

"It's just that in my last unit whenever we were on mission, we never used our real names," she explained. "Not only was it considered sound operational tradecraft, but it reminded each of us we were in a high threat environment of some sort." She shrugged. "It just became my habit. Listen, this is your place, not mine. If you want to call me by my first name, call me Lore."

"Sound operational tradecraft," Mal mused. "What do you think of that, Munro?"

"I think she has a point, sir."

Munro was older than sergeants she'd come to know in the American military. He was probably forty or close to it. But then she remembered that their rank system was a bit different and that sergeant was often much harder to attain.

"I think she has a point too. We can always learn from our young cousins in America." He turned to Preacher's Daughter as the pilot spun up the helicopter. The sergeant sat across from them, already strapped in and muttering through comms. "What do you know of the Black Dragoons?"

"Only that you went to the site of the old cistern in Northern Afghanistan after we battled the dervish. Also, that your organization has been around for quite some time. Longer than 77 for sure. Even longer than SEAL Team 666 I believe."

"This is true. Our lineage began in 1689. At the time, we were Sir Albert Cunningham's Regiment of Dragoons and a normal military unit. We were a brigade of heavy calvary that quickly went to work when the dethroned James II of England, with the help of the French, tried to take over Ireland. We fought on the side of William of Orange and helped to defeat the Stuarts. We changed names several times over the preceding years, first becoming the 6th Dragoons and then the 7th Dragoons. We fought in the Battle of Waterloo and in the Crimean and Boer Wars. Probably our greatest battle was during the Charge of the Heavy Brigade at the Battle of Balaclava where we slaughtered Russian calvary forces that far outnumbered us."

"Four hundred years. That's impressive. When did you become a special unit?" she asked.

"When we went to Flanders in 1743 during the Battle of Dettingen. We almost lost that one. Those in the know consider it a lucky victory, but we had to retreat to achieve it. Not often you win on your heels. Besides being overpowered, we had pitiable reconnaissance. Add to that, our food stores were destroyed when golems rose from the clay of the River Main and attacked our rear lines. No one was prepared for that. I mean, there'd been some talk of various supernatural events in the Jacobite Rising, but nothing of this nature. The Black Dragoons were in the middle of reconstituting, so most of us were in the rear when it happened. Had we not been there to put down the golems, the battle might have gone the other way.

"It was then that King George II formed us into a reaction force for supernatural events. Not the whole brigade, mind you, just a core of us in the know. Then in 1922, we were amalgamated into other units and disbanded, but the core remained and we formed our headquarters in Enniskillen where the original Black Dragoons had been formed."

She raced through her knowledge of Ireland based on a trip she'd made and asked, "Isn't that in Northern

Ireland? Wasn't that where…" She trailed off, afraid of bringing up bad memories.

"Yes and yes?" Munro said, his jaw firm, apparently not wanting to add much to the conversation.

"Yes, Enniskillen is in Northern Ireland," Mal confirmed, "and one of the most difficult periods in our recent history."

"I don't think any civilized country goes unscathed in their history. We've had our own issues as we've tried to overcome earlier failings."

"We all try and be better despite ourselves," Mal said.

"One thing is for certain," Preacher's Daughter said, trying to invent her own little bit of hyperstition. "Whenever someone says the country will never be the same again, they're right, but most often it becomes a better country because those who are in the right achieve over those who just want to be right."

Munro laughed. "Deep thoughts. Can we keep her, sir? I like this one."

She laughed too. She felt no condescension in the sergeant's comments. "I'm lease-to-own and I don't know if you can afford me." She glanced down again at her apparel and was once again mortified. "I'm sorry about the way—I mean—I'd meant to purchase clothes once we got to—hell—I'm a soup sandwich. Aren't I?"

Both Mal and Munro laughed.

She blushed slightly, but just satisfied herself by staring out the window as the countryside rolled past below. Copses of trees followed by small towns, followed by more trees. All shades of green like an American park. No huge housing divisions. No gigantic industrial sites. America was a large place that could fit such ugliness, but in England, they'd had to find better balance, which meant fit the ugly between as many green hedges of beauty as one could.

When they were five minutes out, she made the decision to change and fuck the audience. She pulled out her pack, grabbed a tactical shirt and a T-shirt from the Queens of the Stone Age first album. She also pulled out a pair of 5.11 pants, a belt, and a pair of Merrells. All the while with her new team mates trying not to look, she brazenly removed her clothes and replaced them with something suitable. By the time they were ready to land, she had her shirt unbuttoned over her T-shirt and was rolling up the sleeves.

She sat back in her seat with a satisfied sigh just as they then began to descend. She loved helicopter rides. She always had. She especially loved the one from Kabul to Bagram. She'd normally take off from the Green Zone, which meant running to a helicopter that had just landed in the middle of a protected soccer field. Normally, there would be two contract pilots and a door gunner. By door gunner she meant an operator in a monkey harness around his waist and a long rifle. But that was the end of the military of it. The ride was normally smooth, flying over farms and homes, and family compounds; ranging over the country at the foothills of the Hindu Kush, it was hard to believe from a thousand feet that there was a war going on. But then they'd land at Bagram and the fuel and rubber smell from the various aircraft and the acrid cancer-causing stench of the ever-present burn pits would slam into her and she'd know once again she was in a hell created a thousand years ago by a then invading force and that hell would continue for another thousand years.

Afghanistan was like Milton's *Paradise Lost*.

Abandon All Hope Ye Who Enter Here.

And every country who ever invaded, ensured that paradise would forever be lost in their search of an eye of a needle large enough to pass through with the spoils of a war the country never deserved.

CHAPTER 5

As IT TURNED out, the main headquarters for the Black Dragoons was also in a castle, something right out of *Game of Thrones*. Called Caverswall Castle, it was a fourteen-bedroom castle that had been for sale by a family who had to give it up for taxes. Being temporarily owned by the government, it wasn't long before the Black Dragoons found it and forcibly moved in. Munro gave her the ten-cent aerial tour as they landed, explaining to her that it had always been a private residence. Built on the foundations of a thirteenth century castle, the current mansion was renovated in the 1600s, and had a moat and towers at each corner. It had served several families of High Sheriffs of Staffordshire and looked exactly to her what a castle should look like. The modern problem was that civilization had grown around it and the castle now found itself squatting on the edge of Stoke-on-Trent, surrounded by a park on the west and several churches and a pub. The major selling point for Mal's predecessor had been the moat. Besides salt, it was amazing what creatures were unable to cross simple water, which made

71

the headquarters one of the safer places for the Black Dragoons to make their home.

A young Indian man dressed in a DayGlo pink shirt and tight shorts greeted them as they landed in the courtyard inside the castle walls and before the front door. He offered to help her out, but she declined and jumped out on her own, then grabbed her bag. When she stood on the ground beside him, she realized that he was easily a foot taller.

After Munro and Mal exited the helicopter, they exchanged greetings.

"Preacher's Daughter, this is JigJat Chaterjee, but we call him Jagger. He's our comms specialist, loaned to us by the Navy."

The young man grinned, his dark skin and darker hair making him a handsome albeit leaner version of McQueen—the comparison only because of his pink shirt and the compassion that lived in his eyes. This pleased her and she self-consciously wondered if she might not be projecting her memory of her dead friend and teammate.

"I have the rest of the team inside and waiting, sir. We have an issue, I'm afraid."

Mal's eyebrow did what it did.

Munro grinned from ear to ear. It was clear he was the type that loved field work.

Didn't they all, though?

Inside, she was told to drop her bag. They'd show her to her digs later. For now, they had a mission brief.

Evidently, something else had come up besides a missing village in the center of England.

A formal dining room with parquet floors and thirty-foot ceilings had been transformed into an operations center with seven giant screen displays and an equal amount of computer systems. Tapestries still hung on the walls behind the screens, showing various hunting scenes with dogs and horses. Two other men and a woman sat at terminals, madly typing away, until they heard the group come into the room. All of them disengaged and stood, oddly formal, as if coming to attention.

Mal said, "As you were. Waterhouse, what's the situation?"

A tall but younger version of Mal nodded and with barely moving his lips was able to say, "Knockers, sir. Hundreds reported at Geevor. Come up from underground. Scared a bunch of tourists."

"Hundreds?" Munro said, as if the number was astronomical.

Mal turned to one of the screens that showed a map of England. "Is that what we've become? The Home Office solution to the tourism industry?"

"They killed one, sir and bit off the toes of another," Waterhouse said. "Not good advertising for the UK."

"Nottingham, what's the response so far?"

A black body builder with a crewcut shave and arms the size of regular people's thighs stood with his hands behind his back. His accent was pure cockney with accentuation on the leading vowels. "Local police have a cordon. Scotland Yard's been hammering at MI5 Special Office to handle the situation and that means us."

"Patterson, what's the plan?"

A heavyset woman with dark curly hair frowned. "Chopper is getting refueled. We have weapons and kit ready for all of us, but Ms. May still needs to be certified. Until she obtains special service weapons certification, reads the regulations, and gets her unit qualification signed, she's going to have to be a bystander." When there was no immediate response, the older woman added, "I recommend we leave her back here where she can't get her nails broken."

So, it was going to be that way.

Never once did the woman named Patterson look at Preacher's Daughter. If there was one thing she hated it was being talked about in the third person when she was in the room. Was there animosity coming from the woman or was she just over zealous?

"Who's *she*? The cat's mother?" Munro asked, eyebrow raised.

"She'll be fine, Patterson," Mal said. "Make sure she has a kit."

"But, sir, Home Office regulation states that she has to—"

"I said she'll be fine. In fact, let me introduce United States Army Reserve First Lieutenant Laurie May from Special Unit 77. She prefers to use her call sign when operational. I think that would be a good idea for all of us. Maybe reaffirm our professionalism. Isn't that right,

Barbie?" Mal said, looking at the woman.

Preacher's Daughter inhaled slightly as she saw the anger flare in the woman's eyes. If anything, she was the opposite of a Barbie, if one thought the term represented the ideal unreachable figure some toy maker once decreed that all woman should replicate. For Patterson, it was surely an insult. Was that how they developed their call signs around here? If so, maybe it wasn't a good idea for them to identify using them.

Waterhouse looked pained. "Must we, sir?"

Munro grinned. "It's on like Donkey Kong."

Waterhouse closed his eyes as if he couldn't stand the thought of being seen.

She decided to do something about the situation. "Hey," she stepped forward, careful not to overstep her bounds. She could already tell this unit was a lot more military than she was used to. "If I may, sir," she said to Mal. After a nod, she continued, "We probably do things differently in America."

"You think?" Nottingham asked.

She ignored the comment. "We choose our own call signs or have them given to us, but we always tend to agree to them. I don't want anyone to go around insulted because of a tradition I come from."

Mal stood a little straighter. "There's no insult. Each member of the team earns their call sign, isn't that right, Mr. Waterhouse."

"That's right sir," Waterhouse said tightly.

"Good then. Let me properly introduce everyone then."

For the next few minutes, they had proper introductions, then they were off to get kitted up. Besides body armor and light helmets with comms units and lights, they were issued L22A2 assault rifles with short barrels. Munro and Nottingham carried Benelli M4 Super 90 automatic shotguns. They all also wore Sig Sauer P226s in cross draw holsters affixed to the molles on the front of their body armor. After comms and weapons checks, they boarded what looked like the same helicopter they'd landed in and took off. Their distance was a little over three hundred miles and would take roughly two hours. Most everyone had already settled in, but Preacher's Daughter's head was still reeling from the introductions and the complications of the new mission—not to mention her lack of sleep.

Lieutenant Colonel Malcom McDonnell aka Mal had the call sign Bad Times. He'd spent most of his career in Special Forces and waxed poetic about Afghanistan as if he were the long-lost great grandson of Rudyard Kipling. Mal attended Eton College, which was actually a boarding school, then went on to graduate from the Royal Military Academy at Sandhurst. Although he didn't look like he came from money, he acted like it and seemed to prefer strict military order, even in a unit as unconventional as the Black Dragoons.

Captain Ethan Waterhouse, for all intents and purposes, seemed to be a younger version of Mal. He'd also attended Sandhurst, but four years earlier. He was also British Army, but he was an Engineer specializing in the rebuilding and taking down of enemy infrastructure. By the jibing of his mates during the introductions, it was clear that Waterhouse came from money and a lot of it. It was also clear that he was uncomfortable because of it. The biggest surprise was his call sign. Donkey Kong. Why someone was named after a 1980s video game she didn't know. She knew there had to be a story behind it and looked forward to when he might tell her about it— if she was ever able to break through his stony exterior.

Lieutenant Abbie Patterson was going to be trouble— she fell short of saying nemesis, because that would mean that there was a mutual dislike for each other. Still, by the comments and the piercing looks, it was clear that Patterson did not like that there was another female in the unit. In fact, she seemed not to like the fact that she herself was a female in the unit. She had broad shoulders and a broad waist and man's features, which is why Preacher's Daughter couldn't help but feel that the call sign Barbie was a mean attempt to make fun of her. Body-shaming had never been in her top ten things to do when you're bored and she didn't want to start now. Unlike the two men senior to her, Patterson didn't wear her schools on her sleeve, so Preacher's Daughter could only presume that she had a modest education. Patterson's background was intelligence, like her own.

Andy MacKenzie was the lone Scotsman on the team and was by far the easiest to work with. With his fair demeanor and easy smile, he seemed capable of defusing many situations. He'd tested his mettle as a Royal Marine

Commando in various campaigns throughout Africa and the Middle East. A professed animal lover, his idea of going on holiday was flying out to Mozambique and providing sniper fire to take out elephant poachers. His call sign was Munro, which was confusing, because it seemed just like another name. She'd have to ask what it meant or else remain confused in the interim.

Viceroy Nottingham was the only black man on the team. He had the sort of body she suspected took four hours a day in the gym to prepare, not that she minded by the look of his muscles. He also had a ready smile and was also Royal Marine Commando. But while MacKenzie had been stationed with the 45 at RM Condor in Arbroath, Scotland, Nottingham was with the 40 in Somerset. Also, a senior sergeant, Nottingham was the team's weapons specialist, ensuring that they had the latest and greatest and was all in working order. He had the most obvious call sign, Sheriff, referencing Robin Hood and the old Sheriff of Nottingham.

Finally, JigJat Chatterjee. Of British Indian descent, he was their communications specialist. His rank was Leading Hand, which she understood to be the Navy equivalent of corporal. He seemed studious and serious, but generally interested in the well-being of his team mates. He was the tallest of them, but very thin to the point of his health being worrisome. His flamboyance wasn't lost on her either. A few extra rings here, a bracelet there, an ear ring there, penchant for bright colors, all made her homesick and missing McQueen who'd died a short six months ago. JigJat's call sign was Jagger, as in the lead singer of the Rolling Stones.

She glanced across at Patterson and wondered why with all the choices in call signs they had to name her Barbie. Not that she even knew, but she was getting pissed off for the other woman.

CHAPTER 6

JAGGER GAVE HER a rundown of the history of Cornish miners just prior to landing which she appreciated. Not only did she not know a thing about mining, but she'd also never been to the southwestern tip of England and Cornwall, only having seen it in war movies and briefly in the socio-political historical television series *Poldark*. As it turned out, Cornish miners had been famous the world over. Even during the California Gold Rush, American speculators had hired Cornish miners to sail to America and work in mines. This coincided with a decline in tin mining in Cornwall, thus leading to a Cornish diaspora as miners left for any opportunity to ply their trade. There's a Cornish saying that 'a mine is a hole anywhere in the world with at least one Cornishman at the bottom of it!'

Unlike many of the mines in Cornwall, Geevor Tin Mine, where they were going, was fairly new. It had provided roughly 50,000 tons of black tin from 1910 to 1990. Most of the then modern equipment was still in place as a museum and United Nations World Heritage

Site. Unlike what she'd seen in *Poldark* with men climbing down tunnels supported by beams, Geevor had become more and more automated towards the end of its lifespan. But there were still parts of the mine hearkening back to the nineteenth century, and it was in these parts where the Knockers had been reported. Specifically, in Wheal Mexico, which still had dirt and stone floors and walls and ceilings propped by timber.

She knew what a Knocker was from her research. Although seen in underground locations in the United States—probably brought over by immigrants—they were predominant in England. Their appearance was startlingly similar to that of a homunculus, except that all their faces were supposed to be aged and covered in white whiskers. The name Knockers comes from the knocking on the walls of a mine which usually preceded a cave-in. While some of the miners believed that the Knockers were warning them of impending doom, others believed that it was the Knockers who caused the cave-in, this making them malevolent.

"One thing is for certain. We've not had reports of them gathering in such large a group before. I went through the archives. It's as if something is driving them up," Jagger said.

"You saying something might be coming up beneath?" Sheriff asked.

Jagger shook his head. "Not saying anything of the sort. I'm just speculating."

"Let's keep the speculations to a minimum," Mal said.

"We'll have enough time to figure out why they are there after we assess the situation."

Preacher's Daughter wanted to interject that they could be doing both, but she'd already felt the hard vibe that to dissent with unit command was the absolutely wrong thing to do. She glanced at Patterson to see what she was thinking and was rewarded with an angry glare. What the hell was up with that woman?

"Preacher's Daughter?"

"Yes, sir."

"I want you hanging back," Mal said. "I'm sure you can take care of yourself, but we have a way of doing things in the Dragoons."

"I completely understand, Mal. I mean sir." She grinned sheepishly. Fuck me running. She wanted to make a good impression but she seemed to be failing at every opportunity. "I'll stay out of everyone's way."

They landed in a light rain. The wind coming off the Celtic Sea cut through it like a razor against the face. She couldn't help but open her mouth at the surprise her body felt. It was like a reverse sauna. People sure didn't seem to act like it was this cold on *Poldark*.

Jagger ran over to one of the police officers, while the rest of the group moved towards the stairs leading down the cliff face to the entrance of Wheal Mexico.

From the back, Preacher's Daughter had a view like she was in a First Person Shooter.

Munro and Sheriff led the way, each with a combat shotgun.

Barbie followed behind with her combat rifle, with Donkey Kong and Mal behind her.

Jagger soon caught up and fell in line, bringing everyone up to speed as they descended the stairs.

Preacher's Daughter couldn't help but admire the vista of the waves slamming into rocks and the cliff face, sea birds screeching, wind howling. If it wasn't for the thuggery of a wind, it might be a certain paradise.

"Bobbies say that no one was hurt, but a family sure got scared when they saw them," Jagger said. "Was a dog missing, though. Says one of the little buggers came and snatched it."

"Nothing should eat dogs," Sheriff said.

"Doubt they were eaten," Jagger added. "Knockers like to play around. More a nuisance than anything else."

"If they are so much a nuisance, why are we here in battle rattle?" Munro asked.

Good question, thought Preacher's Daughter.

"Because Home Office said so," Donkey Kong said. "Also, remember that they killed one man and mauled another."

One person was killed by imaginary creatures? Preacher's Daughter tried not to roll her eyes. She thought this was going to be a serious mission. Mal was right. It looked like they just might be working for the tourist industry.

"Turns out the dead man probably had no wounds," Jagger said. "The police pulled him out an hour ago and the undertaker said there wasn't any marks anywhere on the body. He thinks it might be a heart attack."

"My mum would have a heart attack is she saw a Knocker coming up through her floor," Munro said.

"You'd have a heart attack if you saw your mum's knockers," Sheriff said.

"Enough," Barbie said. "Concentrate on mission."

Both the sergeants shut up.

"I also heard that the man missing half a foot tried to kick one of the Knockers," Jagger said.

"So, it's self defense then."

They'd reached the entrance.

The door, which had been made of metal, had been ripped off the hinges. Inside was a waiting area which had been trashed. Everything that could have been broken had been. Papers were scattered about like confetti at an end of the world rave. Signs were ripped from the walls. A brochure rack had been reformed into a ball of intertwined metal. A turnstile had been ripped from its moorings and slung through the wooden ceiling.

Munro and Sheriff were posted at the entrance to the mine shaft, which was a sloping walkway filled with gravel. Every ten feet were wooden piles, shoring up the walls and roof and along the floor. Lights still hung from the walls in places, unbroken and providing illumination. "What'd you think?" Sheriff asked.

"No movement as far as I can see. What do you think, boss?" Munro asked.

Preacher's Daughter couldn't see Mal's face, but she

imagined his eyebrow raising and falling as he considered his options. He was certainly more thoughtful in his actions than Boy Scout had been.

"One by one. Rotate. Move out."

Munro went first, racing down the shaft in a combat crouch. When he'd gotten meters, he stopped, and called into his microphone.

Sheriff followed, pausing at Munro's position, then moving another ten meters.

They did this two more times, going lower and lower, until the shaft began to slant in a different direction. Mal commanded them to stop. Sheriff squatted farthest away.

Mal sent Barbie and Donkey Kong next, who repeated the efforts of the first two.

Then he sent Preacher's Daughter and Jagger, each leap frogging the other until they were down with the others.

Mal came sauntering down last.

As far as Knockers, they hadn't seen nor heard a one. The mine was as silent as it was deep.

"Munro, report," said Mal in an even voice.

"Shaft curves. Can't see more than ten meters. Several doorways off the main shaft."

"Those would be display rooms," Barbie commented, looking at the small tablet attached to her forearm. "Each room is about fifteen-by-ten feet."

"Commandos, clear those rooms," Mal said.

Twin rogers were the replies as the two sergeants moved out.

Barbie and Donkey Kong moved forward to take their place.

Preacher's Daughter and Jagger moved where they had been.

Then everyone stopped as they heard knocking.

The moment threw her back to the first time she read *The Fellowship of the Ring* by J. R. R. Tolkien. She found herself under the mountain in the Mines of Moriah, the fellowship trying to make their way through Khazad-dûm, the old Dwarven Kingdom from the First Age. Sitting by the fire, fearful of everything, the knocking coming from far away. Was it a warning? Was it a threat? Was their location being communicated like some Morse code? Perhaps Tolkien had fashioned whatever it was making the noise after the Knockers.

The knocking stopped and she realized that she'd been holding her breath. She forced herself to breathe and counted silently. By the time she got to thirty, the knocking started once again.

"Khazad-dûm," she whispered dramatically into her microphone.

"Good Tolkien reference," Jagger said.

"Nerd points for her," Munro said.

"Keep it down," Barbie said.

Preacher's Daughter stared an Exocet missile into the back of Patterson's head. She must have felt it, because she turned to look. Preacher's Daughter didn't dial anything down, she kept right on looking. They were both lieutenants. They were both women. Just one was being an asshole. Two could play it that way.

"They're letting us know that they know we're here," Preacher's Daughter said evenly.

The knocking continued, not in any pattern, but rather the sound of hundreds of different hands beating against something.

"She's right," Jagger said, working on a hand-held vid screen. "I'm running an algorithm to see if there's any code built in we can decipher."

Gazes still locked, Patterson nodded slightly, then turned back to attend what was in front of her.

Sheriff shouted once, but then was cut off.

"Sheriff, report," Mal commanded.

"Fuck me. He's gone," Munro said, for the first time, fear sliding into his previously calm voice.

"What do you mean he's gone?" Donkey Kong said.

"Silence," said Mal. "Report."

"I was watching his six, sir, and then it was like something jerked him. Poof. Gone."

"Barbie. Support Munro."

Patterson stood from her semi-kneeling position and lumbered forward. When she got to the sergeant, she continued until she stopped short of where Sheriff had been positioned.

Preacher's Daughter had to give it to her. She wasn't afraid. That was for sure.

Munro rushed down to join her.

"I want the lights off," Mal shouted.

Donkey Kong spun and ran back the way everyone

had come. Within forty-five seconds, the lights were off, probably switched from the master panel in the office up shaft.

Preacher's Daughter lowered her NODS and switched to infrared. Unlike their systems in Special Unit 77, they didn't have a way to tie in the feeds, or if they did, she didn't have access to the master feed—what she would do to find out what Munro and Patterson were seeing.

The knocking suddenly became louder.

Sheriff screamed as if he were in the walls right next to them. His scream skipped by them and kept on going up the shaft.

Everyone spun around to find the source of the sound.

The knocking was so loud now she wanted to cover her ears with her hands. The walls rang with the sound and the lights quivered on the walls. She was about to lay down her weapons and do just that when the knocking abruptly ceased.

The first thing she heard in the silence was her own breathing.

No screams.

No knocking.

Nothing.

Then...

...a whisper through comms.

"I—I see something."

She'd not heard Munro sound scared before.

"It's one of them," Patterson said, awe-filled.

"It's coming towards us," Munro said.

"Don't shoot," Mal commanded, voice even, like he could have also said, "Drink milk."

"It's a Knocker. Three feet tall. Arms long enough to touch the ground," Munro said breathlessly. "Stout legs. It's wearing some sort of clothes and has a mouth full of shark teeth. Blimey. It's like the fecking pictures."

"What's it want?" Jagger asked.

"I dunno." Munro said.

"Why don't you ask it?" Jagger asked. He glanced at Preacher's Daughter with a grin on his face and shrugged.

She didn't grin. She was worried, having recently been in a room with three-foot-tall creatures who wanted to maim, fuck, and kill. She was afraid for the Scotsman. She was more afraid for Sheriff. What'd happened to him? He sounded like he'd been in the wall.

"Who are you?" Munro asked.

There seemed to be a response, but too muffled to hear.

"What about our friend?" Patterson asked.

Good. Preacher's Daughter gave the woman points for remembering.

Another muffled response.

Then, "Fuck."

"Munro. Report."

"Sir, we got a Knocker here. Says his name is Sloath. Says he needs to come with us."

"What about Sheriff? What happened to Sergeant Viceroy Nottingham?" Mal asked.

"Sir, I don't really understand what he said about him. It doesn't make a whole lot of sense."

After a few moments, Mal asked, "What did he say?" the strain to be even evident in his voice.

"Sir, Sloath says that Sheriff doesn't exist anymore."

"What the hell does that mean?" Donkey Kong asked.

Preacher's Daughter stared at Jagger, who had his hands on the walls, testing different places, sometimes knocking. He seemed to be trying to listen, but who could listen through rock?

Munro spoke, "Dunno, just that he doesn't exist."

"Does he mean that Sheriff is dead?" Mal asked.

Munro asked the question and she heard a short-muffled response.

"He doesn't know what dead means, sir."

"What did he say exactly?"

"He said, *Dead No Understand. Him not exist.*"

"Who the hell doesn't understand what dead means?" Donkey Kong asked.

After a moment, Preacher's Daughter replied. "Maybe someone who lives forever."

CHAPTER 7

SLOATH WALKED IN such a way that his arms and legs swung on the same side instead of opposite. He walked with a lumbering gait that made him seem larger than he actually was. Still, he was as intimidating as a three-foot-tall being could possibly be. Both Patterson and Munro hugged the walls, training their rifles on him, as he strode between them up the shaft. Besides his long arms, his body was well proportioned for his size. He wore a stern look on a face that was mostly human. His mouth had too many teeth, all misshapen and ending in points. His lips seemed incapable of covering them. His skin was gray with green splotches with enough wrinkles to make it seem like he had more skin than he needed. His eyes were deep black with no whites but twice the size of normal ones. Pointed ears poked from beneath a leather skull cap that hid whatever hair he might have. On his body, he wore a patchwork of leather that seemed to have been harvested from a myriad of creatures, the ensemble creating a shirt, pants, belt, and shoes.

He passed Preacher's Daughter and she detected the smell of wet rock mixed with old cheese.

When he finally stopped, it was in front of Mal.

They stood facing each other for a long moment.

Then Sloath beckoned Mal to lean down.

Mal set his jaw and leaned at the waist until his face was next to Sloath's.

The two seemed to speak for several minutes. When they were done, Mal stood and backed away a few feet until his back was to the wall. When he touched it, he flinched, the reaction as unusual as anything she had seen.

"Jagger, come to me," Mal ordered.

Jagger flashed a nervous grin at Preacher's Daughter, then headed up shaft. He had to crouch because he was so tall. He passed beside Sloath, but didn't show any fear. Mal spoke to him for several moments, then Jagger ran the rest of the way up the shaft and outside.

She'd tried to hear what was being said, but they hadn't opened the line, nor was their body language a giveaway. She was stymied and out of the loop and she didn't like it one bit. There was a democracy of ideas on her previous team. This team's decision-making process seemed to be very top down, meaning everything and anything came from the top. Still, she would continue to maintain her bearing as best as possible, recognizing that the Black Dragoons had been doing business for an impressive amount of time and surely knew what they were doing.

Jagger appeared ten minutes later with a large plastic

wad under his arm. When he unrolled it, she realized it was a body bag. Oh Jesus, were they to recover Sheriff's body? She glanced back down shaft. But as she returned her attention up shaft, she saw Jagger laying out the body bag. After several words with Sloath, the Knocker climbed inside. Jagger zipped it up.

Her comms crackled and Mal said, "Everyone move out. Munro, get the other end of this."

Munro rushed by her and grabbed the back end of the body bag.

Jagger grabbed the front.

They both lifted.

Munro grunted, "Weighs more than two drunk Irishmen."

"Stop talking about your dates," Patterson said, pushing past Preacher's Daughter.

Munro and Jagger followed Mal up the shaft.

The rest trailed after.

Within moments, they were back in the helicopter and returning to the castle.

Several times Jagger and Munro tried to start a conversation, but each time they were silenced. All everyone did was sit and watch the Knocker in the body bag as it rolled back and forth with the pitch and yaw of the helicopter, occasionally shifting, each movement sending shivers down Preacher's Daughters spine.

When they finally landed back at Caverswall Castle, Munro and Jagger removed the bag on Mal's orders and rushed inside. Patterson and Donkey Kong left the helicopter without a word leaving Preacher's Daughter sitting inside wondering what the hell she was doing in this outfit. She remained sitting and fuming until the pilot asked her through the headset how long she planned on staying. After that, she got off the airframe and trudged through the front door of the castle.

Jagger waited for her.

"The commander apologizes but circumstances aren't normal right now. We've been told that Sheriff is still alive. Right now, things are political. Home Office is sending someone out and until then we are to stand down. Can I please show you to your room?"

She nodded, too tired and frustrated to argue.

He took her to the second floor where she was given an immense room with thirty-foot ceilings and a four-poster bed that could be the centerpiece of a romance novel. He took her gear back to the armory, and left her to her own means.

She thought about taking a nap or washing up or getting a beer or eating something, but every time she settled on something, she decided immediately that she didn't want to do that. One reason she left the active-duty military was because of the stove piping of information. She preferred to be in the middle of things and her frustration was about to spill over.

Thankfully, her phone buzzed in her pocket.

She answered it and felt relieved to hear a friendly voice.

"How are you holding up?" Poe asked from five thousand miles away.

"Things… things are different here."

"I was worried you'd have a problem reintegrating into a real military unit," he said.

What could she say to that? "No problem. Just some getting used to. How's my replacement?"

"Fitting in nicely. I have him on mission right now. He likes it over here."

"Glad someone does."

Silence on both sides drew out almost a full minute.

"We've been following your mission. Is everything okay?"

"How much do you know?"

"Enough to know you have an unseelie."

She paused and wondered how they knew. Was it her? Was her phone transmitting information? "Things are pretty fluid right now."

"Which means they left you in the dark."

"More like the abyss. Information is like the Crown Jewels here. Only a rare few get to see it."

"Once they know your value and worth, all that will change."

"Do you really think so?" she asked.

"If it doesn't, you can always come back."

She thought of the missing town in South Dakota and its missing twin in England. They'd yet to even address the reason for her mission yet. No, she needed more time. Somehow, she felt that the situation was much more dire than it appeared to be on the surface. "How goes it there?"

"We've been interviewing the survivor from the Amish fiasco."

Amish Fiasco. That must be the official term for the last mission she commanded. Great. "And?"

"The interview isn't what I expected. She doesn't remember anything. She claims she was never involved in the occult. Lie detector and PCASS substantiate her claims."

While traditional lie detectors and the relatively new PCASS—Preliminary Credibility Assessment Screening System—weren't allowed as evidence in court procedures, they were definitely helpful as indicators of deception. Especially the PCASS that also measured electrodermal and vasomotor information from an examinee's hand, using silver/silver chloride and photo-plethysmography sensors. To say that there was no indication of deception was as good as being certain.

"What's the hypothesis then?" she asked.

"We're looking at the property now and seeing if there might not have been some outside inducement." There was a pause. "Some other events have transpired."

"Other events? Like what we just encountered?"

"We didn't," he said. "Listen to this, though. I've had reports from Germany, France, Belgium, the Czech Republic, and Greece that other unseelie have been reported massing in large groups and coming to the surface. It's not readily apparent why this is happening."

"Something might be coming up underneath the unseelie."

"What's that?"

"Just something one of the team said here. What if they are coming together in large groups in response to some external stimuli?" she asked.

"That's a great hypothesis, but what stimuli?"

She thought for a moment. "I don't know, but I'm afraid all of these are like tremors. The big one is still coming."

"Maybe the big one is already here and we don't know it."

"The missing towns?"

"Exactly," Poe said. "There could be hundreds—thousands even—and we just don't know it."

"But why? What's the purpose to make a town disappear?"

"Maybe they didn't disappear. What if they are still there and being used by something else?"

Six months ago, she'd dipped inside Space Cowboy books with the cowboy hatted-owner, Jean Paul, to escape the crippling desert heat near 29 Palms, California.

Jean Paul had seen them kitted up, and to be a smart ass she'd asked, "Got anything on Zoroastrian demons and how to defeat them?"

Without missing a beat, he'd said, "Not sure I have—"

Then he held up a hand and stood. He scanned two cases, then reached in and grabbed a thin, dog-eared title. "Try this one. It's The Cosmic Puppets *by Philip K. Dick published by Ace in 1957. It's about a man who returns home only to discover that the town is missing things. Turns out there's a war between two Zoroastrian demigods and they've altered reality in their attempts to outdo the other."*

Not exactly about a missing town, but about a town missing things that should have been there. Still, there were some consistencies between the book and the events at Iron Hat. She mentioned the book to Poe and he said he'd get copies and have their specialists read it to see if there was anything they could glean from it. As they both knew, in situations such as these, they often could obtain more useful information from fiction than non-fiction because fiction often covered more hypothetical ground. Then they exchanged a few more niceties, Poe urged her to do her best, and they said goodbyes.

Could it be that easy? she wondered.

Could the answer have been in a book the entire time? Something written all the way back in 1957? She'd researched books far older for less information that was for sure. She went online and went through the process of downloading an electronic copy and began to re-read it.

Then she said to the room, "I mean, shoot. I have nothing else to do but sit on my ass and read a seventy-year-old book." Then she raised her voice in case someone might be listening. "It's not as if I'm sort of an expert in this supernatural shit. It's not as if I'm not an expert in interrogation."

She listened to see if there'd be a response, then slumped down onto the wing backed chair beside the bed and turned to page one.

CHAPTER 8

THREE HOURS LATER, she decided that she'd spent enough time acting like a sullen teenager. She went looking for companionship and alcohol. She found both almost at once inside a library on the second floor that had been converted to a bar. All of the books and tomes were still in place and along with the rich wooden ceiling and floors added a Victorian element to the presence of the giant screen television playing music videos. She felt Rickrolled the moment she walked in because Rick Astley's 'Never Going to Give You Up' video was playing as she entered. She almost turned around and left, but Munro was drinking a beer from the bottle at a table and waved her over.

Donkey Kong sat at one table with a tablet and what looked like a small glass of claret.

Patterson was also in the room, sitting the furthest away from the door. a bottle of Tequila and a shot glass in front of her.

Preacher's Daughter was the last person to judge. How someone made it through the day was their own business as long as it didn't affect the mission. She moseyed on over to the bar and found a wine fridge. She selected an American Chardonnay from the Russian River Valley, filled a wine glass and sat down across from Munro so she could see the other two and still have the video in her line of sight. Although the music was turned down, it was just loud enough to be heard and understood.

She noticed that Munro was drinking an American IPA called Voodoo Ranger.

"Cheers," she said, as she took a moderate and totally refreshing sip of cold wine.

"Cheers back, mate." He took a sip himself, leaned back and watched the video.

"American IPA?" she asked.

"It's an acquired taste, I know. Not as smooth as many of my favorite English beers, but if I'm drinking to think, then I like IPAs. If I'm drinking to get drunk, then give me a pub beer or something from DC Brau like Stone of Arbroath. That's an IPA from DC using American hops but Scotch beer."

"I didn't know there was that much involved," she said, sipping and watching him.

He glanced at her and rolled his eyes. "If you've been in the service for as long as your sheet says, I'm sure you know that's not true," his brogue coming out a little bit more with the alcohol. "You know, the more you be by yourself, the better you need to be able to get along."

She sat back. "What the fuck does that mean?"

"See?" he grinned. "That's the Preacher's Daughter we

were expecting. Not the 'fraid of her shadow waif who let herself be told to stay in the back."

She wanted to respond right away, but held back. She drank her glass, got up and poured another, this time bringing the bottle back with her.

"That's the spirit," Munro said.

Changing the subject, she asked, "Who is Monroe? Was that a famous Scottish soldier?"

He shook his head. "Munro was never a person."

"But I know people with that last name in America. It's not uncommon."

"We're talking two different things."

"Then where does it come from?"

"A m-u-n-r-o," he began, spelling the word out, "is defined as any Scottish mountain over three thousand feet in height. Scotland has three hundred and thirty-two munros and I have climbed every one of them, including Ben Nevis."

"Now, that sounds like a person."

He laughed. "There always is. Ben means mountain, while Nevis means malicious. Malicious Mountain. That used to be my call sign before I retired it. Now I am simply Munro."

She sipped more of her wine. "I don't think simply is an adequate word. Why did you retire that call sign?"

He stared at her over his beer for a long moment, then shook his head as if he'd come to a decision. "You're going to have to ask someone else for that. Changing the subject, Preacher's Daughter? I take it your father was a preacher?"

She nodded and sipped her Chardonnay. "He was. I grew up being a pretty serious girl. Good in my studies. Every summer we'd go on a mission somewhere and help out when we could."

"Normally, when a girl is a preacher's daughter, well, she's kind of a wild girl," he said.

"That's why Boy Scout gave me the call sign as a joke. I was never a wild girl until I went through ROTC and then had to hold my own and show who I was with the guys."

"So, you're the way you are in order to fit in," he said.

She leaned forward and was about to lay into him, when he spoke first.

"Listen, one thing you haven't figured out yet is that in a team in the UK we are real brothers and sisters and don't let any feelings get in the way. If you're going to be American and act as if you get hurt by what we say when all we are doing is telling the truth then you will never fit in. What is it you 'Muricans call it? Tough Love? Here we just call it love and telling it as we see it. So, get mad if you want to, but that's the way we operate." He snatched his beer off the table and stood. "Be right back. Going to get another one."

She noticed that both Donkey Kong and Patterson were staring at her. When they saw her noticing their attention, they both returned to their own business. Was he right? Was she too uptight? Was this an American thing? She did know that she'd been worried about integrating into the new team—now a second new team in six months. She'd been reserved because she wanted to wait and fit in, but it seems now like they'd expected her to be herself from the get go and stake her place on the team. She grabbed her glass and hugged it to her chest as she leaned back and watched Golden Earring perform 'Twilight Zone', something she really felt she'd stepped in.

Munro returned with a beer and a bowl of crisps. He began to toss them into his mouth as he sipped his beer. He watched the video, pretty much ignoring her.

When the video ended and switched to Rhianna's 'Diamonds', she finally spoke. "I can only guess how easy it is for a good-looking athletic man to become part of a team. It seems like your place is always reserved and ready to be filled. On the other hand, super smart pretty women like myself don't often become part of a functioning front line military unit. There's no rule book how to act. America was founded on Puritan values and most of the time if someone of my sex steps out and tries to act however we want we are called bitch or a slut." She eyed him stonily. "Of which I am neither."

"I never thought you were," he said.

"What you're saying is if I act the way I want to—basically be unadulterated Preacher's Daughter—you'll accept me and not treat me as if I'm trying to be something I shouldn't?"

"Are you Preacher's Daughter?"

"Of course."

"Then you won't be pretending to be someone you aren't. Trust me. We can tell."

"So, everything has been a test."

He tilted his bottle. "Life is a test, mate. Back to what we were talking about. I drink IPA when I'm contemplative. Like, what the fuck is going on with the world and should I be worried contemplative. Look around. The others are doing the same. If we didn't care, this would be a free for all and we'd be like a bunch of your frat boys doing keg stands because we deserve that kind of release after all the shit we've been in.

"But that's not the case. Look at Donkey Kong over there. He's reading Byron, I can guarantee you, because he both wants the poets bedevilry and his humanity. He wants to make sure he has it and understands it and exudes it. Life is getting tough and there are enough leaders from Hollywood who would never work in real life.

"Then there's Barbie. I know you don't like the name, but the reason we call her that isn't what you think. And before you ask, you need to ask her. That's her business. She's sitting over there writing notes in her book about how the rest of us operated. She slow drinks tequila because it's like water to her—never challenge her to drinking tequila—if you do, you'll wake up in your own vomit and with someone else's poodle, but that's another story. My guess is that she even noted your comments and your contributions to today's adventure."

Her mind was spinning. She was kicking herself for never really realizing how deep and how professional everyone was. She'd shown up with her own ideas and thought that everything was about her. Clearly, getting used to a new unit was a talent she had no talent for and she was thankful that Munro or Andy MacKenzie or whoever the Malicious Mountain was that he had taken the time to mansplain. She'd spent a good portion of her time thus far tiptoeing around everyone. From now on, she'd be pure and adulterated Preacher's Daughter, whatever that meant. She'd give them as good as she got and then take as good as they gave. They'd probably appreciate her honesty.

Munro glanced at his watch. "I gotta run. I need to put in at least five miles before bed."

After mission.

And after beers?

He nodded to her, grabbed her shoulder in a friendly grasp, then left the room.

Prince was on TV now singing about Little Red Corvettes.

When she got done listening to Prince singing code for vaginas and condoms, she glanced over at Patterson who was drinking a shot and also watching Purple Royalty on the big screen. If Preacher's Daughter was going to make a change, she might as well do it with the toughest person in the room, so she got up, grabbed her half-filled bottle, and sauntered over to where Patterson was sitting.

"This seat taken?" she asked.

"It is now," Patterson said, trying her best to ignore the other woman. "What do you want?"

"A little respect," Preacher's Daughter said. She

grabbed the bottle of tequila and tipped it to her mouth and took a hit. The warm white liquor seared her throat and sent fireworks into her brain. She coughed once, which she was proud to do because her entire body wanted to rid itself of the vile liquid.

"Not exactly chardonnay," Patterson said, a ghost of a grin behind her normal frown.

"No," Preacher's Daughter coughed. "Not exactly."

She watched to see if the other woman was going to open up, but it might as well have been Fort Knox. Instead of speaking, she turned to watch the screen and they both watched Madness singing 'Our House'. Preacher's Daughter tried to make sense of it, but it was as nonsensical as the problem at hand. On the surface all of the mundane activities seemed somewhat normal, but the continuous refrain about the middle of the street lent an unneeded confusion.

When the video finished, Preacher's Daughter turned back to the table and took a sip of her wine. What she really wanted to do was wash her mouth out with gasoline to get the taste of tequila out of it. Tequila had always been an acquired taste and one she'd never acquired. Patterson continued to jot in her notebook, not once looking up.

A dozen questions went through Preacher's Daughter's mind which she rejected for being either condescending, ill-informed, or petty or combinations thereof. She wanted to break the ice, but she didn't know how. Munro had all but said that she was pretending to be someone she wasn't. Perhaps that was the problem. She'd so closely identified with who she'd been while in Boy Scout's unit that outside of the organization she still struggled to be herself.

Who was Preacher's Daughter?

Maybe the best way to see who you were was to look at you through other's eyes. If that was the case, she didn't like what she saw. She had too many faults and needed to own them more quickly. She also needed to stop waiting to be heard. From now on, she told herself that she would act and react with her previous speed and efficiency. And if they didn't like it then she'd find a way to adjust. She had only to make sure she wasn't allowing complacency and her need to get along to color the way she should be acting.

CHAPTER 9

SHE WENT TO work out but couldn't find the gym—at least she supposed there had to be a gym? So, she did Tabata and Yoga for an hour, then found the mess hall and had a dinner of curry chicken and mashed potatoes and gravy from the buffet. Not that it went together, it was just what she ended up grabbing. In fact, she smelled the curry from down the hall and that had been the lure that showed her where the buffet was located. She'd noted they also had some pre-chewed peas and some chips, but had left them alone.

She was just finishing when Donkey Kong came and sat across from her. He didn't say a word, just sat and ate what looked like bird food that included an inordinate amount of vegetables. He was pretending at being so healthy it made her feel guilty for not adding anything green to her plate. He never looked at her the entire time. When he was done, he got up, took his plate to the cleaning window, and left it there. He glanced back at her and cocked his head to say that she should follow.

She hurriedly dumped her own tray and rushed after him.

Past oil portraits of owner's past, they wound around the stair until they reached the third story of the castle. The walls were covered with tapestry showing various hunting scenes. The floor held well-worn hand-made rugs. She recognized many of the tribal designs from northern Afghanistan as well as Bahktiari province in Iran. The smell of fresh cut grass came through the window to cover the dead scent of old mildewed rock.

Waterhouse opened a non-descript door and she followed him inside. The humidity of the room was a physical thing that stuck to the skin. Her nostrils filled with the heady aromas of various plants and the humidity of the enclosed space. The windows were frosted for indirect light. Ferns from knee- to chin-high were ranged in pots around the room. A fan in a back corner caused a breeze to stir the leaves and fronds of the ferns and flowers like a sirocco from a far off sea. The floor had long ago been stained from water and dirt giving it a well-worn patina much like that favorite pair of jeans. Cages hung from chains with exotic birds. She recognized a hummingbird and an oriole and what looked like a deep red parrot.

It was an aviary. She'd read about how some of the old mansions used to keep exotic birds. During the dull and gray winters of England, there'd have to be some sort of indoor solution to keep the birds alive. She couldn't help but smile in delight at how special this room was and almost spun with exuberance.

But it was the fourth cage in that strange third floor house-bound forest that snatched and held her gaze. Inside of the gilded metal sat a prim little lady upon a chair in front of a doll size vanity with a mirror. She combed her hair with a tiny brush and whistled like a bird, the notes low and somber, as if she were sad and maudlin. Her butterfly wings were a gossamer shade of green, the color barely visible in the spidery veins of the magical appendages.

Preacher's Daughter could hardly breathe. "Is that—"

"A fairy. Just so," Waterhouse said. He approached the cage and leaned forward slightly, more the look of an ornithologist with a bird pinned to velvet than a regular human observing a supernatural entity with awe and wonder.

The cage was a work of marvel itself. It had two floors, the upper for sleeping and the lower for living. The filigree and the workmanship of the metal was as artistic as she'd ever seen before. The creature within looked too perfect, her skin like porcelain and the wings fully formed. She seemed to be wearing a gown, but it continued to move and shift as if it were made of fog or a wisp of imagination. A voluptuous version of Tinkerbell—or Tinkerbell if drawn by Frank Frazetta on an acid trip while listening to 1970s Pink Floyd.

"What am I seeing?" she asked.

"It is a sylph. We call her Madeleine. She's been with my family since 1917. This is her room. She will occasionally speak, but it's been years since she has. So, we just keep her as happy as we can in an environment she appreciates."

The fairy was like the sole occupant of a supernatural zoo. Preacher's Daughter couldn't help but wonder how lonely the creature had to be.

"Have you considered releasing her?"

"Once, when I was thirteen years old, I took her on a train to Cottingley Woods, found a secluded glade, and opened the cage. She refused to leave. I waited hours until it was time for my return train. I assumed then that she was happy with her lot. She definitely isn't wanting for anything. If she wants to leave, I will be the first one to release her."

"Wh- What does a fairy eat?"

"She eats butterflies. To watch her you'd think she was a wild animal. It's bothersome really. Normally, I leave one for her and then let her alone to do what she does."

"How did you come about her?"

"My great grandfather captured her one night in Cottingley. He'd been out drinking, passed out in a fairy grove, and captured her using his hat. He believed it would make him a wealthy man."

Passed out in a fairy grove like it was a normal occurrence.

"And did it?"

Captain Ethan Waterhouse turned to her. "Yes. She informed him of a place where there was over a million pounds of lost gold dating back to the War of the Roses. He dug it up, had it appraised for its antique value, then my uncle arranged to have it given to the College of London. The treasure trove finder's fee came out to nearly three million pounds. Hence, my family is now monied, where before we were penniless."

The new information came as a surprise to her. He acted like old money. Of course, she didn't really know what new money looked like, but she imagined it would be loud music, louder clothes, and fast foreign cars. Seeing Waterhouse in corduroy pants, brogues, a button-down brown shirt beneath a cardigan, he was anything but new money.

"She made you rich?"

"It made us rich," he said. "Yes. Don't forget for a second that it is not a male or a female. It is a fairy."

The tinkling of glass breaking in an echo chamber turned out to be the tiny laughter of the fairy as it shook its head and regarded them. It had flown to the bars and was gripping them with one hand as it hovered above the floor of the cage. Its hair flew backwards, taken by an invisible wind.

"Have you ever heard of the Cottingley fairies?" he asked.

"I think I read something about them being fake."

He nodded. "That's the official story. But how can two teenagers with a new camera and a fairly new technology fake enough pictures so that even Arthur Conan Doyle believed in them?"

"I read that in the 1980s the sisters admitted to faking the pictures."

"For money, yes. They were broke and would have said anything for a few pounds. But they also hedged their bets and said that the fifth picture of the set wasn't a fake, arguing over who had actually taken it." He sighed. "I hope more people believe that it was a fake because Cottingley Woods is an extremely active seelie zone, which was why my great grandfather was so easily able to capture one, even while he was stumbling drunkenly through the woods."

"It doesn't paint a great picture of the man."

"He was a disgusting drunk who beat his wife, but he took care of us. Oldest story in the book."

She didn't want to delve too far into his past, but he'd said something that had interested her. "You mentioned seelie zone. I also heard the word unseelie used before. They represent good and evil fairies, no?"

He looked at her a moment, then returned his attention to Madeleine. "The terms are Scottish and are a generalization for good and evil. But good and evil are human ideas. Fairies have other ways to categorize their own. Madeleine is a fairy. Had she no wings, she would be known as a sprite. But again, those are just words. Our own philosophical and religious constructs color our ways of thinking. There was and is a belief that fairies are demoted angels. Another is that they are uplifted demons. Yet another is that they were the deities that were worshipped before man became so plentiful and since the advent of monotheism, have become merely shadows of what they once were."

She found herself nodding as he spoke. Her studies had by and large passed over English mythology because of the popularity of Harry Potter and the Narnia movies, but she was familiar with the basics. She could wax poetic about ancient religions from around the world, but when it came to the UK, she was a newb. Still, the absorption and syncretization of religions was nothing new to her. She could speak at length about how the Virgin of Guadalupe was a syncretic manifestation of Catholic and Aztec beliefs in order to get the Aztecs to transfer their worship of Tonantzin to something more Catholic. She could apply what she'd learned about the way other cultures dealt with their beliefs to what she was learning about English beliefs.

"Seelies or the Seelie Court," he continued, "are supposed to be the good guys. While the unseelie are the bad guys."

"So, Madeleine is a seelie," she said.

"Conventionally, yes, but since she's become part of the family, my great grandfather died within two years of achieving his wealth, my father died of the flu, his brothers were killed in a train accident, my brother and my sister were struck by lightning on two separate occasions. My brother died. My sister is in a convalescent home and drinks her dinners through a straw. Sure, she's a seelie. She's a good fairy, isn't that right, Madeleine?"

Again, the sound of broken glass in an echo chamber.

Preacher's Daughter detected the mocking in the music of the fairy's laughter. "I've found that the reality of the supernatural is so far from ours that to try and compare the two is a loser's challenge."

He turned to her. "That's genius. Exactly how I feel. I've been waiting for the other shoe to drop for a long time. She's in complete control of my family. I don't know why the others were killed, or almost killed if you think of my sister, Alice, but there had to be reason."

She set her jaw and leaned over to look at the seelie. "Don't be so sure there has to be a reason."

The fairy locked eyes with her and in that moment, she noted how alien they were—how alien it was. This creature might look like a little princess, but it was far from even being human. Anthropomorphizing was a dangerous business and they needed to remember that.

"What's going on with Sloath?" she asked.

"I'm not sure," he sighed. "I'm as in the dark as you."

This surprised her. As second in command, she imagined that Waterhouse would have access to all the information.

"Is the unit usually this tight with information?"

He jerked his head around at the word *tight*.

"If you were a part of my unit, they'd let you know pretty much everything," she said. "Not knowing where the solution to a problem might come from, hoping that by broadly disseminating whatever information we had that cause a solution to rise more quickly."

"You Americans and your democratization of information. We're a little different. When Malcom wants us to know about it, he'll tell us."

"Meanwhile, his best brains are in the dark when they could be working on the problem."

His back stiffened. "That's like arguing about the answer when you don't even know what the question is."

"If we knew the answers, we could figure out what the questions should be."

Again, with the tinkling of broken glass.

"Let's leave Madeleine alone for now," she said.

He agreed and they both left. She followed him to a room two doors down. He invited her in. It was clearly his domicile. Twice as large as hers, it had a fireplace and a separate sitting area with hundred-year-old lush and sturdy furniture. Pictures of him in different uniforms in different countries along with awards lined the walls. This was definitely a place he'd been in for a while. She noted one of the awards had a Kukri and another held a Fairbairn-Sykes fighting knife.

"This is bigger than my apartment," she said, noting the twin chandeliers.

"Mine as well," he said. "Truth be told, I'd be homeless if it wasn't for the Dragoons. There is no family estate. I pretty much leave the money alone."

"Afraid it might be tainted?" she asked.

He gave her a quick glance. "Something like that." He pointed to the sofa for her to sit, which she accepted. He walked over to an Edwardian side table which held a bottle of red wine and crystal glasses. He poured two and brought them back, handing one to her, and keeping one for himself. He sat in an old chair with wide wooden upholstered arms.

Was it her or did he seem more human? He'd seemed so distanced with his Clark Kent looks and his very proper behavior and way of speaking. But now he seemed—well—like an actual person instead of a Stepford Brit.

"I gotta ask," she began, and she laughed as he closed his eyes and shook his head ever so slightly. "Sorry," she said. "Never mind."

"No. It's fine. All super heroes have origin stories, you might as well know mine." He took a sip of his claret and took a moment to savor it. "My bachelor's degree is in game theory. Not that I'm a gamer, but I think there's something to be said about the way people approach games replicated with how people approach life."

"I didn't take you for a gamer," she said.

"I'm not. But it's the approach to games that interests me. There's going to become a time when those who have gamed will outnumber those of us who haven't and they will invent a world we don't understand. The way they think and approach a problem will be unique to them. I studied applied probability, machine learning, optimization, sequential prediction, and statistical learning theory. Game theory is also about the process of modeling strategic interactions between two or more entities in a situation containing set rules and outcomes. It could be people, corporations, or countries."

"It suddenly doesn't sound as fun as gaming," she said.

He grinned sideways. "What I discovered was

that I was a savant when it came to platform action puzzle problems. The first one was *Frogger* and then came *Donkey Kong*. I did my Master's Thesis on the Predictability of Rhizomatic Learning and *Donkey Kong*."

Her amiable grin fell away. She never considered that she might not be the smartest person in the room, much less the unit. That had never happened before. Rhizomatic learning? Was that plants? "Okay. I give in. I have no idea what that is." She bowed from the neck. "Please, explain to me."

"Wikipedia probably explains it the easiest," he said, grasping the stem of his glass with two fingers from each hand. "Rhizome is a philosophical concept developed by Gilles Deleuze and Félix Guattari in their project called Capitalism and Schizophrenia back in the 70s. It is what Deleuze calls an 'image of thought,' based on the botanical rhizome, that apprehends multiplicities. As a model for culture, the rhizome resists the organizational structure of the root-tree system which charts causality along chronological lines and looks for the original source of things in order to predict the pinnacle or conclusion of those things. *Donkey Kong* was the perfect game to demonstrate the theory."

Now she knew how the others felt when she was able to disgorge her learning in a machine gun answer.

"Think of our normal organizational structures. They are hierarchical in nature with a headquarters, below that will be squadrons, then platoons, then squads, and so on.

In civilian life if you include the corporate structure, it includes a chief executive, a committee and its members, different offices to conduct various works, and within those offices, sub-offices. Classic organizational charts. Can you see it?"

She certainly could. She'd come to know military org charts like the back of her hand. To know a unit was to know the organization above, below and lateral to it.

He took a sip of his wine. "But Rhizome theory says that's all hogwash. Deleuze and Guattari arrived at the rhizome by way of analyzing modes of thought associated with a tree. The tree image is their chief contrast against the rhizome, and much about the rhizome can be understood through this opposition. The tree plainly represents a hierarchy, but it also refers to binary systems, because every new branch ties back in some essential way to the root that makes all growth possible.

"The tree has become the dominant ontological model in Western thought, exemplified in such fields as linguistics, psychoanalysis, logic, biology, and human organization. All these are modeled as hierarchical or binary systems, stemming from the tree or root from which all else grows. One of Deleuze and Guattari's criticisms of the tree is that it does not offer an adequate explanation of multiplicity. A political implication of the tree is that it reinforces notions of centrality of authority, state control, and dominance; it is perhaps no coincidence that this theory challenging the tree emerged in France shortly after the elections of 1968 and the ensuing unrest.

"Deleuze and Guattari thus posit another type of organization. Unlike the tree, whose branches have all grown from a single trunk, the rhizome has no unique source from which all development occurs. The rhizome is both heterogeneous and multiplicitous. It can be entered from many different points, all of which connect to each other. The rhizome does not have a beginning, an end, or an exact center. The rhizome is reducible neither to the One nor the multiple... it is comprised not of units but of dimensions, or rather directions in motion. This inter- or trans-dimensionality is an important component of the rhizome, and separates it from a mere system made up of components or structure made up of points.

"Rhizome is defined solely as a circulation of states that are able to operate by means of multiplicity, variation and expansion. Deleuze and Guattari describe a mode of organization in which all individuals are interchangeable, defined only by their state at a given moment—such that the local operations are coordinated and the final, global result synchronized without a central agency. Although a rhizome can be broken or injured in one location, it will merely form a new line, a new connection that will emerge elsewhere."

She took a sip of her own wine and realized that she'd been sipping all along and the glass was empty. She sat the glass on the table beside her. "You're describing organizations with no leader other than an idea. Al-Quaida, for instance. They were a rhizomatic organization even though they had a figure head."

"Indeed. The figurehead, in the case of Osama Bin Laden, did little to direct the organization. Rhizomatic ontological relationships have been used to describe Jihad writ large. You can't map it. It just exists. If we could map it, we could cut off the head and take it out but it's not hierarchical."

She nodded. "It would be easy if it was. So, the study of rhizomatic organizations has told us what about the problem set at hand? I assume you've been trying to work through it."

"I understand the question. I'm trying to apply it to the seelie and unseelie organizations. Although there's a Seelie Court, I think that was a projection rather than a reality. I don't think there's Seelie royalty other than perhaps the oldest of a seelie type and if that's the case, then their organization can't necessarily be hierarchical." He sighed heavily. "It means our understanding of the Fae—as we popularly refer to it—is completely wrong. There is no king and queen. There is no cast system. What if the Fae's organization was like the idea of Jihad or Al Quaida?"

He held up a finger. "Look at it this way. If the world before humans or in the infancy of human existence had Fae throughout the world, why are we assuming they'd conform to human organizational models? Why would we believe that we conformed to theirs? Do we think the Fae would have feudal states that would fight one another? What would bring forth the necessity of such a state? No, I think they lived and performed actions specific to their Fae specialties and lived harmoniously with each other until there was an exertion of an outside force."

"Humanity?"

"Could be. Or another Fae force that pre-existed."

"A force the Fae encountered that made them change their organization?"

"Or made them hide their organization," he countered.

She got up this time and refilled their glasses. When she returned and sat, she said, "Certain things give me pause."

"I can imagine a lot would give you pause," he said.

"I'm thinking of the seelie and unseelie. Why two organizations? Do you think they might be the same and it's us who separated them?"

He liked to nod as he thought out loud and he did so now. "Little known fact is that the Fae cannot tell a lie. Perhaps they let us believe using our organizational constructs that there was not only good and bad but there were kings and queens."

"I can't help but remember that reading about the Queen of Fairies when I was a child. And wasn't it Shakespeare who had the King of Fairies?" she asked.

"Oberon. Yes. What if the fairies took on the hierarchy that would best allow them to interact with us?" he posed.

"So then, Sloath?"

"Exactly. Why did he give himself up? Why did the Knockers show themselves? Why did you encounter so many homunculi?"

"But the homunculi are created by a human," she said. "I wouldn't categorize them as the same."

"Fine. Noted," he said. "But if you did, then how would they fit in."

She told him what she'd learned from Poe about the other countries in Europe.

"I should have known," he said. "These can't be isolated incidents. If there is a pattern then there is a plan. Always. If I was to spend time building a predictive model it would show that these are indications of another action."

"That's the action we're waiting for, aren't we?" she asked.

"Yes, and I hate waiting to know what's going to happen when it can be predicted."

"What's keeping you from predicting? Data points?"

He tipped his glass to her. "Exactly that. Think of a mathematical equation with all the letters. We all know after our mind-numbing classes in secondary school—your high school—that those letters represent data points. I've begun to fill in some of the data points, but I still need more data."

"The missing town. I am going to get briefed on that, yes?"

He waved his hand. "Yes. The missing town. That will give us more data. It's very unscientific for me to link the missing town with all the other data without proof, but my gut tells me that there's a connection."

She finished her claret. "You can't quantify gut instinct. That's kept me alive more times than raw data."

"Same with me." He grinned, then got serious. "Listen, if you want information, go and get it. Ask for it. You are what we need. Malcom is a great sort but he's old school. Everything you do can be forgiven." He laughed. "Information in the British military is hierarchical."

"Of course, I am the loud American."

"If you've got tits, then use them," he said. Then he closed his eyes and lowered his head. "Oh my god, I am sorry. It was a metaphor. I didn't mean to use your tits, I just meant to—"

She couldn't help but burst out laughing and it was during the laughter that the door opened.

Jagger stood at parade rest.

"If you two have your clothes on, the commander wants to see us all."

She took one look at the wink in the eye of the hot gay Indian man and the look of absolute mortification on the face of Donkey Kong and cracked up all over again.

CHAPTER 10

THEY MET IN the operations center. Preacher's Daughter and Donkey Kong were the last to arrive. They took seats at the central work table and spun them around.

Everyone had a chair except Mal who stood in front of the screens—definitely the man in charge. With his back straight and his chin up, he was the model for a military officer. She'd seen enough officers and NCOs throughout her career who aced tests and physical fitness training but knew little about actual work or leadership. She'd once had a sergeant tell her that young officers were like Yugos—the car that was so popular in the 1990s. He'd said, "It looks grand in the showroom, but take it out on the road and it performs like shit."

Jagger wore paisley workout clothes, his shorts not even reaching mid-thigh. She had to admire his long legs though. She wished she had them and if she had, she'd be showing them off as well.

Munro sat next to him wearing a Commandos T-shirt and shorts. But where the Scotsman looked like he'd just come from working out, Jagger looked as if he was about ready to go out on the town.

Patterson sat behind Munro. Her hair was covered by a baseball cap for a team Preacher's Daughter didn't recognize. She looked as if she'd hit the gym as well, her sweatshirt and sweatpants ragged about the edges. Sweat rings under her arms, near her stomach, and around her neck indicated she'd just come from working out. She wore Hokas on her feet which told Preacher's Daughter that the other woman understood good brands and the relative healing qualities of zero drop technology.

There was no sign of Sloath. She couldn't help but wonder where the unseelie was being kept. Perhaps a larger version of the cage Madeleine was in. She was still a bit gobsmacked about the age of the fairy. If Donkey Kong was to be believed—and there was no reason not to—Madeleine had been captured in 1917. She was at least over a hundred years old, making Preacher's Daughter suspect that Fairies might have some sort of eternal life.

"Let's get down to business, shall we?" Mal began, hands folded behind his back. "Prior to Preacher's Daughter's appointment with the Black Dragoons then our trip to Cornwall, we were discussing the missing town of Graves Hill. Major Waterhouse, can you bring us up to speed?"

Donkey Kong stood and moved to the front of the room.

Malcom stepped to the side.

Donkey Kong manipulated a giant vid screen with

his hand and brought up a map. He adjusted the zoom using his fingers until where he was looking was the centerpiece.

"Graves Hill is purported to be west of Leicester between Leicester Forest East and Peckleton, just off the M1. It's also just south of Desford. You can see it right here on the map." He pointed to Graves Hill. "It was originally an Abby from 1520, then it became a seminary. In 1970, the graves were moved to a new cemetery when the land was purchased by a speculator. In the 80s, this same speculator turned Graves Hill into a nice little bedroom community for Leicester with its own high-end pubs and businesses. We know this because it's on the internet, but if you ask anyone else on the planet, Graves Hill doesn't and never has existed. Cars and trucks piloted by persons are unable to go into the area. On each and every occasion, the driver inexplicably turns around."

"You said piloted by persons. Have you tried drones?" Preacher's Daughter asked.

"We've been able to conduct flyovers, but there's been electrical interference," Patterson said from her chair, not turning around. "We're trying various different spectrums and acoustics to see if we can't find a way to visually surveil."

"Any idea what's causing the interference?" Preacher's Daughter asked.

"If we knew that, then we'd be able to work around it," Patterson said.

Preacher's Daughter was getting tired of the attitude. She was about to say something when Munro broke in. "At least we should be happy that whoever or whatever is doing this isn't internet savvy."

Donkey Kong whirled on him. "What did you say?"

Munro stood at attention. "Sir. I meant nothing by it."

"Repeat yourself, sergeant. "

"I said at least we should be happy that whatever is doing this isn't internet savvy."

"Whoever. You also said whoever."

"Sir, I did sir."

Donkey Kong nodded, waved a hand, and said, "Relax, sergeant."

Munro exchanged the time-aged glance with Jagger that begged the question, *what the fuck did I do?*

Jagger shrugged, but never dropped his smile.

"We've been acting on the idea that this was a supernatural event based on a location." He glanced at Preacher's Daughter. "A lot of events have been occurring all over the world involving unseelie coming to public notice. What's usually hidden has come into the light, while at the same time at least two places have disappeared from human consciousness."

"Definitely more than just two," Preacher's Daughter said.

Donkey Kong nodded. "Right. But for purposes of this hypothesis, we'll keep it to these two. If it's someone, then why would they want a piece of the world for themselves and only themselves."

"Perhaps it's a beachhead?" Jagger said.

Donkey Kong pulled up a rolling chalkboard and wrote down 'beachhead'.

"That's good, but who would want that beachhead?"

"Someone not from here," Munro said. "I'm not talking aliens either."

"It could be aliens," Preacher's Daughter said. "Who is to say that the aliens have to come from a different planet? They could be alien to us. Having just battled Zoroastrian demons on both the prime material and astral planes, I can say without a shadow of a doubt that if you saw one in real life they would be seen as aliens."

"You Americans would probably arrest them for being illegal aliens," Jagger said.

Munro laughed.

Preacher's Daughter rolled her eyes. "Let's not even start comparing politics or you're going to have to explain Brexit to me."

Jagger held up his hands. "Peace. We all have our own problems, that's for certain."

Ignoring the conversation, Donkey Kong had written the words 'supernatural' and 'demons' on the board.

"You might as well add Fae to that," Preacher's Daughter said.

Donkey Kong turned. "While Fae are a big part of English superstition, I wasn't aware that they were also part of American superstition. Plus, isn't your missing town on an Indian Reservation? That would make it some sort of Native American superstition."

"Sioux. They are part of the Sioux Nation on Pine Ridge. Don't forget there was a mission there where I supposedly spent some time one summer, although I've somehow completely forgotten." She snapped her fingers. "There's another thing."

"What's that?" Mal asked.

"You said that there's still information about Graves Hill on the web."

"You can see it right there," Donkey Kong pointed to one of the screens that had a list of links from a search engine.

"Information about Iron Hat was still available on the web until suddenly it wasn't. How do you know you aren't looked at pages in your cache?"

Jagger turned to a workstation. "All I have to do is a hard reload and—"

All of the links disappeared.

His fingers danced over the keys as window after window, each a different search engine popped onto the screen, each one laying haphazardly over the one previous, all showing nothing returning for the Booleans for 'Graves Hill.'

"Shit. Shit. Shit."

"What about backups?"

"I need to find out where the information was originally stored to know where it was backed up. Cloud storage has its plusses and minuses. One of the bad things is that we don't have clear access to all the backups anymore."

Mal clicked his heels together to get their attention.

"Let's focus more on why or how the information was removed than what the information was," Mal said. "We know the town was there based on information previously known. We have a member of parliament who states unequivocally that it was there and is our only factual human witness. They've insisted that someone go and search the area. If we can find proof of the missing town, then it would help us a long way to determining a possible way to bring it back."

"So much for not being internet savvy," Munro said to himself.

"How would someone go about erasing something from the internet so completely no one knew it existed?" Preacher's Daughter asked.

Everyone gave her a blank look.

"Jagger?" Mal prompted.

"It could conceivably be done, but search engines store URLs for site locations for their own use which would leave residual data that could be traced. There's always the Internet Way Back Machine," Jagger said. "If they have a firewall that can keep whoever or whatever it was from erasing the data, then they might have the original pages."

Patterson sighed heavily. "I think all of you are missing the point. If the missing towns occurred because of someone's or something's superior technology, then don't you think the same superior technology could remove the information from databases?"

"Or magic," Munro said. "It could be magic, as well."

"Arthur C. Clarke's third law states that any sufficiently

advanced technology is indistinguishable from magic," Patterson said.

And then she saw it.

Preacher's Daughter had been taking Patterson's behavior personally. But the Brit was an equal opportunity asshole. She didn't discriminate. She was the same way to everyone. The thought delighted her because now Preacher's Daughter didn't need to feel slighted. Patterson acted the way she did to everyone and everyone just ignored it. She felt a weight lift off her.

"What's that movie with the Coke bottle that falls from an airplane and hits an African on the head and they begin to worship it?" Munro asked.

Preacher's Daughter remembered it well, but she couldn't remember the name of it. She remembered it being farcical and quite a bit patronizing. A Coke bottle is discovered in the Kalahari Desert by a tribe of Bushmen and believed to be a gift from god.

"*The Gods Must Be Crazy*," Jagger said, his smile dropping. "Written as a political statement by a South African director during Apartheid."

"I didn't know the politics of it," Munro began—

"Said no white man ever," Jagger added.

The Scotsman swung his chair around. "Hey, bro. We're all just talking. I don't mean anything."

Jagger shook his head. "I know. You're right. I'm just thinking about Sheriff. He'd be giving you the same shit."

Munro nodded. "Brother's not out of my thoughts for a moment. And you're right."

Mal cleared his throat. "It's clear we still need information. Donkey Kong and Preacher's Daughter, I want you to interview Sloath."

Donkey Kong began, "But Madeleine and I—"

"Which is exactly why I don't want you talking to her. She has an undue pull over you. I'm having Patterson and Jagger talk with her. I want to know if either of them know what's going on. I'm pretty sure Sloath does, but talking to him makes my head hurt."

"What about me, boss?" Munro asked.

"You and I are going to visit Graves Hill."

The Scotsman punched a fist into his hand. "Hell yes. It's about damn time. Enough of this brain stuff."

Donkey Kong laughed. "Spoken like a Marine Commando."

CHAPTER 11

THEY HELPED MUNRO and Mal prepare for the mission. The Home Office still wasn't sure what was going on, and didn't want to waste more resources on it, but they finally relented on sending MI5 agents and the use of a tactical surveillance van with a host of various drones. If that didn't work, they were going to get as close as they could to the situation and conduct a foot reconnaissance. Preacher's Daughter wished she could go with the pair. As much as she liked the 'brain stuff,' as the Scotsman put it, she also appreciated the physical. Taking down a few bad guys was better than any gym workout. It was like two leg days and a chest day all in one without the next day pain.

But she was an intel gal at heart and knew where her expertise lay. She'd interrogated the worst of them, from suspected child molesters to terrorists and everyone in between. Sloath had come along with them of his own free will, but he and his fellow Knockers had also arranged for the kidnapping of one of the Black Dragoons. Hanging onto Sheriff was supposed to guarantee Sloath's life. She just hoped that the Knockers were respecting Sheriff as much as the Black Dragoons were respecting their hostage Knocker.

She'd interrogate him, but she wouldn't touch him. No stress positions. Nothing of the sort. Just a few questions, a conversation, and then she'd see where it went. He insisted on staying in the darkness in the basement. He couldn't stand man-made light, so it was a candle on an old wooden table that separated him from them.

The unseelie still smelled like old cheese and stone.

They'd set him up in a section of the basement that was unfinished. The floor was composed of dirt worn into a flat sheen from five hundred years of footsteps. The walls were stone upon stone, probably laid by hand as part of the original foundation when the castle was first built. The age of things in England was continually startling her. That the building she was in was twice the age of America really spoke to the youthful exuberance of her nation.

She'd pre-arranged with Donkey Kong how she wanted the session to work. They'd begin with her and her alone. She didn't want any comments from him whatsoever. She wanted to ascertain how Sloath was going to react to being interrogated by a woman. There were men who couldn't deal with it, usually those who thought themselves the most masculine. Then again, Sloath was no man. He wasn't even human. She was just shooting in the dark.

Sloath sat in a corner, the table pulled close enough that running away would be difficult.

She sat in a wooden chair on the left facing him.

Donkey Kong sat on the right in a wooden chair, facing her.

She'd brought along an old school legal pad and a pen. File and dossier approach normally would get the average human used to the idea that providing information was just a matter of fact.

"Before we start, Mr. Sloath, I need some biographical data. Just the normal things. Name, date of birth, place of birth, et cetera. We'll begin with the name. What is your name, Mr. Sloath?"

He stared at her, face wrinkled, teeth overlapping in a mouth too small for all the teeth. His nose was more that of a bat's, barely more than two slits. His skin was gray with green splotches and wrinkled like a Sharpe dog's. Double-sized black eyes stared unblinking. Pointed ears poked from beneath a leather skull cap. He sat completely unmoving with his hands at his sides.

"Mr. Sloath, can you please state your full name."

A moment passed, then the Knocker said, "Sloath."

"Right, got that." She said, smiling, then returning her gaze to her paper. "I meant your full name. What is it your parents called you? Your elders?"

Another moment then he said, "Sloath," but this was followed by aspirated coughing.

She nodded again. "Got it. Sloath," then she tried to mimic his aspirated coughing.

Did she note a twitch on the Knocker's face? Was it anger? Humor?

"And what is your birthdate, Sloath?"

"Hole in the world," he said, no inflection, just a cavalcade of consonants.

"What's that?" she asked.

"Hole in the world."

She scribbled the words across the page.

"What does that mean, Sloath? What is a 'hole in the world?'"

His eyes blinked in such a way she was reminded of a frog. "Hole in world. Fae," aspirated coughing, "Fae."

"Are you saying the Fae are making a hole in the world?"

"Warn Not Fae. We knock. We warn."

She'd lost full on and complete control of the interrogation. He wasn't answering questions but following his own agenda. Still, he was here of his own free will. Perhaps this was reason all along. What was it about the Knockers and the Cornish miners? They helped them find new veins and kept miners from dying in cave ins.

"Why do you warn us? Er—why do you warn Not Fae?"

"Hole in world. Destroy. Hole in world. Kill Not Fae."

"Let me jump in a moment, PD," Donkey Kong said.

She leaned back, hugging the paper to her chest, nodding.

"Sloath. Where is hole in the world?" he asked, speaking like he might to a child.

"Hole in the world here," Sloath said, for the first

time, moving, his right hand now on his chest. "Hole in the world hurts."

"There's a hole in you?" he glanced at Preacher's Daughter. "Does it hurt, Sloath?"

"Sloath always hurt. Knockers always hurt. We take hurt." His eyes narrowed. "We not Not Fae."

"Why does it hurt, Sloath? Why are the Fae making you hurt?"

"Hole in the world. Must escape. Something comes."

Preacher's Daughter exchanged a worried glance with Donkey Kong.

Something comes was never a good thing to hear.

"What's coming?" she asked. "What's chasing the Fae into the hole in the world?"

Sloath pinned her with his wide eyes. "Formori. Formori come to eat Fae. Hole in the world. Escape." He placed both hand on the table. "Hole in the world escape."

Her mind swirled with the history of the world's religions and mythology, the two often dovetailing into each other. What she knew of the Formori, if they were the same as the Formorians, was that they were a race of giants who preceded the Tuatha Dé Danann of Ireland. There'd been centuries long arguments whether the fairies or Sidhe of Ireland were different from England with not many prevailing resolutions, but from a scholarly perspective, they probably had all of the same fairies just known by different names. The Formori, like the Jotun of Norse mythology, were believed to be larger than life, hostile, and ugly, but that point of view was presented by those who had conquered them—the Tuatha.

"What of the fairy upstairs, Sloath? Can you feel it?"

"Fae. I feel. Not Fae. I feel."

"Does the fairy upstairs know about the hole in the world?"

"All Fae know. It draws. Want hole. Takes them new place. No Formori."

"So your sylph has known all along," she said to Donkey Kong. "How is it you communicate with it?"

He blushed and looked at the floor. "Let's talk about that later, please."

She gave him a long wondering look, trying not to imagine what sort of Fae-human interaction would make him blush, then returned her attention to Sloath.

"Back to something you said before. You said, *hole in the world, kill Not Fae.*"

"Fae live beside. Beside. Sloath live beside. Sloath not live with. Formori want live with."

Beside? Like some sort of slipstream pocket universe? She'd heard fairy mounds being referred to as pocket universes in fiction and folklore, so why couldn't that be the truth? And if the Formori wanted to live with—she tried to imagine a race of hideous giants living among the men and women of a Midlands village and could only imagine the carnage that might create.

The unseelie suddenly stood.

"Sloath go now."

"Wait," Donkey Kong said, standing as well.

Preacher's Daughter joined them. What was the Knocker thinking? He couldn't leave. He was part of a hostage exchange.

She asked. "Where are you going, Sloath?"

"Back. Back in urth."

"Uh, Sloath, we can't let you go," she said.

"Sloath go," he said, blinking wide eyes, mouth opening revealing his oddly-shaped sharpened teeth.

Donkey Kong pulled back his shoulders. "Sorry, Mr. Sloath. We thank you for the warning, but you can't leave until you return our man to us. That was the agreement."

Sloath turned to him, eyes blinking again in that contemplative froggy way. "Hole in the world come. Hole in the world kill. Must stop."

He pushed the chair into the table and backed into the corner. He began to be lost in a shadow that she could have sworn hadn't been there before. As the shadow deepened, Sloath lessened.

Donkey Kong grabbed the table and shoved it aside. He lunged to grab the Knocker, but he was too late. His hands disappeared in shadow up to the elbows. He jerked them back, gasping, and stared at them, moving his fingers back and forth. "The pain." He inhaled. "I thought I'd lost them."

Sloath was gone, absorbed into the stone, like he'd never even been there in the first place.

Donkey Kong turned to Preacher's Daughter, frustration on his face, eyes wide, shaking his head.

Then she saw it.

"Wait. Look." She rushed around the other side of the table. As the darkness began to dissipate, a figure began to appear. Knees to his chest, arms around his knees, short black afro. Sheriff. They'd given him back.

He still wore his gear. His weapon was slung across his back.

When she touched him, he opened his eyes and said, "'ole in the world." His breathing got shallow as if he were finding it hard to breathe. Then his eyes widened until they seemed as if they might pop out of his skull.

"It comes," he said.

Then he fell over, unconscious, eyes rolling back inside his head.

CHAPTER 12

THEY DIDN'T WAIT for an ambulance or the helicopter. They carried Sheriff up the stairs and out the front door. They had a choice from a line of cars parked to one side, but they threw open the doors to the Range Rover and slid Sheriff's limp body inside. Waterhouse ordered her to stay behind and brief the others on what had happened. He said it was less than a twenty-minute drive to the Royal Hospital in Stoke-on-Trent and they had a special suite of rooms on standby for their use. Then he was off, speeding across the drawbridge and skidding into The Square Road, just missing a well-dressed family leaving St. Peter's Church.

Preacher's Daughter watched the empty space where they'd turned, fear consuming her. How Sheriff had appeared virtually out of nothing bothered her less than his unconsciousness. She'd lost team members before and didn't want to lose any again. Ever. After several minutes of worrying her hands, she turned and went back inside.

Barbie and Jagger were upstairs and Munro and Mal were on mission, which left her alone with her thoughts.

She thought of breaking into the meeting upstairs, but she realized it wouldn't do anyone any good. So, she did what she was best at. She paced the first floor, her brain trying to wrap itself around what just happened and figure out what the hell it meant by there was a hole in the world.

She decided to give Poe a call. The phone rang several times. When he answered, it was clear from his groggy voice she'd woken him. She briefed him on what was going on as he got up and made a pod of coffee.

When she was finished, she asked, "Did those words ever come up? Hole in the world?"

"The young girl, Christine, was too distraught. When she learned that her parents and her brothers had been ritually murdered, and that it might have been her, she lost it. She's been completely incommunicado since."

"Do you think she did it?"

"No. And I can't seem to make her understand that. We're going to have to turn her over to Child Services soon. We don't have the bandwidth or the legal right to hold onto her."

Preacher's Daughter thought about the girl going into the foster system at her age and it wasn't good. She was messed up and the last thing she needed was to be put in front of more predators.

"Can you hold onto her until I get back?"

A long pause on the other end of the line. "I suppose we can. What do you have in mind?"

"I want to see what I can do. I'm due some time off.

When this is all over, maybe I can help get through to her."

"She's still going to have to go into the system," he said.

"Perhaps. Let's change the subject. Any new evidence from the Amish Fiasco?" she asked.

"Not everything there was a homunculus," he said. "We found several unseelie or what was left of them. We believe them to be kobolds or something similar."

"Wait? Kobolds? Since when have we had kobolds in America?"

"They've been here since the first immigrants brought them over, but they're not centralized and they are few and far between. Checking in Special Unit 77 records, we've come across them on eight other occasions over the years, but those were always solitary encounters. This was the first time we've noted them working together."

"How many were there?"

"Three and a half."

"A half?" she laughed. "Why a half?"

"We don't know. Cleaved cleanly right down the middle."

"Fascinating."

"That's why you don't get a lot of dates," Poe said. "You find these things fascinating."

"I don't get a lot of dates because I have little patience for big muscles and small heads."

A pause at the end of the line was punctuated by a fake cough.

"You know what I mean. And hey? Why didn't you call me about the kobolds?"

"Things are pretty fluid here. We're doing sweeps around the perimeter of Iron Hat and looking for evidence of any other infestations or presence of anything supernatural. I was going to bring you up to speed."

"I'd be interested to know what the kobolds were doing with the homunculi," she said. "Why would they be involved with an alchemical creation? Why also were they working together?"

"All good questions we are trying to figure out. I'll bring the team up to speed about this *hole in the world* idea and see if we can't figure it out. We'll let you know if anything comes up."

They said their goodbyes and hung up.

She'd been pacing aimlessly during the phone call and now found herself in a room she'd never been in before. Turning around, she realized that she'd had to open a door to get in. She was on the other side of the operations center and what looked like an odd pairing of a small library and a child's playroom. Not only were there floor to ceiling bookshelves filled with leather bound tomes, a green felt card table with several chairs, but in the far corner by the window stood a three-story Victorian doll house.

What drew her eye were the lights on in several of the rooms as if someone lived there. Who put lights in a doll house, she wondered? Hell, who even had a doll house? She'd never had one growing up, wanting to be outside more than inside, so she'd never seen the fascination. Then she saw movement.

She drew her pistol from her side holster.

She considered saying something like *freeze* but she didn't think whatever it was would understand. She ran down the list of zoological possibilities and stopped at rat. An old house like this probably had a mischief of rats, scratching their way through byways in the walls that had been scratched by rats for hundreds of years. She lowered the barrel of her pistol. She wasn't about to be the one to freak out and shoot a rat inside the Black Dragoons HQ. She'd be a laughing stock and probably become a warning lesson to be laughed about over ale.

Movement in one of the windows again.

But she couldn't leave the rat to its own devices. She glanced around the room at all the antique books and papers. What if it got into them? What if it destroyed something valuable? She sighed. She hated being the rat catcher.

She angled towards the doll house, admiring the workmanship. It looked absolutely like a real house. Working lights. She'd laugh if it had working plumbing. Now close enough to touch it, she thought she heard music, tinny, and on the edge of her hearing. She couldn't help but detect the source as coming from the doll house.

She straightened and glanced around for cameras.

Was she being punked?

Sure enough, in the one corner of the room was a camera near the ceiling aimed at her and the doll house.

Or was it just aimed at the doll house? She moved aside and the camera did not move with her so it was fixed and not directed by motion. So, it was to observe the doll house. Why would someone go to the expense to monitor an old doll house?

Unless maybe it was haunted.

The Haunted Doll House of Stoke-on-Trent.

She cocked her ear and listened for the music again. She heard it and followed the sound. She could have sworn it sounded like 1980s Blondie. She decided to peek into one of the windows. It appeared to be a bedroom, but the bedsheets were rumpled and the bed was unmade. Clothes were scattered across the floor. Tiny pieces of jewelry were piled on a vanity table. It looked like any single woman's room. It could have been anyone's bedroom in miniature. She had to give the designers credit. Whoever created it sure paid attention to detail. It was a miracle of microstructure.

She moved over a room and swung her gaze into a bathroom. Since when did doll houses have bathrooms? She saw a tiny toilet and a sink and a clawfoot bathtub complete with a doll inside of it.

Then she stared for a cold ten seconds.

Her eyes widened.

A doll that moved.

A naked doll that was washing itself.

Long blond hair. White skin. Tiny features.

"Who in the bloody hell do you think you are?" came a voice to her right;

Leaning out a second story window was a second doll—er—woman—er—small person. This one had dark hair pulled back in a ponytail.

"Fucking Peepin' Tom is who you are. Show some fucking respect for your elders."

Preacher's Daughter backed away, blinking rapidly. She looked down at the pistol in her hand.

"Oh no. Is the giant woman going to shoot the little pixies? Well, come on then. Let's have it."

Preacher's Daughter holstered the pistol, backed into the edge of a chair, turned it around and sat down. Then she began to laugh. The more the pixie cursed the harder she laughed until tears were coming out of her eyes. Whether the Black Dragoons wanted to or not, some of their secrets were beginning to get out.

Of course, they had Fae in the house. Not only the sylph, but now these two pixies.

As she watched the one that had been in the tub wrap a towel around her hair through the window, she wondered what other surprises she might find in Caverswall Castle.

CHAPTER 13

IT TURNED OUT their names were Thrash and Trash. The blonde was Thrash and she was almost as talkative as Trash, who was the one who had lit into her in the beginning. They'd lived in the castle for several hundred years and it was part of the deal that they were kept fed and housed. In exchange, they kept the place free of rodents and other pesky Fae.

"You should have seen the look on your face," Trash said.

Preacher's Daughter had never been this close to a pixie. She'd read about them since joining Special Unit 77 and had seen pictures of them, but to actually interact with an entity like the Fae was beyond her expertise. The *daeva* certainly didn't count. Those had been giants. These pixies were the exact size of Barbie dolls, except they were totally alive. If she hadn't been in the headquarters of a unit designed to protect the United Kingdom from supernatural attack, she would have thought she was going mad. Instead, against all of her notions, she was actually enjoying herself.

"Patterson is your caretaker?" she asked, clarifying what Thrash had just said.

"She's no one's caretaker," Thrash responded in high-pitched tinkling English, her hair still wet but in pigtails. She wore jeans with a miniature Led Zeppelin shirt and sandals. "We call her Mama Bear. She'd do anything for us."

"Caretaker implies we need taking care of," Trash added. "No one puts Pixies in a corner. Mama Bear knows that. She makes sure that other Hooms like that Malcontent don't use us as test subjects."

"Guinea pigs."

"Experiments."

"Lab pixies."

They continued to go back and forth, derivating synonyms while Preacher's Daughter grinned in delight. By Hooms she figured they were referring to humans. And Malcontent could only be Malcom, who probably, upon recognizing that the castle had its own pixies, had wanted to begin studies immediately. Preacher's Daughter imagined frames of pixies pinned to a felt background much like Victorian lepidopterists used to have framed collections of butterflies.

"Subject."

"Case."

"Victim."

"Testee."

"Did you just say testee?"

They both cracked up and laughed, the sound small

but authentic and like the tinkling laughter of children locked behind glass. Thrash punched Trash in the shoulder. Trash grabbed Thrash's arm and they both began to wrestle on top of the green felt table.

Just then the door opened.

The handsome Indian's gaze glommed onto the table, then shifted to Preacher's Daughter and back and forth at the pixies.

"Oh, shit. I was afraid of that."

"What? That I'd find out about our castle pixies?" she asked innocently.

"Noticed you on the surveillance system when we finished with the—ah—interview of Madeleine."

"Interview with Madeleine," cried Thrash. "Did she sex you?"

"Tell us," said Trash, rolling onto her stomach and putting her hands beneath her chin. "Tell us how she tried to sex you."

Jagger's face turned a solid red and he looked away. "Listen. We have news. Can you join us in operations?" He pointed at the pixies. "I'm talking to Preacher's Daughter, not you."

They both looked at her.

"That's your name?" they asked simultaneously.

"That's amazing," Trash said. "A preacher's daughter."

"That's beyond awesome," Thrash said. "All naughty girls."

She stood, caught between a hard place and a pixie.

"Let's go," Jagger said.

She nodded, then gave the pixies an amiable salute. "Catch you two later."

As she left the room she heard, "Did you see how hot she was?" and "But her legs are a little thick, doncha think?"

She found herself looking at her legs as she entered operations, wondering what the pixie meant. Too much wine and not enough working out? Maybe she should run five or ten kilometers. She shook her head. Why was she even listening to the body shaming of a twelve-inch twist of ornery?

Patterson sat in her spot in the operations center with a face only a bulldog could love. Her frown folded the light and captured shadow.

"Are you done snooping?" she asked.

"I wasn't aware there were areas off limits to me," Preacher's Daughter said, her languid feeling scalded by the pot of boiling vile.

"Doors are usually in place for a reason," Patterson said.

"Am I part of the team or not?" Preacher's Daughter asked, realizing she was getting far madder than she should be getting. "I mean, you have been the ultimate super feckless bitch. I figured if there was a place you didn't want me to go, you would have shoved it in my face."

She felt at once like covering her mouth with her hand and laughing at the look on the other woman's face.

The room was completely silent for a full minute.

Jagger was the first to speak and as he began to back out of the room said, "I think I'm about to leave."

Both Barbie and Preacher's Daughter pointed at him and said, "Don't you dare."

He stopped at the door, frozen like a cod jumping out of the water in a sub-Arctic freeze.

"What did you call me?" Barbie said, each word like a gunshot.

"You heard me. Do I need to repeat myself?" Preacher's Daughter crossed her arms and shoved her tongue into her cheek.

Barbie stood, reaching a full six feet, her broad shoulders as large as any man's. "I knew you'd be up to no good. I read your file and saw the debacle you led in Pennsylvania. You come in here with the intention of sleeping with the lot of them, bending them under your wing. You want everyone to think you're the perfect little preacher's daughter, but I know what you are."

She'd felt the heat rising during the whole time the other woman spoke. Now, her entire head was in flame. "What am I?"

"We had a term for you in college, the sort of girls who would hang out by the men's locker room. We called you athletic supporters. What do you call them? Jock straps?"

Preacher's Daughter dropped her arms and balled her fists. "You have got to be fucking kidding me," she said, advancing on the woman.

"Bring it on," Barbie said, putting her fists up like a prizefighter.

Jagger jumped in between the two women, terror in his eyes, but a firm determination in his jaw. He was much taller than either one, but still thin as a willow. "Enough of this. What has gotten into you?"

Suddenly, both the pixies rolled into the room. They ran between Preacher's Daughter's legs, then dove under Barbie's chair. They peeled a little person from beneath and wrestled with it for several seconds. It was clear to Preacher's Daughter that both of them were well-versed at jujitsu, simultaneously throwing the other figure into both an arm bar and a leg bar until it squealed, the sound like a baby pig in distress.

Jagger grabbed the being by the neck and lifted him up for all to see. Slightly smaller and wider than one of the pixies, it had pointed features, a beard, and a small cap. "A lutin," he said. "That's what's got everyone riled up." He laughed forlornly. "I bet the little guy was sent in here to spy and it couldn't help himself."

Thrash and Trash high fived each other, then climbed onto the table beside Barbie.

"Sit down, Mama Bear. It wasn't you but the lutin made you do," Trash said.

Preacher's Daughter felt an immediate calm fold into the room.

"What is a lutin?" she asked.

"An unseelie who loves to get into other people's business," Thrash explained. "He likes to influence people and make them mad. He gets off on it," she said, making a jerk off motion with her right hand.

Preacher's Daughter shook her head. She wished that she could unsee what she'd just seen, but she felt better. Why she'd gotten angry so quickly she could only attribute to the creature.

"Barbie, listen, I am sorry I said those things," she began. "I didn't mean them at all."

"The thing about a lutin," Barbie said as she sat back down, "is they only magnify what is already there."

Preacher's Daughter found a chair and fell into it, the wheels letting her roll back a few inches. "So, you really do think I'm a jock strap?"

"You really do think I am a feckless bitch?"

She smiled sadly. "I think I actually called you the ultimate superior feckless bitch. Not just any old feckless bitch," she said.

"I can be a bitch now and then," Barbie said. "I haven't exactly been welcoming. I was sort of pissed when they took my partner and replaced him with you. Nothing personal."

So, that's what the situation was. At least it wasn't personal or something they couldn't come back from. Had they come to blows, who knows how bad it could have gotten? Her guess was that she'd have been on the next plane smoking west. If it hadn't been for the two little punk rock pixies, that's exactly where she'd be.

Preacher's Daughter apologized once more, while Jagger took the lutin to a glass cage on the floor in the corner of the room, then explained to them what had happened with Sloath and then at the end, how Sheriff had appeared. "I still don't know his status, but I'm sure Donkey Kong will let us know as soon as he can," she said. "What about you guys?"

Jagger had somehow found a beer and sat down at his workstation sipping it so it wouldn't spill.

"Commander doesn't like drinking in ops," Barbie said, not really meaning it.

Jagger handed her a can and then threw one towards Preacher's Daughter, who caught it. "Then don't drink it. Use it as a paperweight." He nodded to the American. "You want to tell her, or do you want me to?"

"Are you sure you're up for it?" Barbie asked.

"He got mind sexed," Thrash tittered.

Jagger blushed.

"Got a sticky wicket?" Trash asked.

"It wasn't exactly pleasant for me," he mumbled in the direction of the pixies. Then, taking a deep draught, told Barbie, "Maybe you should answer this one."

To her credit, Barbie opened her beer and took a sip, then placed it down on her desk. "Old Madeleine admits there's something going on. My guess is that she knows a lot more than she's letting on. She might tell Waterhouse, I'm not certain, but for sure, she knows something. She as much as told us that she was holding back because she wasn't allowed." She glanced at Jagger. "But then again, one never knows. She communicates in an—ahem— different manner than we are used to."

"It's gross, is what it is," he said, shaking his head and shivering his torso. "Can't she just talk?"

"That's not how sylphs work, you know that."

"What's the plan?" Preacher's Daughter asked.

"I'm going to recommend we go to Cottingley Woods," Patterson said. "We'll bring along the Twins and see if they can't scare up some interest. I'm thinking that there are those who will want to talk. Explain to us why they are afraid of the Formori and maybe tell us exactly what it is about them that they are afraid of."

"Don't you have them listed in a database somewhere?" Preacher's Daughter asked.

"The Formori are definitely old school," Jagger said. "They date back almost before recorded history. What we have is merely a scattering of reports that have probably been changed and enlarged over the years."

"What is it you have? I mean, anything right now would be better than nothing," she said.

Jagger shook his head. "While I appreciate your excitement, what you said isn't exactly true. Just having more information isn't helpful. Knowledge isn't power. Knowledge is a deficit. Wisdom is power. Having a random assortment of facts at hand is what creates the crazies on the internet. They believe that by reading a blog or watching a video that what they have just done is research. They don't understand how to differentiate the data. They don't understand about writing abstracts, random sampling, original source reviewing, or how to perform independent probability statistic generation. They don't look at the source of the information and question why the source reported the information in such a way, nor do they wonder if the information wasn't loaded in such a way as to conform to preconceived ideas. Basically, they don't do any real research that a kindergartner would do, yet they call it research."

"I think I'm a little savvier than a kindergartner," Preacher's Daughter said, impressed and a little intrigued by Jagger's sudden slam on information.

"You've hit on one of my pet peeves," Jagger said, for the first time, not a trace of a smile on his dark brown face. "The democratization of information was seen as a great thing. And it should be. But people don't treat information the same way they treat bullets and acid and hand grenades. They are all dangerous. The worst thing you can tell someone is to research something themselves. When you do, they will almost always reinforce the idea they were researching because they don't know how not to look for information that doesn't support their idea."

"It sounds like something personal," she said.

"I guess we all have the horses we ride." He licked his lips and sat forward. "Looking at me, who do you see?"

"I'm not sure what you want me to say."

"I want you to give me unvetted access to your mind."

"You don't want to know what's in my mind. Bite a chunk off my PTSD and you'll never sleep again."

He paused and regarded her. "Okay, not your mind. But how you think of me. Please. For my own sake. Be honest."

She looked him up and down. He was a handsome man, no doubt. Was he conflicted? She couldn't tell. He was no McQueen, but certainly McQueen had a few decades of hatred and experience to deal with whatever internal problems he'd had to conquer.

"Okay," she began, leaning forward she grabbed his hand and held it. "I see a younger man. Six foot three or four inches tall. Not athletic enough to be a basketball player, but you probably exceed in volleyball. I can see you doing well in a team sport, but not individually. You're from a single parent home and were raised by your mother. Your father for whatever reason was out of the picture. How am I doing so far?"

"Scary."

She nodded.

"How did you know I was raised by my mother?"

"You are also gay. Had you been raised by a father, your demeanor might be different. But you seem to like yourself enough. I don't detect a hateful bone in your body. You strive to understand which makes you a great communicator, hence your job with the Black Dragoons.

"Your ancestry is Indian from the subcontinent. You are second or third generation British. Now for the big question. What religion are you? India has one major religion and many others. You don't seem to be practicing the Hindi religion, although you could be a non-practicing Hindu. Still, I'm not feeling it. You also aren't Muslim because I see you drinking beer.

"I think you are a Sikh. Most believe that all male Sikhs grow their hair and wear turbans, but that is not always the case. There are those of you who do not wear turbans yet who still follow the faith. This probably puts you at odds with your uncles and other men in your family, but then again you were already at odds because of your sexuality and your individual beliefs. Sikhism is a uniquely monotheistic religion in that it talks about the marriage of two souls, but doesn't genderize the souls, therefore although homosexuality might not be condoned due to other social practices, the religion doesn't deny its allowance."

She looked him the eyes, noticing the wetness in them and his open sensual mouth and asked, "How did I do? Is that about right?"

He pulled his hand away and wiped his eyes with his palms.

"You should take this act of yours on the road. What did you do? Have your CIA run a bio on me?"

She shook her head. "I don't know anyone in the CIA except for an ex-boyfriend and we're not going to be talking anytime soon. During interrogation instruction we are taught to pay attention to tells. We're also taught to understand interpersonal dynamics. All I gave you were educated guesses based on your own behavior."

"If that's true, you should charge for appearances. Go to Vegas or something." He sniffed. "Sherlock."

She laughed. "Sherlock it is."

CHAPTER 14

WATERHOUSE CALLED FROM the hospital. Sheriff was going to be alright. He was severely dehydrated and required several bags of saline. The doctors wanted to keep him overnight. They made sure to post a guard, then Waterhouse returned to the castle. By the time he arrived, Mal and Munro were returning with a new man. They were all dressed in fatigues, but it was Mal who looked the worse for wear. His chest had been hastily bandaged and was still bloody from where something had ripped through the material of his body armor and his uniform. Munro had a long stare and no trace of a smile. The new man looked very corporate—body armor and uniform fitted by a Saville Row tailor.

None of them said a word until they'd gone into the mess, grabbed some cold cuts to make sandwiches, and ravenously eaten them with crisps and ice-cold beer. When they were done, they all sat back, closed their eyes and let their breathing slow.

Preacher's Daughter knew how they had to unwind and slough off the adrenaline. She'd been in the same situation enough times to know that they needed space and time from what had happened to get it right in their minds.

An hour after they finished eating, they retired to their rooms to clean themselves, announcing that there'd be a meeting in operations at midnight. Whatever the meeting was going to be about, she knew things were ramping up. She felt it. What had been a series of slow-moving events had morphed into something faster and with faster came danger.

She went to the armory and prepared individual weapons. She'd gone out with someone else's kit on the mission to Cornwall. As ill-fitting as the body armor was, it had done the trick, but she wanted something sized to her as well as a weapon that was hers and hers alone. She grabbed a rifle, pistols, body armor, helmet, and coms, and began preparing, knowing that they'd probably be going out in the morning. She wanted to be ready and she wanted to be comfortable. She stripped the pistols and the rifles, ensuring they were free of any grit that might cause a jam. There wasn't a pistol or rifle short of a sniper rifle designed to penetrate the Level IV hard plate armor. She'd been struck once by 7.62mm rounds while on mission outside of FOB Joyce in Afghanistan and the bruise had stayed with her for two weeks.

Originally designed as a Forward Air Refueling Base or FARP, FOB Joyce was comprised of helicopter mechanics and refuelers from the Washington and California National Guards. These were logistic soldiers and weren't trained in kinetic operations. But when the shit hit the fan on May 6, 2016, they were forced to defend themselves from a larger force. She'd been assigned to Special Operations Task Force comprised of four rangers, two Special Forces, and eight Afghan Ktah Khas soldiers, two of whom were women.

The FARP had been a staging area for Apache helicopters to interdict Taliban crossing the Pakistan border, but after a week of heavy rains and being grounded, Taliban approached and began raining down mortar rounds in an attempt to destroy the gunships and the tens of thousands of gallons of fuel at the FARP. Her small unit was able to take out the mortars, but not before she got shot in the chest and back by a half dead insurgent carrying an AK47 older than she was.

Although bruised the color of indigo for weeks, she'd come to count on the body armor for protection. She knew there were some special ammunitions that could penetrate the armor. A .50 caliber round would shred it. But for most things she was going to encounter, the body armor was her best friend. So, she removed all the ceramic plates and carefully inspected them for pitting, as well as scrutinized the plate carrier for ripping or snagging. The front and back plates were curved to fit the contours of a body. Each one weighed just over six pounds. The rectangular side plates weighed three pounds each.

About halfway through her inspection, Munro arrived carrying armloads of equipment from him and the others. His eyes were haunted as if he'd done something for which he was ashamed. He wouldn't look at her, but waited expectantly at the edge of the table.

She hastily made room on the center work table by pushing her equipment to one side.

He dumped his gear onto the table and began to pick through it, arranging like with like.

She continued her own work, exchanging her black plate for a new one on a shelf at the far end of the room. When she returned, she reintegrated the plates back into the plate carrier and began to rearrange the straps.

After a few moments, Munro put both his hands flat on the table and began to breathe through his nose. "You would not believe the shit we went through."

"What did you see?" she asked, glancing at him, then back to her own work.

"See? We saw nothing except for a demonstration. Madness from Leicester. The locals think there's a secret government project. They had a fucking riot of people there."

"But nothing is there."

"Just so. As it turned out, some locals were following us. They ignored the missing town soon enough. They don't know why we insist something is there so they think something sinister is going on."

"Something sinister probably is going on but it's not what they think." She reached over and held up Mal's ripped and ruined body armor, noting that something had cleaved right through the ceramic chest armor. "I can't believe that was from the riot."

Munro let out a chunk of air. "That's the big question of the moment." He gathered himself and began sorting, actually putting the things that needed maintenance in one pile and those that didn't in another. "Something picked him up and slammed him down. We have it on camera, but there's nothing in the visible spectrum. All I can say is the footage is being processed to ascertain whether or not something will become visible in the other spectrums."

She began reassembling her rifle, but kept her eyes on him. Munro was usually the man with an easy smile, but he seemed to be avoiding her gaze. It was clear he didn't want to talk. So, in the best interests of his feelings, she ignored them and asked anyway.

"What is it? What happened out there?"

He sighed. Let his hands go still. Looked up at the ceiling. "There's a reason I volunteered for this duty. You see, I love my job. Being a commando is everything I ever wanted and more. We trained harder, we fight harder, we party harder—we're just harder."

"Then what's wrong?" she asked.

"I don't like working against people anymore, especially my own."

"You spend your off time shooting poachers," she pointed out.

"Poachers aren't people to me. And in the scope, I can't see the expressions on their face when I hurt them. Same thing in Afghanistan. They're terrorists with guns approaching a position I'm detailed to protect." He shook his head. "I'm not saying it right."

"The rioting. You said there were a lot of people there."

He nodded. "They started to get violent and I had to put some of them down."

"You didn't—"

He shot her a frown. "Of course not, but I had to hit a few fine upstanding Cheezits with the butt of my rifle."

"Cheezits?"

"Leicesterians. We call 'em Cheezits because when they ask *how much is it* sounds like the cheese puff."

She shook her head not getting it at all. "You had to put them down, yes?"

"I didn't have to do anything. It just came automatically. We were being attacked and outnumbered and I reacted. I couldn't help myself." He picked up an L22A2 from the table and butt-stroked air. "One for the grandma." He butt-stroked another. "One for the bloke at the pub who drank too much." Yet another. "One for the man too deep in his G&Ts to know better." He slammed the rifle back on the table. "They didn't deserve that shit."

"Like you said, you were being attacked and you were outnumbered."

"That's just it. Nothing about it made sense. If they didn't know nothing was there then why would they complain about something not being there?"

An idea came to her. "The pixies found a lutin in the castle. Do you think that maybe—"

He shot her a steady glance. "You know about the pixies?"

She half smiled and cocked a leg. "If you mean Trash

and Thrash. Hell yeah. They're my new besties."

"And a lutin, you said?"

"Made me call Patterson a supreme feckless bitch or something like that."

Munro snorted a laugh. "They don't make you do anything. They just amplify." He shook his head. "What did she say?"

"Called me a jockstrap or an athletic supporter. Said I was only around to hold up everyone's—"

He held up a hand. "I get it. I truly do."

She glanced at her watch. "Hey, we better hurry or we're going to be late."

CHAPTER 15

When everyone was situated, Waterhouse stood at the front of the operations center. Mal was nowhere to be seen, but the new man sat on a chair next to Donkey Kong. Everyone else was present, including the pixies who sat on the edge of one of the tables swinging their legs like a couple of teenagers.

"I know it's late but things are beginning to move fast. Consider this an After Action for the cockup near Leicester and a mission brief for tomorrow morning. Before anyone asks, Lieutenant Colonel McDonnell is in the hospital. It seems the bruising to his ribs and sternum was worse than we believed and his right lung has collapsed."

Several sharp intakes of breath.

Everyone glanced at everyone else for a moment as they took in the news.

"In the meantime, I will be in charge. All mission briefs and requests will come through me. MI5 is also involved now that we have some proof that something is happening. As you know, the Home Office was reluctant to commit based on the word of a single MP—especially one who spends most of his waking hours trolleyed."

"Don't you love working for an organization that fights things that its government doesn't believe exist?" Jagger asked no one.

Ignoring the question, Waterhouse continued. He pointed to Preacher's Daughter. "She will be my second. The time to include her is well past. Whatever she needs to know, we tell her. Whatever you think you know, you tell her. She can't make a decision without knowing."

Preacher's Daughter wasn't sure what to think. She glanced at Jagger who grinned back at her.

"Let me introduce to you our MI5 liaison. This is Intelligence Officer Lamar Crookes."

The corporate man stood. His hair was cut short and elegant. He had a way of moving that appeared effortless. He reminded her of a dark-haired version of the actor in *The English Patient*. What was his name? Ralph Fiennes.

"Greetings, fellow hunters. You don't know me but I know each and every one of you. I am pleased to be working with you and will do all I can to make life and your missions easier. Know that you are the tip of the supernatural spear for Her Majesty and she is proud of you."

Jagger was still turned towards Preacher's Daughter and he rolled his eyes.

"My call sign is Ghost Hunter," the man continued. "I come from a long line of hunters. I'm excited to tell you that using our state-of-the-art surveillance equipment, we've discovered what attacked Lieutenant Colonel McDonnell."

He snapped his fingers.

Jagger spun his chair around, tapped a few keys and an image appeared on the screen behind Ghost Hunter.

The image looked like it had been drawn on a radioactive Etch-a-Sketch. Humanoid in shape, it had an extra-long torso and short legs. Instead of hands, a single arm emanated from the torso and ended in a short-fat blade. Features on the head couldn't be made out except for a gaping maw and glowing eyes.

"Who's the punter?" Munro asked.

"How'd you take the photo?" Preacher's Daughter asked. "I thought the creature was invisible."

Crookes put his hands behind his back and leaned forward slightly. "Ah, the American. Welcome aboard as they say."

"I've already been here and on mission," she said flatly. Why is it that some British just pissed her off?

"Just so. We have systems available that can test the entire electromagnetic spectrum. Although this beastie wasn't available through visible light means, we were able to use gamma radiation and track it using a gamma ray spectrometer. This image was rendered using computer simulation of the data received."

"Then you have a fairy version of the Hulk," she said.

He straightened and blinked.

She guessed they didn't have comics at the all-boy's schools he'd probably attended, so she attempted to help him out. "Bruce Banner? Gamma radiation? Became the Hulk? First he was gray, then green, then gray, then green again."

Crookes shook his head and remained silent.

"She's talking the MCU," Thrash the Pixie said. "Marvel. Hulk is a green superhero created through the gamma radiation."

"Comic books," Trash said. "Don't you know who the Hulk is?"

"Comic books are for children," Crookes said.

The pixies looked at each other.

"He's the punter."

"Comics are for kids. Didn't he ever read *Sandman*?"

"Probably jerks off to the *Financial Times*."

"Comics are pop culture metaphors for social injustices and situations," Thrash said, addressing Crookes now. "Racial inequality is at the heart of the X-Men franchise."

Trash stood on the edge of the desk. "Or Superman as a commentary on illegal immigration yet becoming a contributing member of society."

"What the hell are they talking about?" Crookes asked.

Barbie turned to her pixies. "Hush, you two, or I will cut your telly allowance, which means no *Game of Thrones*."

Thrash seemed about to say something and Trash threw her hands around the other's mouth.

"No problem, Mama Bear. We got it."

She spun the other pixie around and they both began to whisper and gesture madly.

Patterson turned back to the front. "Sorry about that. But they're right. You really should read a comic book or two. At least *2000AD* or Judge Dredd or something British."

"I asked who the punter was?" Munro put in.

Gathering himself, Crookes gestured towards the screen. "That is a Marrow."

"What is a Marrow?" Jagger asked.

"One of the unseelie," Donkey Kong said. "They are a sort of trow or troll. Words basically mean the same thing. They were formed with shadow magic, according to the mythology. Since they didn't have access to science in pre-history, we can assume that shadow magic was used to describe anything that wasn't able to be seen in the visible spectrum. In the case of the Marrow, gamma radiation."

"Is there any information in the Black Dragoon database?" Preacher's Daughter asked.

Jagger and Munro laughed.

"There is no database," Barbie offered, with air quotes. "We have a private library with two pensioners working there who we call when we need information."

"Why can't they digitize the information?" she asked.

"Then they'd be out of a job," Barbie said simply.

Preacher's Daughter opened her mouth to argue the point, but snapped it shut instead.

"But yes," Donkey Kong said. "We do have information. The Dragoons have encountered these creatures before. Once at Dunnottar Castle in 1697 during a thunderstorm. The creature was struck several times, which is how they knew the shape of it, especially the hands. No one except a young boy witness survived. And another in Staiths, Yorkshire, in 1917. It was thrashing about the harbor and was defeated by gunboats."

"How do we know it was defeated if we couldn't see it?" Munro asked.

"It stopped thrashing, I supposed," Donkey Kong said.

"Maybe it just got chased away," Jagger said.

"Or decided to leave," Munro said.

"Be that as it may," Donkey Kong said through gritted teeth, "these are the only two occasions where the Dragoons officially encountered a Marrow."

"How did they know it was a Marrow?" Preacher's Daughter asked.

"The hands and the size. Pict artifacts show the Marrow standing twice as high as a normal man at the time, which was considered to be five feet. So, we believe a mature Marrow stands at least ten feet tall. Then there is the distinct shape of the hand. We already saw what it did to Level IV body armor."

Jagger brought up several different photos of stones that had carvings of the beast. Several had smaller men for reference. All, however, had the same diagram.

Preacher's Daughter pulled out her notepad and made a copy of it, then asked, "That symbol. It looks Persian. What's it doing there?"

Barbie nodded, half turned in her chair and grinned. "When the Romans came, they brought their own religions. One was Mithraism. Are you familiar?"

Preacher's Daughter nodded. "Oh, am I. In Zoroastrian cannon, the *daevas* were gods that preceded even Mithras. We—I mean my previous team—encountered them in a valley in Afghanistan and were held spiritual hostage by a crack squad of insane Sufi dervishes. Mithraism was a Roman Mystery Cult passed along by the Romans when they came through doing their normal pillaging and burning and occupying and exploiting. Plutarch believed that the Romans first encountered the religion when they encountered statuary in Turkey. Mithraism first came from Persia where they worshipped Yazata. Ahura Mazda was the highest of Yazada. Think of him as the king god of the Zoroastrian religion. Mithras was a yazata as well, but much lower on the totem. Mithras was worshipped as the god of cattle, oaths, and the sun."

Barbie chewed on her cheek. "That sounds about right."

"Are you telling us that this Marrow and the daeva are the same?" Munro asked.

Preacher's Daughter pulled out her phone and thumbed up a picture and passed it around. Everyone took a turn, including Crookes. The image showed an elongated ten-foot-tall creature that resembled a gray alien for all intents and purposes. This one was dead, but alive it held a blue aura.

"Was it invisible some of the time?" Jagger asked.

"Only when it was in a vimana. That's a flying ship or flying shield. It could be visible or invisible. Incidentally, Alexander the Great and Socrates reported seeing these vimana in the same location we found them in."

"Did you go searching for them?" Barbie asked.

Preacher's Daughter shook her head. "I wasn't with 77 then. Different unit. We were just in the wrong place at the wrong time."

"Been there and done that," Munro said.

"Got the T-shirt," Jagger added.

"But it is interesting that there are two giant beings—these are clearly different based on the shape of the hands—that have links to an ancient Persian religion," Donkey Kong said.

"The Marrow has those cleavers for hands. We see what it can do," Munro said. "Does the daeva have any powers?"

"Death rays from its mouth."

The Scotsman's jaw dropped. "Oh, yeah. I suppose that's a power."

"Back to that symbol."

Crookes spoke up, curiously happy to once again have something to say. "They call it the double disc symbol. It's often overlaid by a Z-rod. No one really knows what the meaning is but it's been posited that it has to do with the multiple faces of god."

She nodded slowly having other things on her mind. "I'm sure it does. Say, can I get a map of everywhere those symbols have been found?"

"Everywhere?" Waterhouse asked.

"Everywhere."

"Maybe that's something the database can do," Barbie said.

"What are you thinking?" Donkey Kong asked.

"That there might be a link. Mind if I contact 77 with this? We can get their computers working as well."

Waterhouse glanced at Crookes who shrugged slightly.

"Not at all," Donkey Kong said.

"Good," Preacher's Daughter said, checking her watch. "It's getting late. Can we get on with the mission brief?"

Everyone looked at her for a moment, then returned their attention to the two men in front of the room.

For the next forty-five minutes Preacher's Daughter didn't say a word. Truth be told, she barely listened at all. Instead, she doodled, creating various versions of the symbol, manipulating it, trying to figure out if there was a link between Flesh Road and Iron Hat and Leicester and Grave Hill.

CHAPTER 16

THE UNIVERSE WAS completely white.

No floor

No ceiling.

No walls.

No structures.

Just white.

She looked down, unable to see even herself. She'd been here before. Or was this before? Was she in a memory or was this new? She tried to remember but her mind was as white as the universe, void, and without form. She felt an intake of breath where she had no breath. Was she back inside the cistern? Had she never escaped? Part of her wanted it to be real because if it was true and she was still locked in the mind of the daeva, that meant that the others were still alive. Bully. Narco. Criminal. McQueen. And maybe Boy Scout. Where he'd gone she still didn't know. He might be dead. He should be dead. That she was the sole survivor was an impossible nightmare to live.

Then she remembered. She had complete control. All she had to do was exert it.

She held nothing out in front of her and willed it to be her hand.

It formed in a blink.

Then the arm.

Then the rest of her body all the way to her feet.

She blushed without a face when she realized she was naked as the moment she was born. She willed clothes and they were there. Finally, fully formed, she was the only aspect within the white. Alone, this was a universe of only her.

Why had they sent her before?

To find Rumi—Jal l ad-D n Muhammad R m —a Persian poet whose mind had gone missing in the 1200s because he'd uploaded it to the White. The memories were returning. They'd shot down a daeva, but then been captured and were used to find the long-lost icon of the Mevlevi Dervishes, their minds dangling like bait for the spirit to use.

Boy Scout had found him on several occasions—or Rumi had found him—they'd never been sure of the sequence. Rumi had appeared to him in the guise of famous photos. Once as Phan Thị Kim Phúc—better known as the Napalm Girl—running down a war-torn Vietnamese road, napalm exploding behind her. Another time Rumi had appeared as both General Nguyễn Ngọc Loan and Nguyễn V n Lém—both executioner and executed in the famous black and white picture. And finally, Rumi had visited him as Thích Quảng Đức—known as the Burning Monk—who set himself on fire in the middle of a 1967

Saigon street. Why Rumi had appeared in the guises of Vietnam War tragedies they could never figure out—but appear he did and he always had something to say.

What Preacher's Daughter had never shared with Boy Scout was that Rumi had appeared to her once. He hadn't appeared to her as a famous person of Vietnam War history, though. Instead, he'd come to her as Robert Mitchum or rather the character he'd played in the old black and white movie—the Reverend Harry Powel, with LOVE and HATE tattooed on the knuckles of each hand respectively. The movie was *Night of the Hunter* and Rumi had inhabited a black and white Mitchum who'd spoken to her directly about Love and Hate and the nature of Good and Evil.

Why she'd never told Boy Scout she did not know. It just didn't seem relevant. He'd thought he'd been the only one chosen and she hadn't wanted to take that away from him. Or was it that she wanted to keep her own secrets?

She spied a black spot on the horizon. Whenever she'd seen one before, she'd run or willed herself to move. That's right. She remembered that the White was a universe of thought. Whatever one imagined could be. She could will herself to move away from the blackness coming towards her and move at the speed of thought, but she was more curious than anything else. She'd easily survived her last encounter so why not this one as well? So, she paused, and waited and it only took a moment for the incarnation to appear.

Once again, the image was from a black and white movie. Whoever or whatever chose the form must have had access to her mind. It had chosen Robert Mitchum the first time because of her obvious affinity for preachers. This one also came from her mind. It was a young version of actor Sidney Poitier. But he wasn't alone. He was dragging a corpse behind him that was attached to him by a chain around his wrist. She remembered the movie. *The Defiant Ones*. About two escaped convicts, one black, one white, who must learn to work together or else they might get captured again.

Her gaze went to the body being dragged.

The white one.

Tony Curtis.

Eyes staring.

Mouth agape and bloody.

Dead.

"He's not as heavy as he looks," said Sydney Poitier in his slow soft voice that she had come to love the first time she'd ever seen *To Sir, With Love*. "In fact, he's not heavy, he's my brother."

"What is it you want from me?" she asked.

Poitier straightened and dropped his grip on Tony Curtis' arm. "I was going to ask the same thing?"

"You came to me," she said.

"Are you certain? Are you so certain you didn't come to me in my universe? How can you be so sure that you were here first?"

She remembered how much she hated the constant

circular reasoning of the White. What had Boy Scout called it? Fortune Cookie Logic. Yes.

"Does it matter who was first?" she asked.

"That is my point exactly," he said. Then he nodded to Tony Curtis. "What do you think of this one?"

"I don't remember him being dead."

"Only a temporary state. He's coming alive again. Do you think I should be worried?"

"Why would you be worried about him being alive, unless perhaps it was you who killed him?"

Poitier grinned, showing his stunning white teeth. "Wasn't me who killed him. It happened so long ago no one remembers. But when he wakes, he's going to want what I have."

"You're chained together. He already has everything you have?"

"This is not a chain. It's a gateway," he said.

Suddenly, his mouth formed an O. His skin went gray. His lips lost color. His teeth blackened. His eyes became watery, then marbled into a light blue. He fell to his knees.

"Bloody hell."

Then he fell on his face.

Tony Curtis stood, looking no worse for wear. In fact, he pulsated with new vigor.

"What'd I miss?" he glanced down and saw his partner dead on the ground. He pointed with a finger. "That guy's a pain in the ass. I'm now going to have to drag him everywhere."

"He dragged you here."

"I appreciate what you're trying to say, but just because one does something, it doesn't mean we all have to appreciate it."

"I don't understand."

"Neither did he."

"Can you explain?" she asked.

"I can use small syllables and talk slowly if that helps."

"I liked Poitier better," she said.

"Everyone likes him better," the fake Tony Curtis said. "It's not my fault I am who I am. I was written this way."

"This wasn't part of the movie. No one is writing what you are saying to me."

"Sugar. Everyone is always writing what everyone else should say. It's all pre-planned, pre-canned, and pre-packaged pablum. Just when you think you are a master of yourself, someone else comes to cause you to behave differently. Cause and reaction. It's not just an idea. It's science."

"You're a metaphor aren't you? You're the double disc."

"Well, look who just took a heaping spoonful of smartness!"

"You're two people linked together. But what are the people. What does the chain represent?"

"You don't know, yet?" Curtis asked.

"You're the Double Disc," she said again.

He grinned showing off improbably white Hollywood teeth. "Not the double whopper with cheese?"

"No. The Pictish double disc symbol separated by a—a—"

"Spit it out, girl!"

"Not a chain. The chain is a metaphor too." She remembered how Poitier had lost his lifeforce and how Curtis had come by it. "Like a straw or a tunnel."

"There you go. Now you're figuring it out."

"Why are you helping me?"

"How do you know I'm helping you?"

"The wound is the place where the light enters you," she said, remembering how it had come to her during her fugue states and had ended up being the key to their survival.

"That one's not going to help now."

"No shit, Sherlock. What will?"

"Aw, hell."

Curtis' face turned ashen. His eyes marbled to blue. His lips turned gray. His mouth cracked and bled. He fell to his knees, then hit the ground with his face, already dead.

Poitier stood slowly, then wiped himself off.

"That's always a pain when it happens." He glanced down at Curtis. "Poor fellow. He means well."

"What just happened? Are you both dying to let the other one live? Why can't you live together?" she asked.

"And that is the question that must be answered."

"What is the question?"

Poitier shrugged. "Sorry. Maybe Robert Mitchum might have helped you more. We're just two prisoners chained together, unable to break free, but with just enough life for one to live."

"What question!"

"The one you already asked. The one the answer came for before the question."

Fucking Fortune Cookie Logic. She wanted to raise a hand and bitch slap the actor or whoever it was.

Then a sound intruded on the otherwise silence of the White.

The sound of thumping edged into her senses and soon overwhelmed her.

CHAPTER 17

"WAKE UP. WE'RE five mikes out," Munro said, nudging her with his shoulder.

Strapped into the helicopter and on the way to the mission she immediately remembered where she was. She snapped her lips together several times. Her mouth was as dry as seven miles of desert road. She grabbed the canteen at her waist and wet her mouth enough to make it feel like a desert after a thunderstorm, images of Sidney Poitier and Tony Curtis dying over and over chained to her brain. She blinked several times to clear her head, then put away the canteen and focused on the mission at hand.

She adjusted the balaclava over her nose and mouth. It was designed like her shirt and her pants with a fine steel mesh running through the center of the fabric. With mesh gloves, a helmet, and shooting glasses, there wasn't a piece of skin available for Fae contact. They liked to poison using natural herbs and solutions made from insects and fungi. She also wore body armor. Presumably, the Fae were unable to pick up most human weapons because of their aversion to iron and their slightly less aversion to steel. But thanks to Glock and some more inventive gun manufacturers and the advent of ceramic weapons, they were able to now wield firepower almost equal to what a modern military could.

The team had also been issued a different weapon set. Instead of the L22A2s, they were only using pistols because of their proximity to inhabited neighborhoods. It appeared that in the hundred plus years since the Cottingley Woods pictures had appeared, people migrated toward the area, built homes, stores, pubs, churches, and even golf courses, one of which was on Black Dragoons' previously-designated Fae lands. So, it was in the best interests of those they were trying to serve not to give chances for stray bullets to intersect their lives.

The most interesting weapon she carried was the sword. She'd never anticipated, nor planned on, ever carrying a sword into battle. It wasn't a long sword, mind you, but it was a sword nonetheless. Patterned from a Roman gladius, the sword had a polymer handle, a steel body, and edges on each side with embedded iron shavings. She'd swung it a few times back at the castle and hoped that if swinging a sword like a baseball bat was the way to do it then she'd be fine when the shit hit the fan. She stored the blade in a sheath on her belt.

MI5 had the mission of convincing the local populace to remove themselves from harm's way. They hadn't a lot of time to put everything in place but the local constabulary had evacuated much of the area claiming there'd been a HAZMAT spill upwind, telling residents, for the sake of their well-being, to leave their homes until cleared by chemical specialists.

The day was heavily overcast. The fog-shrouded forest rolled out before her, bordered by narrow thin roads, so unlike those she was used to seeing in America. Where she'd become accustomed to the garish sometimes ostentatious advertisements that had been planted along every possible roadside like improbable capitalistic flowers, it was rare to find its like in the Midlands, the English settling for a smaller square sign with enough data that the locals would feel comfortable.

The plan was for her and Munro to infil by fast rope near a place known as St. David's Folly. They'd explained to her that England was so old that people actually built buildings that were in ruins to make them look like they'd been around for centuries. Hence the term folly. The ironic thing was that the folly was built the same year America was founded, but made to look like something much older. Located on the southwestern edge of the wood, it would give them immediate access and allow them to press inside.

Meanwhile, the helicopter would insert Donkey Kong and Barbie into the field just south of Shipley Golf Course. They would move north and west.

Of special interest was Jagger's job. He was to provide surveillance and comms for the entire team, using not only real-time satellite imagery, but the pixies as well. Each of them would be riding their own quad copter which they would pilot, until such a time when they transitioned to combat and remote drone operations would be provided by Jagger.

Their purpose was to meet a particular dryad who had her pulse on the way of things all Fae. Donkey Kong had spoken to her on multiple occasions. She lived in a particular tree in the center of what was left of the wood. If they could reach that and secure the area, then they'd be able extract needed information for part two of the mission.

"One minute!"

The doors opened and the wind rushed in.

The sound of the helicopter immediately quadrupled— the *thwacka thwacka thwacka* of the rotors making any real conversation difficult.

She stood and attached the clips to her harness. She checked Munro and in turn, he checked her. They both gave each other a thumbs up. One last check of comms through their helmets and each of them was standing at the opposite door. She spied their target as they rushed towards it. The helicopter flared and hovered.

"Go! Go! Go!"

She leaped into the air and twisted, letting the rope catch her. She snapped as the descent negotiator engaged, allowing her to descend quickly and steadily, with relative safety. When her booted feet hit the ground, she squatted, removed the harness, letting it fall to the forest floor, then stepped out of it and away.

A moment later the harness was rising as was the helicopter.

She and Munro met and proceeded forward.

Each drew a pistol.

They listened to the background chatter in their comms.

She swept her area with her pistol, but found nothing moving. The path to the folly was well-kept and when they made the structure, Munro cleared the inside, and then they waited for the others to touch down.

Ten seconds later, they heard the all clear from Donkey Kong.

The pixies deployed, flying at fifteen feet and conducting their own recon through the trees, each one lying flat on her stomach, guiding the drone with pedals for her feet and levers for her hands. Shouts of excitement and a few *yippikiyas* were silenced by a stern warning from Barbie, but the exuberance of the pair of Fae wasn't lost on anyone.

The pixies reported all clear then hovered in their prescribed positions.

Preacher's Daughter didn't really expect any contact. They had no identified enemy. They had no intelligence or reconnaissance indicating that there would be any threats. Nor did they have reason to believe anything was going go wrong. Still, their plan was to go in force with the possibility that bad things could happen and if that meant that some golfers had to miss their day at golf and some locals had to leave their homes for half a day, then so be it.

She and Munro moved from the folly to their second location roughly one hundred meters away. They kept low and moved from tree to tree. Preacher's Daughter was no expert but it looked like a combination of old and new forest. The meandering ground was covered with leaves and moss while the pines grew straight and true. At times the trees seemed as if they'd been planted in a pattern and at others it seemed as if seeds had been scattered by an absent-minded child.

They made their second planned stop without incident, a knoll overlooking the area they would descend into. Infil Team B had further to go, so they waited until they'd arrived at their predetermined spot as well. Theirs would be closer to the target area so they wouldn't move until Infil Team A was within fifty meters of the target. The pixies conducted a circular flight of the area, then returned to their station keeping.

Crookes was in the helicopter and wanted a check-in, so they gave it.

Preacher's Daughter and Munro began to move when Jagger broke into comms. "We have infrared movement to your right. It's not moving, but it just popped up on satellite."

Both she and Munro paused, sweeping their own areas and taking visual, but they didn't see anything.

"How far out, Jagger?" Munro asked.

"About two hundred meters."

"Trash, why don't you fly over and see what you can see," Preacher's Daughter said.

"Copy. Roger." The pixie sounded remarkably military.

"Stop trying to suck up," Thrash said.

"Up your nose with a rubber hose," Trash said.

Preacher's Daughter rolled her eyes. She had been military. Now she was just a snotty teenager.

"Trash, report," came Jagger's command from the helicopter.

"I don't see anything, but there's a disturbance in the force."

"A disturbance in the—does that mean you feel something?" Jagger asked.

"Yes, a certain *je ne sais quoi*."

"Keep eyes right," Munro said. "I trust her instincts more than I trust a satellite."

"Affirmative," she said, trying to keep all of her responses brief.

A few tense moments later, Donkey Kong said breathlessly. "In position two."

"Position two. Affirmative." Preacher's Daughter nodded to Munro.

They'd moved fifty meters when Jagger jumped on comms.

"Break. Break. Movement to your front right. Counting five targets moving online."

Preacher's Daughter tapped Munro.

He moved five meters to his left.

She moved five meters to their right.

She found a tree and a fallen branch and used it to balance her pistol. She felt for the other magazines strapped to the side of her chest and silently went through the mental process of stripping an empty mag, letting it fall, ripping a full mag from her chest, slamming it home, and sending the charging handle forward.

"Do we have any indication of the size or shape of the enemy?" she asked.

"Negative. Foliage is too heavy. All I have is infrared movement."

"No visual here," Munro said.

"Shhh," came a whisper from Trash. "It's wabbit season. I count four bockles and a hobber."

Preacher's Daughter wished she had studied a zoological index of mythical British creatures because she had no idea what the hell a bockle or a hobber was.

"Weapons?" Munro asked.

"Sticks and stones."

"Switching to blade," Munro said.

She decided to stick with what she knew.

"Advancing," Munro said.

"Stay out of my line of fire," she said.

She watched as he stood with his back to a tree, slid his pistol into its holster, then pulled out his gladius. He looked over at her and winked as he kissed the blade, then he slunk around the other side of the tree and disappeared into the ferns.

"Donkey Kong, you have movement as well. Imagery from north near Thrash's position as well as south. Unable to identify."

Donkey Kong sent the pixies to check out both locations, leaving Infil Team 1 without any direct overwatch.

She kept her gaze across the top of her pistol, aligning

the front aiming point with the two rear aiming points. If anything got within her range of fire it was going down.

"Contact imminent," Munro said. The sound of grunting and effort. "One down. Oh shit. Coming your way."

Her heart leaped into her throat and all of her careful breathing went to hell. "What happened?"

"Trash missed one. Fachan. Fachan alert everyone."

"What the fuck is a—"

A giant with one leg, one arm, and a single eye in the center of its head pushed its way between two trees. Four three-foot-tall, brown clothed things ran beneath him, while on his shoulder stood a man-sized creature with a face like a rabid bulldog snapping at the air. The giant was easily ten feet tall and should have been seen from space. For some reason, although the great beast only had one leg, she was reminded of an Imperial Walker from *Star Wars*.

She aimed at the Fachan's single great leg and missed because it moved faster than she could imagine. It didn't hop, but moved forward, defying all gravity. Instead, she shifted her aim to its chest and emptied her clip of iron-tipped bullets. By the time she'd emptied it, several of the small men wielding branches with stones on the end were upon her, snatching at her hair and grabbing her.

She was hit in the chest, thigh and back by the three bockles.

She spun, kicking out, catching one of the creatures in the face.

She took two more hits in the back, spun again, but this time missed. That was okay because she'd managed to rack another magazine and immediately fired at her attackers, taking two down, and a third with a shot through the eyes.

Then she turned and ran, following Munro to the target area.

"Three down. Bockles I think. There's still at least one bockle, the fachan, and whatever is riding it," she said, while running and breathing heavily.

She spied Munro waiting behind a tree and ran past him. After ten yards she turned and was gratified to see his blade come out and decapitate the bockle that had been chasing her.

But another hobber dodged past. She grabbed it and began to kick, trying to knee it in the chest even as it sought to choke her., But try as she might, it kept squeezing. Finally, she managed to pull down her balaclava by moving her chin up and down and bit the hobber's wrist. It growled as it tried to jerk free, but she kept her jaw locked around the tendons of its hand and it finally released her.

Grabbing blindly at her side, she found the sword and ripped it free. She brought it across the hobber's face, putting as much weight as she could behind the stroke with her back on the ground.

The hobber screamed, drenching her with sick hot blood. It rolled off her and slammed into a tree. It scrambled to its feet and fled into the forest, ricocheting from one tree to the other, its howls echoing into the gloom.

"To me!" shouted Munro.

She tried to get up. It took two attempts. One hand smeared her face clean of the hobber's blood, while the other still held the sword. She shoved it back in the sheath, not even trying to clean it. Stumbling against the tree, she almost slipped and fell. Her chest felt like it had been cracked asunder, but she knew it was merely bruised.

She stagger-ran to where Munro stood, staring up into the face of the fachan.

"Why isn't it moving?" she gasped.

He shook his head. "I can't be sure. It's like it was just turned off."

He was right. The giant half creature stood, facing towards them, but looking past them. It didn't even seem to breathe. It appeared to be more a statue now than an actual Fae creature.

Something whirled past her face.

Then another.

Then another.

She went to swat the next one but missed.

She was suddenly swarmed by what seemed like a conflagration of butterflies, swatting, spinning, slapping, smacking, even karate chopping the intrusive little cockroaches with wings. "Munro, what the fuck is going on?" she asked.

"Sylphs by the smell of it. Get your balaclava back on. Something's stirred them up."

And there it was. The aroma of lavender which was the calling card of sylphs in the wild. She'd only seen Madeleine in person, but had learned more about them in the short time she'd been in the castle. Looking up, she noted that the fachan's face was covered with fluttering sylphs. The juxtaposition of the tiny winged fairies against the fierce visage was stunning. She could see now the tiny arrows sticking out of the fachan's face and neck. The sylphs had done their job and stopped the giant it its tracks.

Bur for what reason?

Feelings swam past and through her. Desperation. Fear. Hatred. Sorrow. All of the emotions so strong they almost stopped her in her tracks.

"Barbie's wounded. We're going to need an evac," came Donkey Kong's voice.

She shook herself free. "Moving your direction." To Munro she ordered, "Watch our six."

She searched the ground, found her pistol, snatched it, and began to trot in the direction she knew the others were. From somewhere up ahead she heard the most horrific scream.

"Pixies, report!" she said.

"Trouble from the north. Hobbers and a banshee," Trash said.

"Some bogies as well, but two of them seem to be fighting the others," Thrash said. "I don't know what they are doing."

"Munro. Bogie?"

"Think Ewoks who can talk."

"Ewok. As in *Return of the Jedi* Ewok? Fucking *Star Wars* Ewok? Little furry balls of George Lucas cuddliness Ewok?"

They'd given up stealth and were flat out running for Infil Team 2's position.

"Same. Probably copied Ewoks from bogies. But they talk."

"You keep saying that."

"They're ruthlessly obnoxious. Like parrots with brains."

"Parrots already have brains," she reminded him.

Then they saw the others. Patterson was down on one knee, choking out a hobber with her left arm across its throat. Donkey Kong had a pistol in one hand and a sword in the other. Beneath him lay five bockles in varying states of dead. Even as he fired, he brought his foot down on the face of one of the bockles that was still moving.

"Where's the wound?" Preacher's Daughter asked, skidding to a stop by the others.

Patterson shoved the unconscious hobber away, where it slumped to the ground. Then she looked at Preacher's Daughter, revealing scratch marks across both of her eyes. One eyeball was hanging free on the optic nerve. She'd seen this happen once before after an explosion in Iraq. The overpressure had caused the eyeball to bulge free.

"All the mascara in the world isn't going to cover that up," she said.

Patterson laughed. "Then I'll become a pirate." She raised her pistol and fired at a hobber running on all fours towards her. The beast took two in the face then went down. With her left hand she pushed the eye back in the socket.

Preacher's Daughter reached into her first aid pouch and grabbed some gauze. She quickly wrapped it around the other woman's head, tying it in place to keep it snug.

"Gonna need to have that looked at," Preacher's Daughter said when they were done.

"I'll keep an eye on it," Barbie growled.

"Enough chatter," Donkey Kong said. "Just over the hill there," he pointed.

They followed him, heads on swivels, waiting for danger, creeping from tree to tree. But other than the occasional sylph, they didn't see anything until they crested the hill. What they saw made them halt in their tracks.

It wasn't the two pixies who'd leaped on the back of a bockle and were strangling it against the ground.

It wasn't what could only be two Ewok-looking bogies nut-gouging a hobber.

What made them stop was the immense tree in the middle of the clearing, denuded of leaves, rotting, the figure of an ancient naked woman at its center, her face split open as if by an axe.

"Who would do such a thing?" Preacher's Daughter asked.

She stumbled towards what was left of the dryad.

It was the sort of tree that would inspire entire cultures to worship, perhaps wondering if it were the first tree. So great were its branches that each one was as big around as a man. Standing beneath it, the limbs seemed to hold up the sky.

"Why didn't we notice it earlier?" Preacher's Daughter asked, her voice hushed, solemn. "I'm sure we would have seen it in imagery."

"It had a glamour," Donkey Kong said, all but sagging. "You had to know it was here to see it and even then the dryad's magic was so powerful it was almost impossible to see."

Preacher's Daughter walked forward, noting the maggots writhing along the ground, eating through the root system. "If her magic was so strong, then what happened?"

"The thing about strong magic is there's always something stronger."

The wind shifted and the stench of old death wafted over her. She brought her arm up to cover her nose and mouth and backed away. A sadness overcame her as if something unique had been lost to the world and she was witness to it. She felt her throat tighten and her eyes begin to water. The first sobs took her as she was running away.

CHAPTER 18

An MI5 CLEANUP team arrived to remove not only the dead dryad and her tree, but all the dead Fae from the woods. It just wouldn't do to have a pensioner walking his or her dog only to find a dead bockle stinking up the path.

A medic on scene helped Patterson with her eye. The socket had swollen around the orb and the swelling would need to subside before they could set it back in permanently. She wanted to leave it in place and ignored the order to go to the hospital.

The pixies were beside themselves and locked themselves in their doll house, each of them with their own airplane bottle of vodka. The loss of the dryad sent shockwaves through the Fae and they felt the sickness bone deep and were trying to do anything to dispel it.

A report from an outstation in Ireland that another dryad had been found dead sent the team into the operations center where they began to track and match all known dryad locations. So, while the others were doing something beneficial, Preacher's Daughter was stuck, sitting on an uncomfortable metal chair in the garage watching the two bogies argue amongst themselves. It turned out that they'd witnessed the dryad's murder and didn't want to be a part of the unseelie who'd been involved.

Ironically, they wouldn't speak to anyone except her. She was finding the job of keeping them on task quite impossible. Donkey Kong neither believed the bogies nor did he trust their intentions, so they weren't allowed in the castle proper. Instead, he had an iron holding cage inside the garage that they'd used on occasion when they'd captured an unseelie and needed a few words out of them.

The bogies seemed to have latched onto her because she was American. Evidently, they'd once lived in a home where the elderly owner had watched nothing but old 1980s American police dramas. She was the first real life American they'd ever seen in person and all they wanted to do was watch her.

They also insisted on being called Crockett and Tubbs.

They lounged against the back of the iron cage as she sat watching them, her foot tapping angrily on the concrete floor. She'd been able to deposit her gear and was down to a sweat-sodden T-shirt, pants and her boots. Her chest still hurt when she breathed and she knew her ribs were bruised. Her impression of the bogies wasn't improved by their constant bickering back and forth. Munro had called them parrots with brains. Now she knew why.

Boggarts was their official name. They lived in

households, usually older ones and lived for the sole purpose of creating enough mischief to make the homeowners want to move. The boggarts preferred to live alone and didn't like the presence of humans. That was until their last homeowner began watching cop dramas. They couldn't get enough of them. So, when one of the bogies would do something to disrupt the life of the homeowner, the other would go around and fix it before the homeowner even knew what had happened. This went on for a decade until the homeowner eventually died of old age. They tried to get the next homeowner to watch the same shows by switching the television, but it never worked. The new people just weren't interested in 1980s cop dramas and preferred Teletubbies to Tubbs and crocheting to Crockett.

"Who was it who destroyed the dryad?" she asked for a fifth time. She wondered lamely if bogies could be waterboarded.

"Maybe we should have her read us a story," Crockett said to Tubbs. He had a wave of lighter hair on his head than the other.

"Her voice makes me swoon. She sounds like Sheena Easton. Remember her?"

"How could I forget? She died in your arms, Crockett."

The Crockett bogie shook its head. "Was a sad day, that, Tubbs."

The reverse anthropomorphization of the characters played by the actors on *Miami Vice* into these two bogies was driving her absolutely crazy. She really didn't want to deal with it, but knew her job as intelligence officer was to extract actionable information. Since direct questioning and threatening hadn't worked, perhaps some incentivized questioning might do the trick. Basically, she'd treat them like children. If you want B then give me A.

"You tell me who killed the dryad and I will give you *Miami Vice*."

"How can you do that?" Crockett asked.

"Technology. Like the TV you watched it on. I can give you your own TV that plays nothing but *Miami Vice*."

"But how?" Tubbs asked.

"How can you walk through walls?" she asked.

They both shrugged, then they stood.

"We just do," Crockett said.

"How will I give you *Miami Vice*?" she asked. "I'll just do."

They looked at her for a long moment, then crossed their arms, glanced at each other and nodded. For an odd second, they looked exactly like the Ewok versions of Don Johnson and Philip Michael Thomas, as if they were leaning against a Ferrari and regarding her in Miami's South Beach. The only thing more ridiculous would be for Trash and Thrash to show up and then watch all four of them walk to prom.

"It was a Marrow," Crockett said.

This was the second time in the last twenty-four hours that she'd heard of a Marrow. All she knew of it was what she'd been told by Munro and about the attack on McDonnell, so she asked, "Do you know which one?"

Without missing a beat, Tubbs said, "There are five of them. This one is called Mirth."

Five of them. Mirth. What a lark to call it something that meant funny.

"Why did it come?" she asked. "Why did it kill?"

"They're all killing... The Marrows," Tubbs said.

"I get that, but who's directing them?"

Crockett shook his head. "We don't know."

"Who are the Marrow?" she asked.

"They are Formori," Tubbs said.

That was now two unseelie who'd mentioned that the Formori were returning. If that indeed was the case, could the Marrows be shock troops? They seemed too powerful to be simply reconnaissance. If so, then the Formori already had a plan and it was in action. They weren't trying to figure anything out. They knew what they were doing, which meant that Special Unit 77 was already two steps behind and a day late. But that still didn't explain the missing towns. If only she could figure out why they were going missing, she might be able to determine what the ultimate goal of the Formori was.

She regarded her two bogies. "Why did you help them?"

Crockett shrugged. "We are unseelie. They called upon us. We do their bidding."

"How did they call you?"

"Through the hum," Tubbs said.

"And the shimmer," Crocket said.

"But you are not Formori. Don't they want to kill all seelie and unseelie?"

"Just seelie. Just dryads."

"Why the dryads?"

"They are the heart of all seelie. They are the holder togethers. They are the memory."

"Who are the Formori?"

"The makers of hum," Tubbs said.

"The makers of shimmer," Crocket said.

"Those who came before," Tubbs said,

"Those who will come again," Crocket said.

She couldn't help but note the similarities to Christian biblical references. Then there was the hum and the shimmer. Was it a way the supernatural communicated?

"Where are the Formori?" she asked.

"Coming," Crockett said.

"Where are they coming from?" she asked.

Crockett and Tubbs looked at each other. "We have no words for it."

Of course, they didn't. Their vocabulary was based on 1980s cop dramas. Not much chance on *Miami Vice* or *Magnum PI* for interdimensional monster travel. She could only think of one other question to ask.

"What is it they want?" she asked.

"To be back," Tubbs said.

Jagger poked his head into the garage. He gave the two bogies a questioning stare, then looked at her. "Got a second?"

She stood and stretched. "I sure do. What's up?"

"We're going in."

"By in you mean—"

"The town. We need eyes on and you and I have been nominated."

She did the mental gymnastics and didn't have to achieve a high score to win. "You mean we are the most expendable. I'm a foreigner and you're the lowest rank."

He flashed a grin. "What? Don't you think we'll succeed?"

"I just hate being fodder."

"Well, if it makes you any happier," he said, pointing at the two bogies, "they are going with us."

"Crockett and Tubbs?"

"Most definitely. Home Office has decided that the unseelie have an unusual covenant with the Formori and what's going on and will be able to identify any threats that might be coming our way."

"*If* they decide to cooperate."

"You do realize that we are listening, right?" Crockett said.

Jagger ignored them. "Powers that be said we are to literally latch them to our sides and make our way inside the perimeter of Graves Hill."

"Lash them. But that would be using iron or else they could merge through."

"You're not putting handcuffs on me," Tubbs said.

"Do you want *Miami Vice*?" she asked.

Crockett punched Tubbs in the chest. "I told you she was going to be a hardass."

CHAPTER 19

MUCH LIKE THE tree in which the dryad had lived, Graves Hill had a glamour around it. It was why cars turned away and delivery trucks suddenly had more things to deliver and they didn't know why. Only birds and animals seemed unaffected by it according to the surveillance team. But the team themselves were affected. They had to keep reading a script every twenty minutes to remember what their mission was. So powerful was the glamour that without it, they would have packed up and gone home. Even so, they didn't really believe in the mission, merely reported the information as their script told them to.

There was also great concern about the status of the people who lived in the village. What happened to them? Were they all dead? Or were they blissfully unaware of their changed existence much like the population of P.K. Dick's Millgate, Virginia, in his novel *The Cosmic Puppets*. Or possibly worse yet, they knew and were trapped in the reality, unable to break past the glamour. The discussion lasted several hours with the members of the Black Dragoons constantly being referred to a slide from an overhead projector reminding them that there was indeed a problem. Although they hadn't had any problem remembering the mission before, it seemed that the more they concentrated on the town, the more the very idea of its existence seemed to fight against their own memories.

Interestingly enough, Preacher's Daughter didn't find herself having the same problem with this town, but she still didn't remember ever having been to Iron Hat before. What was it that made her different? Was it her background and having been living in the mind of a Zoroastrian demon? Or perhaps it was her understanding of the doorway theory of forgetting. For whatever reason, she, the pixies, and the unseelie were the only ones who seemed to be immune to the universal glamour associated with the missing towns.

Jagger had written on his hand in Sanskrit to remind him of the missing town. Something he could look at and discover anew every time he read it.

They couldn't exactly walk into the place hand-in-hand with the unseelie. Regardless of what was going on inside the boundaries of the glamour, such a sight would be a dead giveaway that something was going on. Luckily, the unseelie were of a size and fit snugly into large military packs. They dressed in regular clothes instead of military gear. For Preacher's Daughter that meant a Fu Manchu band shirt, jeans, tennis shoes, and a denim jacket. For Jagger that meant green pants, purple button shirt, a matching green jacket, and purple glitter tennis shoes.

Munro said Jagger looked like an aubergine—which he quickly explained was what Americans called an eggplant—and Preacher's Daughter couldn't disagree.

They did bring along a set of comms. The nature of their trip was such that they couldn't wear them all the time. Unlike on television and in the movies, people noticed when someone else was wearing an earpiece and speaking into a sleeve. The logic of Hollywood didn't work IRL and she doubted if it would work at all on the other side of the glamour.

They rode with Munro to an Esso fuel station, or petrol station as the Brits called it, on the corner of Hinkley and Desford Roads. It was a four way stop and the traffic on three of the ways was constant. But as Hinkley Road continued to the southwest, it was as empty and clear as a desert highway. Nothing moved along the narrow road as it lifted to a rise at which point the road disappeared from sight. The demonstration from the night before that Munro had witnessed had dispersed as the glamour took hold of each and every one, making them wonder why or what they'd even been demonstrating.

Munro had turned the engine off, but then turned it on and said, "Well, that's it. Anyone up for some chips?"

"Wait a moment," she said. "We're not going anywhere."

"What? You want to hang out at a petrol station?"

"We have a mission, Munro." She nodded to a note taped to the dash. "Read that."

He did, then scratched his head. "Are you sure about this?"

"Absolutely," she said.

"But this makes no sense."

The glamour had really taken hold over the space of forty-eight hours. As far as she knew, only she and the MP were consciously aware of the missing town, although the members of the Black Dragoons were trying different mnemonic devices to help them master their own memories. If they could pin down how the glamour didn't affect them, they might be able to provide defense to the others. But until then, the others just had to trust her that she wasn't insane and that there was a missing village. One thing was sure, she reminded herself. No one was going to be coming to her rescue if she got in trouble.

"Can't we get some chips?" Jagger asked.

"Read your hand, friend."

Jagger did as he was told, then nodded. "Right. Let's get to this."

She opened the door to the car and went around to the boot. She and Jagger removed the heavy packs and slid them on, using the back of the car as a lever. She walked around to the driver's window.

"We'll see you soon."

"Sooner than you think," Munro said, giving her a look like she was crazy. "You'll see. There's nothing there."

They headed southwest on Hinkley Road.

"Whatever happens, Jagger, I want you to stay next to me." She took several more steps and asked, "How are you two doing back there?"

"There's a Marrow nearby," Crocket whispered.

She stopped. "Is it Mirth?"

"This one is called Madness," Tubbs said. "It's looking for a way in."

"Do you mean the glamour is keeping them out?"

"It wants in. We can feel its anger. Its frustration," Crocket said.

"The hum and shimmer," Tubbs added.

"Will it attack us?" she asked.

"It senses us, but it won't attack," Tubbs said.

"How can you be so sure?" she asked.

"We can't be," Crocket said, "but it's the wrong hum. It's not the death hum."

"Not the murder shimmer," Tubbs added.

She continued down the road until she reached the crest of the hill. Her view was blocked as if a mirage had become a wall, blocking even sunlight from its natural ambience. She could see the curve of it to her left, but not to her right where it continued along an old stone fence line.

She grabbed Jagger's hand and pulled him along. Their cover was as boyfriend and girlfriend hikers who got lost. If they could make it past the shimmer, they needed to play the part, even if he did look like a glitter-footed eggplant in his green and purple getup.

"Hurry. The Marrow comes," Tubbs said from the backpack.

They walked faster. Whatever the Marrow was it had to be invisible. Having seen what one had done to

McDonnell's body armor and the dryad, she didn't want to bear witness to what one could do to unprotected human flesh.

When they reached the shimmer they slowed, not because they shortened their steps, but because the air had a viscous quality. She turned her head to look at Jagger and she shouldn't have. Her brain didn't understand the movement and sent the wrong signals to her stomach, which instantly revolted. But they kept moving and it was three seconds later that she managed to step through. The problem was that Jagger wasn't with her. He was stuck inside the shimmer, frozen like a fly caught in amber.

She still had a grip on his hand. She tried to pull, but he wouldn't budge. He couldn't even acknowledge her much less say anything. He let go of her hand and began to turn away. Should she go back after him? Would she be able to return?

Someone tapped her on the shoulder.

"You're a new one then, aren't you lass," said a middle-aged man with a beer belly and a pock-marked face. He wore a John Deere green and yellow baseball hat.

She forced her frown of worry into a grin. "I think I'm lost. Looking for Grave Hill."

Over his shoulder she spied a pub—The Bull's Head. An old white plaster building. Beneath the sign it said Fine Food and Local Cask Ales.

"This be it. Wonderful place now, isn't it?"

"I suppose it is. Thought I might go to the pub."

He waved at her and stumbled a bit.

That's when she noticed his reddish cheeks and his generally unwashed appearance. He was clearly drunk and a bit unkempt.

"Tell them Oliver sent ya. Not that it matters. What with the changes, everything is free now."

He staggered away, heading vaguely west and into the town proper.

She spun around to see if she could still grab Jagger, but he was gone.

"Do you know what happened at the shimmer, Crockett?" she asked the bogie.

She felt him shift slightly as he answered. "Wouldn't let him through. He didn't believe."

"But you made it through."

"Of course. Why wouldn't we?"

She headed to the pub. *Of course, why wouldn't we,* she repeated to herself. There was a solution to a mystery in those words if she could ever figure them out.

As she approached the pub a pair of women about seventy left arm and arm singing 'I Am the Walrus' in an adorable off key acapella.

So far, everyone seemed to be happy in Grave Hill. But did they know what's going on?

A waft of lavender caused her to turn and she noted a sylph standing on a bird feeder and watching her. She felt the concern of emotion from the little Fae and part of her wanted nothing more than to bring her hand down on it like it was a mosquito with attitude. Could it feel the presence of the unseelie? Would it matter?

She opened the door and went from church quiet to rowdy in a heartbeat. The place was packed. Eight to eighty, blind crippled and crazy, everyone was drinking, carousing, and eating as if this was the smorgasbord at the end of the world. The noise was thunderous in the way a hundred low conversations and rattling of cutlery can only make it. For some reason, she smiled. She felt right at home.

The Bull's Head was old school all the way. Although she felt like a Connecticut Yankee in King Arthur's court, everything she saw matched with the images she'd anticipated based on pop culture television and movies. The pub could have been from the set of *Shaun of the Dead* for all she knew and have been the inspiration for The Winchester. She loved it.

She grabbed a paper menu from the table that said Free Specials at the top and had Fish and Chips with Mushy Peas, a Fish Finger Sandwich, a Steak and Ale Pie, a Red Leicester Cheese Toastie, and something called Bubble and Squeak. She couldn't help but smile. She'd once dated a Scotsman who loved spending his days making fun of the English, especially their food, seemingly forgetting that his own national dish was haggis.

"Gotta put that load somewhere, luv, else you'll be knocking people down."

A waitress had paused to scold her. She had a tray of dark beers in one hand and pointed to the door with the other.

Preacher's Daughter unhefted her pack and leaned it against the wall. "Don't do anything I wouldn't do," she said quietly as she let it go.

She nudged her way to the bar and once the bartender saw her, she said, "Beer. Dark. Cold."

He returned a moment later with a tall sudsy glass of frosted malt goodness. She could almost taste it and she did, leaving a little mustache of foam under her nose that she licked away.

He stood tall and thin with a white towel over his shoulder. "Didn't think we'd get anyone else after the world ended, much less an American. Welcome."

The world ended? Was that their logic for not being able to leave town?

"Seems pretty crowded," she said, but the bartender was already serving someone else.

Still, a woman her age inched closer. "Been living here for years and it's the first time I saw you."

"I'm new. My boyfriend and I got lost. We were hiking across England."

The woman smiled and sipped her own beer. "Where's this boyfriend of yours."

Preacher's Daughter turned to the woman. "He got stuck. He didn't make it through that thing surrounding the town."

The woman nodded sagely and slammed her Irish whiskey down. "The shimmer. It's been what's keeping us safe."

"Who's this, Maeve?" a younger man asked, Patagonia shirt and hat, hipster beard.

"Dunno. What's your name, lass?"

"Laurie. I'm American."

"You don't have to tell us that. We can tell that a mile off. Your kind are easy to spot."

She laughed. "My kind? I wasn't aware that I had a kind."

"Of course, you do. The way you keep back your hair like it's an enemy. You should let it fly free. Do what it wants."

Preacher's Daughter couldn't help herself and lifted her hand to her hair. It was pulled back in a ponytail because that was a tactically sound decision. She'd never really considered her hair. She rarely ever let it down—or to be free as Maeve said. She made a quick decision, pulled at the bands securing her hair, and shook her hair loose. Light brown with streaks of blonde, it fell just past her shoulders.

"How about now?" she asked.

"Lovely," Maeve said.

The young man nodded. "Where'd you come from?"

"Leicester," she said.

All conversation around her ceased. It was like someone had thrown a cone of silence around her. She could see others in the pub continuing to talk, but couldn't hear a word they said. Like God had pressed the mute button on everything.

But not everything.

"That's not possible, dear," Maeve said. "Leicester doesn't exist."

Preacher's Daughter gave her best trust me smile. "Sure, it does. I was just there."

The man leaned forward and sniffed her like a dog might the base of a tree, lingering long enough to make her feel uncomfortable. "I smell unseelie. Seelie as well. I also smell rot." He jerked his head back and gave her a startled look. "Who are you?"

"I'm Laurie May. As I said." She smiled sweetly but felt her face begin to crack. "I don't understand what's going on here."

"Oh, I think you do, honey," Maeve said.

The young man adjusted his cap and as he did so she noticed that his ears weren't quite as round as they should have been. "You were there, weren't you—when they killed Epiphonia?"

"I don't know—"

"Enough of your lies. I can smell her on you. I can smell her death. The rot of it. The horror of it."

Preacher's Daughter sighed. She took a drink, glanced at the other customers cavorting in complete silence, then turned to the pair. "It was terrible. I've never witnessed anything so gruesome in my life. I was told that it was a Marrow. One called Mirth."

"Mirth," Maeve said, looking knowingly at the young man.

He nodded. "It's as we suspected."

Maeve stood and as she did, she seemed to grow, not in mass but in presence. Her eyes turned fierce and her countenance was carved with annoyance. "Who are you really?"

"I'm Preacher's Daughter. Formerly of Special Unit 77,

I am now working with the Black Dragoons to determine what happened to Grave Hill." She glanced around. "Looks like the people are still here, although they've been told it's the end of the world."

"All that will change later. Everyone will be okay once we're finished," Maeve said.

"What is it you're doing?"

"I say we get rid of her," said the young man.

Suddenly the smell of lavender was overpowering. A pixie stood atop a pair of sylphs, one leg on each, reins going to the chests of each sylph. It hovered for a moment, then went to Maeve and spoke to her in hushed tones. When it was done, the pixie riding the sylphs spun around and zoomed back the way it had come.

"Chigas. Move. We have a breach."

His eyes widened. "Where?" Then they landed on her. "You caused this."

Preacher's Daughter remained perfectly still.

"You brought them here. You are the reason. If any of us die, it will be on your head."

"Chigas," hissed Maeve. "Move out."

The glamour surrounding the young man evaporated and in his place stood a tall willowy creature that seemed to be half man and half tree. His skin was burled and his eyes were obsidian orbs deeply set into wood. A cape ran down his back. No, not a cape. Wings. He ran to the door, opened it, and took flight.

She turned back to Maeve.

"Is there anything else you aren't telling me?" the

woman asked, as she let the cone of silence shatter and the noise of the pub once again become part of the landscape.

Preacher's Daughter shook her head.

Then someone shouted, "Who the fuck changed the channel?"

She turned to look and instead of the football she'd seen on the television when she'd walked in, there was now the flashing of pastels and beautiful women. She recognized the synthpop of Jan Hammer and the sparkling lights of Miami's South Beach. Another beautiful woman. A car. Then Sonny Crockett and Rico Tubbs.

"What the hell is that?" shouted a young kid, too young to be in the pub, but drinking and sloshed just the same.

An older man laughed. "*Miami Vice.*" He laughed again. "It's fucking *Miami Vice*. What will the elves think of next!"

CHAPTER 20

THINGS HAPPENED QUICKLY after that.

Everyone human froze in mid-movement.

The old man who'd recognized the TV show had begun to slosh ale into his mouth, with even the liquid frozen in a forever waterfall.

Another young boy, frozen looking down the dress of an older woman sitting on a bar stool.

A young girl in the process of slapping someone who'd just laid a hand on her ass.

Everyone and anyone caught in a single instant.

Preacher's Daughter knew exactly what had happened, but Maeve and the others didn't know the particulars. What they did know was that an unseelie was present and the pixies began to hunt. She counted more than a dozen of the pixie-sylph chariots flying through the air as if on an unseelie patrol.

A naked girl stepped through the doorway, her hair alive, obscuring her skin at times, caressing those she passed. Her eyes were large ovals in a pear-shaped face. Skin alabaster white. Although she appeared to be a teenager, she had an animal quality to her that belied her humanity. The way she stepped between the stilled humans, moving with a cat-like grace, ignoring everything except the long peacock feather she carried in front of her, made her seem anything but human.

Preacher's Daughter was reminded of an aunt she'd had in the mountains of East Tennessee. Not that she'd pranced around naked ever, but she did have her quirks. One of which was she never wore anything but nightgowns. The other was that she could find water in a desert with a simple willow branch. She was a famous dowser who everyone came to see when they needed water, her magical talent to be able to find it even in the high scrub of the hills where there seemed to be nothing but rocks and dirt.

The girl was like this. Preacher's Daughter corrected herself. It had to be some sort of Fae—perhaps a nymph—who had the ability to track. And in this case, her heart dropped, because she knew exactly what the nymph was tracking.

The unseelie.

Crockett.

She glanced to where her pack was and saw it sagging empty against the wall beside a side door.

Of course it was.

Watching the nymph was hypnotic, each of her steps chosen seemingly absently, but perfectly placed. She never used her hands to touch a single person or thing, both grasping the peacock feather like she was an acolyte carrying a processional cross, but her hair seemed to search, touch, feel, taste, caress those she passed. Preacher's Daughter wondered if somewhere in the recipient's frozen minds, they felt the intrusion.

She began moving past the fat man and the boy looking down the woman's shirt. The nymph's eyes were on the tip of her feather, nowhere else. Her concentration was so absolute that Preacher's Daughter found her own gaze drifting to the feather, wondering what it would do if it was ever to find the unseelie for which it was dowsing.

Then the nymph was in front of her.

Her gaze shifted from her feather to Preacher's Daughter. Her head shifted like a bird, twitching sideways, regarding her from first one side and then the other. The nymph's gaze raked her from stem to stern, the peacock feather quivering, for the first time moving as if it could feel the taint of the unseelie on her.

The nymph pursed her lips and whistled, the sound also birdlike, fluid and musical.

Maeve moved nearer Preacher's Daughter. "Where's the unseelie?"

The nymph moved to the backpack and her feather lowered and shook. She whistled again, the notes rising and falling.

"Oh, *that* unseelie." She shifted on her stool to make the Glock in the hollow of her back easier to grab. "What about him?"

"Why did you bring him here?" Maeve asked.

"I wasn't sure what I would find."

"Why do you align yourself with evil?"

Preacher's Daughter regarded the other woman-Fae. "Good and evil? Really? We going to play that game? The Christian church would call you both evil."

Maeve spit on the ground. "Fuck the Christians."

Preacher's Daughter nodded. "I've heard that before. Sometimes I agree with you. But your problem with the unseelie is politics and not G vs E."

"G vs E?"

"Good versus evil, ma'am."

The nymph was on the move, following a scent or something similar, weaving through the frozen men and women. She passed several tables, an ATM, a lotto display, and then spun a hundred and eighty degrees. She whistled twice and then the feather began to vibrate, the barbs flecking off until all that was left was the eye, standing on the feather stalk like the Eye of Ra. The barbs fell upon an umbrella holder which immediately caught fire, snapping and popping, then smoking.

The boggart stumbled forth, patting its fur, a smoked Ewok, smacking at singed hair and dampened pride. Almost all of the fur had been burned, as if someone had taken a razor to the creature in an attempt to give him a millennial shave.

"Well, shit," Crockett said. He glanced around. "Talk about arriving for the wrong wedding."

"You brought this into our sacred place?" Maeve asked Preacher's Daughter.

"Do you mean, did I bring a friend of mine into a town

that you've stolen and lied to everyone about saying that it's the end of the world? I guess I did."

Maeve regarded her for a moment, and Preacher's Daughter thought that maybe her comments might have gotten through. But then the Fae's eyes narrowed and fury etched her face.

"You will not bring an unseelie into my presence."

Preacher's Daughter stood, drew her pistol, and took two steps, pressing the barrel against the right cheek of the Fae-woman. "I think it's a little late for that. Crockett, get over here by me."

The bogie scrambled madly through the legs of the stilled and grabbed the tail of her shirt when he arrived at her side. "Is this the way you thought it might turn out?" he asked.

"Yes," she said. "A girl has to be prepared." She adjusted her grip and pressed a little harder into Maeve's face. "Now, this is what you are going to do. You're going to let us go back through the shimmer and we'll be on our way."

Maeve growled. "Did you think it would be that easy?"

"I figure you might not want to be shot in the face. I have iron-tipped bullets in this. I'm told that they might hurt."

Maeve's eyes would have melted Preacher's Daughter if her gaze were acid. She seemed to be about to say something, but the door slammed open and a swarm of pixie-sylph chariots flew into the pub. All of the pixies carried tiny bows. Preacher's Daughter had no doubt that each arrow was tipped with poison.

"You little bitches shoot me and the old woman gets it," she said. "Watch my six, Crockett?"

He grabbed a chair, slammed it against the ground to get the broken pieces and came up with a length of wood. "I got it."

For one brief moment she felt empowered, ready and eager to prover her mettle against a host of unseelie. Then she was being shot by dozens of toothpick sized arrows in the side of the neck and face. She thought about turning her head. She thought about saying something. Because all she could do was think. She was unable to move at all, frozen like the Fachan in Cottingley Woods.

"Now, dear. It's not nice to use that sort of language," Maeve said.

The pixies on their sylph chariots shifted their attention to Crocket.

He threw the wood at a pixie, taking her right off the top of the sylphs. Then he backed into the wall and disappeared.

"I see the unseelie are as loyal as always," Maeve said.

Preacher's Daughter tried to answer her, but it only came out as a series of mumbles.

"You want to know what we are going to do with you?"

She tried to call the Fae-woman variations of a female dog.

"Language, my dear," she said, knocking on Preacher's Daughter's forehead with her knuckles. "We talked about that. A lady. Must. Watch. Her. Language."

She mumbled what she would do to the woman when she was finally freed.

"That's it. Be optimistic. You'll get your freedom eventually. I know someone's going to need your blood sooner or later." Maeve stepped back, removed the pistol from Preacher's Daughter's hand, and held it as if it were a stinky load of diapers between her two fingers.

"Now, will someone please help me get this trash out of here?"

Preacher's Daughter felt herself being tilted and rocked, forward and backward. Then suddenly she was falling forward. She watched as the floor came up to greet her and smack her in the face.

Then all went black.

CHAPTER 21

HER NOSE FELT as if it had been slammed in a door a dozen times. She could barely touch it. Even the anticipation of a touch made it hurt. So, instead of touching her nose, she touched the cheeks around it. She'd had broken noses before and she could feel this one radiating right through her cheek bones. She looked at her hands. In the dim light she could see the bindings were made of vine. She pried at them, but they tightened on their own as if they were alive.

"Those won't be coming off anytime soon," came a voice out of the darkness.

She peered into the gloom. The floor was made of dirt. Her back appeared to be against something wooden. "Who's there?"

"Nobody."

She sneered and in the doing of it pain lanced her face. "Does nobody have a name?"

"A friend. At least I think I am. If the enemy of your enemy is a friend."

She closed her eyes to parse the meaning of the words.

It was a man's voice, the words easy, almost like he was southern but not quite. He was definitely American and she said so.

"You're American," she said.

"As are you." After a moment, "Do you have a name?"

She was well aware this could be some sort of interrogation technique. "You can call me Preacher's Daughter."

Laughter from the darkness. "Sounds like code."

"Oh yeah, then what's your name?"

"Francis Scott Key Catches the Enemy."

"That's a mouthful." Then she understood the man's speech pattern. She'd heard it before. "You're Indian, aren't you?"

Again laughter. "If you mean the ones with feathers and not dots, then yes."

She tried to move her legs, but they were bound at the ankles and just above the knees, the vines tightening as she squirmed. "Alright already. You can ease up. I'm not going anywhere." And the vines loosened.

"Took me two days to figure that one out. Took you less than five minutes."

"Let's just say this isn't my first supernatural rodeo."

"You've done this before? Been captured by fairies?"

She thought of the way they'd been tricked back in Afghanistan—more than six months of their lives wasted as they squatted in an ancient cistern beside a captured supernatural entity. "Not by fairies, but it's close enough, I suppose."

"Looks like they worked you over," said the voice in the darkness.

"Face-planted. Pixies shot me full of arrows. Some sort of paralytic."

She heard the sound of the man scooting forward along the ground. He growled at his bindings, then complained to them. The vines must have thought he was trying to get away. A face materialized through the darkness. Black hair long enough to make her jealous hung raggedly over a broad chest. His reddish skin was wrinkled by both the sun and age. He wore a blue flannel shirt opened to reveal a yellow and blue stylized jackrabbit with the words SD STATE above it and JACKRABBITS below. He had contemplative eyes and the curl of a lip that seemed ready to laugh in an instant. He wore old jeans and had red Jordan basketball shoes on his feet.

"Pixies got me too," he said grinning. "It's been a long time, Ms. May. Or do they just call you Laurie."

Her jaw dropped. How did he know her? But then she looked closer. He looked familiar as well. She knew him, but from where? From the television. She'd seen his report. Was that it?

"I helped your dad out, Ms. May. Back when you were in Iron Hat."

"I've never been to—" but she knew she had. Poe had shown her the evidence. Still, if she could only remember.

"You used to follow me around when I was working. You called me Chief Frankie Scotty."

Chief Frankie Scotty. Of course. She grinned. She hadn't

heard those words in twenty years. Francis Scott Key. She'd loved it because he'd had two first names. He'd also been in the Army. Desert Storm if she remembered correctly. And her father had been livid when he found out she was calling the young Indian man chief.

"My father was so mad I called you that," she said.

"You were only twelve years old. You didn't know any better." He paused, glanced at her, then clasped his hands. "How are your parents?"

"Dead," she said, simply.

"You don't seem too broken up about it."

"A lot of water has gone under that bridge."

"Was it placid water or tumultuous water?"

She eyed the Indian man, his face half in shadow. "You seem unusually interested."

He shrugged. "I never thought I'd see that young girl grown up. I was just wondering about her life."

"It all seems too perfect. My hypothesis is correct in that there's a pathway between the two missing towns."

His face disappeared and she heard a slight snoring coming from the darkness.

"Francis Scott Key?" Had he fallen asleep? "Chief Frankie Scotty?"

The snoring was soft and regular. He'd fallen asleep. How strange. Still, his presence brought back a lot of the memories she'd forgotten. Her father hadn't been the normal missionary, building churches and proselytizing whenever he could. Instead, he'd build gymnasiums so that the kids would have some place to congregate.

Everyone liked to play basketball and it was in coming together that they could achieve fellowship. Of course, the gyms were multiuse and could also be houses of worship.

They also drilled for wells, the aquifer sometimes four-hundred feet down. Summers on the Great Plains could be as forsaken as summers in the desert. Water was a necessity that was becoming increasingly hard to come by.

"Ms. May," came the Indian's voice.

"You fell asleep."

"Narcolepsy. I hit my head in Desert Storm and sometimes get tired. How long was I out?"

"Maybe five minutes."

"I saw your TV interview, but didn't recognize you from that," she said. "How is it that you were able to remember the missing town and no one else was?"

"That is a fine question, Ms. May. I wish I knew." He tapped the side of his head. "Perhaps it's because I'm broken."

"That's a definite possibility."

Then why was she able to enter? Perhaps her interaction with the *daeva* and living in the White for so long had somehow reconfigured the way she perceived things.

"Was there anyone else you knew who realized Iron Hat had gone missing?" she asked.

He shook his head. "Only me. They thought I was crazy. But they were my best friends so they trusted me."

"A lot of blind trust."

"When it's you against the world, it's easy to trust." He glanced at her, then back down at his hands. "How did your mother die?"

"I don't know."

He looked up sharply. "You don't know? I thought you said she was dead."

Preacher's Daughter shrugged. "She's dead to me. She left us—my father and me. One day she was there, the next she left, never to be seen again." She changed the subject. "How'd you get to England?"

His eyes narrowed. "Is that where you think we are?"

She glanced around but there was no evidence to support her assertion, just wooden walls and a dirt floor. "Of course it is."

He scratched the side of his face. "I wouldn't be so sure."

"Why? Where were—They captured you in Iron Hat, didn't they?"

He nodded. "I pushed through some sort of barrier. Got far enough to notice a bunch of new trees in the middle of town, then it was lights out." He chuckled. "Woke up here."

"How long has it been?"

"A day. Maybe two. They feed me fruit and seeds. They also leave me water."

"Have they shown any indication of what they are doing?" she asked.

He shook his head. "Nothing. They just stole the town." He paused. "You say you're from England? Did they steal one there as well?"

She nodded. "And other places too. Something is going on with the Fae and I don't know what."

He grinned again. "Ever consider asking them?"

"We tried once, but an invisible giant Formori killed her before we had the chance."

He seemed about to say something, when his eyes rolled up in his head and he began to shudder. Five seconds later, he fell forward onto the side of his face. For a moment she was worried be might have had a stroke or worse, but then he began to snore softly. Fast asleep like a baby who'd been kept awake too long.

She leaned back and knocked her head against the wood softly a few times in frustration. Her ignoble attempt to enter the town without being seen had been a complete failure. Then again, she hadn't thought she'd have been up against such powerful magic. It occurred to her that Maeve could probably have just frozen her in place like she'd done the rest of the people in the pub, but the Fae-woman had wanted to listen to her—had wanted information. They were just too powerful. What would it take to stop them short of a nuclear bomb?

She shook her head. She couldn't think that way. The Black Dragoons had been working with the fairies for centuries. They had to have information that would help her. That is if she could get free. Here she was stuck somewhere she did not know with a man she hadn't seen in twenty years. What were the odds that she was back in America? Could she be in South Dakota?

Her head whipped around. She heard momentary

scratching from the other side of the wall. It was miniscule, but was just there above the silence. She strained to hear it again. She closed her eyes to better focus her senses. And there it was again. Scratching. There was definitely a rhythm there. It couldn't be organic. What was the rhythm?

When it came again, she had it. She let the scratching finish, then she added her own, finishing the intro beats of Jan Hammer to the theme song for *Miami Vice*.

Crockett materialized through the wood.

He glanced around, noted the sleeping Indian, then turned to her.

"Couldn't be sure where they kept you. This was the fourth place I tried. I was about to give up." He sniffed at her. "You smell different."

She grinned so wide she thought her face might crack. She threw her arms around him and hugged the boggart to her chest. He smelled of pine, earth, and sweat and she didn't care. "I can't believe you came back for me."

"I couldn't leave without you. The shimmer. It won't let me through."

"Whatever. Are we still in England?"

He gave her a look. "Of course, we are."

She let him go and held out her arms. "Can you do anything about this?"

He touched the vines and they writhed away into the corner like terrified snakes. He did the same to the ones on her legs, which tightened momentarily, cutting off her circulation, then unfurled and fled after the others.

"Seelie magic doesn't like the touch of unseelie," he said.

"What sort of guards are outside?"

"No guards. Everyone is passed out or sleeping."

"What about the seelie? What about Maeve?" she asked.

"There was a disturbance in the shimmer. A Marrow. Tried to follow us in."

She nodded. "I bet that got them riled."

"I must be dreaming," came a voice from the other side of the room. "I see an Ewok speaking English."

Francis Scott Key was awake. He rolled over and sat up, wiping the side of his face with his bound hands. His eyes had narrowed, then he looked at Preacher's Daughter.

"What's going on?"

"We're going to escape," she said. "We're taking you with us."

"You're going to have to explain this to me. Especially how Ewoks are real."

"No time for that." She directed Crockett to remove his vines. Then she began searching the room. They'd brought her in, so there had to be a way out. She'd checked the walls but the seams between the boards seemed too tight. She couldn't see anyway of escaping.

Francis Scott Key was a head taller than her and lean like an elm. He gently pushed her aside and began tapping on the area beside her. "This is where they came in to give me food and water."

She turned to Crockett.

The bogie was already ahead of her. He melted through the wall and within ten seconds, they heard a click from the other side of the wood and a door opened. She and the Indian slid through and found themselves in the cool hours of a new morning. When Crockett had said that everyone was either passed out or sleeping, he hadn't been joking. It seemed as if no one had gone home. Then she remembered that there had to be a certain number of people who were from other places and had been trapped in the village. Then again, everyone thought it was the end of the world because that's what they'd been told, so they were living a last chance bacchanalian existence.

People slept on stoops and on benches.

Five slept in a tangle on a square of grass.

One had passed out with her head inside a trash can and by the smell, it was no wonder why.

They saw all this and more as they ran-walked down the street, heading towards the nearest shimmer. They reached it without intrigue. She and Francis Scott Key each grabbed Crockett's hand and pushed their way through.

The moment they touched the shimmer, Crockett began to scream. His hair began to sizzle.

An alarm went up from somewhere behind them.

She smelled lavender and ducked, the arrows flying into the shimmer.

She pushed through as hard as she could, screaming as she did.

Francis Scott Key screamed as well.

And they didn't stop screaming until they pushed free into the cool Leicester night.

Crockett slumped between them. He'd lost all of his hair and looked like a giant bipedal weasel. He started to talk, coughed once, then sagged to the ground. She knew then that he needed help or he was going to die.

CHAPTER 22

MI5 AND THE Home Office had brought in a squad of Royal Marines who found them within minutes and escorted them to waiting vehicles. Within an hour, they were being medically triaged and after that released. No one asked about the strips of white tape across her nose and her double black eyes. No one asked about the American Indian she had with her. No one asked about the hairless Ewok. Everyone was hush hush as if they'd been read onto the Dragoon's missions and knew better than to ask. Still, the three of them stumbling out of the mobile medical facility and into the waiting Land Rover driven by Munro had to be a sight to see.

They didn't go back to the castle. Instead, Munro drove them to Leicester railway station. As they were hustled through a side door she noted a sign that said the building had been built in 1832. She couldn't help but shake her head. Even British train stations were older than most American cities. They boarded a private train car with blacked out windows, red carpeting, smooth mahogany walls, and eight deep leather chairs.

Preacher's Daughter found one and sank into it, rattling an audible sigh as she did. Glancing over she noted that McDonnell was present, as was Nottingham. Jagger and Tubbs sat together in a chair, the Bogie resting on the wide leather arm. Barbie and Donkey Kong sat in other chairs. Barbie wore a patch like she was a pirate in training. Preacher's Daughter could only wonder how much the other woman's eye hurt. Crookes along with McDonnell leaned against a bar talking with someone she'd never met. It seemed to be one big happy family with only the newness of a Sioux Indian and a blistered Ewok to make things different.

The train lurched once, then twice, then settled into a rattling amble down the tracks.

Preacher's Daughter closed her eyes. Damn but if she wasn't exhausted. Funny how being unconscious wasn't restive. She supposed part of her had been awake and worried the entire time. She didn't know where they were going or what they were doing and at this point, she didn't care. Maeve was what worried her. Maeve had an amazing amount of power, yet what she was doing with it seemed simple enough.

"Allow me to introduce Lord Charles Windsor-Sikes," McDonnell said after clearing his voice. He still wore a bandage around his torso beneath his jacket and held a cane that seemed more than artifice. "He's come from the Queen and speaks with her voice. Although the PM deals with the day to day, the Royal Family maintains continuity over—let us say—some of the things that make Great Britain more interesting." He nodded and then stepped aside.

Perhaps seventy and dressed in a slick form-fitting suit with white shirt and tie, the new man stood well over six feet tall and held himself with a confidence for which the other men in the car could only strive. He nodded to McDonnell, placing a hand on the man's shoulder for a moment, then stepped forward.

"Before we begin, I'd like to hear from the American, if we can. Is it true your name is Preacher's Daughter?" he asked.

"It's more what I am called—I am more than what my given name is. Preacher's Daughter seems to suffice, if it's okay with you." She didn't know if she was supposed to end her sentence with *your majesty* or *your eminence*. Her education on how to address a royal was severely lacking. Hell, she didn't even know if he was a royal. For all she knew she should have been standing and for the insult the man was going to have her beheaded.

The silence in the room seemed to stretch out. She sat up and gave the new man a fierce look.

"Fine then," he said, his words smiling. "Why don't you back brief us so that we can all be on a level playing field?"

She sat up, but she wasn't going to curtsey. "Jagger and myself along with two bogarts tried to pierce the veil surrounding the missing town of Grave Hill. Only myself and Crockett were able to make it through. For some reason Jagger couldn't make it. Everyone inside was partying like it's an end of the world rave, which it might be for them. Everything is free. There seems to be a host of Fae who are running things led by a Fae named Maeve who has the ability to put everyone to sleep and possibly stop time. During my brief tenure, this included myself."

She nodded to Francis Scott Key. "There's another missing town linked to this one in America. On an Indian reservation called Pine Ridge in the state of South Dakota. Of interest is that my new friend here somehow traveled from there and arrived in Grave Hill where he was incarcerated. He also mentioned that there were large trees in the center of the missing town in America—trees I can guarantee you weren't there before this started happening."

All through her brief, Windsor-Sykes stared intently, not moving, nodding, or even acknowledging her words. No one spoke for almost ten seconds before he seemed to come back to life. He nodded sharply and placed his hands behind his back. "Right. I see. This is unusual but as we expected."

McDonnell straightened. "Sir? You expected this?"

"The Royal Dryad has been sick these last few months and been relatively incommunicado."

Royal Dryad, she thought. Of course, they had a royal dryad. *I mean what royal court wouldn't have one.*

"She's been trying to communicate with us, but even the other seelie get sick when they are around her so it's been—" He cleared his throat. "Rather difficult.

What we have discovered is the dryads are under attack. Crooke's report from the events of Cottingley backs this up."

"It seems that they've been under attack by Marrows, a sort of giant invisible unseelie," Preacher's Daughter said.

Windsor-Sykes nodded. "Indeed. It seems that the seelie have created a redoubt of sorts. Something to protect them."

"Like Rorke's Drift," Waterhouse said. "Only this redoubt has a veil and magic behind it."

"My presumption is the magic of forgetting was to confuse the unseelie as much as humanity," McDonnell said. "Even now, we're having trouble remembering Grave Hill. If it wasn't for the mnemonics we have set in place to include pictures on almost every wall of the ops center, we'd forget as well. It seems the only one capable of remembering successfully is Preacher's Daughter, but even her memory has been affected regarding her past residence at the location in America."

Windsor-Sykes gave him a look followed by a swift nod. "That would seem to be the case. I believe your initial mission set was to ascertain the reasons for the missing town and determine whether it's a possible threat to England. I think we've determined that it isn't. So, now we are going to support our second position."

She couldn't help herself. "Second position?"

Everyone turned to her.

She'd been totally slouching in the chair with a leg over an arm. She removed the leg and sat like she was addressing a grade school nun with a ruler. "Second position, sir? What is that?"

He raised a single eyebrow. "I'm not sure of your knowledge of our history, young lady," he began, "But it's the nature of—"

She interrupted as she recited, "Willie Willie Harry Stee; Harry Dick John Harry three; one two three Neds, Richard two Harrys four five six... then who? Edwards four five, Dick the bad, Harrys twain, VII VIII Ned six the lad; Mary, Bessie, James you ken, then Charlie, Charlie, James again. Will and Mary, Anna Gloria, Georges four, I II III IV Will four Victoria; Edward seven next, and then Came George the fifth in nineteen ten; Ned the eighth soon abdicated. Then George six was coronated; after which Elizabeth, our reigning queen." When she'd finished she felt proud. Like the Pythagorean theorem, she never thought she'd ever use the mnemonics to remember the kings and queens of England. That she still remembered and was able to demonstrate her proficiency baked steel into her spine.

Windsor-Sykes gave her a deadpan glare as he said, "So, essentially your knowledge of our history is what every primary school student learns in their second year." He paused for dramatic effect, then said, "Swell."

Her pride collapsed like a stack of hard-shaken Legos.

"Have you at least heard of the Jacobites?" he asked.

She stood and as she did, Crockett came to her side like a beaten dog, but ready to defend her. "That was a rebellion of the Scots, yes?"

"Yes. We made a treaty with the Fae that they wouldn't take any side in the conflict. They were set to work against us and support the Scots. In fact, had they not decided to recede into the background and leave humanity's business to humanity, the Battle of Culloden would have ended dramatically differently, rendering your childish mnemonic very different as well."

"What does that have to do with this second position?" she asked, and then it dawned on her. "The treaty was more than just the Fae not supporting the Scots wasn't it? It was an alliance. Any enemy of ours is an enemy of theirs and vice versa. Is that it?"

"The Queen considers the Fae to be a national treasure. Although the UK is quite a technical country, we have tried to keep places like the Cotswolds, the Yorkshire Dales, and the Moors as pastoral as possible. The UK is essentially a giant landscaped garden. Human encroachment has always been an issue with the Fae. They used to fight against it, but now they accept it as long as we have a place for them."

Francis Scott Key chuckled. "I see here even the supernatural are relegated to a reservation."

Everyone turned to him as if they were just now noticing him.

"What? Did you think I didn't speak English?"

Crookes sniffed and said, "I wouldn't exactly call that English?"

Francis Scott Key grinned, showing several missing teeth. "Careful white man. Me no scalp 'em you... yet."

Preacher's Daughter laughed out loud.

Francis Scott Key winked at her. "The irony is that it seems the English Fae are leaving their reservations here to live on our reservations back in America."

"Not too many trees from what I understand," Jagger said.

"I think they brought the trees with them," said the Indian. "Or are they dryads?"

"And we can't have that," Crookes said. "As I mentioned. The Queen considers the Fae to be a national treasure. As such, we need to protect them. We can best protect them here."

Waterhouse asked, "What are you proposing, Lord Windsor-Sykes?"

"We're going to bring back those who left and protect those who remain."

Francis Scott Key Catches the Enemy shook his head. "Some things never change."

CHAPTER 23

IT TOOK THREE hours to reach Edinburgh by high speed rail, then another hour to reach a small store along the Royal Mile that looked as if it had been there for a thousand years. It was just after one in the morning and it was raining. Everyone had rain jackets, including the pair of bogies who wore rain ponchos that drug on the ground behind them.

Lord Windsor-Sykes led the strange entourage out of a Mercedes van that had been waiting for them at the station and knocked on the door. No sooner did he raise his hand than the door opened and they were ushered inside. The store seemed to cater to tourists who wanted kilts and *Sgian Dubhs*.

The man who met them at the door looked as old as the building and had actual cracks in his face and hands. Preacher's Daughter knew right away he couldn't be human but didn't dare ask the question. At this point, she was along for the ride. While the members of the Black Dragoons knew her enough to understand her sense of humor, it seemed as if the royal messenger they had with them found her absolutely incomprehensible. She didn't want to be relegated to a desk somewhere out of the way. She wanted to remain on the front lines of the situation, so she knew she needed to watch her words.

But as much as she tried, she couldn't tear her gaze away from the man's face. It looked human and moved like leathered skin instead of porcelain, but it had cracks like a dinner plate might have, one jutting through an eye socket to his forehead.

"We're here to see the Centaur," Windsor-Sykes announced.

The man nodded but kept his eyes down. "He's been waiting for you, my lord."

"What's up with cracked face man?" Francis Scott Key asked, voice barely above a whisper.

"He was grown, not made," Crockett said from beneath the layers of cloth.

Preacher's Daughter looked closely. She spied tiny green leaves sprouting from the man's wrists just inside his sleeves. Is that what the bogie meant? That the cracked face man was a grown thing with some sort of mask?

Crockett added, "He smells like you."

The cracked face man led them to the rear of the shop, where a service elevator awaited them. It was large enough for all of them to get on, which they all did. She glanced down at the scuffed wood of the elevator floor as they descended. It could have been ten, a hundred, or five hundred years old. It held the scuffs and stomps of innumerable people. Hoof prints were prominent, half-moon shapes making a mosaic of shuffling. The man pressed a button and the door lowered.

As the elevator descended, music played in her head. Soft jazz. Like she was in a department store. She also felt an itch at her left wrist. She scratched it and came away with a tiny leaf. Had she got it from the cracked face man? What an odd thing. She wadded the leaf and rubbed it between her fingers, then dropped it.

Crockett picked it up and ate it without comment.

Bogies. She had no idea about their culture or their diet. All she knew was that two of them had decided to partner with her and she'd so far benefited from the relationship. They'd both disappeared for a while during the train ride which had given Preacher's Daughter a chance to speak with Barbie.

"I just want to point out that you get a couple of bad ass Pixies that bonded to you and will keep you out of trouble, while I got the Laurel and Hardy of the unseelie who ended up watching too much 1980s television and decided to live their lives as the main characters of *Miami Vice*."

"At least you don't have a sylph who only communicates with you during simulated sex," Barbie said. "It's sort of embarrassing when Waterhouse comes out of a meeting with his fairy because we all know how gross the situation was."

"What do your Pixies have to say about the Sylph?" Preacher's Daughter asked.

"First of all, they aren't my pixies. What do they say?

They call her the old woman who loves humans too much. That's why she had all of the other men in the family killed, you know. She got jealous. As long as she lives, Waterhouse can't have any other relationship."

"Oh." Preacher's Daughter blinked. It had never occurred to her that the link to the deaths had been anything more than bad luck. "Really?"

Barbie stopped cold. "You weren't really thinking..."

"Me? Oh no." But she had been thinking that. A little bit. It hadn't been front and center in her mind, but the more she'd gotten to know Donkey Kong, the more the attraction grew. Not that she'd ever seen herself ending up with a stuffed shirt Englishman, but she'd had her share of flights of fancy. She guessed that's all they would be as long as Madeleine was around. And who was she kidding. They had a mission to prosecute. They needed all hands on deck and a distraction of that sort would just cause problems.

The elevator jarred to a stop, making them all take a step for balance—all except for the cracked face man who had his hand on the lever that lowered the contraption.

The basement—if that's what it was called—had the earthy smell of a barn. The floor was littered with enough straw that it had a bounce to it. The walls were comprised of exposed rock the same color as the volcanic plug that Edinburgh Castle sat on. She was aware that the castle had been built on the pinnacle of an extinct volcano, but it was hard to think of the United Kingdom as a land of volcanos. Their imagery belonged in a more equatorial zone, and not the cold misty days of Scotland.

Cracked face man led the way.

She hung back with the two bogies.

This didn't feel at all like her scene.

Francis Scott Key Catches the Enemy followed her lead and stood beside her.

Double wooden doors opened before them and they all piled inside. The room was larger than she expected, but then when she saw the figure that dominated the center of the room she knew why. They'd mentioned they were going to meet the centaur, but she'd thought it was a nickname. The four-legged equine with the head and torso of a human told her otherwise. His body was jet black with a sheen from being brushed. The man part was dressed in a tartan vest with a white shirt, sleeves rolled up revealing bulging forearms. The head was a little longer than a normal human's, but the face was beyond handsome. Black eyes set over a patrician's nose and a jet black goatee that came to a point. His lips were a deep red, but she doubted he'd needed makeup to achieve the effect. His ears were pointed and poked through thick black hair that had been pulled back into a pony tail.

Cracked face man bowed deeply and said, "The man from the Queen, my lord." Then he backed out the door without straightening.

All eyes fell expectantly on the centaur who stood heads and shoulders taller than Jagger, the tallest of them. Other than a side table with crystal glasses and a half full scotch decanter, the room was empty.

"Things must really be in the shite if you're coming to me," he said, voice bone deep, Scottish brogue deeper.

"The Queen has concerns," Windsor-Sikes said.

"She should. The Formori have returned and there doesn't seem to be any stopping them."

"If we had known sooner, we could have helped."

"Tell that to the dead dryads," the centaur said, tail lashing angrily.

The two stood nose to nose or rather nose to chest, neither backing down.

McDonnell cleared his throat, but didn't say a word.

Windsor-Sikes was the first to back away by a single step. He scratched the side of his head, then shook it. "We shouldn't be at odds with each other. That will get us nowhere fast. We need to find a way to work together. Which means—"

"You've not wanted to work together in the past," the Centaur said.

"Which means," Windsor-Sykes reiterated, "that we need to put past differences behind us and look ahead to solving the problems at hand."

The centaur began to pace, which pushed everyone to the edge of the room. He eyed each and every one of them. When he saw Crockett, he couldn't help but chuckle. Both bogies had removed their rain ponchos and looked like a before and after version of a seared and singed Ewok. Then he noted Preacher's Daughter and completely stopped. He stared at her so long she felt uncomfortable. She glanced at Munro and Jagger, but both of them seemed as concerned as she was.

Then the centaur pointed at her.

"This one will speak for you."

"But Arthur, she is a guest and—"

"I invoke the old ways. You may have one ambassador and this is it."

"But the Queen sent me," the lord said.

The centaur whirled and he gestured towards the door. "The rest of you. Out!"

Windsor-Sykes stared lasers at Preacher's Daughter, but all she could do was shrug. She hadn't done anything.

Waterhouse attempted to come to her, but the centaur stepped into his path. He gave her a sympathetic look, but was helpless to do anything.

The more people appeared worried, the more worried she became.

The centaur gave the two bogies a withering look and spoke in a language filled with coughs and grunts.

They responded to him, but neither seemed ready to leave her side. At that moment, not even knowing what the centaur was about to do with her, she loved the little fuckwits for all of their murmuring chicanery. Crockett seemed to stand up straighter as he replied with his own series of grunts and snorts.

The Indian didn't know what to do, but he did stand taller, chin up.

The others were already on the elevator.

She turned to her retinue. "I'll be alright, fellas. Why don't you go with the others?"

"I'm not sure this is a good idea," Francis Scott Key Catches the Enemy said.

"What he said," Tubbs added.

Crockett just looked beat, but wasn't about to leave her.

Where did she get off having such admiration?

"Really, let me handle this." She gripped the Indian on the shoulder and gently nudged him towards the elevator.

Reluctantly, he went, watching her through the slats as the elevator ascended.

The bogies remained, however.

Finally, the centaur shook his head and sneered at the two unseelie. He went to the side table, poured himself two fingers of scotch and slugged it down. He poured two more fingers, turned around and offered her the same glass he'd drunk from.

"Here. Might as well have a drink."

She stared at the glass for a hard moment, then marched across the room, grabbed it, downed the tawny liquid, and handed him back the empty glass. It tasted like a stronger version of scotch and almost buckled her knees. She never took her eyes off of him and wouldn't give him the satisfaction of knowing she was terrified. She reminded herself that she'd done battle with giant Zoroastrian demons, so this fellow with four horse legs wasn't about to intimidate her.

And it almost worked.

"So?" the centaur boomed.

"So what?" she said in return.

"You're supposed to convince me to help you."

She narrowed her eyes. She hated bullies. She swept past him, poured herself two fingers of scotch, downed it, poured another, then handed it to him.

"Here," she said, trying to copy his intonation and inflection. "Might as well have a drink."

He glared at her a moment longer, then took the glass, downed it and hurled it against the wall above where the two bogies stood. They both flinched, but didn't move.

"What's an American doing with that bunch?" he asked.

"At first we were trying to figure out why a town went missing," she said. "But you already know that."

"Yes. Of course, but why you? Why an American?"

"We had a town go missing as well. We had an exchange of sorts."

"Oh, that. That accounts for the Indian."

"And what's with me supposed to be convincing you to help us?" she added, feeling a little juiced from the scotch. "You should be begging us to help you."

His eyes blazed for a moment, then he laughed. "You're a rough one, I'll give you that. Even the boggarts think so and they don't like humans much at all." He glanced at them as did she.

"What did they say to you?" she asked, wondering if he'd answer.

"I told them to leave or I'd cook them and stuff them in my haggis."

"What did they say?"

"They said if I did, they'd crawl into my throat and make sure I choked to death."

She couldn't help but grin. She nodded to the bogies who gave each other a high five.

"I don't know why they hang around me," she said.

"It's your aura. It's completely different than everyone else's."

She was taken aback. "My aura? Is that even a thing?" It sounded like something like her old friend Charlene might say.

"If you can't see them then you wouldn't understand the difference. Just know that it is different and it's imbued with several things you'll learn about in the near future."

"Wait. That sounds like you do know."

He shook his head. "The business at hand."

She glanced around at the empty room. "Oh, yeah. I can see how busy you are. Unless you're having a game of twister with a pod of pixies in the other room, I think you can spare the time."

"You Americans really are disrespectful aren't you?"

"If you mean why am I not going on about lord this and lord that and bowing or curtseying or whatever the fuck I'm supposed to do in the presence of another country's royalty, then it's because I am from America and we did away with all of that bowing and scraping more than two hundred and forty-five years ago."

"I watch your television. When the French gifted you

the Statue of Liberty they weren't kidding when they said bring me your poor and hungry, because the amount you have in your country is, frankly, staggering."

She held up her hand. "Let's just say we all have our own political problems, Captain Brexit, and leave it at that. Now, why don't you want to help us help you? It seems as if your Fae are doing a Brexit of their own."

He glared at her, but then softened his look. Clearly he wasn't used to being spoken to in this way but was coming to terms with it. "They have to do something or else they will all die."

"The Fae? Will all die? How is that possible?" she asked.

"Where shall I begin? Are you aware of interdimensional topology?" he asked.

She blinked hard. She wasn't expecting a centaur in a basement of an Edinburgh men's dress store to begin a conversation with high order math. "I understand the concepts of topology," she said slowly. "You can say that I traveled to a pocket universe created by a supernatural being on a previous occasion."

He cocked his head and laughed. "You're not simply a pretty American spy, are you?"

"I'm not a spy, I am a soldier."

"I've read your dossier. You're a member of the intelligence service and belong to Special Unit 77."

"How did you get my—" She shook her head. "We protect American interests," she said, "Much as the Black Dragoons protect the interests of the United Kingdom."

He waved her response away with a hand. "Pocket universe is the perfect description. Most of the seelie and unseelie live in such places. Call them cul-de-sacs of time and space if you will. They can move into and out of them regardless of where they are. The problems are with the Marrow. They can sniff out such places and have been doing so at an alarming rate in recent years. They've also come to understand something which we've kept to ourselves in that the dryads, seen once as lowly seelie locked into an existence based on their link to different aspects of nature, are actually the lifeblood of the seelie and unseelie alike."

"Then why were the unseelie fighting against us in Cottingley Woods?"

"Like any marginalized group they can be made to believe what those in power want them to believe. It has nothing to do with intelligence or lack thereof. It has to do with their desire to leave the margins. The Marrow are being directed by the Formori. Chasing down all of the pocket universes was taking too long so they figured that they could hasten their plans by destroying all of the dryads."

"But why the missing towns?"

"Each one is located at a pole of inaccessibility. You'll note that each town is as far from the coast as possible. The Formori are of the oceans. They draw their strength from the tides and the ebb and flow of the currents. They are weakest when they are farthest away. The Formori are creatures the Fae drove away eons ago so that humanity could be allowed to flourish, instead of hiding in caves and behind walls made from stone. Now, they've returned for their pounds of flesh and in this case, they want the dryads."

She thought about this for a moment, then thought back to the Pict symbol they'd all been studying. Then her dream about the White—or her transition to it—where she'd met Tony Curtis and Sydney Poitier in their roles from the movie *The Defiant Ones*. They were the double disc connected by the tunnel. That's what the missing towns were—of course. They were the discs at the end of the zag. The Picts knew all along. They understood before science was even formalized into a body of collected knowledge, and represented the way to transit interdimensional topology through a symbol. She should reach out to Dr. Fields so he could validate her hypothesis.

"The trees Francis Scott Key saw. You're moving the dryads to a safe place. You're trying to save the Fae."

He grinned and stomped a hoof. "An irony is that we're moving the lifeblood of our species to a place where your military has been known to indiscriminatingly kill Native Americans, or what you call Indians."

"That was a hundred years ago. Buffalo Gap, Stronghold, and Wounded Knee were the last in South Dakota."

He smiled like a mother might to a child. "Time is different for our kind. That's almost yesterday for me."

Her mind was racing. "So, Maeve is organizing the evacuation."

"She is."

"And who is Maeve in all of this?"

"The fairy queen herself."

She remembered the conversation she had with Waterhouse about fairy kings and queens and how they conformed to the human construct. She said as much to the Centaur.

"Queen. King. They are shorthand. A true term would be New Mother and New Father, but those beg explanation. Why use those when I can just say King and Queen and everyone knows what that means?"

"Who is the king?"

"Killed by a Marrow."

"These Marrow, how powerful are they?"

"They can be killed," he said. "Our problems like when the first Formori came to the UK. They will come from the ocean and they shall be like kaiju. They will be monstrous and will destroy everything in their path."

"How did you defeat them before?" she asked.

"It took time. We grew the dryads who influenced the land, making it poisonous for them to live here. Even the touch of our soil would sizzle their skin and they were forced to be driven back into the sea, into their own pocket dimension. Then they grew the Marrow, an abomination of Formori and unseelie created using shadow magic, outlawed by the Fae."

"Without the dryads, they can return. Aren't you helping them by removing the dryads?" she asked.

"Hence the problem." His tail flicked back and forth.

She was beginning to recognize it as an indicator of his mood.

"What if we can kill the Marrows before the Formori arrive?" she asked.

"Then the dryads can return and the Formori won't be able to inhabit the land."

She tapped her forehead with a finger and said, "Then we have to make the Marrow come to us."

"How are we going to do that?" the centaur asked.

She turned to her bogies. "What would Crockett and Tubbs do?"

"Set a trap," Crockett said.

"Set a trap," Tubbs said.

She turned back to the centaur. "Then that's what we're going to do. We're going to set a trap. Let's plan this."

Thirty minutes later, she knew what she was going to do.

Or at least she thought she did.

CHAPTER 24

ALL OF THEM ran through the rain the short distance to Victoria Street where they filed into an apartment that had been reserved long ago as a safe house. It had a host of bedrooms, a single bathroom, a living room, and a large dining room. But there was no kitchen. A nearby restaurant called Maison Bleu was said to provide food if needed. Jagger went about sorting just that, while Munro procured a case of water and three bottles of Speyside scotch. He found a mish mosh of glasses and tea cups and spread them out on the table for all to use.

No one had spoken to her after her conversation with the centaur except for a curt, "Let's go," from Windsor-Sykes.

She found a bedroom and threw her coat on the bed. She stared longingly at it, wishing that she could just fall onto the cushion and close her eyes to oblivion for a while, but she knew that she had to deal with the Queen's man. She longed for her last unit. Her relationship with Boy Scout and McQueen was perfectly clear. They trusted her and wouldn't dare even think of questioning any of her decisions. But here she was a Connecticut Yankee in King Arthur's Court. While they seemed to trust her acumen, they didn't appreciate her authority or the authorities thrust upon her.

She went into the bathroom and examined her face. Her nose had now been broken twice in a week. She looked like an alien raccoon, black beneath both of her eyes turning to green. Her nose was swollen and her eyes were puffy. She took her time washing her face with the soap at hand, then ran her fingers through her hair several times and reset her pony tail.

Staring into the mirror she told herself that she would play well with others, regardless of the assholes they appeared to be.

In the living room she plopped into a chair with a tea cup full of scotch. At this rate, she'd be plastered before they even had any food.

Windsor-Sykes came in and sat across from her, hands empty, closed into fists. His face was almost purple with pent-up frustration but he said nothing.

She really wasn't feeling like a confrontation. She knew it was inevitable, but she wasn't about to be the one to speak first. Whoever did that would lose the opening salvo. So she let him fume while the room filled with the rest of the crew. Clearly, this was going to be a spectator sport.

It was Donkey Kong who finally broke the burgeoning silence.

"So, you and the centaur had a conversation," he said letting the word trail off.

"Arthur and I had a lot to talk about. But first, riddle me this, Batman. What is it he said about invoking the old ways? Why did he choose me?"

"Because he believed he could get from you that which we have held back in the past," Windsor-Sykes said.

"Hmm," was all she said.

"The old ways state that anyone present can be selected as ambassador for each party. Because it was only him, he was ensured that he and he alone spoke for the Fae."

"So, had the cracked face man stayed, we could have chosen him?" she asked.

Waterhouse nodded. "Not that he knows anything, but yes."

"Somehow the centaur had already gained access to and seen my dossier. He knew my qualifications. He knew my history." She watched as Windsor-Sykes fought and lost the urge to not roll his eyes. "He chose me because he didn't want to deal with his usual ambassador. No offense to you, sir."

The Queen's man's stare softened. "What's done is done. The insult wasn't to you. It was to the Queen and of course me, because I get to return and explain to her that I've failed at my single job at the court." He sighed heavily, seemingly resigned at the outcome. "What is it you spoke about?"

Now, she understood. The centaur had taken the rug out from under him and insulted him intentionally. He'd ignored the highest ranking person in the room only to select a foreigner and a woman. The entire scenario had been nothing but a poke in the Queen's eye and Windsor-Sykes would have to return to the palace and let Her Majesty know that he'd let it happen. Politics. She had little need for them, but they were what they were.

She told them all what went on with the centaur, answering their questions as they came. Sometime, during the conversation, Jagger appeared carrying bags of food, which he left in the dining room. She smelled their aroma and her mouth watered. But instead of everyone taking a break, they continued their verbal head to head.

"We decided the best way to stop the forced emigration of the Fae to America is to track down and kill the Marrow," she said.

"We don't even know how many there are," Jagger said.

"The bogies think there are five. Crockett and Tubbs are tracking them down now."

Everyone looked around as if just now noticing that the little creatures were nowhere to be seen.

"The centaur has a two-phased plan," she said.

"The centaur has—" Windsor-Sykes now did roll his eyes.

"It's a solid plan," she said.

"How would you know?" he snapped. "What operational training do you have?"

"Six-hundred and forty days in Iraq and Afghanistan plus another hundred and eighty days transiting the mind of a captured demigod. What's your experience?"

His back straightened. "The Falkland Islands."

She grinned. "Were you aboard ship or on the ground?"

"I was a naval officer," he said.

"I see."

"And how long was the Falklands War?" she asked.

"Ten weeks."

"So, roughly seventy days from start to finish," she said.

Waterhouse cleared his throat. "What's the plan?"

Windsor-Sykes shot him a withering look. "More likely what did you give up?"

"Listen, Lord Stuck in the Mud, I didn't want to be in the position I was in, but I was put there by some crazy tradition that allows the other team to select their opponent. Like it or not, the centaur and I had a negotiation. The Queen wanted her national treasure and we discovered a way to make that happen."

Waterhouse offered a weak smile. "We might as well know what's being proposed before we decide not to go with it, don't you think, my lord?"

Windsor-Sykes closed his eyes.

She could tell he was fighting an internal battle. Not only had he been outmaneuvered by the centaur, but he'd also been marginalized. She couldn't imagine that a man of his pedigree was used to such a thing. So, she tried to give him the benefit of the doubt. She tried to act civil, even though she felt about as uncivil as a felon in a money counting house.

"The Formori are still incapable of landing on UK soil," she began. "The dryads are still able to hold them off by their very presence. But the Marrow are targeting each one and trying to remove them, thus clearing the way for the Formori. The centaur admitted that there were eleven dryads left. We can't protect each one, but we can concentrate on the oldest and most powerful."

"And where would that be?" Windsor-Sykes asked.

"Glen Quoich has one," Barbie said.

"What? Aberdeenshire? There are barely any trees there," said Munro.

"She's in a protected grotto. Under a glamour," Barbie said.

"Any other choices?" Windsor-Sykes asked.

"Killiehunty," said Barbie. "They're both in Cairngorms National Park."

"Which one do we go to?" Jagger asked.

"Glen Quoich," said Preacher's Daughter. "I just mapped it on my phone. It's near Scotland's Pole of Inaccessibility where the Marrow will be the weakest."

"How are we going to get the Marrow to take the bait?" Windsor-Sykes asked.

"The bogies are going to let it be known that we are moving her. They believe that the dryads are weakest when they are outside of their protected glamours."

Everyone nodded as they envisioned their own piece of the mission.

"Wait," Donkey Kong said. "You said two-phased."

She nodded and took a final sip of her scotch. Any more and she wouldn't be able to feel her face. "While half of us guard the dryad with a squad of Royal Marines, the other half returns to Grave Hill and susses out how to bring back the dryads who have already emigrated to America. We'll need a good negotiator for that because they'll have to deal with Maeve."

"Maeve," Windsor-Sykes murmured. "She's worse than the centaur."

"Maybe this is your chance to make it up with the Queen, my lord," said McDonnell.

"Maybe you're right. Okay, sort out the men and give me some backup."

"I'll come along," McDonnell said. "Jagger, Munro, and Nottingham you are with me. That leaves Barbie, Donkey Kong, and Preacher's Daughter. Waterhouse. You are in charge. Crookes. Can the Home Office support my people?"

"Already called and have them on standby," he said.

"What about me?" Francis Scott Key asked.

Everyone turned to him as if just now realizing that they had an Indian in their midst.

Her inclination was to send him back to the reservation, but that grated on her in a personal way. She'd give him a choice. "What do you want to do?" Preacher's Daughter asked.

He looked around at the others then finally nodded. "All of you are warriors. I am no warrior. Sure, I was in Desert Storm, but that was an easy war conducted largely by weapons across great distances. I've never been an in-your-face sort of warrior."

"That doesn't make you any less of a warrior," she said.

"Thank you, Ms. May. I think I'd like to go back. Before this is all over, the war is going to come to my lands. I want my people to be prepared."

She grinned. She'd never thought of it in that way, but having an opposing force prepared in the event they might need one was of utmost importance. Plus, they'd be protecting the young dryads who had already moved through the hole in the world.

"So, it's settled then," McDonnell said.

"When's the last time you used a machine gun? Please say it wasn't Desert Storm," she asked.

"We know our way around weapons on the Res," Francis Scott Key said.

"Then it's settled," she repeated. She glanced at Munro who seemed a little sick. "You okay?"

He gritted his teeth. "Fine. Just a little cold."

Dark circles hugged his eyes and his skin looked pallid.

Everyone began making their way into the dining room to grab a paper plate and some food.

She stood to join them, but found her path blocked by Windsor-Sykes.

"We're not done here," he said.

"Listen, I am tired and hungry and more than a little drunk. Can we do this some other time?"

"Just tell me one thing," he said.

She sighed. "What?"

"What did you promise him?"

She shrugged. "It's no big deal."

He moved to stand in her way.

"Listen, Lord Speed Bump. I'm hungry. Drunk. And did I say hungry?

"What did you promise the centaur?

"He said he wants the Green Man."

His face went white. "He said that?" He grabbed the chair for balance. He looked at her, mouth open. "And you agreed."

For the first time she felt worried. She hadn't expected so simple of a request to be that big of a deal. "You said the Queen wanted to take care of her national treasure. I supposed this was a priority."

"But the Green Man. You promised him the Green Man?"

"Who is this Green Man?" she asked.

"The devil himself."

CHAPTER 25

"Tell me about the Green Man," she said. "Can't be as bad as all that."

Her head felt like it had been bashed into a wall, then bashed again. She hadn't thought she'd drunk that much last night. Right now she could barely hold the steaming cup of tea her hands were shaking so badly. God she wished for coffee.

Windsor-Sykes sat across the table from her but said nothing. He was dressed immaculately in a suit and tie. She wondered how he'd gotten it. She didn't remember him having a stash of clothing during the run through the rain the previous evening.

Jagger poured him tea and laid out a tray of croissants and jam.

Waterhouse sat next to her, eyeing her as he drank his own cup of tea. He, at least, was still dressed in yesterday's clothes.

Patterson paced in the other room, arranging something on the phone. Her voice rose and fell. Clearly, she wasn't getting what she wanted, but Preacher's

Daughter had no doubt that the woman would find a way to get it.

She'd been informed that the others had left earlier in the morning.

Jagger offered her a croissant and she felt her bile rise. She gestured with a free hand to take it away and brought her knees up into the chair. She hugged them and let the steam from the tea wash over her face. God, she felt like hell's half acre.

"Let's run through everything that happened one more time," Donkey Kong said. "Begin from when we were ushered out."

"We've done this," she said. "Must we plow it into the earth?"

"Every little detail helps. All we want to know is what happened. Last night you were a little, how should we say, under the weather."

She laughed hoarsely. "If that's how the English say flat ass drunk, then yes, I was a little under the weather."

"Were you given anything to eat or drink?"

"No. Nothing. Nothing at all," she said.

Donkey Kong stared dejectedly at the table.

"Well, I did have a glass of scotch."

He looked up sharply. He glanced quickly in Windsor-Sykes' direction, then returned his attention to her. "And you drank it?"

"It seemed like a good idea at the time. Plus, I was cold and wet and not exactly feeling my best. I needed a warm up."

Windsor-Sykes grinned as he typed something into his phone.

Donkey-Kong shook his head. "You never agree to drink anything from a centaur."

"What? And you didn't tell me? No, *See you later love, and don't drink anything he gives you*?"

"Some things should be obvious," Windsor-Sykes said without looking up.

"Don't be a catty lord," she said. Then she added, "You really should have some sort of Fae warning guide or some other type of briefing about the do's and don'ts of Fae-human interaction."

"We have that in the library back at the castle. You're supposed to read it and sign off on it prior to going on mission," Barbie said, entering the room, grabbing three croissants.

No one told her that. "What was in the drink?" she asked.

"Centaur semen," Barbie yelled over her shoulder, as she returned to the other room, the phone wedged between her face and shoulder.

Preacher's Daughter snorted tea and spit-taked into the cup.

"What the hell?" she said, wiping her face clean with her sleeve and setting the cup down. She put both feet on the floor and both hands on the table to steady herself.

Donkey Kong couldn't help but grin. "No one really knows what it is he drinks. He tries to get everyone to drink when they get there. None of us has ever tried it."

He spread his hands on the table. "I mean, there could actually be centaur semen in the drink, but I really doubt it."

"Have you ever considered that he was just being hospitable?" she asked.

Jagger sat down with them. "Remember that movie, *The Princess Bride*?"

She blinked at him. "Of course."

"Remember the scene where Vizzini, the criminal mastermind hired by Humperdink to capture Princess Buttercup, is speaking with Wesley, who's masquerading as the Dread Pirate Roberts?"

She looked at him blankly.

"Vizzini said, *You fell victim to one of the classic blunders, the most famous of which is, never get involved in a land war in Asia, but only slightly less well-known is this, never go against a Sicilian when death is on the line.*"

"What does that have to do with anything?" she asked.

"Had Vizzini not died because Wesley switched the cups of poison," Jagger began, "you would have learned the third classic blunder people make. Never drink the jizz of a centaur named Arthur."

She stared at him coldly. "You just made that up."

Jagger grinned then busted out into a fit of laughter. "I might have."

She turned to Donkey Kong. "So, he drugged me is what you're saying."

"More than likely. I haven't known you long, but you seem pretty capable of holding your own with alcohol."

"I've been known to plant a squad of marines in the ground and walk away. Yeah, maybe too much," she grumbled. Then she sighed. "Clearly, I fucked up royally. Tell me what I've done."

Donkey Kong glanced at Windsor-Sykes, who nodded in return.

"The Green Men are proto-sapiens, much like the monster Grendel, only Green Men can wield a strange sort of natural magic."

"Green Men? Plural? I thought there was just the one. And didn't he have other names?"

"The Green Knight. Jack on the Green. Some say the legend of Robin Hood originated with the Green Man of England, but we think otherwise. The Green Man we have in custody doesn't care for humanity and will do pretty much anything to get rid of us, which is why it took us several hundred years and a lot of dead Black Dragoons before we were able to capture it."

"You said you have one. What of the others?" she asked.

"There's evidence of Green Men all over the world. Most of the representations are on churches. Ever wonder why? Because historically it was believed that the church could save someone from the Green Men. Churches all over Europe, Jerusalem, Turkey, Borneo, Lebanon, Japan, Iraq, Indonesia, Papua New Guinea— the list goes on. Every major culture and society has Green Man mythology."

"I've never heard of one in America."

"What about Bigfoot?" Jagger offered.

She looked at him. "No way." She waggled a finger at him. "Plus, I am not trusting you."

"The Green Men don't all look the same," Donkey Kong continued. "But the one thing they have in common is their magical ability to commune with nature, be one with it, and derive magic from it. Jury is out on Bigfoot. That's your problem anyway, Ms. America. As you see, we have enough going on to keep our little happy family busy."

"Proto-sapiens? Are you saying that they predated humans?" She couldn't help but also be reminded of the Zoroastrian *daeva* who predated humans and how powerful they were. Remembering her studies, she said, "The Ahmarian, Bohunician, Aurignacian, Gravettian, Solutrean and Magdalenian cultures had their own ideas of worship and intermingled as they travelled across the Levant to various parts of Europe."

She looked up trying to dredge up a memory from her master's classes on world religions. "That would have been about forty-five thousand years ago. The Middle Paleolithic Period which runs from about fifty thousand to two hundred thousand years ago really didn't have much religion except for animal culture. Although we don't have any written texts, we can track the advent of religious ideas that the body is special by tracking the dates of burials. We don't have actual religious texts until the proto-Egyptians in twenty-five hundred BCE.

"And you're saying that these beings, the Green Men

predate all of this. Then they'd have to be supernatural."
She turned to Donkey Kong. "And they live forever."
She turned to Windsor-Sykes as the truth of it presented
itself like God's own thesis. "Is that one of the reasons
that the royal family spent hundreds of years trying to
capture a Green Man. The Fountain of Youth?"

The lord shrugged. "Who doesn't want to live forever?"

"Essentially," she began, "to make sure that England
doesn't lose the Fae, we need to give them the Green
Man." She nodded her head. "It's almost like they'd
planned it this way all along. Wait? I thought you were
going to Grave Hill."

"I am," Windsor-Sykes said. "The Queen just wanted
to hear the story."

She glanced from him to the phone in his hands. Had
the Queen been listening the entire time? The actual
Queen of England? Mortification began to set in as she
realized everything she'd just said and how she'd said it.

"Wait... that was her on the phone?" Preacher's
Daughter asked, remembering she'd discussed centaur
semen. She blanched and closed her eyes.

"More importantly, we know that you were drugged
by the centaur. That voids any agreements you made.
I'm going to go and have a little chat with him before
heading over to Grave Hill. Mr. Chatterjee, get something
appropriate to wear. We are going to be representing the
Queen."

Jagger looked up in surprise, then snapped to it, leaving
the room in a rush.

CHAPTER 26

Two MK1-Wildcats met them at the Meadows just south of the University of Edinburgh. Six Royal Marines were on one. At the second, she was greeted by the same handsome tanned and blonde pilot who had picked her up at the airport. The rest of them boarded that one. Once strapped in and with their helmets on, she toggled the command channel for the pilot.

"How long until we arrive?"

"Forty minutes, ma'am."

The plan was for the marines to hit the ground first and secure the area. All of their rounds were iron-tipped and steel gladii hung at their sides.

"What's the channel to the marines on the other helicopter?" she asked.

The pilot gave it to her and as they lifted off, she discussed tactics and techniques with the squad leader. She wanted to make certain that he knew what they were going after wasn't merely another target, but a nasty hybrid of unseelie and Formori. He assured her that he had knowledge of the target, but several of his men hadn't and he'd already briefed them on combat techniques.

"We'll be going up against a Marrow," she said, speaking over the sound of the rotors. "They will be invisible. We have a method to make them visible. My recommendation is to not fire until that happens. Just keep your marines out of the way. Conserve ammunition. Once it becomes visible, you will know what to do."

She signed off and leaned back. She'd gone out hungover on missions before, but it was never good. She was always a second slower to think and respond. Plus, her face hurt and her eyes burned. She didn't feel 100 percent. Had she been back with her old unit, Boy Scout would have read her the riot act. But Waterhouse—aka Donkey Kong—had merely looked her up and down, nodded curtly, and pursed his lips. She didn't know what was worse. The silent treatment or the loud treatment. Either way, she vowed not to be a hindrance on the mission.

She glanced at Donkey Kong who seemed as fresh as a daisy. He'd pulled a small book of poetry out of his cargo pocket and was reading it with a pair of glasses as if he were on the commuter train bound for London.

Barbie looked like the hatchet faced hard-ass she'd always been, staring out the window, probably imagining how she was going to kill her next target. Her part of the battle was perhaps the most important. Hopefully, she was running it back and forth through her mind to find any inconsistencies.

Preacher's Daughter checked her weapons. Like before,

she had the modern version of the SA-80 with iron-tipped rounds and four mags of ammo. She shrugged into her body armor which had been modified after McDonnell's got split in two. In modern times, they'd used a composite material because it was lighter and allowed the wearer to move around. But now she wore iron at her front and back and the weight went straight to her feet. She struggled to adjust it across her shoulders, then finally gave up when she saw she was going to have to lug it or slug it.

They received the word that they were ten minutes out.

Donkey Kong casually replaced his book and secured his glasses into a case, both going in his cargo pocket. Then he donned his own body armor, not even blinking at the additional weight.

Preacher's Daughter wondered what she would have to do for him to display any emotion. He was like a robot from *Westworld* and couldn't be bothered to show anything other than a flat, calm countenance. His demeanor was both infuriating and soothing.

The helicopter rocked with turbulence, then settled.

Still, no reaction.

Barbie was another thing altogether. Her emotions ate at her face regardless of what she was doing. It was as if she didn't care what she was doing or what people thought about her. Preacher's Daughter couldn't help but admire the trait. So many folks spent their lives trying to impress others by looks rather than deeds. Barbie was all deeds. Then again, had she the looks, who knows.

The Royal Marines landed first and fanned out.

Once their MK1 flared away, the second one landed in its place.

The door flung open and Preacher's Daughter got out and spun around. Donkey Kong and Barbie began to toss her small bags. She caught each one and tossed it behind her. When it was all said and done, they had a pile of forty. Just enough.

Donkey Kong and Barbie followed after.

The MK1 flared, and left them in the noonday sun. Or what Scotland had for a noonday sun, the bright orb held tight in a gray blanket of sky.

No tourists were out walking today. MI5 had shut that down. The place didn't seem as if a Dryad lived there. Mostly flat and treeless, Glen Quoich trail was roughly eight miles, circling the glen itself. But this wasn't their destination. Off to the left stood Braemar Castle which was built in the 1600s. It was a favorite of Queen Victoria, because it gave her access to the River Dee and the Linn of Quoich. Mainly, so she could consort with the Dryad.

The Royal Marines led the way, moving in a quick overwatch. They headed north to what was known as the Punchbowl. Inside, behind a glamour, lived the Dryad Quoich.

"Any sign of the Marrow?" Preacher's Daughter asked.

Barbie answered negative. Her pixies and a few of their closest friends were flying overwatch using quadcopter UAVs and were looking for abnormal movement within the flora. Although invisible, it was believed that the creature couldn't merely pass through things.

They arrived at the Punchbowl without incident.

But nothing was there.

Just a confluence of water in a ravine. Tall and lusty pines grew along the confluence. These conifers were probably the largest she had seen. Perhaps the presence of trees indicated the presence of the Dryad?

Donkey Kong pulled out a piece of paper and began to read it aloud.

Preacher's Daughter recognized it as Old English, but couldn't understand a word of the syllable-thick language. His voice rose and filled the hollow, drowning out the sound of the rushing water. Like a preacher, his cadence was reverent, careful to pronounce each word. A sizzle began to fill the air. She felt the skin on her arms rise and her hair begin to dance. She glanced over and Barbie's hair stood on end, her mouth grimacing.

Then like a curtain dissolving, the view changed. Gone was a scene of merely water and a confluence. Now, the center was filled with a great tree, limbs as big around as a man, rising to several hundred feet. The face was old, but beautiful in only the way a seelie can be beautiful. But the eyes were anything but inviting.

The Dryad spoke in Old English and suddenly it was as if Preacher's Daughter could understand it. Clearly, it had to be seelie magic, but she wasn't about to question it.

"What is it you come to disturb me?" the Dryad asked, her words slow, ponderous, beautiful.

"We come to protect you," Donkey Kong said in Old English.

"Who says I need protection from humans?"

Several of the Pixies descended and landed in her branches. They disembarked their UAVs and lay down upon them and basked in the aura of the Dryad.

"The Formori are returning," he said.

The Dryad laughed. "They cannot as long as I am here."

"There lies the problem," Donkey Kong said. "They've created a special monster called the Marrow. He has been killing your sisters and is coming for you."

"Yes. I have felt a change in things. A loss perhaps. Who have they killed?"

"The Lady of Cottingley Woods and several others."

"I find that hard to believe."

Preacher's Daughter stepped forward and spoke and was stunned to hear Old English come out of her mouth. "It is true. I saw it myself. The Marrow. We feel now it is coming for you."

"And what is it you will do, my pretty?"

Preacher's Daughter straightened her back. "We will protect you."

The Dryad laughed again. "But it is I who have been protecting you all these eons."

"Perhaps it's our turn to protect you," Preacher's Daughter said.

Barbie spoke through the headphones. "It's coming."

Preacher's Daughter whirled. "From where."

Barbie searched the horizon, turning a slow 180 degrees. Then she stopped and pointed. "There."

Preacher's Daughter spoke through the head set. "Marines, to the front."

They moved quickly, making a semicircle in front of the Dryad to block attack from the indicated direction. They had their weapons up, ready to fire.

The pixies mounted their UAVs and began to circle high above.

Then Preacher's Daughter saw it, like an invisible King Kong. The Marrow moved aside the tree limbs and leaves at a twenty-foot level. She could almost hear the thunder of its feet, but that was her heartbeat instead.

The creature moved within fifty feet of them and then stopped.

They waited ten, twenty, thirty seconds.

Suddenly, the Dryad behind them screamed as one of her great limbs were hacked to the ground.

Everyone whirled.

How had the Marrow gotten past them?

Donkey Kong commanded, "Barbie, let it fly."

Using hand signals, she caused every pixie to open the bags that were suspended beneath their UAVs. They'd affixed them upon landing and were integral to their plan. In titters of laughter and barbarian screams, the little seelie swooped and swirled.

The Dryad screamed again as another limb was severed.

The marines dare not open fire because their rounds would harm the Dryad just as they would the Marrow.

"Release them," Preacher's Daughter yelled, unwilling to bear the death of another Dryad.

Barbie shouted as well and the pixies opened their parcels.

Glitter rained from the sky, catching on the great form of the Marrow. More fell to the ground, but enough attached itself to the outlines of the beast that they were able to make it out.

The Marrow had two great legs, rising to a waist that began taller than a man stood. Tentacles that waved madly in the air ran from each shoulder. From the center of its sternum, however, came a single great arm with a cleaver at the end of it, this one now raised for another blow. Impossible muscles bulged from everywhere. Its head was the shape of a hammerhead shark with a mouthful of fangs that ate God knew what. Black hair like kelp shot from the top of its head and down a spiny dorsal back.

"Open fire!" Preacher's Daughter screamed.

The marines did as they were commanded and released magazine after magazine into the Marrow.

It charged, grabbing several of the marines in tentacles, but it was clearly wounded. The Marrow was made for magical combat. Nothing in its creation had anticipated 5.56mm iron ball ammunition at subsonic speeds.

One of the marines was able to unsheathe his sword and sever the tentacle that held it. He fell hard to the ground on his back, rolling to the side in pain, but alive.

The other was not so lucky.

Now that the Marrow was away from the Dryad, Preacher's Daughter and Barbie added to the fusillade.

The great beast fell to one knee.

Two of the marines ran towards it and began to hack at its back with their swords.

The remaining two fanned out to the sides so they wouldn't shoot their comrades and kept firing.

The Marrow fell face first into the ground, but still breathed.

Donkey Kong ran up its back, drawing his sword as he did, and planted it hilt deep in the back of the Marrow's neck.

The creature shuddered twice, rattled its tentacles on the ground, then stilled. And like a phantom, it came into existence, the magic of its invisibility gone with its life.

Preacher's Daughter realized that she'd been holding her breath and inhaled deeply.

Then she turned to the Dryad.

Two great limbs had been severed, like two arms. Green-like blood seeped from them. The Dryad's eyes were heavy, mouth downturned.

They'd killed the Marrow, but was the Dryad to die as well?

CHAPTER 27

DONKEY KONG ORDERED the surviving marines to grab handfuls of mud from the bottom of the confluence. The chore wasn't easy because of the rushing water, but they formed a line and soon began to make a pile. As they did so, the pixies grabbed tiny handfuls of the mud from the pile and flew them up to the wounds. They cried as they flew, the aura of the dryad having changed from one of regal confidence to one of fear and death. Once at the wounds, they packed them, attempting to staunch the flow of putrescent green blood, caressing the tree as they left, singing to it in forlorn voices, much like a nurse or a mother would a wounded loved one or patient.

The wounds the Marrow had managed to cause were terrible and might be enough to kill the dryad if they couldn't staunch the bleeding. Still, even if they were able to save the great seelie, its ability to protect was surely diminished. In that, the Marrow had been successful. Now they had to worry about another attack. According to her unseelie, there were five in total. Now there were four. Preacher's Daughter had no doubt that the Formori would send another Marrow to attack the Dryad of Glen Quoich. The task would be easier now because of its grave wounds.

By the time the dryad seemed as if she would survive, Barbie had called in for additional support. The first helicopter to land unloaded ten Royal Marines and uploaded those who had been in the battle, including the wounded and the dead. The sergeant leading the first crew insisted on staying so he might pass on the best TTPs—tactics, techniques, and procedures. Donkey Kong briefed them on their mission to guard the area. By that time, the magic he'd invoked to reveal the dryad was gone and all they saw was a glen and a confluence of water.

Preacher's Daughter hid her grin. She could tell by the way the marines looked at each other that they had no idea why they were protecting some random spot in the middle of nowhere. But like the marines they were, they'd do what they were told.

She strode over to the Marrow and examined it. Its skin seemed to be made up of black and gray scales, much like that of a fish. It smelled of the sea with the rankness of something rotten, like something captured in sea kelp and floating for days. She hadn't noticed before, but it had hooks on the heels of its webbed feet and hooks also at the knees. What she'd taken for dorsal hair was more than merely hair. Each strand was as stiff and deadly as wire and could be used to slice or impale. She couldn't see the arm that was pinned under it, but she noted the tentacles—each one about eight feet long with suction cups containing circular rows of little sharpened teeth. She shuddered, remembering the marine who'd been plucked away and killed. Then there was the head. Its dead eyes stared openly from the ends of the hammerheads. Its pupils were blown red. So imaginatively strange seeing a hammerhead on a bipedal creature, albeit one that was twenty feet tall if it was an inch.

Next came a Chinook—an immense cargo helicopter.

It hovered over the Marrow. Ropes were lowered and along with them came the load master. With the help of the marines on the ground, they secured the dread beast and within twenty minutes it was in the air and heading towards an MI5 facility near Glasgow. She watched it as it hung dead, arm secured, but tentacles catching the wind. To think that this creature was purpose made to kill dryads made her sick to her stomach. The dryads were the essence of good— She corrected herself—they were good for the land. She doubted that the dryads cared much for the people.

Donkey Kong came up to her.

"Ugly mutt, don't you think?"

"Ugly isn't the word," she said. "But it'll do."

"When's the next inbound?" she asked.

"Five mikes. Then off to Killiehunty. We already have pixies and marines on site waiting for us."

"Hold on. I'm not getting something. Why two dryads so close together?" she asked.

"What do you mean?" Donkey Kong replied.

"Tell me if what I'm saying sounds off."

He nodded.

"The dryads add a certain magic to the land that makes it poisonous for the Formori to touch it." She grabbed a stick and got down on the ground. She cleared away a patch revealing dirt and drew a rough outline of England and Scotland using a twig. "If this is the UK and these are the locations of the dryads that we know of, Cottingley Woods, Glen Quoich, Killiehunty, then where are the dryads to the south, southwest, and south east."

"I'm not sure what you are getting at," he said.

She pointed to each of the known dryad locations. "If these dryads protect central and north," she said, drawing interlocking circles around them, "then what's to keep the Formori from just taking the south right now. Brighton to London could be theirs."

Donkey Kong knelt down beside her. "I see what you mean." He snatched a twig for himself and marked as he spoke. "There are also younger dryads in Snowdonia in Wales. Dardmore for Cornwall and Exeter, North Wessex for the central south, Wakehurst Place, and the Royal Botanical Gardens at Kew for London." His concentric circles around those locations interlocked the whole of England and then some. "Additionally, there are even younger dryads along the coast in some areas that the Formori cannot know about."

"Who's protecting these others?" she asked.

"MI5 and the Home Office have contacted Marlborough Lines who are deploying several regiments using our newly developed TTPs to guard the better known dryads I mentioned. We don't have pixies, but we do have night vision and infrared, so we'll be able to see them coming."

"And the glitter?" he asked.

"Will be deployed by micro-UAVs."

"Looks like you have everything planned."

He gave her a concerned look. "You don't think so?"

"We don't have a backup plan. We're merely reacting to the situation as it unfolds. That's always a reason to make me nervous."

He looked at her in part exasperation. "We're working with the information we have at hand," he said.

"As an intelligence officer, I'd have more assets trying to get more information, like how is it that Maeve knew before all of us that this was going to happen? How was she able to create a hole in the world to transit through without us knowing about it?" She stood and tossed aside the twig. "If Windsor-Sykes is so tied in, then how did he not know what was going on? Or did he and has he been trying to ameliorate the situation on his own before it got completely out of hand?"

Donkey Kong stood as well. He stared into the distance. "That's an excellent possibility, but we'll never find out. This isn't America. Lord Windsor-Sykes has the authority to do whatever he deems fit. But you do have a good point. We have an A Plan but no B Plan." He flicked his wrist around. "Let's reverse it. If the Formori's A Plan is to take out the dryads and they are unable to do it, then what would be their B Plan?"

This was more like it. Preacher's Daughter needed this kind of brain challenge. Like so many times before, she'd been in reaction mode. Wouldn't it be nice to be in pro-action mode? She thought about what Donkey Kong said. What would be the Formori's B Plan?

"Right now, they are attacking one at a time," she began. "We've killed one of the five that we know about. If they don't already know through their own magical zeitgeist, they will soon enough when they discover that their target is still alive, which is why we've surrounded her with Royal Marines. We've already venned out the maximum effective ranges of the major dryads. There might be a space or two uncovered, but you assured me that those are covered by younger dryads. So, then what? What do you think the Formori have planned? You can't tell me they've been waiting a millennium and only have a simple plan."

"Ever since I learned about Maeve and her hole in the world, I felt it was a bit pre-emptive," he said. "Her fear seems unreasonable to the threat."

"I was thinking the same. And she didn't want me anywhere near the situation."

He stared at her thoughtfully. "As an outsider, why do you think the Fae would want to leave?"

She twisted her lips. "Could it be the ownership?"

He looked at her with wide eyes. "Ownership?"

"The Queen owns some pretty obnoxious things."

Donkey Kong visibly shuddered "Obnoxious?"

"Sure? I read somewhere where she owns all the swans

on the Thames. All the sea beds. The Cliffs of Dover. Uh, all the dolphins around the UK and I think all the gold mines in Scotland. I get the gold mines and the sea beds. Those can easily be monetized. But the dolphins and the swans? Seriously?"

"It's to protect them."

"What's not available on Google is the Queen's ownership of the Fae. Sure, they're a national treasure, but do you believe that they want to be owned?"

"Well, as I understand it from the records, it was either to be protected, or to be removed."

"*Protected*. I think I read that term somewhere in my own history books about slaves in the American South. They were certainly protected."

"Hey, that's not fair. Our Fae are protected. Your slaves were monetized and, according to our history books, were the reason for America's economic dominance in the 1800s without a major navy."

"Not arguing with you, DK, but I just want to point out that one of the reasons people come to the UK is because they see it as the old world. And part of being the old world is the idea that magic still exists. If you think your Fae aren't being monetized, then I think you're being intentionally obtuse."

He blinked at her, clearly not appreciating the term. Then he sighed. "Let's just say you're right. Let's say that the Queen has been monetizing the idea of Fae. What is Maeve's end game?"

She tapped the side of her head with a finger. "I don't

really think she wants the Fae to end up in America. The part of South Dakota that has been opened for the Fae is treeless and mostly barren except for plains of wheat. That doesn't make much sense. I think she's trying to renegotiate the terms of the contract."

"You seem pretty sure."

"I've been thinking about this. How come it's taken so long for the Formori to attack? You mentioned that there was an aborted attack by a Marrow a hundred years ago. Why was it aborted? Why didn't they all attack?" She glanced back at the invisible grove. "Here's what I think. I believe that the seelie helped defeat them. From the selkie to the pixies, they were all involved. But now there's no seelie to help. They've abandoned the United Kingdom or are in the process of doing so."

"They sacrificed the dryads? All for political leverage?"

"Can you think of another reason?" she asked.

"It's—it's unimaginable," he said. "What about the Centaur?"

"What about him? My guess is that he's the go between? I don't think he likes it but doesn't have the power to stop it."

"So, he's their ambassador."

Barbie came running up. "Come on, you two. We have to go. Killiehunty is under attack."

They all looked to the sky as the sound of their helicopter came to them.

Would they even have time to save the dryad?

CHAPTER 28

THE MK1 SCREAMED as it tore through the sky at max speed. Killiehunty was on the western edge of Cairngorms National Park and just over the Munro Braeriach. Fifteen minutes of hypersonic hell, the rotors spinning so fast that the entire airframe shook like a battered beast. The helicopter had to clear the third highest point in the UK and roller coasted over 4,300 feet before arrowing down to nearly sea level where the action was occurring. Even from on high, they could see the battle transpiring. Five marines were down, pieces of them scattered across the field. Two glittering monsters hacked savagely at a diminishing green tree.

The helicopter flared fifty feet away on a flat area and before it could even touch with skids down, the occupants were off and running towards the battle.

Preacher's Daughter screamed as she ran, raising her rifle and shooting the nearest Marrow in the back with a full magazine.

Donkey Kong ran beside her doing the same thing.

Barbie kept to the rear, sniping head shots on the other one.

The Marrow nearest them turned and advanced on them.

Preacher's Daughter emptied her magazine. Out of the corner of her eye, she noted that the tree was being hacked into nonexistence and it enraged her. She let the rifle fall on its sling and drew her sword. She was about to hack at one of the glittering legs, when she was snatched high in the air. She gasped at first as she rose so fast her head spun, then she felt the pain as the suction began to bite into her skin. She found that she still had the blade in her hand and she began to hack at the tentacle that held her, all the while screaming her rage and anger.

Below her, Donkey Kong was also grabbed by the second Marrow and slammed to the ground until he was unconscious.

This wasn't going as planned—like they'd actually planned anything.

She hacked at the tentacle holding her until it let go. She fell for one brief instant, then was snatched by yet another tentacle, this one attaching to her leg, and swung back and forth like a mad pendulum. She screamed her frustration as she swung her blade madly, trying to get to the length of Marrow that held her.

On the ground, the marines were scrambling out of the way of the two creatures as fast as they could. The Marrows weren't moving normally, but surging forward, almost teleporting from place to place, which, Preacher's

Daughter realized, explained how the one at Glen Quoich had managed to get behind them. The movement made her dizzy, moving from one location to the other without so much as a step. The marines were falling like bowling pins, however, not knowing where the Marrow would appear or disappear to. In fact, they were too busy trying to get out of the way of the spiked heels and knees to actually fire or bring their blades to bare.

This was not the laconic Marrow kaiju attacking like at Glen Quoich. These Marrow were berserkers and not allowing anyone to get a bead on them. Every now and then, they'd surge towards the dryad, cut away a part of her, then surge back, like duelists in a one-way sword fight. Green liquid seeped from two dozen places on the dryad. It couldn't possibly survive the attack. Sylphs swarmed her wounds, but were swatted away by tentacles and hatchet-shaped hands.

Horns blaring in unison as if announcing the arrival of royalty sounded from behind the Marrow that held her. She couldn't make out what it was, but the Marrow momentarily paused and in that pause more than twenty small arrows found a home in its chest and head. It dropped her.

She managed to twist so she landed on her side, but the ground still came up too fast. All the air was knocked out of her. Even so, she had the wherewithal to roll several times out of the way until she felt she was far enough that she wouldn't get crushed by the Marrow's feet or slashed by its heel. Her side aching from the collision with the ground and her head spinning from all of the rolling, she managed to get to her hands and knees and looked to see who'd just joined the party.

Red hats. Ten. Twenty. Thirty. Maybe fifty of them. Gnomes bearing miniature crossbows who were even then running through a rift in time and space. And behind them, in all of his glory, came the Centaur, whitish green swords in each hand bellowing a thunderous barbaric *yawpp*.

The Marrows backed away, but only succeeded in getting shot by the remaining marines and the host of Redhats. Standing a little over two feet high, they were more like armed Yorkshire Terriers, but the fierceness in their faces and the rage in their eyes, coupled with their iron-tipped quarrels, made them much deadlier.

One Marrow went to one knee.

The other turned and ran, surging a hundred feet with every teleport.

Half of the Redhats chased after it, moving spritely on their short legs, while the other half continued to fire at the wounded Marrow before them.

The Centaur galloped full speed towards the beast. Gnomes parted like a red sea. The Centaur swung both blades, severing the great hammer shaped head from its body. Blood spurted skyward in a Quentin Tarantino-esque waterfall of crimson effluence, then dissipated as the Marrow sagged dead to one side. The earth trembled beneath its fall.

The Redhats cheered.

Preacher's Daughter scrambled to her feet and ran over to the Marrow. She didn't hesitate as she shoved her blade into one of its eyes. It met resistance at first, then slid in up to the hilt. She kicked it for good measure, then turned to see where Donkey Kong had landed. He was surrounded by Redhats.

She ran over, shouting, "Out of the way. Waterhouse. DK. Are you okay?"

He managed to sit up, his hand going to the side of his head. "Feels like I drank two bottles of gin and slammed my head into a brick wall."

"A Marrow slammed you into the ground," she said.

"That sounds about right." Looking around at the Redhats, he asked, "Did we win, or are these some crazy looking angels?"

"We drove one off and killed the other?"

"What about the dryad?"

She glanced over her shoulder. The tree was now the size of a bush, a pool of green blood surrounded it. "Gone."

Horse clops made her turn over her other shoulder. The Centaur stood with his two bloody swords down at his side, wearing chainmail with the crest of the Royal Family. "There was a time when I'd ride into battle with whomever was king at the time. Damn, but I miss those moments."

"The Centaur..." Donkey Kong said.

The Centaur bowed, then began to clean the blood from his blades with a piece of sheepskin.

Preacher's Daughter stood. "You knew about the attacks all along." She pointed at the shrub that had once been a great tree. "Look at that. Look at her. You caused this. You and Maeve."

Without looking up, he said, "I'm trying to fix everything. I'm trying to be in three places at once so I might fix the situation."

"How in the hell are you going to fix it, you jackass?"

The Centaur now looked at her and shot daggers from his eyes. "Watch who you are talking to."

"I see who I am talking to. How can I miss you?"

"I'm detecting anger in my direction," he said. "And I don't understand it. After all, I just saved you."

She sputtered. "Saved me? This wouldn't have even been an issue had you come clean last night and told me what was really going on."

He sniffed and looked away. "I'm sure I don't know what you mean."

"I think we have an idea about what Maeve is doing," she said.

The Centaur looked at her. "Do you think this is the right place and time to talk about it?"

"Where else would you have us go to?"

"You two follow me," he said, pointing to Donkey Kong.

"Centaur here wants to have a word with us."

She helped Donkey Kong to his feet.

"This has got to stop," he said.

"Not here." The Centaur clopped several feet over and

made a gesture at the air, which resulted in an unzipping noise. "Follow me." He stepped through and was gone, but the vertical line in the sky remained.

DK reached up and felt for something around his neck, then turned to Barbie.

"Get back to HQ and find out what's going on. We're going to need a report when we get back."

She fired Preacher's Daughter a look but said nothing to her. "Yes, sir." Then she turned towards her pixies.

Donkey Kong reached down and grabbed her hand. "Follow me."

She let him pull her through and felt the sizzle of fire across her skin. But it was more a tickle than a burn and she quickly managed to dispel it, appearing once again in the foyer of the Centaur's abode.

CHAPTER 29

HE WENT STRAIGHT for his decanter and poured himself a drink. He glanced over his shoulder. "Do either of you want one?"

They both shook their heads.

The Centaur beckoned and the cracked face man appeared. The Centaur ordered scotches for all of them.

The cracked face man bowed and went through the double doors where Preacher's Daughter had yet to go.

The Centaur stood where he was, sipping at his drink and staring at them.

A few minutes later, the cracked face man returned with a tray and two drinks. One was darker than the other. He passed this to Waterhouse. The other he held out for Preacher's Daughter.

She took a suspicious sip, then followed it up with a fuller one. She found the Scotch pleasant and burning, not like the firewater the Centaur had given her the night before.

"Now that everyone has a drink, let's retire to my lounge." He clopped to the double doors, which were opened by the cracked face man.

Inside the carpet was a conglomeration of layers of Afghan and Persian carpets, making it seem as if one was walking on a sponge. She'd seen the same set up in family tents in the Hindu Kush, but the brightness of the colors of these carpets demonstrated that they'd never had to survive any element except the feet of the Centaur. A set of two Edwardian leather chairs sat against one wall. The Centaur gestured for them to take it. Several chandeliers lit the room. Across from the chairs were a tall desk and a wall-to-wall ceiling-to-floor bookcase filled with all manner of tomes and papers. The walls were smooth rock. The ceiling was wooden beams. The Centaur continued to the rear of the room where a pile of sheepskins awaited him. He sat, pulling his equine legs beneath him. He faced the pair of humans, a look of satisfaction on his face.

Cracked face man entered and helped him out of his chainmail. Beneath the Centaur wore a simple red shirt, coated in sweat.

Preacher's Daughter couldn't take the ridiculous pomp and circumstance any longer. "You have no right to be so smug," she said. "Dryads are dying because of you."

The Centaur raised an eyebrow. "Because of me? What is it you think that I did?"

She sat her glass down. "We've figured out your plan—you and Maeve."

The Centaur held up a hand. "Wait a moment. Maeve does what she wants. She always has. There are times where I might go along, sure. But there are also times where I try and reduce the damage her decisions might cause."

"Like the dead dryad. Is that a reduction in damage? She was beyond old and could have lived forever."

"Have you ever thought that there comes a time when someone or something doesn't want to live forever?"

She sat back turning the question over and over in her mind.

"Are you saying that she wanted this?"

"I'm saying there was an inevitability to it all and that she would rather die and let someone younger take over. There's only so much an immortal can take, after all."

She chewed thoughtfully on her lip, then took a drink. The Centaur seemed so sure of himself. But then again, she felt certain she'd sussed out what was going on as well. Had the dryads really given themselves up for a larger good, knowing, perhaps hoping that everything would turn out as expected. They certainly didn't want the Formori to take over or the seelie to be destroyed, so that had to be the case if the Centaur was being truthful.

"I need to get a message to McDonnell," Waterhouse said. "He needs to understand what's going on."

The Centaur nodded slightly. "And I need to speak with Windsor-Sykes. I know he's been looking for me, but I've been busy. But now that we have the attention of the Marrow, it's time."

"Are you really telling me that everything was planned?" She waggled her hands. "All of this. The attacks. The dead dryads. Are you telling me that you let Royal Marines be killed for a plan?"

The Centaur stared at her like she was an interesting

knickknack. "Is there a difference between planning and anticipating?"

"There is if you cause those anticipating to act."

"Then I suppose it was planned to a degree."

She balled her fists." You—You—You're not—"

"Human? No, Ms. May, I am not human. Part of me might appear to be human, but don't mistake that for me being like you. I will never be like you. I shudder to even think of the possibility of the weakness humans have to endure their entire lives. No, I enjoy who and what I am."

"And that would be alone," she said, standing.

To this he frowned and she knew she'd gotten in a blow, no matter how petty it was.

"Sit down. I'd like to explain some things to you."

"What are you going to explain?" she asked, feeling petulant.

"Stop acting like a child and sit down," the Centaur said. When she wouldn't, he turned to address Donkey Kong. "It wasn't a coincidence that Maeve's hole in the world took her to Pine Ridge Indian Reservation."

"Of course not. It's a pole of inaccessibility and safer from the Formori," Preacher's Daughter said.

"There are plenty of poles of inaccessibility, my child."

"Don't call me 'my child.'"

Ignoring her comment, the Centaur continued.

"Maeve could have chosen Canada or South America or anywhere in Asia or Africa. All of them have poles of inaccessibility. But she chose Pine Ridge for a reason. It is a place where your kind sanctioned the indigenous peoples.

You forced those who came before you from their lands and put them in a place where you felt they couldn't do any harm. A throwaway place. A place that you didn't care about."

"Don't categorize me," she said. "I don't represent all humans."

"Just as I don't represent all Fae."

She sighed. "Touché."

"The point is that the Fae feel that they have a relationship with your indigenous peoples."

"The difference being that the Fae have magic," she said.

"There was a time that your indigenous people had magic. Some still do, but it is a rare thing indeed." He paused to sip his elixir. "Maeve chose Pine Ridge because the humans there are like us. They are unwanted in a general sense, seen as a nuisance, even made fun of. But when it comes time to convince visitors to visit an area, they are suddenly important. *Come to Cottingley Woods and see the pixies. Come to South Dakota and see the noble Sioux Indian.* Is there really that much difference?"

"Do they really want to leave or do they want to renegotiate their status?" she asked.

"Who is they? The Sioux or the Fae? I think the answer is the same for both. They want to stay nearest their lands. They just want to be treated differently."

"And killing dryads is your negotiating tool."

"Not having seelie to help out is the negotiating tool. If the Queen doesn't want to help us, then why should we help her? It's not like she's really our monarch. All of us are much older than she ever will be."

"Where does the Green Man come into this?" Waterhouse asked.

The Centaur grinned. "You never take your eye off the ball, do you?"

"My degree is in game theory. At the end of a string of a million *If Thens* is always the goal one desires. I hear that the Fae desire a change in status, but there's more than that. Maeve has been without her consort for hundreds of years. I am sure she wants him back. The question is, if the Queen releases the Green Man, what will he do to benefit the crown?"

"To benefit the crown?" The Centaur tapped a finger on his glass several times. "Perhaps nothing. Perhaps everything. But I can tell you what he will do. He will send the Marrow back whence they came. As long as the Green Man is able to plant himself and commune with the land, the land is safe. It always has been as long as he's been around."

"Wait? Is he like a super dryad?" Preacher's Daughter asked. "Is he a male version of a dryad?"

"He's both that and more," the Centaur said. "Think of it this way. If you need to define his role using human terms, then consider him the King of the Dryads."

"We have two issues in play," Donkey Kong said. "The most important one is the defense of England. The Fae have been keeping us safe for over a thousand years. I have no doubt that the British military could bring any Formori threat under control given time—"

"You should have doubt," the Centaur said.

Ignoring the comment, Donkey Kong repeated, "I have no doubt that the British military could bring any Formori threat under control given time, the problem is that there would be significant loss of life before we are able to turn the tides. So, the best chance to save lives is to have the Fae present and doing what they have always done. Act as a deterrent."

"You said two things," the Centaur said.

"While we don't want the Fae to leave, the negotiations for future treatment are left up to Windsor-Sykes. What we can do, however, is free the Green Man if that would sweeten the pot and allow the Fae to better protect us."

"Wait a moment," Preacher's Daughter said. "I thought you said that he's dangerous and doesn't care for humanity." She left out the part about how they were probably experimenting on his blood to try and develop an elixir that would allow the royals to live forever. Such an operation, if real, would make him hate humanity even more.

Without breaking eye contact with the Centaur, Donkey Kong said, "We are not in a place where we can negotiate. This is but a temporary solution. Once the Fae have returned and the Formori have been vanquished, we'll revisit our relationship with the Green Man and hope that he will be willing to listen."

A phone buzzed in Donkey Kong's pocket.

He answered it, turning halfway from the others in the room.

His face blanched.

"Are you certain? All of them?"

He wiped his forehead and looked down. "We're going to Warwick Castle. I know. I know. But we're going. Meet us there after you call Barbie and let her know." Then he hung up.

When he looked at the others his face was blank and his eyes were wide.

"What's wrong, DK?" she asked.

He could barely speak. "It's McDonnell. McDonnell and Nottingham. They're dead."

CHAPTER 30

"THEY MADE IT through the veil, but on the way back out they encountered a Marrow," Donkey Kong said flatly. "It just tore them apart. They said—they said pieces of them are scattered everywhere."

She closed her eyes and tried not to imagine a Marrow tearing a man apart and failed. She tried not to imagine the handsome Nottingham ripped to shreds and failed. She attempted valiantly to ignore the images crashing through her mind of Malcom McDonnell's head skipping across the earth like a mad-thrown bowling ball and found it futile.

"What about Munro and Jagger?" she asked, voice barely a whisper.

"That was Jagger on the phone. Munro is in South Dakota with the Indian you brought through. But that's not all of it." He clearly wanted her to ask because he didn't seem to have the effort to say what he wanted to on his own.

She gulped. "What aren't you telling me?"

"Lord Windsor-Sykes."

"Is he dead as well?"

"No, but Maeve won't allow him to leave."

"He's been kidnapped?" she asked, feeling suddenly elated that he wasn't dead either, even though she found him unsufferable.

"He's being held as a negotiating tool, it seems," he said, staring at the ground in front of him.

"Then who's going to negotiate with the Queen?" she asked.

He shook his head. "I guess that will be me." He sighed deeply, wiping at an eye. "Dammit. I seem to have sprung a leak." Then he looked at her as he tried to compose himself. His features collapsed once more, but he did not shed any more tears. Instead, he set his jaw and asked, "What about your bogies? I thought they were supposed to be telling us where the Marrow are."

"This wasn't their fault," she said.

"Wasn't it? We've known where the Marrow were without them. All we had to do was look for a dryad. Your two personal *Miami Vice* bogies were of no help whatsoever. One must wonder what they were really doing all of this time."

She admitted to herself that she felt an unusual sense of ownership over the bogies even though she didn't really know them, but she couldn't let his statement stand. "We're all angry right now. It's the second stage of grief. We're going to be angry for a while, but let's not take it out on things we are unsure of. When Crockett and Tubbs come around again, we'll have a conversation.

Until then, let's control the things we are able to control. That means freeing the Green Man." She paused. "Are you going to clear it with the Queen?"

He glanced nervously between the Centaur and Preacher's Daughter. She could almost see him going through the machinations of *what ifs* and *if thens*. He put a hand to his head and closed his eyes. A full minute passed without anyone saying anything.

"We have a saying in America. It's better to ask forgiveness, than permission."

He opened his eyes and glanced at her. "We have the same saying."

"Is there history in the records of the Black Dragoons taking situations into their own hands?"

"There is. Extenuating circumstances have created necessities to act before consultation. But that was before cell phones and instantaneous communications. Those who did so didn't last. They either died during the operation, were jailed, or were put to death."

"I can't see the Queen putting anyone to death," she said.

"Have you ever met the Queen?" he asked.

"No, but in this day and age of paparazzi, if such a thing happened, it would be all over the news."

"Keep telling yourself that," he said. Then he added, "I really need to coordinate this."

"Let's role play," she said. "What happens if she says no?"

He didn't hesitate. "The remaining Marrow will most

certainly gain a beachhead so that the Formori can land in the UK."

"Then what's the issue. The Queen doesn't realize it, but she can't say no."

Waterhouse straightened his shoulders. "She can always say no and then I have to abide."

She shook her head. The glory of being a stranger in a strange land. "Well, I don't have to. Maybe I should run the op from here on out. Let you drag your feet and coordinate."

"Let you run the operation?"

"Don't you see? I don't answer to the Queen."

He stared at her for a long moment, then nodded briskly. "I'm going to go to the veil and see about recovering the bodies. Jagger is expecting to meet me at Warwick Castle. I will text you the release code for the Green Man. I will probably be unavailable for contact in the next twenty-four hours, at which point I will confer with Her Majesty on my plans."

The Centaur laughed out loud.

Preacher's Daughter didn't find it funny at all, and was relieved to be able to proceed with the plan.

With that, Waterhouse, aka Donkey Kong, left the room, head down, deep in thought.

She waited until she could hear the sound of the elevator operating before she addressed the Centaur. First, she looked him up and down. Never once in her life had she ever thought she'd be conversing with a centaur, much less one as magnificent as this one. Still, he had an otherworldly quality about him, a monstrous strangeness that kept her feelings in check.

He said, "That was some disingenuous manipulation you accomplished."

"Don't pretend that you don't like it," she said.

"Oh, I'm not pretending. I'm just not used to a human with the compelling capability of Fae."

She didn't know if that was a compliment or an insult and she didn't really care. "Where are you in all of this?" she asked.

"I need to speak with Maeve—to try and make the road easy for you. She wants no truck with humans. She is tired of them."

"And you? Do you want truck with humans?"

"Humans give me no end of entertainment."

"I see that," she said. She eyed his glass and the liquid within. She was not going to mention the jokes about centaur semen. Since he drank it himself, she was in serious doubt that it was one of the secret ingredients. Still, she wanted to know. "What is in that anyway? It hit me like a load of bricks."

"A brew that has been in my family for a millennium."

She made a surprised face. "I didn't know you have a family."

He was stone faced as he said, "Not present tense. Past tense. I used to. I don't anymore. I am the last of my kind."

She kept her jaw from dropping with effort. "But you raced into the battle with little account for yourself. You could have died."

"We all will die someday. I'd rather die in battle, than die down here in an Edinburgh basement on the Royal Mile feeling sorry for myself."

"Do you often feel sorry for yourself?" she asked.

He turned away. "I've said too much and you are too excellent a listener."

"Do you have any friends besides the cracked face man?" she asked.

He grunted, then offered a short laugh. "Is that what you call him? I suppose it fits. He's a simulacrum I created long ago so that I might have something to talk to."

"I never heard him speak."

"It's because he can't. Still, it pleases me to be able to converse with him at times. It makes me feel a little saner than speaking to a wall."

She regarded him a moment, then said, "Why are you sharing this with me?" Then she hurriedly added, "You don't seem like someone who's overly share-y."

He sighed. "Let's just say it's easier to speak with you because, like me, you are an outsider."

"I've felt like I've been an outsider my entire life. My father wanted me to be a missionary like him. I wanted to be soldier."

"Why is that? Why be a soldier?"

"*Black Hawk Down*. It was a movie and I saw it as a child and cried. I wanted to be able to go into harm's way and save people. Missionaries save people. It's sometimes the same thing. But in some places, missionaries are killed."

"I can say the same thing about soldiers, albeit it's a problem they face more often."

"True. But a soldier can fight. A soldier can be proactive in what they protect. A missionary finds it necessary to have someone or something else to protect them."

"When you say 'something', you must mean God."

She ignored the comment and said, "So, instead, I became a soldier."

He stared at her for a long moment, then said, "Perhaps you are a missionary after all—just a missionary with a gun."

She thought about that for an instant and wished her father was alive so she could share the idea of it with him. But he died long ago and his disappointment in her was a continuous shroud around every memory she had of him.

She shrugged away from her thoughts and asked, "Why does the cracked face man have a cracked face?"

The Centaur looked down and closed his eyes. "It was my fault. I did that to him."

"Why would you do such a thing?" she asked.

"I molded him. I created him. Then in a fit of anger, I broke him."

"What made you so angry?" she asked.

He stared at her then shook his head slowly. "That's a question for a different conversation. If you survive. If I survive this, ask again. I might just answer."

She stood and took a couple of steps towards him. "Does that mean I will see you again?"

"Who knows? Perhaps. Perhaps not. I will say our conversations have been interesting."

She shrugged. "At least there's that. One more thing."

He sighed. "What is it?"

"Why didn't you fix him?"

"To remind me why I was angry." He gestured for her to stand back. "Allow me one final gesture," he said. He stood and moved into the foyer.

She followed him.

He faced a blank wall, spoke a few unintelligible words, and a rift opened.

"This will take you to Warwick Castle."

She started towards the vertical slice in reality.

"One thing," he said. "If the Green Man gets out of control, know that he is afraid of dandelions."

"Dandelions? I find that hard to believe."

"Just so. He is."

She stared at him a moment. "Why are you telling me this? Aren't you on the side of the seelie?"

"I'm on the side of balance. England has been functioning fine the last five hundred years or so. I'd like to keep it that way. Which means, although the Green Man might have his own ideas, I don't want to see them come to fruition."

She shook her head. "You are the strangest being I have ever met."

He cocked his head. "Am I really? I thought the things you met in Afghanistan were the strangest?"

"How do you know about them?"

He grinned. "You'd be surprised what I don't know about you, Ms. May." He gestured towards the rift. "You better get going. I can't hold this open for too long or something might come out of it."

She glanced at the rift in momentary horror, then closing her eyes and gritting her teeth, hurried through.

CHAPTER 31

THE RIFT DEPOSITED her at a shrubbery three times the height of a man. It was so green and thick it seemed impenetrable. An older couple who had been walking together, turned around at her arrival, looks of surprise on their faces. She made a gesture in the air she'd seen Obi-Wan Kenobi make and muttered, "These are not the droids you are looking for."

The woman gave her a horrid look, tugged at the man's arm, and they hurried away.

Preacher's Daughter looked around. She was still wearing her sweat-soaked T-shirt and body armor. She wore 5.11 pants and Merrell shoes. Her arms were uncovered and she found herself chilled by the gray English weather. She walked several paces, then saw a break in the shrubbery. She glanced through first, and upon seeing no threat, stepped to the other side where she beheld an immense castle. It was far larger than she thought it was going to be. It was surrounded by surreal green grass and a small river on one side.

Flowers had been planted around the trees, creating

a miasma of scents that drifted languidly on a breeze. From somewhere, she smelled the unmistakable odor of cotton candy. She also smelled cooked sausages from a grill. The aroma made her mouth water. She tried to put her hunger aside and approached in awe, her eyes alight, remembering the tales she'd read about knights and ladies. This was the sort of castle that reminded her of such a place. She soon found herself in a crowd of tourists who were doing much the same thing. This couldn't be the right place. She saw men dressed as knights and serfs and women in all manner of medieval clothes as if this was a jamboree for the Society of Creative Anachronism right out of her imagination. Was this where they were holding the Green Man? She'd heard of hiding in plain sight, but this was too plain of sight.

She felt a presence to her right.

"Keep walking," came a voice she recognized, hand on her elbow for a moment.

JigJat Chatterjee.

"I take it I'm in the right place," she said.

"This place is more extensive than it looks. We've expanded the dungeons beneath it. You're in for a surprise."

"So, you've been here before," she said.

"We all have." They walked past a few pensioners feeding pigeons. "I take it you've heard."

She lowered her eyes. "Yes. I am so sorry, Jagger."

"This mission is a bad one."

"Understatement of the year. Any word from Munro?"

"He's working with your boss, Poe."

She stopped. "Is he really?"

"Yes, but I hear he's sick. There's something wrong with him."

"What could be wrong…" She glanced around and saw a large tree. She stepped beneath it and leaned against it. "Keep anyone from bothering me for a few moments, will you?"

He nodded, turned and stood with his hands crossed in front of him, looking for all the world like a security guard.

She hit speed dial and listened as the notes of the numbers emanated from the speaker.

Two rings later, Poe answered. "I was wondering when you were going to call."

"How up to speed are you?"

"You've killed two Marrow and lost three people including an English Lord."

"Yep," she said. A squirrel was pestering the shit out of a blackbird. "You're pretty much up to date. I was wondering if you've had any action on that side of Maeve's hole in the world."

"A few have bled through. Your friend Sergeant MacKenzie calls them Knockers. Little ugly things is what they are."

"We call him Munro. MacKenzie, I mean."

"What the hell is a Munro?"

"It's what they call mountain tops in Scotland."

"You operators have weird call signs," Poe said.

"Said the world's oldest lieutenant."

"I hear he isn't doing well."

There was a pause, followed by, "He's infected with something we don't understand."

"Is it affecting his operations?"

"Not so far. But the Indians have been talking to him. Touching him. Your friend Francis Scott Key has been working with him."

"Then I take it he's not contagious."

"He doesn't seem to be."

"What is it you are doing over there?"

"Right now, just trying to keep these unseelie from coming through. It's pretty barren in this part of South Dakota, but if they are able to get a foothold..."

"So, true. And they live underground, so I'd be on the lookout for them going to caves. As I understand it, once they've been to a place, they can just appear there."

"Just appear?" Poe asked.

"Sure, like Scotty beaming them somewhere."

"Noted." Then he paused. "Seriously, May. Are you doing okay? I remember your last team and what happened. Seems like the same thing might be happening."

"What's that? People dying around me?" She laughed softly and watched as a child ran after a soccer ball. "I'm a regular Typhoid Mary."

"Do you believe that?"

"Not really. The others were in the wrong place, wrong time. They weren't prepared."

"And you are?"

"I think so. Are you on the reservation?"

"I am. Some place called No Flesh Road."

"He was a famous warrior. Went to Washington, D.C. He became a scout."

"I thought it was a condition. I didn't know it was a person."

She noted a pair of cops coming her way. They must have spied her body armor and wanted to know what was up. Jagger intercepted them and began to speak. He pulled out his wallet and showed them something. Probably a badge of some sort.

"Have you talked with Norris about the veil and his topological models?" she asked.

The police kept pointing at her and Jagger began arguing fiercely enough so that his head jerked as he enunciated each word.

"You mean Dr. Fields? Yes. He heard from Munro your topological thesis and the Pictish symbol and thinks there's something to it. He believes that all seelie and unseelie have the ability to accomplish this."

"So, the big time Doctor believes the MA in Religious Studies. Boom."

"Must you be so petty?"

"Can't I just enjoy being right?"

Poe sighed, but didn't answer.

"But it's Maeve who can create the veil to keep the others out—to a degree," she continued.

"That's what he thinks as well."

Jagger made an exaggerated act of making a phone call and pointed to it with a finger.

The police glanced at each other, then shook their heads.

"Listen, I need to go," she said. "I'll probably be seeing you soon."

"You going into Grave Hill?" Poe asked.

"I'm going to try. I'm on a detour though."

"Need to talk about it?"

"Not really."

"Then be safe."

She wished him the same and hung up.

Poe and Special Unit 77 had their own issues to deal with. The last thing he needed was for a flood of Fae to come his way. Not that they'd find much at the Pine Ridge Reservation. One of the reasons the U.S. government settled the Indians there was because it didn't have many resources. The fact that there were Knockers was worrisome however. As far as she knew, Grave Hill was only inhabited by seelie. The presences of unseelie meant that there was a hole somewhere in the veil.

She approached Jagger, who had finished speaking to the bobbies who had grudgingly turned away.

"What did they want?"

"Just the usual. Why there was an American woman with body armor and a 9mm standing under a tree and talking on a mobile. That sort of thing."

She glanced down. "Oh shit." She'd forgotten she had a chest holster with her 9mm. She removed it, holster and all, and placed it in a cargo pocket. "Wait. How did they know I was American?"

"Your clothes. No one dresses like you do in England. Plus, it's your swagger."

"I have swagger?"

He nodded. "You have swagger."

They began walking again.

"I never knew." She couldn't help but grin. She liked the idea of swaggering.

They entered under the portcullis and Jagger paid their entry fee. Inside, it was as if a street fair was occurring. Performers sang and danced, while earnest shopkeepers sold wares designed to symbolize what would have been the height of fashion half a millennium ago.

"Oi! Oi!" said a woman. "You need to be wearing one of my dresses, darlin'. Make your mate happy."

Preacher's Daughter offered the woman a dangerous smile and continued on.

"I need to make my mate happy. Bollocks," she said. "Where did this place come from?"

"Warwick Castle. Built as a wooden fort in 1098 by William the Conqueror, it was rebuilt in stone two hundred years later. It is the oldest continually running castle in England. It is the archetype of 14th Century military architecture and the style of castle most seen in your American Hollywood movies."

"Another one of England's treasures," she said.

"What?" Jagger gave her a look. "Of course, it is. What of it?"

She smiled wanly. "Of course."

"You don't sound as if you agree," he said.

"Not my place. Plus, it's a long story." She glanced around at the mad activity. "Where to now?"

"See that door over there?" he nodded.

"The steel one?"

"Yes. Head there."

They almost made it to the door before two men appeared as if from nowhere, each in full black battle rattle, serious looks on their faces. One was white, one was black, and both looked as if they had jaws carved from granite.

"Piss off," said the white guy.

She raised an eyebrow and thought of a lot of things she could say. Instead of giving back to him, she merely said, "I have a password."

"Odd time to be using it. Can't you come back after closing?" the black one said.

"No time. We need to use it now." She glanced around and seeing no one, said, "Oscar Five Seven Nine Three Bravo Sierra Foxtrot."

The guard who had told them to piss off, opened a tablet, keyed it up, and dialed up the one time use code. He asked her to repeat it. She did. He showed the result to his partner. Both of the men gave her a surprised look, then they stepped aside.

One of them removed a remote control from his body armor and depressed a button.

The steel door snicked opened.

Jagger shrugged. "I guess we're doing this."

She stood staring into the darkness of the doorway.

"Have you ever seen him?"

Jagger shook his head slowly. "Never. I can't even tell you what he's like. He's been redacted from the records and any information about him is beyond my classification."

"He's a regular boogeyman," she said.

"I don't think there's anything regular about him."

'Fair point."

She entered first, noting that there was no light for the first five meters. When she turned back to check behind her, the entrance which was a brilliant square behind her closed with what felt like a permanent snap. A series of rectangular lights came on above her as she walked, revealing a long industrial hall one might find in a NYC high rise but not a thousand-year-old castle. She led, feeling comforted by the sound of Jagger's steps behind her. She didn't know what the Green Man was going to be like. He was either going to be a Shardik or a Baba Yaga. She secretly feared he might be both.

The hallway ran for ten meters, then hit a set of basalt stairs that looked as if they'd been made when the earth was still cooling. She took them one at a time, pulling her 9mm from her cargo pocket and replacing it in the chest holster—not that she believed that a bullet would affect the head of the King of all Seelie, but it felt better to have it than to not have it. Then again, it was iron-tipped, so there was that.

The walls were likewise rough, seemingly dug out of the earth. Her overactive mind thought some of what she saw might be claw marks, but she knew they'd been made with trowels and lathes that had been forged before the United States was even a thought. She descended the granite steps and entered a darkness lit by solitary lights. She continued by idea of the way rather than any direction. Empty cells with thick bars stood at corners of other passages, but she could detect a particular scent that seemed to be her destination. There, in the bowels of a thousand-year-old stone castle was the aroma of trees and old soil and freshly cut grass. It could only come from one place and after walking for a few minutes, she finally turned the corner and saw a man-shaped figure standing inside of a large pot, behind a weaving of bars that left little space through which to see. A single pinpoint of light shone on its face, just enough to illuminate it like a laser pointer might at a briefing.

He was truly the Green Man. His hair stood straight like roots from a tree seeking water. His face was contoured like the skin of a birch tree, white with pieces that would just as soon fall off as to stay. If she had to use pop culture references, she'd reckon he was a mix of a giant-sized Groot from *Guardians of the Galaxy* and DC's Swamp Thing. But in his presence, she felt a majesty that she would never feel with those cartoon-spawned creations. Something special and with gravitas surrounded him, even as he stared at her with two maleficent eyes.

"You are too late," he said, his words both regal and sickening to hear.

"I can't be too late. Maeve is still alive."

"Maeve," he said, love and hatred consorting with the vowels. "I have felt her movements."

"Have you also felt the Marrow?" she asked. "Have you felt what they have done to the dryads?"

"Euthanasia."

"Are you saying it was assisted suicide? That the dryads wanted it? I was there. I saw them. I heard their screams. I felt their deaths."

"And did you feel the longing for nothing?"

"I felt no such thing," she spat. "I felt the inequity of their lives and the need to remain alive."

"Inequity. Appropriate. Not enough of the world knows the service they provide."

All the while he spoke, his movements were fluid. Not fast. Not slow. Just the result of a mystical breeze only he seemed to be able to feel.

"They were murdered. They were chopped down like trees."

He turned to her and his green eyes beheld her. "What would you have me do?"

"What would you do if you were free?"

"Free? There is no such thing."

"Of course, there is. We could walk out of here right now."

"They would stop me."

"Not this time."

He looked at her—really looked at her—appraising her. "You don't look like much," he eventually said.

She thrust out a hip. "I could say the same about you. I'd been hearing tales of the Green Man and now that I see you, I wonder how much is exaggeration. To me you're just a runtish tree ent."

"The memories of man tend to make things more fascinating than they ever were," he said. "Some things were as they always were despite the fascination of a subspecies."

"We need your help," Jagger said, speaking up for the first time.

"Your consort speaks," the Green Man said.

"I'm no one's—"

"Many things have changed. When was the last time you had company?" she asked.

"The one called Victoria. She was much like you. Older. But sure of herself. And of course, her consort, just as you have."

"Munshi," Jagger said with a grin. "He's talking about Munshi."

"That's it," said the Green Man.

"What is a *munshi?*" Preacher's Daughter asked.

"A clerk. A man servant. A confidant. He was Queen Victoria's man for her last dozen years. He was South Asian like me."

"He seemed much more than a clerk," said the Green Man.

"You haven't had a visitor in over a hundred years?" Preacher's Daughter asked.

"I don't need visitors."

She stared at him a moment. "What would you do for sunshine?"

His head snapped around. "I've given up all hope for such a thing." He glanced ceilingward until the pinprick pierced the space between his eyes. "They left me this as a mad joke."

"Then I am not too late. You haven't given up."

"There's no one to give up to," he said. "I also cannot die, even though I can suffer." He glanced down at one leg which was withered and brown.

"Then you shall be free once more."

"What's the trick?" he said.

"There is no trick. We just need to keep the Formori from landing."

His eyes narrowed, the green pupils spun to yellow. "Formori, you say? They are back?"

"They are trying to get back. They have sent creatures called Marrow to kill the dryads. Once they kill the dryads they will kill the seelie. Once the seelie are gone, they will destroy humanity."

He blinked as if thinking and nodded his head. "I'm beginning to understand the words now. The Marrow. My sisters. The Formori."

"We need you to save Britain," she said.

"Britain has never been mine for saving," he said.

"How about this? Let's go save your dryads and if Britain is a reluctant recipient of your patronage, then so be it."

He was silent for a full minute, glancing around at

his cell, moss on the walls, moisture in the air, a single pinprick of light. Then he nodded.

"I might need some help getting out of here," he said, staring at the dirt that surrounded his feet.

CHAPTER 32

THEY LEFT BY a different door that deposited them outside the castle near the water. Probably the old bolt hole for when the castle was overrun and the royals had to escape. There was no indication from the outside a door even existed. Where the Green Man strode the grass grew like mad, leaving a trail of opulent growth behind him. Seeing it rise was like viewing time-stopped footage. Still, he limped, however, one leg black and withered. He walked straight for the water; a narrow slip of confluence too large to be a creek but with not enough energy to be a river where Preacher's Daughter came from.

"Oi!" came a masculine voice. "What are you three on about?"

"They's cosplaying. Look at Swamp Thing. Not a bad outfit."

She turned and spied four young men dressed in sports shirts—light blue Coventry United shirts that were too large for them. They all wore jeans that were too loose and sagging down their butts like they lived in Compton. They all wore clearly faked Air Jordans.

Jagger grabbed her shoulder and said, "They're wannabe hooligans. Football thugs. Leave them be. I'll handle them." Then in a louder voice, he addressed the four. "Leave off. This is official business."

"With Swamp Thing? I fucking doubt that," one said.

One was black, the other three were white with red hair and freckles.

"I want that costume," said one of the red-haired kids.

She figured they were twenty if a day. Preacher's Daughter rolled her eyes at the audacity of four adolescents to attack a soldier with a pistol, a freakishly tall south Asian, and a monster. So, instead of engaging with them, she sought to ignore them.

The Green Man stood in the middle of the water and she watched as the water swirled around him in a vortex. His ruined leg was now as green as the rest of him. Birds and insects were drawn toward him, some landing on him. The sound of their whistles was mesmerizing and delightful at the same time.

Everyone was watching in awe for a moment.

"How does he do that with the birds?" the black hooligan asked.

"He probably glues feed to his dress. Like your mum does with a pork chop around her neck so your dog will lick her."

She heard shoving but promised herself she wasn't going to get involved.

"I said this was official business. If you don't want to be disappeared by the Home Office, I'd advise you to—"

She heard the hit and knew immediately what happened. So, when she spun around and saw Jagger falling stiff-legged to the ground, she knew that he'd been cold cocked.

Two of the ruffians drew knives and so she drew her pistol, shaking her head as the old adage *don't bring a knife to a gunfight* rattled through her head. Who did these punks think they were and why were they intent on messing with them when the fate of Great Britain relied on their ability to reconstitute the Green Man and get him back on track? Was there madness in the air? Did the mere presence of the Marrow inculcate a certain evil— promote it—invite it to come forth? She remembered the homunculus and the other creatures in Europe and Asia that Poe had reported as swarming. There was definitely something wrong with the Force.

She pointed her pistol at the ground between two of the redheads and said, "You all need to get the hell out of here."

"She's American," one said to the other. "I told you she was."

"What does that have to do with my ability to kick your ass?" she asked.

One of the thugs with a knife kneeled and put his knife to the side of Jagger's neck. "Drop your pistol or he gets it."

Her trigger finger itched like mad and wanted nothing more than to be released, but she held back. She removed the magazine from the pistol and popped the round out of the chamber. She threw all three in different places. She didn't really feel like she needed the pistol as a weapon, but she was beginning to appreciate the distraction from the Fae these young men were making. The irony was that she was trying to protect all the people in England. Even these thugs. But they'd never understand. They were too concerned about the now.

Still, she had to try and play nice.

"Why don't you fine boys go find yourself somewhere to go." She left off *so you won't get hurt* because she didn't want to egg them on. She really just wanted them to go away, but it seemed as if they were spoiling for a fight.

"There she goes. That's more like it."

"I've never done it with an American woman before," one of the redheads said.

"You've never done it with a woman," another redhead said.

They pushed each other for a moment, cursing and verbally sparring, then moved towards her.

The knifeman removed his weapon from the neck of the unconscious Jagger and she soon found herself surrounded. The thing about martial arts movies was that people who have never fought don't realize that most fights happen that way. Not the all-out brawls where snot slings, curses are hurled and people lose all composure. No. But when you have someone who knows how to fight and how to manipulate others to fight, it's a different thing altogether. The group dynamic of wanting to win against all costs goes out the window and instead it becomes displays of personal expertise—one's own martial prowess—or a demonstration of an inconvenient lack thereof.

Had she presented herself as helpless, they would have gang tackled her and she'd have little chance at success. But she portrayed herself as a professional and looked the part and each of the boys harbored dreams of undoing her—and in the end it would be their undoing. Plus, she was a woman and what twenty-year-old hooligan believed that she couldn't be taken? So, she stood with her legs shoulder-width apart, her arms loose, and channeled her very best Bruce Lee—she especially liked the group fight towards the end of *Fists of Fury* where he hadn't fought for the entire movie, and then the necklace that represents his promise to his sister to never fight again is ripped away.

She imagined herself in the ice factory, surrounded by dozens of knife-wielding thugs. Then she let the deaths of all of her friends flow into her, from Criminal, to Narco, to McQueen, blessed McQueen, and Nottingham, McDonnell, and even Windsor-Sykes. All of them died for a purpose, their deaths never in vain but at the very least used as a motivation to live.

She was attacked from the left and let the weight of the man-boy propel him into the man across from him, his arm wrenched from his shoulder for his efforts. He and the other boy disentangled themselves while the black kid attacked, kicking and punching like he knew Tae

Kwon Do. The problem with that art was that there was little in the way of defense. She blocked, then grabbed an arm and snapped it at the elbow.

She spun to the last hooligan standing, who ran towards her with knife raised. She almost yawned as she fell to the ground, scissored his feet with her own, then launched herself on top of him, giving him a throat punch that would leave him hoarse for weeks. She grabbed the knife and tossed it into the water.

Still, he'd been able to slice her forearm.

She'd been too confident and the incandescent pain from the slice almost to the bone reminded her that she wasn't immortal.

She rolled to her feet and glanced to where the other two had been, left hand on the wound to staunch the flow of blood, but the Green Man had pummeled each of them to the ground, his arms now like tentacles, elongated and slamming them until their faces were unimaginable and their heads were dashed into the shapes of squashed gourds.

"Stop!" she cried. "They're just bullies."

"They attacked. I attack back."

The boys had never stood a chance. They'd not only faced her, but the indomitable judgement of a godlike being whose idea of right and wrong was binary.

She approached the black kid who tried to skitter away from her.

"If you don't let me help you, he's going to kill you."

His face was drawn and grave both from pain and

from the stunning violence of it all. "I thought it was a game," he said.

"Don't you all." She helped him to his feet, careful to not touch his detached elbow. "Go, now. Run."

He began to and then an arm reached out from the water and grabbed him. He glanced back at her as if he wanted to say something, then he was yanked into the air, only to be slammed down into the water next to the Green Man. He held the kid there, staring at Preacher's Daughter, as alien a creature as she had ever seen or met.

Fuck.

Even the daeva had common concerns.

But the Green Man was solitary.

He suddenly went under, straight down, and never came up.

She fell to the ground, staring at the spot he'd just been. Two thoughts crossed her mind at the same time.

Where had he gone?

What had she done?

CHAPTER 33

She ran to Jagger and helped him to his feet. A golf-ball sized bulge had grown on the right side of his head. His right eye was already starting to blacken. He wobbled a bit. She found it hard to hold him up. Right beside him, she'd forgotten how tall he was. Drool dribbled out of the corner of his mouth and blood bubbled from his nose. She glanced around and saw the remaining thug, grabbing his throat coughing and gagging, trying to breathe.

She balanced Jagger, prayed he wouldn't fall, then went to the thug.

"Stay down," she said, "Or you'll be next."

She ripped his shirt and came away with a length of the light blue material. She wrapped her own wound, cleaning it before she covered it. Then she ripped free another length. She returned to the tall man just as he was about to topple. She wiped Jagger's face, careful around his nose and mouth. "Gotta watch your six, my friend."

"I was too busy watching yours," he coughed, smiling grimly.

"Well, that'll teach you."

Shrill whistles sounded out from the direction of the castle's entrance, followed by another, then another.

"Looks like we've been found out," she said after a glance and seeing the two bobbies running ungainly towards them across the wide expanse of grass. "Can you walk?"

He nodded and grabbed the cloth from her hands.

She looked around and found her pistol and the mag she'd ejected. She didn't bother looking for the round. She inserted the mag, and shoved the pistol back inside her holster.

"What happened to the others?" Jagger asked, looking at the gasping thug. "I thought there were four."

She shrugged. "Took a trip with the Green Man, I guess."

She searched for an avenue of escape. They had a choice. Run away from the bobbies, find a way to scale the castle walls and fail like so many armies before, or take a pleasant dip in the River Avon.

"Can you swim, JigJat Chatterjee?"

He stared at the water and stuttered, "I'm—I'm in the Navy. Of course, I can swim." Then he added a meek, "Mostly."

"Then come with me if you want to live," she cried, and took a running jump into the river. She gasped at the temperature and then sunk like a rock. She kicked her way back to the surface, fighting to stay afloat with her body armor. The water numbed her wound and she hoped it would slow the blood flow.

She watched as Jagger hesitated, then he took big ambling giraffe-legged gaits and jumped awkwardly into the water. He landed on his back and the air left him. She grabbed his collar, partially to help him, but also to use him as a floatation device. As soon as she grabbed him, she felt the ease on her legs and no longer had to kick like she was sprinting. She lay on her back and kicked towards the middle of the Avon. He kicked as well. Soon, they were in the current being swept downstream.

Behind her the bobbies ran to the river's edge and glared at them. Had this been America, they would have been armed and maybe shot them in the water. Thankfully, England had a more practical approach to subduing criminals and it was to their favor. They floated for ten minutes and gradually kicked themselves to the far shore.

They interrupted a fly fisherman who was in the middle of a cast. His look of surprise turned into anger as they pulled themselves out of the water near enough to him to spook any chance of him catching fish for the next hour. He wore at least five hundred pounds' worth of gear and his pole looked like it cost twice that much.

Dripping wet and exhausted, but feeling clean for the first time in a long time, she helped Jagger out of the river.

She turned to the fisherman and asked, "Is this the mermaid crossing?"

He gave her a baleful look and spouted something in a dialect she couldn't fathom.

She laughed, then she and Jagger sloshed up the bank and onto the grass.

She heard cursing from behind and the sound of a man throwing down a thousand-pound fishing pole in a tantrum of spite and anger.

It appeared that they'd come out near some cabins that looked as if they belonged to the castle. Five of them. She checked and saw that two were unoccupied. She elbowed open the glass on the window of one with a subdued crash, reached in, and opened the door.

Jagger went in first, shivering uncontrollably, arms wrapped around himself, body quivering.

She glanced around, then went in next, locking the door behind her, wedging a chair under the doorknob. She checked her phone which had been turned into a water-logged brick. So much for waterproof. She removed the battery, then tossed it into the fireplace, and turned on the gas which activated it with a click. Fire whooshed to life and she watched with satisfaction as the plastic began to melt.

The inside was meant to look like a room from a castle. The ceiling was made from wooden beams with white lathing in between. The walls were stone and wood. The floor was slate with thick pieces of carpet scattered here and there. The furniture in the living room was so blocky it seemed as if the building must have been built around it. Everything smelled like a cocktail of old wood and modern cleanser.

She turned to Jagger who stood in the middle of the room shivering.

"Don't just stand there, take off your clothes."

She began to do the same. First her body armor, which she threw on the couch and then her T-shirt.

Seeing that Jagger hadn't moved, she said, "Listen my gay friend. I'm not going to jump your bones. We're clearly not each other's types. But if you want privacy, then go into one of the bedrooms.

He glanced behind him, nodded, and did as he was told, timidly closing the door behind him.

She ripped off her bra, then concentrated on untying wet shoe laces so she could pull off her boots. She'd removed one, then was halfway through figuring out the knot on the other, when she was interrupted.

"She looks more and more like Sheena Easton," came a recognizable voice. "Do you see all that skin?"

"Naw, Tubbs. She's too skinny."

She glanced up and saw her two personal *Miami Vice* bogies staring at her. They leaned against the chair blocking the front door. Tubbs wore a pink jacket. Crockett wore a blue jacket over his singed fur. Where they'd gotten them, she had no idea. Wherever it was, they were certainly trying to live their *Miami Vice* fantasies.

"You two getting an eye full?" she asked. "And where the hell have you been?"

She pulled off both boots, her socks, and her pants, but came short of removing her underwear for no particular reason other than the four alien eyes ogling her. She laid her garments out next to the fire, then went over and knocked on the bedroom door.

"Give me your clothes."

The door opened slightly, then a handful of garments came out. She grabbed these and laid them out as well. They really needed to move on, but they had two problems. One, they couldn't do it soaking wet or they'd catch pneumonia and two, they had no clue where the Green Man had gotten to.

In the kitchenette she found a coffee maker. After a moment, she had some brewing. She didn't know how long they had before the authorities found them. She guessed not long, once they met up with the fisherman. She shouldn't have said anything, but that couldn't be helped. Once the coffee was brewed, she poured a cup and knocked on the door again. It opened slightly and she passed it through.

"Take a hot shower, then wrap yourself up in something and come out here when you are done."

She poured herself a cup, found a stool, placed it as close to the fire as she could, and sat on it. She examined the cut on her arm. It wasn't as bad as she'd thought it was. In fact, oddly, it had almost healed. So strange. She alternated between sipping the hot beverage and wringing water from her hair. Finally, when she'd gathered her thoughts, she addressed the two bogies. The only way she could speak to them was in terms of *Miami Vice*. She vaguely remembered that Edward James Olmos played their boss, but it took a few moments for her to remember what his character's name was on the show. She'd never put *Miami Vice* up on her top 100 and had only seen maybe a dozen of the shows, usually when laying on the couch and too hungover to reach for the remote to change the channel. She would freely admit that Don Johnson and Philip Michael Thomas weren't hard to look at, but she also reminded herself that the show as at least forty years old.

Sitting on the stool, she was aware that she was almost completely naked. Elbows on her knees, breasts dangling precipitously, she gave them both a look.

"Okay, boys. Pretend I'm Lieutenant Castillo and you've been undercover."

They each perked up.

"I want you to brief me on your comings and goings. I want to know who you talked to. I also want to know what you found out. And finally, I want to know how you knew where I was."

They began talking at once, using both the guttural language of the unseelie and their own accented English. She let that go on for about thirty seconds, then held up a hand.

"One at a time."

They both began to answer at the same time again.

She sighed.

Jagger peeked his head out the door. When he saw that she was near naked, his eyes widened.

She waved him over. "Come on. Join the party."

"I can't possibly. Not with your—your—"

"My what? My breasts?" She rolled her eyes. "Fine then. Throw me something."

His head disappeared a moment, then reappeared as he entered the room, averting his eyes, arm holding a sheet outstretched.

She took the sheet, and made a toga out of it, tying it off near one shoulder. "Is this better?"

He glanced at her apprehensively, then full on. He sighed. "So much better."

"Find a seat, Jagger. Now, that the world is no longer hanging in the balance of my breasts, we can move on." She pointed. "You, Tubbs. Answer."

The bogie straightened and actually looked proud at being chosen. "We went everywhere. We spoke with other bogies. We spoke with Knockers. They've been promised... free rein... is that how you say it?"

Preacher's Daughter nodded.

"They were told when the Formori arrive that the humans would be slaughtered in the streets and in their caves and in their trees. If they would help do this, then they could do as they wished. Like the times before the times when humans were not here and this was merely a land for the Fae."

Streets and caves and trees. She surmised that translated to in the open and in the homes and in the high-rises. "What of the Marrow?"

"Two are gone. One is wounded. One is trying to breach the veil."

"Where is the fifth?" she asked.

"Creeper. He's creeping."

She felt a shiver coming through the toga.

"You, Crockett."

The bogie stood forth.

"Where's the fifth Marrow?"

Crockett lifted his head, "Creeping, like Tubbs said, Lieutenant. We're not sure. It's creeping for sure. Could be anywhere. Could be outside right now and we'd never know."

Jagger jerked his head to the window as if he could see an invisible creature.

"Who did you speak with to discover this information?"

"Bogies and Knockers. We speak with banshee too." He shivered. "Revered banshee. Ruler of the air and scourge of man. The banshee know the skies and know the birds. Birds tell them about Marrow. Birds see everything."

So, the banshee had a tie to the birds. Preacher's Daughter had always wondered if the birds weren't the best natural surveillance method, if only they could find a way to harness them as a resource. They wouldn't have to rely on cutting edge electronics or electricity.

"What's to fear of the banshee?" she asked. "I didn't think Crockett and Tubbs were afraid of anything."

"Crockett. Tubbs. We no afraid. We live forever. We *Miami Vice* bogie. But banshee take our breaths and keep. Not give back. Banshee end life. Never give life."

That there was a specific type of unseelie that terrified another unseelie was something she hadn't considered. Of course, like any community, there were those who were worse—those on the fringes that no one wanted to be a part of. She'd never seen a banshee in person, but she'd certainly seen them in popular fiction and they seemed like something that shouldn't be trifled with.

Tubbs added, "Missing children are taken by the wind."

"The banshee take children?" She glanced at Jagger whose eyes were wide. "What is it they do with them?"

"What does the wind do to the ground? What does the bird do to the seed? What does the fox do with the bird? What does the hunter dog do with the fox? What does man do with his dog?"

She could think of a dozen answers and all of them made her vaguely ill. As much as she wanted to chase this information down this particular rabbit hole, she knew she needed to concentrate on the problem at hand. Two members of the Black Dragoons had perished, as well as a lord had gone missing. Dryads had been destroyed. The remaining seelie, at least those who weren't being used as shock troops, were hidden behind a veil and possibly hiding in South Dakota. And they'd lost track of the solitary being who might be able to put a stop to the entire situation.

"Both of you. We care about the banshee, but that's for another time. For now, who is leading the unseelie."

Tubbs turned to Crockett. "She asks the question."

Crockett nodded. "She asks it and we must answer."

"But she will find us."

"Who will find you?" she asked. This entire conversation had taken a turn for the crazy. "What is her name?"

"We don't know her name," Tubbs said. "We know her as The Shrews."

"What is The Shrews?" she asked.

"She takes what sinks and remakes it. The bog is her mouth and she chews bad things to life."

Chews bad things to life. Sounds like a television advertisement mnemonic for the world's worst children's present. This Shrews sounded like a witch of sorts. There'd been a moment in her life when Preacher's Daughter would have said witches weren't real. But that was before she carved and wrote arcane sigils over her body, wrapped herself in tinfoil and plastic, and slammed herself around the inside of her trailer. She knew witches existed, but thought them to have more of a *locus magicus* surrounding them. For one to have a reach throughout a country meant she was very powerful indeed.

"Does this witch have a name?"

"We dare not say it," Tubbs said, shivering.

"Crockett?" she asked, expectantly.

The bogie shook his head. "To say her name makes her get you. Her mouth is the world and her stomach is hell. I do not want this." He took a step towards her. Jagger jolted like he was going to intercept, but she held up a hand. "I do not want you to do this. Marrow and banshee are not Shrews. They're different like the sky is different from the ground—like the water is different from blood."

"Where is she?"

"The bog. She minds the bog near Mercia or Cun."

"What is it she is doing?" she asked.

"Organizing. She organizes for the unseelie," Crockett said. "She tells us where to be and what to be."

"She also makes us—something like us but not unseelie," Tubbs added.

"She makes you?"

"Terrible things from pieces of other things. Not pure like Fae. This is unFae."

Preacher's Daughter was beginning to understand. They definitely had a new target.

"I could work with a team of soldiers from the regiment," Jagger offered. "We could go and investigate."

She remembered what had happened to Delta and Norris when she'd been in charge of their last mission. She'd split them off then and now one was dead and the other was mutilated for life. There was no way she was going to make the same mistake twice. If her urge was right and this Shrews was indeed a homunculus factory, then they could try to send in some conventional forces. Even if they couldn't remove her from the board, they could slow her down. Meanwhile, where were her creations going and how were they to be used?

"How can her creations move so fast?"

"The unseelie. We can move things with us. We can take you with us."

That was more like it. As much as she wanted to get a few rounds into this witch, her number one concern right now was the Green Man.

CHAPTER 34

THEY ARRIVED AMIDST the cacophony of a battle of incredible size. Like days of old, two forces were arrayed across a field, clashing in the center. Bodies lay in varying states of destruction, sometimes in piles, and sometimes in singles. Arms, legs, hands and even feet were being used as bludgeons by both sides as their spears and knives were either broken or lost inside the gullet of an enemy. The field had once been green, but now ran red, colorful because of the variances of the uniforms of the dead. Preacher's Daughter had been in her share of firefights and knew the sounds of screaming and firing whether it be one of the big guns or an individual weapon. The bucking of the weapons of warcraft and the sucking of the foul air into lungs created a heady rave that had many invitations but few survivors. But this was altogether different. No big guns belched and no machine guns whirred. Not a single explosion lit the field, except when groups of five of more ran together at full force. So, when they materialized behind seelie lines on the side of a heather-combed hill, it was to these screams she was welcomed—but more than a hundred times those of individual firefights.

Back in the cabin, they'd dressed hurriedly once the bogies had let them know they could transport them to the location of the Green Man. They weren't expecting a battle—then again, she didn't know what she was expecting. For all she knew he could have been planting himself for sustenance so he could heal beneath a broad blue sky. Instead the Green Man was leading a battalion of gnomes, while in the air, sylphs rained down deadly volleys of iron-tipped arrows, against an onslaught of bogies and Knockers.

If any unseelie got too near, the Green Man would snatch it from the earth and hurl it back a hundred feet where it was sure to strike one of those still waiting to attack. The Green Man's arms were mantis-quick and never seemed to miss a target. In fact, the being seemed to relish the action after so many decades or perhaps centuries of inaction.

Preacher's Daughter seriously doubted that The Shrews and the other Marrow had planned on the Green Man getting in their way on their assault of the veil. But here they were, organized and amplified by the Green Man; his sentence commuted because of the diplomacy of the Centaur.

"Crockett, tell me what's happening," she said, drawing her pistol, and two-handing it at the low ready.

"The unseelie want the Fae to remain outside of England. Those who have left, they are not to return."

"To do that," Tubbs said, "they must kill Maeve. She is the transit. She is the train."

Along the far side of the battlefield, a wedge of Knockers led by some unknown large unseelie with too large of a head plowed into two lines of gnomes. The red hats went flying amid screams and a blood rain.

"What the hell is that?" Jagger asked.

"Goblin," Tubbs murmured as he crinkled his nose. "Never good to see one. Or smell one."

"Like it slept in its own piss and showered in its own shit," Crockett said, wiping away something that wasn't there on his baby blue jacket.

Preacher's Daughter suddenly erupted into laughter. She tried to stop it, but was unable. Her entire visage was hijacked by hilarity. And to think that she'd been naively juvenile enough to believe that the Fae were the result of some millennia of hyperstition and not really there at all. She'd been so completely wrong. The Fae were real. They always had been. They were creatures of the land and air and did not require humans to be alive.

Jagger leaned over and whispered, "Laurie. Are you alright?"

She patted him on the shoulder as the Goblin took another swipe and killed three more red hats. "They asked me to come because of my expertise. They said understanding the doorway effect would help. They said knowing hyperstition would help. They even talked about topological modeling, like the space time continuum meant anything to a mythological creature older than most countries. Not a one of them sat back and asked, 'What it if it's just fucking magic?' you know. Not a single one of them. They didn't think to ask themselves if maybe all of the myths and legends in the Old Country were actually true instead of fodder for a whole host of rather bad made for streaming movies. Next thing you know we'll be fighting Krampus."

"They live on the continent," Tubbs said.

"Laurie, get a hold of yourself."

"Jagger, if I were to hold myself any tighter my head would pop off."

"Then why are you laughing?"

The Goblin noticed them on their perch on the side of the hill, and changed direction, heading for them. Its monstrous features were contorted in both anger and hunger as it galloped on all fours towards them like a giant male gorilla, knuckles pounding the ground, splitting rock. Yellow marbles of eyes, set back in mottled gray skin with white bristly hair shooting from the head, regarded her and the beast roared. Muscles where muscles should not have grown bulged in places that should have never been in an unimaginable show of antagonistic might.

Still, Preacher's Daughter stood her ground and wiped her eyes as laughter still sought to send her rolling once more. She remembered what she'd said before and repeated it now, as she pulled out her 9mm, chambered a round, checked the overall status of her pistol, and took a shooter's stance facing the on-rushing Goblin, her voice near screaming and climbing octaves the closer it came as she repeated the words like an insane professor.

"Hyperstition is a portmanteau of hyper and superstition. The term posits that hyper, which is the state of being abnormally or unusually active, and superstition, which is a widely held but unjustified belief, can come together and become an entity unto itself. Nick Land says that hyperstitions by their very existence as ideas function causally to bring about their own reality. In modern times that would be the idea of Atlantis, which is widely believed but lacking in fact. Or the Bermuda Triangle or the Illuminati.

"The idea is that we brought these creatures to life just by thinking about them and to make them go away is to not think about them." She punched Jagger in the shoulder. "Quick, don't think about the white horse!"

"What? How? White horse?"

"Exactly." She squatted and side-stepped.

BLAMBLAMBLAMBLAMBLAMBLAM, catching the charging Goblin in the face with each round, the iron slamming through the skin, skull, and brain, until it collapsed and skidded to a stop beside her, rolling up turf as it died.

Crockett and Tubbs, fought several Knockers in a hand-to-hand, coming up on the winning side in admirable fashion, but concerned about the ever-increasingly desultory condition of their outfits.

Jagger grabbed a spear from where it had fallen and stabbed as best he could, catching one Knocker in the side and then lodging the tip of the spear in the second Knocker's face.

A bogie smacked him with the wooden end of the spear across his back, causing him to go sprawling into the Goblin.

Crockett came up behind the bogie and stabbed it in the side of the head, then slit its throat. "Damn cave dwellers," he said.

Preacher's Daughter ejected the magazine, let it fall to the ground, and slapped a new one home.

Jagger peeled himself from the dead Goblin. "Oh my god. What is that smell?"

"I think that's you, my friend," she said.

Suddenly, the entire battlefield went quiet as all of the Knockers and the bogies, bar Crockett and Tubbs, vanished.

"Where'd they go?" Jagger asked.

"Follow me," she said, breaking into a run towards the Green Man.

Thirty seconds later, she skidded to a stop and said, "You could have waited for us, you know."

He looked at her as if she were a bug, but left her alone.

"Jagger. Back-to-back," she cried.

"Where'd they go?" he asked.

"What do you think happens when you fight transdimensional creatures? Think they're just going to stand and take it when they are losing?"

"What are you talking about?"

Several hundred Redhats milled around chatting, pointing, even picking up the weapons of their enemies. Many of them chuckled. Several high-fived. It was like watching a garden gnome party in Martha Stewart's garden with inappropriate carnage.

She laughed madly. "They were right. I was the right person to be here. There is topology involved and I know their strategy. Hey, Greenie. They're coming back. Be ready."

The Green Man turned to her.

She snapped her fingers. "Beam me up, Scotty. Don't you get it, you Chia-Fae. They can appear and reappear. Oh, for fuck's sake, will one of you *Miami Vice* bogies explain it to him."

Both the bogies began talking at once. They babbled over each other's sentences for about twenty seconds, when they were swept off the hilltop by a tentacled arm.

The Green Man shouted something unintelligible.

The Redhats halted where they were milling about. Several scratched their heads. Others looked around.

The Green Man shouted again.

As one, the Redhats ran towards him. Soon, they'd formed concentric circles with spears out, prepared for whatever was about to transpire.

"I need more ammunition. I'm completely out," Jagger said.

"Why do you want to bring a gun to a knife fight?" she asked. "Enjoy yourself. We're all going to die anyway."

He turned to her. "Wait. What?"

Then the Knockers and bogies reappeared as one great beast, screaming, ready to throw down and surprise their Redhat brethren. But to their dismay, the seelie were prepared. What had been screams of barbaric joy collapsed all the octaves until it was the low thrum of disappointment, fear, and misrule.

"Hey, Greenie. I think it's time to attack."

Another unintelligible shout later and the Redhats attacked, helped by the Pixies on UAVs who eagerly performed a daring series of coordinated strafing runs.

Twice, Goblins appeared and arrowed towards Preacher's Daughter. Twice, she took them down, the latter with the help of the Green Man as her pistol clicked empty. She shoved the useless iron into her chest holster and grabbed a spear from the ground, stepping on the face of a dead Knocker as she did so. The shaft had been made from bamboo, which accounted for its flexibility and its capacity to fly straight through the air. She knew bamboo to be an invasive species, making it the perfect weapon for an unseelie.

The unseelie made a great coordinated surge on the Green Man's position, but they met an organized phalanx of Redhats and soon fell back. What had seemed a sure thing now appeared to be complete failure. Many of them just turned away, cursing, kicking at the earth. Several got into shoving matches with each other. Within a minute, all of them had winked out and returned whence they came, leaving a battlefield strewn with too many dead and dying. Correct that. Just dead, because a squad of Redhats moved between the ranks of the fallen and ensured none would see the light of day or the dark of their unseelie sun.

CHAPTER 35

EXHILARATION OF THE battle coursed through her veins. This was what she was made for. Not grubbing about some computers in search of esoteric answers to questions they didn't even know they wanted to ask. She needed action. She needed the thrill of combat where reactions replaced actions and her arms knew the maneuvers to deliver the most efficient means of death even before she actively thought about it. Her eyes were wide, mouth slightly open, ready for someone to press 'save game' so she could do it all over again.

Crockett and Tubbs climbed over a series of dead bodies, advancing on her location. Both of them disheveled, their previously pristine jackets untidy and ripped. They clucked at their own state of affairs, while commiserating over their treatment by the Green Man.

"He could have said thank you," Tubbs said.

"He could have shown appreciation," Crockett said.

"But no. He wanted to act like a kingpin."

"If this was the TV show, we'd have a long boat ride with a soundtrack from Glen Frey, then a major battle where we take him down," Crockett mused.

"We'd totally have that," Tubbs agreed.

"Then we'd have a boss fight and take him out."

"He's lucky we're not doing that," Tubbs said.

"What the hell are you two talking about?" Preacher's Daughter asked.

"Our treatment by that one over there. I mean, if it wasn't for Crockett and Tubbs the battle would have been lost."

Suddenly, all the bodies on the battlefield disappeared, leaving a cleaved and trampled expanse of heath. If she hadn't known better, it looked as if someone had used the wide expanse of grass as a pitch and had never cleaned up. Even the blood and offal had disappeared, leaving no evidence of the battle. If you were going to have a mythological Fae, it just wouldn't do to leave their body parts laying all over the place.

"Stop talking about yourself in the third person," she said.

"I think Sheena Easton's mad at us," Tubbs said.

She took a step towards them, was about to say something, then sighed, holding up her right hand and shaking her head. "Don't go anywhere." To the tall South Asian bending over at the waist and out of breath. "Jagger!"

He began to get near and she held out her other hand as a waft of the most terrible aroma she had ever encountered threatened to surround and swallow her. "Don't come any closer. What the hell did you fall into?"

"A dead goblin."

"Another one? Just—just stay over there, will you?"

He stood, pouting, smelling himself and frowning. He was at that stage where he could no longer smell himself, where the stench became part of the person. She wasn't sure if he could be cleaned. Perhaps it would be best to set him on fire and let it burn off, but until then, all she could do was mitigate the results, which meant keeping him as far from her as possible.

"We need to contact Intelligence Officer Crookes. How can we do that?" she asked. She noticed her hands were beginning to shake. Really the result of an adrenaline dump and not fear.

He shrugged. "Both of our phones are waterlogged bricks."

"Crockett, get me a cell phone, ASAP," she commanded.

Crockett nodded, backed up and disappeared. A moment later, he appeared carrying a cell phone. With a sunflower protector and a tasseled chain, it dwarfed his hand. He handed it to her and it was clear he'd taken it mid conversation.

"She'll get back with you in a moment," Preacher's Daughter said, guessing that the phone belonged to a woman of some age. She tossed it to Jagger. "Get us ammunition. Get us out of here."

"Which one do you want?" he asked.

She stared at the Green Man a moment. A shiver ran through her. Was it a premonition or was it adrenaline? Then she said, "Ammunition. I think we are tied to

Greenie for the foreseeable future. Lots of ammunition."

Jagger spoke into the phone for a moment, then covered it with a hand. "They want to know where we are."

No shit, Sherlock. Where were they? She spun around, but everything seemed the same. The same unnatural green. The same grey skies. She literally had no idea where they were. Then she snapped her fingers.

"Tubbs, can you ask a pixie where we are, please?"

Tubbs, who had been sitting on the ground trying to mend his jacket, leaped to his feet, ran a short way, then began to make bird noises. Two pixies flew down and around his head. He continued with his bird noises and had a conversation with the flying Barbie dolls, then they flittered away.

"Makes sense," he said to no one at all. Then he turned to Crockett and began speaking in bogie, evidentially copacetic in his accomplishment of the task. He reached out and touched the other's lapel and they both shook their heads as if commiserating.

"Tubbs!"

"Yes?"

"Where are we?"

"About two miles south of Graves Hill, near Croft Quarry."

"Let's head to the quarry. Crockett, gather everyone." She approached the Green Man who seemed to be standing and staring across what was once a battlefield. "We need to go to a quarry. There's going to be another attack."

His head turned to her, but his body remained immobile.

She could see that his feet had sunk into the loam of the earth. His withered leg was all but healed at this point. "Who will be attacking? I must get to Maeve."

"Easy there, big fella. I really think we should be ready for attack. The quarry would be an easier place to defend. It's just over there," she said, pointing to her right.

He ignored her and headed for the hill next to the quarry which held the high ground as well as a copse of trees. From that vantage point, one could see for miles in any direction. Then it hit her. Of course, the Green Man would eschew the quarry. The hole in the ground was a manmade blight upon the land that would more than likely sap his power instead of refueling it. She followed him and urged the others to do the same.

"Jagger, did you get in contact with the Home Office?"

"They're sending someone to the location of this phone. Location services are on so there's nothing else we can do but wait."

She counted a little over thirty Redhats, and along with her two bogies, Jagger, herself, and the Green Man constituted their ground forces. There were unknown aerial forces—wait. "Jagger, can you contact Barbie and let her know of our situation? Thanks."

She really had two choices. She could abandon the Green Man and she and Jagger could beat feet to the veil and hope to get inside where it was safer. The problem with that plan was that it would leave greater England to attack. Right now, besides those guarding the dryads, hers was the only considerable fighting force. So, what was it she was anticipating? Why was she so sure in her gut that there'd be another attack?

The Shrews.

The moment she'd heard the name, she knew it was going to be trouble. Regular unseelie forces couldn't fight against the veil. It even seemed too much for the Marrow that attacked. So, they needed to create irregular forces— and by create she meant 'create.' Something invented, arcane, necromantic. That could only mean The Shrews creating an army of homunculi, whose presence would even be an abomination to the seelie.

A helicopter buzzed the area once, then twice, then a duffle bag lowered on a safety line. She unclipped it and went right to work getting the bag open as the helicopter flew away. Inside, she found two HK-416 machine guns, along with a suite of 9mm pistols, hand grenades, and magazine after magazine of ammunition. Coms were also inside and she tried this, but she got nothing but static. This told her that the rest of the Dragoons were on the other side of the veil.

"We have an audience," Jagger said.

Several cars had pulled over on the side of the road, their occupants standing beside their vehicles, holding their phones out. She was worried about this. The larger the battle, the greatest chance for them to be discovered. They were bound to be on the news. And then what? Were they fake news? Were they reenactors? Oh, what she'd pay to have some signs advertising the filming of a new movie. Talk about a great cover.

Suddenly, three of the four standing by their cars began to swat at things, moving too quickly for them to see. Then after a moment, they were gesturing angrily to each other.

Preacher's Daughter grinned. If she was to believe what she was thinking, then Barbie had done her job and sent someone to pluck the smart phones right from their hands.

She felt a whir and a titter of laughter by her face, then watched as a pair of Sylphs climbed straight up above the quarry. Once they reached several hundred feet, they let go, the phones clattering to the bottom, snapping into hundreds of pieces as they hit.

But there was something else.

Another sound came from the bottom of the quarry, like the sound of a bell tinkling from far away. Just on the edge of hearing, she was able to recognize it as it became louder and louder. Once again, she was back in the Mines of Moriah. Khazad-dûm, the old Dwarven Kingdom from the First Age gave notice that something was coming, but instead of drums it was the tinkling of bells. First one, then a dozen, then what seemed to be a thousand created a cacophony of sound emanating from the quarry.

Tubbs appeared on one side of her while Crockett appeared on the other and both bogies stared into the quarry depths with her.

"What is that?" she asked.

"It's not natural?" Tubbs asked.

"Are those unseelie down there?" she asked.

"No unseelie. But something else." Crockett straightened. "We should get out of here."

She pointed, "Everyone, to the Green Man."

They ran as fast as they could, tripping over bushes and winding their way around trucks. The quarry was closed for the weekend, so there weren't any workers, which was just as well. If they had been present and working, they would have been run over. If there was one thing Preacher's Daughter didn't want, it was to be caught out in the open by what she knew was coming.

They made it up the hill to stand beside the Green Man just as the first impossibly long arm pulled itself onto level ground. Down below this one, she could imagine hundreds, if not thousands of these creatures surging from the depths of the quarry. How they got there she wouldn't know, but The Shrew ensured that her forces would have access to the veil and this was it. By some miracle of miracles, Preacher's Daughter found them there to act as the tip of the spear.

She glanced around at her forces.

The Redhats.

Crockett and Tubbs—two pain in the ass bogies—but they were her bogies and devoted to her.

Jagger, now in full kit, a machine gun in his hand, steadier now that he had a length of murderous steel in his hands.

And of course, the Green Man. He wasn't used to fighting such abominations. She could only hope that he would react as a master of nature should, by trying to eradicate the unnatural.

"Jagger, watch our six."

He turned and sighted down the rifle, seeking threats.

He could look that way all he needed to, but Preacher's Daughter would bet a paycheck that the threat was all in the quarry. Still, they had to be wary. She didn't know the tactical acumen of The Shrews and she didn't want to find out after the fact that she'd been outwitted.

The creatures began to form at the lip of the quarry facing the veil, which was due north.

She and the Green Man were situated on the high point, due west of the quarry.

They couldn't merely watch it all happen. They had to figure out a way to stop or at least redirect the simple creatures.

She peered through her sighting device on her HK. Sure enough, they were homunculi—or rather golems. But of a sort she'd never seen before. Where the created beings they'd encountered in America came up to one's hip, these simulacrums were almost man-sized, which probably meant that they had a commensurate strength. Her hands were still shaking, but now with anticipation.

"Jagger, are we clear back there?"

"No threats."

"Good. To me then."

He turned, placed the butt of the stock on his hip and asked, "What's the plan?"

"Look at them. They either don't know we exist, or

don't care. They're facing right at the veil as if they're going to rush it."

"Do you think they can get through?" he asked.

"I don't know the nature of her magic, or how strong the veil is. You and I slipped through, but I think that was more luck than anything else. To do the damage they want to do, they have to find a way to rip the veil down, which means getting to Maeve."

"Why are they waiting?"

"Crockett? Tubbs?"

They glanced at each other.

"A Marrow comes," Crockett said.

"And it's coming fast," Tubbs said.

For the first time she noticed that the ground beneath her feet was vibrating. She hadn't been sure how to attribute it, but now she knew. She felt a thrill of fear sear the tips of her nerves. She kept her voice calm by clenching her jaw.

"Jagger, on the count of three, we're laying down grazing fire on those creatures. Three round bursts. Three mags."

She knelt and hurriedly adjusted herself into a prone position. She pulled out two mags, and lay them beside her rifle to ease reloading. She noted that her hands were still shaking almost as imperceptively as the ground.

Jagger did the same beside her.

"Jesus, man. Your stench."

He closed his eyes. "You have no idea how happy that makes a gay man feel."

"On my count, one, two, three, fire."

Three round bursts launched from their bullpup rifles to the waiting hoard on the top lip of the quarry. Every round found a target, knocking some sideways, sending others cascading back down into the hole. But as soon as one fell, another took its place. How long had The Shrews been planning this? How many homunculi did she create and have waiting? Still, their attention wasn't long in coming.

A third homunculus turned from their surveillance of the veil and ran at them, long arms outstretched with claws larger than human hands, spiked teeth capable of ripping and rending, short legs good for sprinting short distances. The problem was the creatures never got tired. They had to be killed or dismembered right away.

Suddenly, the Redhats that had been standing between the oncoming tide and those on the hilltop disappeared.

She cursed as she emptied the third magazine, then stood, pulling a grenade from her pouch.

"Where the hell did they go?"

"Home, if they're smart," Jagger said, getting to his feet and pulling out a grenade.

They each pulled the pin at the same time and heaved.

Both grenades exploded taking a dozen creatures with each blast.

But still they came, an onrushing horde of Shrews-made homunculi. Arms outstretched and ready to rend and rip human skin.

Fuck it. She pulled two more grenades and hurled them

without aiming. Each one took out a dozen creatures, but they still came. And they'd still be coming.

"Jagger?"

"What?"

"Save yourself."

"I'm not leaving you."

She felt a pang of relief. "Then you're stupid." Even if they were to win, it would be nothing more than a pyrrhic victory. She doubted there'd be anyone left to celebrate it. She slapped a fresh magazine home, then brought the rifle up and prepared to fire.

Suddenly, the Redhats returned, but this time behind the homunculi. They immediately began to attack from the rear, shoving iron-tipped spears in so many their shafts were soon breaking, causing them to draw iron-bladed knives.

Meanwhile, Preacher's Daughter and Jagger took their time, popping shots at the voluminous number of heads that were still coming at them.

And it was now that the Green Man unleashed his fury. He spun into the front three rows, grabbing homunculi with his tentacles and raking them against all of those standing, until he had a circle of fallen homunculi. Those who weren't already dead tried to stand, and soon found them joining their partners. Then he did it again, moving like a giant fan blade, the living reaping the simulacrum, leaving lifeless wherever they went.

Within moments, the advancing force of homunculi had been devastated to the point not a single one stood.

Redhats dispatched these one at a time, simple thrusts of their spears through faces and heads.

A sense of elation surged through Preacher's Daughter and she almost high fived Jagger, until she saw that they'd only managed to kill one third of the attacking forces. Ten Redhats were down, as were several Pixies. Half of her ammunition was gone, and she imagined the same was probable for Jagger. Her gaze snapped to the remaining homunculi charging the veil. Then she realized that the trembling of the ground had stopped. In horror, she watched as the Green Man was plucked into the air and it looked as if he were about to be slammed back into the ground.

She ran forward, screaming at the invisible creature to put the Green Man down.

CHAPTER 36

AND IT DID, slamming the supernatural entity of growth and entropy into the ground hard enough to shatter it into a thousand pieces. Preacher's Daughter's jaw dropped at the ease at which the Marrow dispatched an immortal being as old as the land itself.

The invisible creature gave neither of them the time of day and moved to the veil, which was an aurora borealis of impenetrable mist.

Barbie must have seen it happen as well, because it took her several moments to urge her pixies to engage the sparkle.

Preacher's Daughter wished she hadn't seen, because as the monster appeared it was clearly the largest Marrow they had ever seen—half again the size of the last one to attack. It glittered in the sun, winking laughing death across the hundred meters that separated it from their position. How dare you think a Green Man could stop me, its flickering light said. How dare you believe that any pathetic human could ever stop us, the twinkling flashes said. Who did you think you were believing you could bring down such a being as I? the ensemble screamed.

The homunculi scratched at the veil which was nothing more than a shimmer. But the more they interacted with the shimmer, the brighter it became. Hundreds of man-made clawed simulacrum scratched and rattled their hands along the edges of the veil, while the Marrow hammered, the BOOM BOOM BOOM the antithesis of the earlier bells, yet far more deadly.

She fell to her knees.

How could they possibly stop them?

Even the Redhats stood in awe of the singular destructive power of the Marrow.

And if this creature was merely the doorman for the Formori, how much worse could they possibly be?

And then she saw it.

Or at least she thought she did.

Movement in the Green Man's destroyed pieces…

She brought her rifle up and scoped it, zooming in on the image. Sure enough, pieces of green were coalescing like an amoeba, pieces seeking other pieces. Even those that had splashed far and wide slid across the earth and where they slid, the grass grew high. She didn't dare say the words that begged to burst forth. She managed to stand, still staring at the process through the scope.

The Redhats noticed and began to move towards the Green Man as it performed a reverse melting candle, going from nothing to something, as different parts of itself slapped together forming a whole. Once it stood tall again, the Redhats ran full speed, still eerily silent, spears in front of them, their own covert forces on the edge of attack.

A military jet passed low above the fray, causing everyone to look up. But it did not drop any bombs, nor did it strafe any rounds. It probably came in for a sneak and peek, without much of the sneak. With a Doppler thunder, it shot back into the sky and soon disappeared.

Back on the ground, the Green Man reached out at the twinkling giant, arms becoming tentacles longer than seemed possible. Its lower body pulsed and rooted itself deep into the soil. The tentacles wrapped themselves around the Marrow's neck and yanked.

The Marrow flew back over its head, high into the air, only to come down on top of a dump truck in the quarry, flattening it. For one brief moment an alarm went off, then the Marrow was up, shoving the machine into the quarry where it rattled off the sides and disappeared into its depths until it exploded, an orange and blue mushroom cloud rising from the pit, like the belch of a wounded dragon.

Several men ran out of one of the quarry trailers, only to hurry back inside when they saw the almost invisible twinkling monster marching away from their site.

The pixies added more glitter to the beast.

Preacher's Daughter grinned with her teeth showing. Barbie was probably enjoying this.

The Green Man began to grow, pulling nutrients from the grass around him. At first it was the area directly around him, but that soon expanded as the Green Man grew taller and taller until all of the grass was gray and brittle and dead.

But it now stood as tall as the Marrow.

Many of the homunculi turned to attack the Green Man, but roots sprouted forth and grabbed them, slamming them into each other over and over until their bodies and brains became mush. Then the Redhats attacked, spearing the homunculi, demonstrating what millennia of combat and training could do to creatures most recently fabricated. Where the homunculi operated on pure no-living savagery, the Redhats operated on guile. Millions of Americans planted effigies to them in their gardens never once realizing that they represented the foot soldiers of the Fae, ready to stand up and kill, even those loving enough to place them by their grandmother's favorite rose.

The homunculi fought against the Redhats, but for every one gnome, it took three simulacrums just to create a stalemate.

Meanwhile, the Marrow charged, full on, gathering up speed, until it hit the Green Man.

But instead of breaking, the Green Man bent double, as if struck by a sudden gale, the Marrow tumbling over the top and slamming to the ground.

"We should do something," Jagger said.

"What do you propose?" she asked.

"Anyway to get in contact with that aircraft?" he asked.

"What's your plan, conduct a strafing run?"

"It couldn't hurt," he said.

"Sure about that? Look how close the Marrow and the Green Man are."

As if to accentuate the comment, the Marrow roared like a Kaiju as it once again was thrown into the quarry, this time skittering over the edge where it gripped and grabbed, only to fall the rest of the way inside, ricocheting down to the bottom

"At least we have a breather."

A roar came from beneath the earth.

The truck that had fallen suddenly launched up in the air like it had been strapped to rockets, only to flutter, then fall, crushing the trailer flat where the unlucky men huddled.

She winced and turned partially away.

Then she grabbed Jagger's shoulder. "We can't stay here while the big boys fight. We need to get inside."

"Agreed," he said, eyes worrying the landscape. "Do you have a plan?"

She glanced back at the road which was only fifty yards behind them. Whatever magic had been engaged to ensure people ignored the area wasn't working at the moment and people had stopped and were watching. Many of them were pointing and talking to their friends. Still others had their phones out and were recording what they saw. She had little time to worry about social media. If they weren't able to stop the Marrow from killing all of the dryads, then there wouldn't be any social media.

But she did see something.

"Follow me," she called.

Jagger sighed. "Follow me, she says, and then I get hurt."

"Stop being a cry baby," she began to call over her shoulder, but realized he was running beside her.

"You know, one of these days, you are going to trust someone enough to tell them your plan," he said.

"One of these days, I will actually have a plan," she said. "As of now, I'm just winging it."

The crowd saw them and their weapons and backed away.

Preacher's Daughter grinned. "Pretty cool cosplay, isn't it?"

Then she grabbed a 250cc motorcycle and twisted onto it.

A young man in motocross gear stepped forward.

"This yours?" she asked.

He nodded.

"Mind if I borrow it?"

He nodded again.

"Excellent. Thank you." To Jagger, she said, "Climb on."

Jagger hesitated, then did as ordered. With his long legs, he looked like a grown up on a child's toy. He grabbed tentatively until she gunned the bike, then he held on for dear life as she cranked it up to thirty miles an hour, the studded wheels tearing across the grass towards the far right side of the veil surrounding Graves Hill.

She felt him hold on tighter, pinching her left breast, as they plummeted down the hill onto the uneven pasture. She could just see him blushing and grinned wickedly at the idea. From above, the surface looked smooth, but now down on the valley floor, she couldn't help but notice the divots and ruts and rocks, each one threatening to send her ass over tea kettle into the sky if she didn't give the motorbike her full attention.

She had a hard enough time keeping her front wheel aimed for flat ground, the added weight on the back threatening to flip them over or smash them sideways every time she slammed on the brakes or made a hard cut. Jagger's arms were completely around her now. If he was going to fly off, he was going to take her with him, of that there was no doubt.

The fight continued to their left.

The Green Man now stood twenty feet tall, equal to that of the Marrow.

They fought with tentacles, wrapping and unwrapping each other's appendages as they sought better leverage. Like two evenly matched wrestlers, as soon as one was able to grab the other, the hold was reversed and the move given back.

Meanwhile, beneath their feet the Redhats fought valiantly against the homunculi, but it was obvious who was winning. At this point, it came down to numbers and there were just more simulacrums than there were Fae.

With a bellow of rage, the Marrow drove the Green Man to his knees.

Redhats kamikazed into the Marrow's back, jamming their spears in and out as fast as they could move their arms.

But it left their own backs unguarded and they were soon cut down by the homunculi.

Crockett and Tubbs leaped into the fray, small swords in each hand. They whipped and twirled like half-pint ninjas, and where they struck, a homunculus fell. But they didn't fight unscathed. For every two homunculi they brought down, another would get past their defenses and slice them in an unprotected area with arcane claws.

All at once, the Marrow was again flying through the air, this time its limbs limp, head dangling. It landed at the base of the hill they'd been standing on.

Preacher's Daughter grinned. It was all over except the punctuation. Now, almost near enough the veil to touch it, she stopped the motorcycle. Jagger hopped off. They might just survive this after all. Even the homunculi had stopped attacking.

Then came a roar from off to the left, down inside the quarry.

She stared at the dirt on the ground in front of her and watched as the pebbles rattled as if the earth were moving, or something was moving the earth.

The roar came again, this time echoed more weakly by the Marrow at the base of the hill as it struggled to find its footing.

CHAPTER 37

THE MARROW WERE coming.

The Green Man looked exhausted.

There was only so much he could do.

She gunned her motorcycle, then sped towards the homunculi who were overwhelming Crockett and Tubbs. She aimed her front wheel at one of the downed creatures and used it to launch the bike into the air, catching two of the homunculi in the chest. She let the bike continue in its momentum, and pushed herself free. She landed on her side and grasped a dropped spear, which she used to twist and stab at her nearest target.

Then she felt hands grab her, she fought against them, searching for her knife at her side.

Something punched her in the side of the head.

She blocked and grabbed, but the hands moved too fast.

She felt it.

The death she'd always deserved.

She began to kick as well, growling and arguing, urging to be let go.

Then someone picked her up and dragged her through a wall of electricity.

"Let me go. Let go you assholes. I'm going to—" She realized that no one was fighting her any longer. She lay on her back, and stared around her, seeing things she never ever expected she would see.

"You're okay. Let me take a look at you," Munro said, hands gently running up and down her limbs.

"Munro? Where'd you come from?"

"Other side of the veil."

She tried to sit up. "What about Jagger?"

"I'm here," came a voice from nearby.

Munro pushed her gently to the ground as he bound a wound on her left arm

She sighed. "And Crockett and Tubbs?" she asked, popping back up.

"Still fighting," Munro said.

"Let them in," she said. "Before they get killed.""

"Maeve says no. No unseelie allowed on this side of the veil."

"No unseelie—what the hell, Munro. You know they had my back." She brushed his hand away and managed to get to her feet. "I need to have theirs because—"

For the first time she noticed the forces arrayed before her. Indians sat on dozens of horses, Winchesters and other hunting rifles resting across their saddle horns. Many of them wore war paint and had on the same sort of attire they'd worn when they'd torn through Custer and his 7th Calvary. Still others merely wore T-shirts, jeans, cowboy boots and cowboy hats. Six ATVs rumbled along the sides and in the back, she could see them by their whip antennas moving to and fro in the wind. Indians from the Sioux reservation stared down at her, their long warrior faces almost implacable, others grinning, all seemingly ready to fight.

"We have to get back out there," she said. "The Green Man. Crockett and Tubbs."

"This is their fight," said Maeve, striding forward.

"They're fighting for you," Preacher's Daughter said.

"I never asked for them to fight for me."

"Bullshit. You manipulated all of this. If it wasn't for your stealing and hiding two towns, none of them would be here now."

"No, we'd all be dead because no one was preparing themselves for the coming invasion. All of the evidence was there, but no one wanted to look." Maeve gave her a look like she'd just removed her from the side of her boot. "I'm glad that they came during the final hours, but I will not put my dryads in danger."

"Your dryads—Didn't you see what they did to Cottingley Wood? What about Killiehunty? My god, Maeve, you sacrificed them."

"They were old and sanctimonious."

"Sounds like you."

Maeve looked as if she'd been slapped. It took her a moment to recover and when she did, she said, "I never asked for the help. I knew what I was doing.

"Nonetheless, they are helping. We need to help them."

Maeve looked at her as if she were a flea on the back of a dying dog. "They have chosen the fate they most desired to chase."

"They were always the bait. This is what you wanted. With the Green Man gone, you are the most powerful Fae." Preacher's Daughter wanted to spit on the ground but her mouth was too dry, even to accomplish such a simple task.

She fought her way to her feet, pushing Munro aside, although he tried to hold her down. She noted how sickly green he looked and wondered what it was that he had. She also noted that a few leaves had wedged into the cut on her right arm. What had been almost bone deep was now barely a scratch. She tried to use the flat of her left hand to wipe away the leaf, but it wouldn't budge. She actually had to pluck it as if it was growing from her. She shook her head at the strangeness of it and then noticed Munro had similar leaves all up and down his neck.

"Are you okay?" she asked softly.

He gave her a haunted look. "I don't know. I feel... I'm becoming something different," he said.

"Where's Poe? Where's Special Unit 77?" she asked no one in particular.

"They're guarding the American side. Maeve won't allow them in the veil, so they're waiting to see if anything emerges."

She glanced at the old Fae witch. "Fucking Maeve."

Now, standing, Preacher's Daughter sought a familiar

face. She spied him sitting in an ATV, a Winchester 30.30 across his lap. His eyes were closed as if he was taking a nap. Either that, or his narcolepsy had him in its grips.

"Chief Frankie Scottie," she called.

His eyes opened.

"Chief Frankie Scottie, I need you."

Seeing her, he climbed out of his ATV and came over.

"You look at little worse for wear, Ms. Mae. Is everything alright? Are you wounded?"

She tried not to laugh as she mimicked, "Is everything alright? Of course, it's not alright. Who's in charge of your forces?" she asked.

"President Slaughter. We have a Tribal Council."

A man appeared at her elbow. He could have been an American-Indian banker. Slight paunch and balding. He wore a polo shirt tucked into jeans. A Stetson rode his head. Three-hundred-dollar boots hugged his feet. "I'm Rick Slaughter, President, Pine Ridge Tribal Council."

She immediately saw how corporate he was. Where Francis Scott Key Chases the Enemy still held onto much of the tribal history, those members of the Sioux Nation who wanted to move forward had embraced more of a company outlook on life. She imagined Rick had a different name to the one he was given when he was born, but to better assimilate into the culture of money and government grants, Rick was a much safer word. No one would pause at loaning 'Rick' money, but someone called 'Chases the Enemy' would be hard-pressed to receive even a dime of investment money. Her challenge was a way to use that knowledge to her benefit.

She glanced at the gathered Indians. Half seemed to be like Rick and the others like Chief Frankie Scottie.

"Why do you gather so?" she asked simply.

"To protect our own," he said.

"What is it you would protect? What the white man gave you?"

Rick glanced around and noted that the other Indians were watching him closely.

"We have little in the way of land left. We need to protect what we have."

"And if the Marrow get past the veil?"

"Then we'll be forced to fight them."

"Why not take the battle to them? Look out there. They have no idea you lie in wait for them."

Everyone stared through the haze of the veil, the battle still going on. It was clear, however, that the Green Man was losing, as were the last of the Redhats. Crockett and Tubbs stood on a pile of bodies fighting like warriors out of an old epic, but even they were flagging, resting after each swing or two.

"I think we should go," Francis Scott Key Chases the Enemy said.

President Rick shook his head. "This isn't our fight."

"When is it going to be our fight?" Francis Scott Key asked. "We're protecting their dryads. The green women have already improved the land where they rooted. Do you really want to give them back? Do you want to let them take yet something more from us?"

A grumbling could be heard coming from the men on horses.

"Many of us hate the way we live and we tell ourselves, if only we had a chance to fight against it. These aren't the ones who put us on the reservation... they aren't the ones who took away our land... but they are as close as we are ever going to have as a target." He placed a hand on Rick's shoulder. "Come on, brother. Just say the word."

"People might die," he said.

"People will die," Francis Scott Key Chases the Enemy said. "I know that might startle you, but some of us will die. But you know what?" he asked, raising his voice so that all might hear. "I'm good with that. What am I going to regret if I don't do this? What will I regret if I have a chance to change my future and I don't take it? What will I miss if I die? More Jerry Springer on television? More winters where we barely have enough heat to survive? I'd rather miss those things than regret anything."

Several of the Indians made war cries, shoving their weapons into the air as he spoke.

President Rick looked at the men on horseback and on the ATVs. All of them were leaning forward, eager to do something. "The idea is that we just charge right in?"

"Just like the old days," Francis Scott Key said.

"Just like the old days." President Rick nodded and returned to his ATV. Instead of sitting, he stood in the seat. "So, how do we open the veil?"

As one, the Indians sitting atop their horses raised their rifles in one hand and made warrior screams.

The veil dropped.

Preacher's Daughter jumped into the side seat of Chief Frankie Scottie's ATV and pointed at the conflict. "Charge!" she screamed.

And the ATV shot forward, followed by five other ATVs and thirty horses, the sound of their hooves shaking the earth like their own version of a Marrow.

Crockett and Tubbs jerked their heads around and at first seemed ready to run. But when they saw Preacher's Daughter, they held their spears up and screamed with the Indians.

The new Marrow exited the quarry which had become some sort of transit from one place to the other. Above it, the Pixies were prepared and bedazzled it with their glitter. This one was also of the larger size and began to pound its way towards where the veil had just been.

Indians on horseback raised their rifles at full gallop and began to fire at the emerging beast.

It swung at them, but they were too far away, so it did what it could do best. It surged forward, moving one hundred meters in the blink of an eye.

The Indians were baffled at first, but regrouped, now finding themselves behind the dread creature. They put their heels into their mounts and surged back the way they came, firing into the back of the beast, all the while screaming at the top of their lungs.

Preacher's Daughter could only imagine what they

were feeling. Was it the sudden freedom of more than a hundred years of pent-up frustration? It sure sounded like that. Watching them fight, even the ATVs gunning engines around pods of homunculi as their passengers took potshots at their targets, it was hard to fathom that the Indians in America had ever been conquered. Then again, the same thing could be said for the Fae.

Francis Scott Key made a hard turn, wheels skittering to grab ahold.

She grasped the bar above her with her left arm and held on as the ATV made a curl turn on only two wheels.

Francis Scott Key screamed with joy, laughing the entire way.

Everyone was reliving the best battle until the moment when a Marrow swept its arm and three horses went down in squeals and screams. The sound of a horse in pain wrenched through her, causing her to grit her teeth and return to the present, reminding her that this was far from a game. One horse was sliced clean through, its steaming entrails covering a downed rider.

The Green Man stumbled from the gray ground from where he had taken all of the life and into Grave Hill. Where it limped, the grass didn't grow higher. The opposite occurred. The grass browned, then grayed, then died, withering black as the Green Man took his nutrients from nature and the soil. Soon, it was once again a twenty-foot creature with tentacles and arms, waiting for a Marrow to come to him.

From her distance, Preacher's Daughter also spied

Maeve who approached the Green Man and who, herself, grew in size and stature until she was as equally tall. She stood next to him, hauled back, and struck him full force in the face.

What was she seeing?

A lover's spat?

Or something more serious?

"Oh hell. Looks like there's more of them," Francis Scott Key said.

Homunculi of all shapes and sizes were scrambling out of the quarry. Not one was as large as the first group which had attacked, which led her to believe that The Shrews was running on empty—or at least that's what she hoped it meant.

Maeve and the Green Man were going to have to take care of the Marrow. The Indians should form themselves around the new threat, removing the homunculi from existence.

She gestured to the quarry. "There! Take us there!"

But the ATV was slowing rather than speeding up.

She glanced over and saw Francis Scott Key Chases the Enemy with his chin to his chest, eyes closed, hands no longer on the wheel. She grabbed the wheel as they slowed so that they wouldn't flip or tumble. When the ATV came to a stop, she pulled the emergency brake and checked him briefly for wounds. Alas, he had none. He was fast asleep.

She grabbed his Winchester and leaped from the ATV and found a horse with no rider. She grabbed the pommel as it trotted by and used the beast's momentum to launch her into the simple leather saddle. She squeezed with her thighs, remembering when she and the others from her last unit rode with American Special Forces near Mez, Afghanistan, in early 2002, some of the first Westerners on the ground in that god-forsaken country. She checked the rifle chamber and saw that it was loaded. If she recalled correctly, 30.30s generally held five or six rounds so she was going to need to make sure that every round counted.

She raised her rifle, took aim, and fired, catching an arcane creation in the chest, the force of the round sending it tumbling. She took aim again and this time missed, failing to lead it.

Around her, Indians were doing the same. Many were still horsed, but several were on the ground. One was being helped by friends, while another was being ravaged by a homunculus, who kept bringing its fists at the end of long arms, crashing up and down upon the man's collapsed chest. To him she rode. The horse didn't want to cross the body on the ground, but she muscled it and dug her heels in so it took the homunculus in the face and chest, then trampled it as it completed its transit over the body of the dead man and his killer.

She swung back around and saw where Crockett and Tubbs were standing atop a mound of bodies, tired beyond belief, taking turns whacking anything that might try and crest their mountain of arms and legs, then using their weapons as canes to hold themselves upright.

She charged towards them, slowing only when she got near.

"You two need to beat it," she said. "The calvary has arrived." Even as she said it, she realized the irony of calling the Indians calvary.

"It's okay, LT," Tubbs said. "We got this."

"We're doing fine," Crockett said.

She grinned. Next thing he was going to say was that it was nothing but a flesh wound.

Suddenly, something struck Crockett in the face, sending him tumbling down the far side of the pile.

"Crockett!"

Tubbs dove after him.

She maneuvered the horse to the other side of the mound.

Blood poured from Crockett's mouth. His eyes were closed. She couldn't tell if he was even breathing.

"Crocket!!"

Tubbs held him, the other's head in his lap.

"Get out of here," she cried, feeling the tightness of tears about to break free. "Save yourselves."

"What about you?" Tubbs asked.

"I'll be fine." She glanced over her shoulder just as a roar went up, Maeve and the Green Man meeting the final two Marrow in Grave Hill. She turned back. The bogies were gone if they were even there at all.

Now the tears did flow.

It was all too much.

She put the horse into a trot, raised her rifle and fired. Target down.

She found another target. Target down.

And another. Target down.

She tried again, but got nothing but a click instead, so she rode down her target, and grabbing the barrel of the rifle, shattered the homunculus's face with the butt of the rifle. She tossed it aside and drew her pistol, now sweeping the battlefield, making each round count, head shots all. She lost track of how many times she reloaded. She fired until she could fire no more. Then empty of rounds, she let the horse slow to a stop and they both remained in the middle of the battlefield, panting, exhausted.

Around her, the occasional homunculus was chased by an Indian, or a troupe of Redhats. But otherwise, the battle was over.

Behind the veil, there was no sign of the Green Man.

Maeve had returned to normal size.

Preacher's Daughter spied Poe standing atop a boulder, binoculars to his eyes, trained on her.

They stared at each other for a moment, then she offered Poe a tired wave.

He returned it, but made no move to stop watching.

She pushed herself up in the saddle and looked around, searching for the ATV where Francis Scott Key had been. She spied it amidst several piles of bodies, still rumbling in neutral. His eyes were still closed. She urged the horse towards the ATV, then slid off, knees buckling, almost falling. She patted the horse's rump and it left, searching for grass that didn't have blood on it.

She climbed into the passenger seat and sat heavily, breathing a sigh of relief.

The movement must have awoken the Indian. His head jerked up and around. Then he looked at the battlefield.

"Did we do it?" he asked.

"I think so," she said.

"What—what about me? How did I do?"

She laid her hand on his as it rested on the steering wheel.

"You were awesome, Chief Frankie Scottie. We couldn't have won the day without you."

He sat back and grinned uncertainly. "What now?"

"Let's go to America and see the dryads."

He shook his head. "Imagine that. Dryads in America."

She grinned, then stifled back a yawn with the back of her hand. "Yeah. Imagine."

EPILOGUE

MI5 AND THE Home Office had their hands full trying to keep things under wraps. Too many people had seen the battle. Many had posted the information to social media, flooding computers from Edinburgh to Katmandu with images of both small and huge monsters attacking in what looked more like a B-movie than a real-life documentary. Still, with the assistance of Maeve and some other indigenous magical resources, they'd managed to relegate it to a combination of cosplay and games played by reenactment organizations. The finality of the 'evidence' was relegated to conspiracy websites, a good enough place for the information to live in ignominy, fuel to the fire of those who "knew the truth of it all."

The Green Man was nowhere to be found. He'd fought alongside Maeve and they'd taken out the two Marrow, but immediately following the battle, he'd just disappeared. The Home Office wasn't at all happy about that turn of events, but there was nothing to be done about it. Rumor had it that the Queen was livid that she'd lost such a resource.

The Centaur presented new conditions to the royal family, namely that there would be permanent set asides for much of the Fae. The encroachment of humanity was threatening their very existence, and if the Queen ever wanted the Fae to come to her defense in the event the Formori attempted a return, then they needed to have a home they weren't constantly afraid was going to turn into newly developed real estate. In essence, they created their own series of reservations upon which to live, with the guarantee that humanity would never defile the lands.

Ironically, it was President Rick Slaughter who helped the Centaur with some of the wording in the legal arguments. In exchange, the Centaur would assist Pine Ridge in their own desire to renegotiate the terms of their land use, especially since they had new formations that were exciting everyone from hydrologists to tourists.

The Indians returned to Pine Ridge and Maeve severed the hole in the world she'd created. Of the seven dryads secreted to the other side, two wanted to stay and there wasn't any convincing them otherwise. Already, Pine Ridge had discovered a new and mysterious water source that was becoming the envy of non-Indian farmers along the edges of the reservation. People were coming far and wide to see the green veldt. Its popularity had already surpassed that of the Corn Palace in Mitchell.

Jagger, Barbie, Donkey Kong, and Hard Hat, the exchange sergeant who'd been sent to Special Unit 77 in her stead, were none the worse for wear. Munro was something altogether different, which was why everyone was gathered in Cottingley Wood, in front of the ruined corpse of the old dryad, Epiphonia.

Poe was present as well, choosing to stay on this side of the veil. He wanted to confer with Waterhouse and ensure that Preacher's Daughter was alright in the head, something which she wasn't sure she'd ever be after all of this was said and done. One of the more ridiculous things that bothered her was the fate of Crockett and Tubbs. Damned if those two bogies hadn't grown on her.

Munro, on the other hand, needed to be heard and he'd invited everyone to where things started, while MI5 once again ran crowd control so they'd be alone for the time necessary to do what needed to be done. He could barely move on his own and needed the help of a walker.

"I just wanted to thank all of you," he said, his voice trembling and weak. "You have been the best friends I have ever had."

"Why are you talking past tense?" Jagger asked.

"Something happened when I was here last—when we saw her die." He looked to the tree, but couldn't hold the gaze of the dead and accusing dryad.

"She's in you, isn't she," Donkey Kong said.

Munro nodded. "I think so." Then to Preacher's Daughter. "And her to a smaller extent."

Preacher's Daughter glanced at the leaves sprouting from her wound. Silly little things. She picked one and winced slightly.

"Can you give it back?" Barbie asked.

Munro shook his head.

"No. What do you mean, no?" Barbie asked, anguish in her voice. She glanced at the others, suddenly more woman than any of them had ever seen her be.

Trash and Thrash ran up and hugged her legs. "Why is he saying no, Waterhouse?"

Her face returned to its normally angry clench and she said firmly, "Tell him to give it back."

"He means he has no power over it," said Maeve, appearing in vestments made from leaves and vines. Grapes and flowers still grew upon them. They hugged her body like they'd always been there. She brought with her the scent of a flower bed. She approached the dead dryad, tree split by the axe hand of the first Marrow they'd encountered. The dryad's face was still visible on the trunk of the tree, mouth open in a silent forever scream. Maeve allowed her right hand to caress the wood, as gentle and honorable as someone might be to a body laid in state.

Preacher's Daughter shook her head. "I should have known this was something you cooked up."

"This has nothing to do with me. She gave the last of herself to Munro and you so that you would come back and return it one day."

"We never asked for this."

"Does it make the gift any less important?" She faced Preacher's Daughter. "So angry all the time. Why is that? Have you thought about that?"

Preacher's Daughter wasn't prepared for this to be an intervention. She crossed her arms and shoved out a leg. "You don't know me."

Maeve's eyebrow raised. "Don't I?" She approached Preacher's Daughter and placed a soft hand on her shoulder. "Everything is transitory. Everything is transactional. I'm surprised Boy Scout didn't explain that to you."

"Don't speak his name."

"Why not? It's not like he's dead."

Preacher's Daughter shook free the hand and dropped her own at her sides, then brought them up in prayer. "He's alive? You know him? Where is he? Please. Tell me."

Maeve shook her head and pushed aside a length of hair that had fallen free from Preacher's Daughter's ponytail. "I've not met him, but I feel him in the world pulse. He's out there."

A gulf of opportunity and ideas opened up inside of her. Oh, but how she'd missed her old team boss and comrade. But that was another lifetime ago, or so it seemed. He'd left them to move on, so wasn't the idea that she moved on as well? What was it Maeve had said? *Everything is transitory.*

She turned to Munro now. Poe. Donkey Kong. Jagger. Barbie. This was her team now. She wondered how much of her life she'd lived looking back instead of forward. She cleared her throat and wet her lips. "So, how does it work for us? How do we return what the dryad gave?"

Everyone stared at her, but no one said a word.

She put her arm around Munro's shoulders. "How can he return the life that was stored inside of him?"

"What makes you think you can return it?" Maeve asked.

Preacher's Daughter began to pull at the tiny leaves sprouting out of her wound. Each one was a pinprick of pain, wincing with each pull. "Here, let me give these back. Take them," she said, throwing a handful at the tree.

They struck the bark, then fell unceremoniously to the ground.

"Do you understand? I don't want this? I don't want you!" She hammered against the side of the tree. "Take it back." Then, as if to accentuate her frustration, she shouted and pounded at the same time. "Take. It. Back."

Donkey Kong came and grabbed her wrists. "It doesn't want anything from you. What you have is but a side effect of being nearby when it happened. Munro has the whole of it."

Her face collapsed for one brief moment as if to succumb to crying, but then she fought back and found composure. "Oh, Munro."

"Alas, it has taken ahold of him," Maeve said. "The magic is powerful. He has already changed. I bet he bleeds green even now."

Munro feebly pulled free a knife from a sheath at his waist and with a shaking hand, cut his palm long and deep. Green blood pooled in the cup of his hand. He sobbed once, then closed his eyes.

"He's no longer human, no matter what he looks like."

"Can't he remain the way he is, walking around like—like—Swamp Thing or something?" Jagger asked.

"Swamp Thing isn't real, son," Maeve said, touching him on his shoulder.

At the touch, he sobbed as well.

"What am I to do?" Munro asked.

"What is it asking of you? What are the whispers in your head?" she asked. Then she nodded. "Even now you converse. Such is the way."

"They want me to embrace the dead dryad. They want to show me things from the beginning of time. They want me to do things for the land. They want me to protect just as Epiphonia did."

"Is that so bad? To live something larger than you ever imagined?"

He ignored her. "It also wants me to open my veins on my arms, to cut my throat, to release the blood so that it might once again be infused. It wants to peel me inside out and take the life from me so that it might live."

"Munro, you can't," Preacher's Daughter said, voice hitching.

He approached her. "But what if I can do more—what if I can be better?"

"You are already among the best of us," she said.

Waterhouse stepped forward, "Is this something you want to do?"

He stared at him, real fear in his eyes. "I don't know what I want to do. I'm—I'm scared."

"Of course you are," Maeve said, preparing to reach out.

But Barbie blocked her way. "Just go away. We don't

need you. We understand what needs to be done."

"I'm only here to—"

"Please. Just. Go." Barbie stood firm.

For a brief moment, Preacher's Daughter believed that Barbie could actually take the supernatural entity. For a brief moment, Maeve must have believed so as well, because she turned and disappeared into the woods.

Barbie walked up to Munro and put her arms around him.

Jagger did the same.

As did Hard Hat.

And finally, Preacher's Daughter.

"Whatever you want to do," she said, "we are with you."

Munro looked at each of them with haunted eyes. "I've spent my life protecting my country," he said, his voice, barely above a whisper. "I suppose it's fitting to continue doing so," he said, his voice cracking. "This—this is just a different way of doing it."

Transitory.

Transactional.

Preacher's Daughter felt overwhelmed with emotion. Never in her wildest dreams had she imagined she would be witness to such a thing. Part of it seemed so horrific, but another part seemed honorable. She didn't know if she'd ever be able to merge the two ideas together.

"Donkey Kong? I mean Waterhouse? Commander?"

"Yes, son."

"Take this," and Munro handed him the knife.

"What do you want me to do with it, son?" Waterhouse asked as he took the mean blade.

"Cut me fast and deep." He sighed; his entire body seemed to rattle with it. "Cut me fast and deep and don't stop until I live again."

Waterhouse took the knife.

Preacher's Daughter couldn't look. She covered her face and turned, even as the first of the screams split the silent wood.

ACKNOWLEDGEMENTS

No book is ever created in a vacuum. Thanks first to Jonathan Oliver for luring me into the Solaris corona. Also a huge thanks to David Thomas Moore for being there from the beginning. Thanks massively to Michael Rowley, the poor bloke who was given the task of guiding me through the ins and outs of Briticisms. Also thank yous to Paul Simpson, Amy Borsuk and Martin at Amazing15 for the cover art. Thanks to my agent, Cherry Weiner, my wife Yvonne Navarro, and to Boy Scout for allowing me to use one of his team in a brand new advanture. And most of all, thank you to my readers. Without you, I would be the lone man on top of the mountain screaming at the world.

ABOUT THE AUTHOR

The American Library Association calls **Weston Ochse** "one of the major horror authors of the 21st Century." His work has won the Bram Stoker Award, been nominated for the Pushcart Prize, and won four New Mexico-Arizona Book Awards. A writer of more than thirty books in multiple genres, his *Burning Sky Duology* has been hailed as the best military horror of the generation. His military supernatural series *SEAL Team 666* has been optioned to be a movie starring Dwayne Johnson and his military sci fi trilogy, which starts with *Grunt Life*, has been praised for its PTSD-positive depiction of soldiers at peace and at war.

Weston has also published literary fiction, poetry, comics, and non-fiction articles. His shorter work has appeared in DC Comics, IDW Comics, *Soldier of Fortune Magazine*, *Cemetery Dance*, and peer-reviewed literary journals. His franchise work includes *The X-Files*, *Predator*, *Aliens*, *Hellboy*, *Clive Barker's Midian*, and *V-Wars*.

Weston holds a Master of Fine Arts in Creative Writing and teaches at Southern New Hampshire University. He lives in Arizona with his wife, and fellow author, Yvonne Navarro and their Great Danes.

FIND US ONLINE!

www.rebellionpublishing.com

/rebellionpub   /rebellionpublishing   /rebellionpublishing

SIGN UP TO OUR NEWSLETTER!

rebellionpublishing.com/newsletter

YOUR REVIEWS MATTER!

Enjoy this book? Got something to say?

Leave a review on Amazon, GoodReads or with your
favourite bookseller and let the world know!

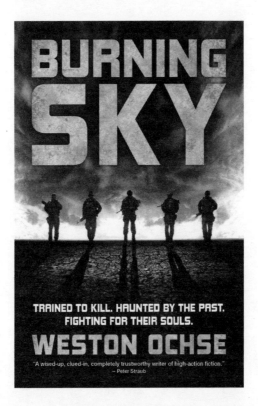

TRAINED TO KILL. HAUNTED BY THE PAST. FIGHTING FOR THEIR SOULS.

Everything is dangerous in Afghanistan, nothing more so than the mission of a Tactical Support Team or T.S.T. All veterans, these men and women spend seasons in hell, to not only try and fix what's broken in each of them, but also to make enough bank to change their fortunes.

But seven months later, safely back on American soil, they feel like there's something left undone. They're meeting people who already know them, remembering things that haven't happened, hearing words that don't exist. And they're all having the same dream... a dream of a sky that won't stop burning.